The Edge of Maybe

A Novel

Ericka Lutz

Last Light Studio Books ~ Boston, Massachusetts

Published by Last Light Studio Books
423 Brookline Avenue #324
Boston, Massachusetts 02215
www.lastlightstudio.com

Book design by Joel Friedlander, www.TheBookDesigner.com

Cover image © Kelly Taylor, licensed under Creative Commons
(CC BY-SA 2.0) http://www.flickr.com/photos/wmshc_kiwitayro/3519423997/

Printed in the United States of America

Publisher's Cataloging-in-Publication
      Lutz, Ericka.
          The edge of maybe : a novel / Ericka Lutz.
          p. cm.
          LCCN 2011934385
          ISBN-13: 978-0-9827084-4-6
          ISBN-10: 0-9827084-4-0
          1. Families--California--San Francisco Bay Area--
      Fiction. 2. San Francisco Bay Area (Calif.)--Social
      life and customs--Fiction. 3. Parenting--California--
      San Francisco Bay Area--Fiction. 4. Domestic fiction.
      I. Title.
      PS3612.U893E34 2012   813'.6
                                 QBI11-600143

In Memory of Bill Sonnenschein
Husband, Reader, Friend

1949–2008

The Edge of Maybe

CHAPTER 1

🌿 KIRA

There were strangers on the porch of their Oakland, California bungalow, a young woman in pink sweats and a small boy in dirty blue pajamas. They waited as Kira and Polly walked from the car to the house, Kira balancing groceries, purse, phone, keys, Polly wearing a backpack too large for her thin, thirteen-year-old frame. The woman sat on the top step, thick-bodied and barefoot; she rested her bandaged right ankle on a dingy canvas bag. The little boy crouched by the redwood planter, breaking Kira's dendroideum succulent. He held each section between tiny thumb and forefinger—*snap*.

Kira winced, a pang of guilt and uselessness: Too shabby for the Jehovah's, homeless people didn't usually venture up the hill… "Can I help you?" she said, her voice shut tight. Fragments of succulent littered the old wooden porch. Behind Kira, Polly had stopped abruptly, too.

"I'm Amber," the woman on the porch said.

"Excuse me?"

The young woman's voice a monotone, "I'm Amber. Looking for Dad."

"Dad?"

"Adam. Adam Glazer. I'm Amber. Sandi's daughter."

It took Kira a moment to register: Dad. Adam. Amber. Sandi. Her stomach turned. What had been swept under the rug was now exposed to light of day—old skin, hair, dust, garbage. The

3

boy stripped years of growth from the succulent—*snap*.

"Please… stop hurting my plant." The little boy didn't turn around. "Um. Please stop him," Kira said to the woman—to Amber—arms full, pointing with her chin.

Amber moved her head slowly to look at the child. "Joey. Told you not to touch stuff." She smacked the toddler across the back of his head and he cringed. "Is Dad home?"

"I'm Kira. I'm Adam's wife. This is our daughter Polly."

"Yeah. I'm looking for Dad."

"Adam's working today. He'll be home in a couple hours."

"Do you got something to eat? I lost my shoes and money and we walked from the Greyhound station."

The Greyhound station, miles away, through grimy downtown Oakland avenues. All the way to Moss Street in her bare feet, carrying the canvas bag with its zipper pinned and gaping, the little boy dragging behind. In early January.

"Mommy?" Polly's voice from behind her.

Kira turned to introduce: "Polly, this is Amber and… Joey?"

Polly silently mouthed, "Who?"

"Polly, c'mere." She set down the bag of groceries on the bottom step and put her arms around her daughter. Polly's head came to Kira's neck now.

Kira took a deep breath. That pause before lake ice gave way underfoot; when lips moved towards each other for the first kiss; when the knife stuck on the bread crust before skittering across to slice into an index finger; when teeth tested the tension of pomegranate seeds before their decisive crunch. She exhaled and spoke softly into Polly's brown curly hair smelling of sweat and tea rose conditioner.

"Amber is your half-sister. She's Daddy's daughter, from a long time ago."

Maybe.

Polly pulled away, eyes wide. The edges of her nose turned red. Then she spun and walked quickly back toward the driveway.

"Oh no," Kira said, starting towards Polly's direction. "Excuse me, Amber."

"Knew it," Amber said, her voice as flat as before. "She didn't even fucking know about me. Okay, we're out of here."

Kira stopped. Yes, go! she thought. She blinked her eyes, willing the porch vacant, problems gone. Opened them. They were still there. She's Adam's daughter, she thought, then corrected: might be Adam's daughter. "No, please wait," she said. Then, "Polly!" Turned to Amber again, "No! Amber… Adam thought… Come in. Excuse Polly, she's just surprised. Joey's your son? Adam gets home in a couple of hours." *I hope.* The child was back to the plant. Each segment he snapped off made a small popping sound. Triage; she'd deal with Polly in a moment. She climbed the four steps to the porch and unlocked the front door of the Moss Street house. "Come in. You must be cold."

Amber and Joey trailed Kira into the house, through the living room, dining room, into the kitchen. "Would you like water? Juice?" Kira said. Her work clothes pressed in on her, a fleeting longing for her yoga pants, a life without negotiations and confrontations and complications. The deep vibrating thrum of chanting monks, dark robes, shaved heads.

"Got a couple Diet Pepsi?"

"No, sorry. Apple juice. Juice Squeeze?"

"Joey, get over here! So, um, when does Dad get home?" Amber stood halfway between the door and the table. Looking closer, past Amber's overflowing body, Kira could see the youth in her forehead strewn with lank bangs, her baby face. Amber caught her gaze, pushed her bangs back with both hands away from her face. "I been on the bus since yesterday."

"He'll be here in a couple hours, 5:45 maybe. Sit down, I'll be right back, okay?" Kira backed out of the kitchen, hesitated—and hurried back out of the house to the driveway where Polly leaned against the car. Polly's pants were too short, her thirteen-year-old legs—Adam's skinny legs—had stretched again. "Polly. You okay, Poodle?"

Polly shrugged. Stared at the ground.

"It was a long time ago. Obviously. Before we were together. I don't know…" How to explain this? "Daddy wasn't sure she was his daughter, still isn't. He's never really been her dad; her mom's sort of… She must be twenty-something now. Twenty-four? Twenty-five? The daughter, I mean. Amber." She stopped, furious at Adam. She'd warned him this could happen; nothing stayed hidden forever. The ragged edges of his life dragging against her because he wasn't here to deal with it.

Polly stared at her, tears welling over. "Why didn't anybody tell me?"

Kira shook her head. "I'm so sorry."

"She's my sister? Who's that boy? He was breaking your plant. He's ugly, Mommy, she's obese, they don't look like they're related to us."

Kira agreed. All three on the short, slight side—Polly with Adam's nose and his dark hair, her own thick curls and slightly bug eyes. "From trying to see too much," her grandmother had said. Amber and the boy so… extra white. She paused again, aware of the three feet between her and Polly, wanting to bridge it; aware of the strangers she'd left alone in the kitchen. The poisons under the sink; the house not childproofed for years: Clorox, Simple Green, orchid fertilizer. "I don't know, honey. I guess, her son? She has an older boy too, I know. She hasn't called your dad in a few years. She lives in Elko, Nevada, that's five hundred miles from here. And then she was in jail; drugs, I think." Her brain spun: the computers. Small things—PDAs, iPods. Their stuff ransacked. "Daddy sent her money for a lawyer but we never heard back," she said. "I think she was in prison a couple of years. She's had a hard life. I don't think your dad's seen her since she was a baby. I'm so sorry. But I need you to help me with this. Polly. Will you come in with me? Help me out with this? Please?"

Polly paused, then nodded. "I'm not going to love them."

"You don't have to love them."

Polly stared at the ground again where the cement pad was cracking, the rust colored paint chipping. Another year and they'd have to paint.

"I'm sorry, Polly. We'll work this out."

"Right." Polly said, obedient but chafing. "Yeah, right, we'll work it out."

In the kitchen, Amber sat at the table and Joey lay on the white linoleum floor, chewing his sleeve. His eyes stared, like a lizard's. They didn't blink. "Nice to finally meet you, Amber," Kira said, taking a chair across the yellow Formica table from her. "Polly? Could you get us all juice? Joey? Do you want juice?" The boy didn't respond.

"He don't like juice," Amber said.

"Milk? Joey, would you like a glass of milk? He's really cute."

"Nah, this one's not cute."

"You have an older one too, right? Another boy?" Kira said.

Polly stood in front of the open refrigerator, staring inside. "We're out of milk."

"Johnny." Amber said. Every word an effort.

"I got milk today. Oh, the groceries. Polly, I left the groceries on the steps. Could you go get them? Johnny. And how old is he now?"

"Seven."

"Mommy!"

"Polly. What."

"I can't carry that big bag."

"It's not that heavy."

"No. I can't."

"Okay. Excuse me, Amber." It wasn't worth the battle. Kira got up and walked out of the kitchen again. Her stomach twisted. Adam was wrapping a shoot today, planning to work straight through. Unreachable. Her hands shook and she had a hard time opening the door. Ravi had dedicated last Friday's yoga class to Gandhi: "'I have so much to accomplish today that I must meditate for two hours instead of one.' Like Gandhi, take time for yourself, just now, just a moment," he'd said, his ugly face radiant—long jaw, large nose, thick glasses, dark hair, deep eyes, a lithe bull with pitted skin—and Kira had felt the tightness in her chest loosen.

The late afternoon sky was just turning towards dusk, clean January Oakland air with a chill wind, gray fog coming in off the bay. A few leaves blew, a gust of dust. At Kira's feet, the bag of groceries sat near the ravaged plant. She stooped and gathered together the broken fragments of succulent and slid them in her blazer pocket, then salvaged the paper bag of groceries and returned to the kitchen. Where seemingly nobody had moved.

Amber sat, a still toad, at the table, Polly stared into the refrigerator, Joey lay on the floor in cobra pose: *bhujangasana*. Kira put the bag on the counter. "Milk." She handed it to Polly. "I could make sandwiches," she said.

"Whatever. Joey likes fish sticks. But he can't have no more tuna fish 'cause of mercury. Or peanut butter, he likes peanut butter. Do you got any of that?"

"Um. Maybe peanut butter."

"Just almond butter." Polly said. "We never have peanut butter."

"You are welcome to whatever we have in the house, food-wise," Kira said in her "that's-enough-Polly" voice. "I'll make us sandwiches. We've got salsa and chips, too. Polly, pour yourself and Joey some milk."

"Where's the bathroom?"

"Go back into the living room. Turn left. You'll see it." Her mind scanned the medicine cabinet shelves. Codeine, cold medicine…"Can I get you anything? I'll get you a towel if you want to shower."

"Look, I just need to pee, lady."

Kira grimaced. *Lady*. She placed the pieces of broken succulent in a pie dish and added a half inch of water. Each one would sprout roots, if she was lucky.

When Amber left the room, hobbling slowly on her injured foot, Joey yelled a wordless howl. "Joey! Shut it!" Amber yelled from the bathroom, and he stopped.

"Mommy. My math homework," Polly said.

"Call your dad," Kira said to Polly. "Please call him, tell him to come home as soon as he can, okay? Use my cell, it's on the counter." Polly nodded, took the phone, and hurried from the room. "Joey, would you like a cookie?" Kira reached in the cabinet. They only had organic fig bars, but at least they were sweet.

The eggplant sandwiches on Acme Bakery pain au levain were not a hit.

In the kitchen: "I can't eat this," Amber said. "My stomach

shrunk. I'm gacked to shit." She clutched her abdomen, a spider with a baby's head. Next to her, Kira felt dainty. Polly and Joey looked frail and pale.

"Want a banana to settle your stomach?"

"Nah. Just chips."

Kira passed the corn chips and mild salsa, deliberately not saying what she thought; chips wouldn't help her feel better. Amber reached for a chip. Kira noticed her pretty hands and nails, perfect half moons, squared off white tips with a French manicure, delicate fingers. Joey wouldn't sit at the table; when Amber tried to make him, he straightened his legs and screamed until she dropped him back on the floor. "It's okay," Kira said. "Let him eat wherever he's comfortable,"—she, still a stickler with Polly for table manners. She passed down chunks of banana to Joey under the table. And felt pleased when he ate them.

Polly wrapped her sandwich in a paper towel and retreated with it from the room.

"Is that him?" Amber asked, pointing toward the refrigerator at a snapshot of Adam on skis at Kirkwood a few years ago, his nose white with zinc oxide, grinning ear to ear. "Do I look like him?"

"Um, maybe," Kira said. The nose? The shape of the eyes? So different otherwise. "I'd have to see you next to each other."

"Can I use your phone?" Amber asked. She'd lost her phone on the bus with her shoes, she said, and what time again did she say "Dad" would be home? The word riled Kira every time Amber used it; as if she was stealing something precious from Polly.

"Of course. Feel free. But let me try Adam again first." She let it ring four times, hung up. Damn him.

☙ POLLY

Polly ran down the hall to her room, slammed the door, threw the sandwich on her desk, and fell on the bed. The pressure burst from her eyes, throat, and nose as tears, sobs, and snot. Nobody followed. Her heart beat too fast. A sick feeling emanated from behind her ears and pooled in her stomach. Polly squeezed her face tight, clenched her teeth. Her head felt like the beginning of a migraine.

They'd lied. Tuesday night. Her mom was supposed to help her with her homework. Supposed to. That was normal for Tuesday. And then they'd go out to dinner, maybe at Mikado. Maybe at Café Gratitude. But now, clearly that was not going to happen. A sandwich. A sister. And a nephew? Is that what that boy was? What else now, oh stupid punk rock Dad, any more extra kids? And no matter how much they all pretended now, it would never be normal again; the egg hatched, the baby born, and you couldn't—no matter how much you wanted to—stuff it back inside. They'd lied to her. Her entire childhood was a lie.

But after a while she was bored of crying.

Forget it. She got off the bed and sat at her desk, but just sitting and waiting for something to happen was boring. Nobody knocked, so she did her homework alone, with the exception of 9-13b in math, which was impossible. She could call Nell or Amanda for help but she didn't want to go out of her room for the house phone, and she'd stupidly left her cell in her purse in the kitchen with the strangers. The eggplant sandwich stared up at her. Polly folded the paper towel over it. Fine then. She just wouldn't eat.

☙ KIRA

Amber talked long distance on the land line in the living room, her voice a sudden shift from monotone to melodious alto. Joey lay at her feet on the floor. From the kitchen table, Kira smelled shit rising from him, wondered about toilet training—he had to be almost four—wondered about diapers, but Amber hadn't made a move towards her canvas bag. Should she offer to go buy diapers?

"If Joey needs to be changed, I'm happy to go get diapers for him, just tell me what to get him," she finally volunteered, sticking her head in the living room between Amber's phone calls. "Safeway's only a couple blocks."

Amber looked up, phone still at her ear. "He's okay." Flat toned again.

"But if you'd like to clean him up, please feel free to use the bathroom."

"Okay."

Kira wondered whether to call Child Protective Services. She walked down the hall, stood in front of Polly's closed door and knocked.

"What!"

"Can I come in?"

"I'm doing my homework."

"Good. Whenever you're ready." Polly did not come out. Kira sat back down at the kitchen table, then got up to put on more water for tea. She tried calling Adam again. Trapped in her own house with the intruders. Wrapping her hands around the tea mug, closing her eyes, she worked hard to recapture the sense of serenity she always felt after yoga class. Instead, the feel of Ravi's torso against her back as he corrected her *trikonasana*.

Amber was still on the phone, the big screen TV blaring commercials. Kira heard only a few of her words and phrases: "… kicked my ass, took my shoes snow or no snow, threw me on the bus, freezin' and tweakin' for days. …Three hundred dollars, that's all we had… Yes, I'm checking it out. Hey, J.J.'s not no trouble, come on now… I know he's my ace… Well, then, what else can I do?" And the phone clicked down. And silence.

CHAPTER 2

◌ KIRA

At 6:20, the light long gone from the winter sky, Adam arrived home, and by the time he did, Kira was dizzy with anger and helplessness. She caught him in the small foyer off the living room—stood speechless blocking his way. They were almost the same height; she wore his shirts to bed; when younger, they'd traded clothes, gotten the same hair cuts. Now they didn't look the same anymore, except perhaps the expressions on their faces, their hand gestures. So many years together.

"What happened? What's the matter?" he asked, moving toward her, as if through her into the living room. She didn't budge.

She hissed. "Amber's here. With one of her kids. Joey. The big kid is Johnny, he lives with her mom. Can you believe it: Joey and Johnny. Nice, huh. All afternoon, Adam. Have we even heard from her in what, three, four years? Since the money for the lawyer thing? What was I supposed to tell Polly? What was I supposed to do?"

"Who?"

"Amber! As in Amber and Sandi, Amber. She's here. From Nevada. If you ever turned on your phone, you'd know about this. Since we arrived home from school. Look, Adam, I had a really hard, hell of a day at The Center: grant apps due and at least ten faculty members including Robison, that idiot, wanted me to walk them through the process, and the visiting artist apps are flying in, I was late for yoga—I hate that, Polly's got a ton of homework, I can't believe Mr. Scott. We need to talk to him, these kids are totally overloaded. And now this." She wanted to hit him, slam him over the head with it. His fault. His problem. "I told Polly. What was I supposed to do?"

Adam turned white. "Oh, fuck."

"Yup."

"Was Polly okay with it?"

Kira shrugged.

"How'd she get here?"

"She was just here, sitting on the doorstep, stinking of cigarettes. The boy destroyed my succulent. He's not okay, there's something wrong with his eyes. He doesn't engage; autistic or something. She's in there, on the couch. She's on the phone to Elko. To her mom. Again. Do you want to talk to her?"

"To Sandi? Psycho bitch from hell?"

"To Amber! Go in there, please. I've had it. Polly's hiding in her room."

Adam looked panicked. "Can I get changed first?"

"Changed? No! It's your problem. They're staying for dinner."

"Dinner? How come?"

"Because she has nothing, no shoes, no money, and there's a little boy involved. She's coming off of something; she seems really zoned out. I hid my codeine, it's in my bedside drawer. Look, go in there and meet her yourself. This is not my responsibility."

He set down the video recording equipment, pulled his sweatshirt over his head, exposing his rounded belly for a moment, the familiar scraggle of gray-black wiry hair. "Give me a break, Kira. Let me catch up a minute. You've had all afternoon to get used to this."

"Don't. You. Even." She wanted to smack him or run, run,

run… a cool forest, a deserted island… she pictured Ravi next to her, easing her back gently into place. "Please, get in there, Adam," she said. "I'm going to do breath work in the bedroom. I have to calm down."

He stopped, reached a hand towards her face. "We'll get take-out, pizza or Japanese. Don't try to cook. I'll call Mikado for Green Dragon rolls or something."

"I wasn't planning on it."

"Look, we'll feed them dinner, and then I'll put them on a bus home." His voice reached for compromise.

"Don't be a jerk," she said. "She's your daughter, maybe. Let them stay the night."

Through the bedroom door: "Polly? Still doing your homework? Are you okay?"

"I'm doing my homework."

"Okay, I'll be in the bedroom. Amber and Joey are spending the night. We're calling out for pizza. Okay, Poodle?" She wanted to see Polly's face, reassure herself that Polly was fine, that this had not hurt her irrevocably… but she would not breach the closed door.

"Whatever! I'm fine!"

Kira leaned her face for a moment against the white painted wood. "Okay," she called, feeling ice floes crack and separate, the dark arctic waters increasing between them. She went into her room to breathe.

❧ ADAM

It was impossible. If he weren't so tired. Part of the issue, Adam thought, looking through the open kitchen door into the living room where Amber sat in profile, was that she was just so fat.

Which implied a whole different mindset. His own child couldn't be fat, in their household where they got a box of organic groceries every week from their local CSA, popped Omega 3 capsules and vitamin C, fucking yuppie that he was. Last year he'd realized, in an epiphany of self-disgust, what a stereotype he'd become: typical middle-class Bay Area family man with Green politics, down to the Prius hybrid in the driveway of their 1917 Craftsman-with-potential. Kira's Saab—bought flat out at least, with a small inheritance after her dad's death—shouting money money money. They'd fought about that. But it was her car, she could drive whatever the fuck she felt comfortable with. Better than an SUV, anyway. They'd even investigated solar for the house; they'd gotten an estimate ($30K, even with the rebates)—sticker-shocked out of that one. Yeah, in about fifteen years it saved you money.

Why was he thinking about solar power? Amber's voice sounded like Sandi's. She was still on the phone. He couldn't quite make out her words, just her emotion, self-righteousness, fatigue, and then just as he finally keyed his ears to hear what she was saying, she said loudly, "Steve, you're a fucking asshole!" and put down the phone hard.

If he could just nap first. Take off his clothes, slide into the sheets, lay his head down onto the pillow. Finish the dream he'd started five minutes before the alarm went off (Bob Dylan singing First Man's anthem in his nasally voice, "*Pipe up, bong down, drive that fucker out of town…*"), a dream of cool water and wind, the sea; and at this point he'd been standing in the doorway too long, looking at what he now realized was the blanketed head of a small child facing away from him. Grandson. The word was impossible.

But she turned and saw him. Round face, not pretty. Dull eyes, lank hair, skin too yellow for the pink sweat suit. Who wore pink? Certainly not pretty Polly, dabbling in Goth. Pink a travesty on this tired, puffy woman.

"Dad?"

"Hi, you must be Amber." Adam forced himself around the back of the worn blue loveseat and into the room. "Nice to meet you. And this is Johnny? Hi Johnny."

"Joey," Amber said.

"Hi Joey."

The boy didn't look up.

"He doesn't talk, really," she said. "The other one, Johnny, J.J., he's my smart boy, sweet one. He's with his grandma. My mom. He lives with her, well, for right now. You know."

"Uh, how is your mother?" Adam stood near the love seat, Amber in it. He and Polly snuggled comfortably to watch DVDs, but Amber was too big to share with, even if he'd known her well. He tried not to notice her sloppy belly, overly big breasts. This was his daughter. Maybe. His mouth felt dry and old. Old man's breath. He took a seat at the edge of the torture chair— great lines, but if you sat down deeply in its receptive wooden slats you had to pry yourself out of it. Perched on the edge, he felt his face's tightness, his human hypocrisy. How to keep look- ing interested and... fatherly when all he wanted was to walk away, out the door, into the car, across the bay and the city, park in the lot to the bridge, face the bracing air and lean against the steel barrier. Just lean.

"Mom? She's okay. Got a new job at the new hospital in town."

"She's a nurse?"

"Nurse's aide at the NNRH."

"Uh huh. Great! Sounds great!" He had no idea what the NNRH was. He sounded completely insincere to himself, trying for a Clintonesque feel-your-pain tone. "And how are you?"

"Not so good, Dad."

The word shocked him every time she used it. Five years ago he'd left a message on Amber's answering machine—Sandi's machine—, "I'd prefer if you didn't call me Dad until we get a DNA test done. Which I am willing to pay for. It might make things easier if we know." He'd tried to picture her face listening to his words, but he hadn't seen that face since she was a baby. And he didn't know if she'd gotten that message or if Sandi had erased it, because the next time she called she was scared, small voiced, twenty-one years old and up for 2-to-5 years on interstate meth smuggling, and it seemed mean and small to mention the name thing or the DNA thing again. He'd wired her five grand for lawyer's fees—a huge fight between him and Kira: "So you're claiming her now?" "I don't know. I don't know if she's mine." "It doesn't matter, Adam. You can't keep dicking all of us around. Claim her or don't claim her, shit or get off the pot."

Poor kid. Even if she wasn't his.

This was his cue to ask her what was up. What was not so good. And why she was here. But he couldn't. "You can stay here tonight," he said. "Tomorrow I'm happy to take you to the bus station, or I can put you on a train, if you like. But you can stay here. Tonight. We'll all have dinner together; you can meet Polly."

"I already met her."

"Yes." He corrected himself. Where was Polly?

"I'm broke." She looked right in his eyes.

"Bus tickets on me, no problemo," he said. Wondering if she'd seen the Saab. "Let me show you the room. I have a t-shirt you can sleep in, I'll get something from Polly for Joey. Do you need a futon for Joey or does he sleep with you?"

Joey was asleep sitting on the floor, his head leaned against the loveseat, making a small boy's sleep noises. Kira was right, there was something wrong. His eyes didn't close.

"Sleep with me? Don't you got a sleeping bag? He sleeps anywheres."

Anywhere, Adam thought. "We'll fix you both up." He stood, the chair cooperated and he didn't fall, but still she sat there.

"Come on, I'll show you the guest room."

"Can we just hang out here?"

"Of course. Make yourself at home." He backed out the door.

Well. That went… terribly. In the refrigerator, he found an old beer in the back. He wasn't much of a drinker anymore but if he had a shot of heroin he would cook it right up in front of the whole family right now, tie off, shoot up, nod out. His face flushed, his hands shook. Something so stupid, and he couldn't even remember much about it—a twenty minute fuck—fucking it all up, all his life, his only life. When what you do early in life backfires, and there is no way out. Cannot do-over though you try. Because it all follows you around.

The first few years, there'd been something of success to it. Knocked her up one weekend in Reno, a sense of accomplishment, a thrill down his torso into his balls, and he stood taller. The reality—he never knew if it was him, or Stan, or even Jumbo the big Indian dude; Sandi got around that weekend. "Because Baby Amber is just like *you*," she'd said when she hitched down to the Haight to tell him a year later. "I know it was you." And then he'd fucked her again, all weekend, her belly a postpartum poof under Indian patchouli-smelling cotton, baby in the corner in a nest of blankets, before she disappeared back to the wilds of an occasional phone call asking for cash, putting the little girl on to say, "Daddy?" Kira glaring at him across the room: "Claim her or don't claim her, Adam. Shit or get off the pot."

Was that before paternity tests existed, or did that not happen with wannabe-neo-hippie hick girls? Five years older than he was, taking advantage. She'd planned that weekend, wanted a baby, knew she was fertile, she told him later, asking for $500 "and I'll never bother you again." Ha. As if. And even knowing it, "I wanna have a baby with you," he couldn't keep his dick in his pants. What did you expect from a 20-year-old guy on the loose? Why had she named him? The whole band had boned her. And the little girl in the annual Christmas photo that he opened and tossed away—Amber—looked more like Stan. Stan's bone structure (big) and high cheek-boned pink complexion. Then again, Sandi was pink too.

For years, he hadn't mentioned it. Kira knew, of course. Stan. Nobody else. Every time he heard Sandi's voice on the phone he felt the same sense of trapped fury. It choked him. You should be into it, man. The inner voice. You stud muffin. Stressed, he sang the blues: *"White Man Tryin' to be a Bluesman and I Ain't Even Black."*

They hadn't called for a long time. Years. Long enough to almost forget.

The beer was gone. He dug another Corona from the back of the fridge and took it with him to his studio where he'd stashed a bottle of tequila. Beer shot. Then he fired up his hash pipe for a hit or two, picked up his guitar. By the time he called Rustica for a pizza delivery, he was more smashed than he'd been in years.

☙ POLLY

Seven o'clock and still no dinner. Not that she'd come out if they called. Polly surfed the Internet, looking at tattoos. Which she was not allowed to get until she moved out of the house, though pierces were "negotiable." After all, her mom had one in her navel, and, if you counted the ones in her ears, most of which stood empty, she had at least five more. "No eyebrows, though," her dad said. The last time they'd talked about it was just a week ago Saturday. They were inching down Telegraph towards campus—slowly because of the traffic, street vendors, and homeless people pushing shopping carts between the cars—and Polly brought it up again as they passed Zebra Piercing and Tattoo. Her dad was doing a used sci fi run at Moe's, and Polly wanted the new Weetzi Bat book. "Not if it's still in hardback."

"I know, Dad."

"And no tongue pierce either," he said. "Messes up your teeth, and you got lucky and got my strong straight ones—let's not even think about your mother's mouth from hell—we're not doing the orthodontia thing because of something that looks cool."

"Nobody does eyebrow pierces anymore."

"And we might consider a nose pierce, but not one of those cow things."

"Okay! So what's left, Dad? A labia pierce?"

"Polly!" To her delight, he looked genuinely shocked.

"Don't worry. I think piercing your genitalia is disgusting," she said.

"Good. Glad you agree. Thank God you agree. You are sensible. All this is contingent on one thing, though."

"What?"

He paused. "Turning eighteen."

"What? But…?!"

"Uh huh, uh huh, oh yeah, that's right." He drummed the steering wheel in victory, opened the car window, and handed a dollar bill to a homeless woman with a caved-in face. "No, don't bless me, curse the system," he said.

"Humph." Polly retucked her hair behind her ears. Grrr, she thought. Contingent on turning eighteen. He always pretended to be so cool, Mr. Rock Star, but he so wasn't.

Now they'd lied to her, broken the *trust* they always said they'd built as a family. She couldn't trust them anymore, fine. So Polly planned her first tat. Something at the base of her spine so it just peeked out of her pants. A "tramp stamp." A runic or Asian symbol that meant Peace or Resistance. Icing on the muffin top, that little nice swell of flesh over the top of low riders. As if she had any muffin to ice.

The awful thing was what she'd seen out of the back of Amber's sweat pants. A whole lot of muffin, white and puffy. And a solid black tattoo, a symbol just like the one Polly wanted.

Polly pushed away from her desk and lay on the carpet, her head on her arms, but the feeling got worse, like she couldn't swallow or breathe. Today sucked worse than any day since Mishka died, hit by a car on Oakland Avenue and put to sleep before she'd said goodbye. First Mishka got hit by the car last July, and when she found a clump of Mishka's hairs somewhere, her stomach still twisted. Now this.

"Polly! Dinner!" Her dad's voice muted from two rooms away.

She could refuse. But then it would be a scene, and lots of talking and concern. She picked herself up and dragged herself out there.

✎ KIRA

Polly was quiet during dinner, though she laughed meanly when Amber asked if they had "a can of parmesan cheese." "We no doubt have Reggiano and a grater," she said. Amber looked baffled, and Polly sighed, "Life with foodies. You'll get used to it."

Kira glared at her, mouthed, "Be polite." But, deep sadness for her daughter.

"What?" Polly asked loudly. "What did I do?"

Joey chewed on bread with butter, slid to the floor. Amber took a few bites of her pesto pizza then went out to the porch to smoke. "She'll get hungry probably tomorrow," Adam said, sotto voce. "It's the meth. It takes away your appetite."

"I know that, Adam. I've done speed." Kira noticed Adam's vague eyes, wondered if he was stoned, decided not to ask. So what if he took a hit or two. She had her yoga; he had his pot. A lifetime together. Whatever kept them serene. She told herself: if I can just get through tonight.

By nine thirty, Amber and Joey were ensconced in the guest bedroom on a single tri-fold futon for Amber and a sleeping bag for Joey on the floor. Amber looked lost but Kira said, "Good night. Get some rest," and closed the door firmly on them. Garbage night. Adam went to bring the cans to the curb. Kira loaded the dishwasher.

"Mommy, look, I hurt myself." Polly pushed a hand near Kira's face. A tiny pin prick on the tip of her index finger. Poor Polly—thirteen-year-olds were one minute adults, the next, back to being two-year-olds.

Kira bent to kiss the boo boo. "Oh, Poodle, put something on that. You know where the BandAids are? Then go to bed, it's late for a school night."

Polly's face twisted and reddened—she pulled away and ran out of the room.

She's in shock, Kira thought. Give her time. They'll be gone tomorrow.

Adam stood near the stairway down to his basement studio. Waiting. "It's a different socioeconomic status," he said. "They're hicks. I don't want Polly hanging out with hicks on speed. She's probably got a hairy biker boyfriend with a Harley and twenty prison tattoos."

"Oh, forget it," she said. "Let's just deal with it tomorrow."

He nodded, and turned down the stairs. Late at night, she felt the bed shake as he slid in behind her.

In the morning, silence from the guest bedroom. The January sky was still dark, almost 7:00, pink dawn clouds through the kitchen window, the garden frosted white in the low areas. Months before she'd be able to get back out there, replenish herself with weeding, planting, harvesting. Kira and Adam, a well-oiled machine, prepared oatmeal and coffee and Polly's lunch. Showers and scurrying to stuff the overfull backpack and "…don't forget your permission slip for the Egyptian Museum field trip!" "Shh, they're still sleeping, Adam!"; cell phones plucked from the vine of snarled charge cords and computer cables on the cluttered dining room table. And off in the Saab: Kira and Polly, the sky brightening. A clear day.

Kira dropped Polly at Pioneer School at 8:30. Polly talked less than usual, the sullenness of new adolescence. They listened to morning drive time silly talk radio—a compromise between Kira's preference of NPR and Polly's insipid pop. Then off to campus, fifteen minutes circling the lots to get a spot even with her staff permit. It was a relief to get to her office at The Center, a small airy room in one of the Julia Morgan buildings on campus; white walls, brown moldings, tall windows, heavy furniture, contemporary art from all the visiting artists in the program she directed. A quick hello to Sarah, her assistant, and booting up the computer with a sigh. Several times during the day-long deluge of email she thought briefly about Adam, home dealing with Amber and Joey, and her stomach clenched. Then she turned back to the endless flow of requests and clarifications, compiling the grant proposal docs, getting Sarah to copy and distribute, fielding the endless calls and emails from nervous or confused faculty and student applicants.

❧ ADAM

All morning, Adam puttered, waiting for them to get up, reading the paper in the kitchen and drinking an extra cup of black coffee, his stomach a queasy mess from the insult of tequila last night, his head too large. Beer, tequila, and a couple of hits—man. Too old for that shit. At ten thirty, still silence from the guest room. Adam went to his basement to check email.

Amber got up around eleven and used the bathroom for a long time, then she and Joey settled into the living room in front of the TV watching Family Feud with bowls of Kashi and milk, still wearing Adam and Polly's sleep shirts. Amber half sat, half lay, eyes closed, against the couch cushions. "Can we maybe wash our clothes," she said, opening her eyes when Adam walked into the room.

"Hand 'em over. I'll take you to get some new clothes when these are clean," he told her. She barely nodded. The dirty sweatsuit and boy's pajamas felt thin and polyester in his hands as he put them in the machine, added soap. She hadn't given him any underwear to wash.

Behind the washer and dryer, a low plywood door led to a dirt-floored crawlspace where they'd stored Polly's old favorite toys in plastic bins: the wooden blocks, the stuffed animals, Groovy Girls. Near the bins, her doll house, her trike. Her old booster seat. They'd meant to have a garage sale with some of this stuff, the rest they'd keep forever or until Polly had kids. *Grandkids.* He cringed in the cold musty space; old cobwebs, insect carcasses, yellow dust. Joey might be his grandson, *might be,* but all he felt was the same vague compassion he felt for the swollen bellied, big eyed babies on the outside of fundraising envelopes.

"Love is a verb," Kira always said. It was woo-woo, but he knew what she meant, that it was actions that counted. He took action. The booster seat. They would need that for the drive to the Greyhound station. The trike, the blocks. The kids books. He brought them upstairs in batches, his brains loose, black jeans tight.

"Hey Joey," softly. "Look at these." Joey licked his sleeve, long slow cow licks. "I'll just leave them here. Amber, feel free to use any of these, Polly's got some cool old stuff here."

"Okay." She didn't meet his eyes either. Shy? Stoned? "You putting us out today? Mom said don't come back to Elko, that it's your turn to take some responsibility."

Damn that Sandi.

Joey was reaching for the box of blocks three feet away, a slow motion reach, thumb and fingers snapping shut again and again. He put his hand around a blue cylinder and brought it to his mouth.

"And Steve's gonna call me here." Amber said it like a challenge. Without looking at him. Stubborn. Desperate.

"Steve?"

"Steve, that's Joey's dad, not Johnny's dad—that's Mike, he's down in Louisiana—he was on oil rigs—don't know what he's doing now, but anyways, Steve and I used to be together for a long time, but he dumped me, but now he's trying to be a good dad so we're still kinda together. Sometimes. His mom's cool. She gives a shit." Her voice had loosened a bit.

She had a pretty voice, Adam realized. But a face for radio. "Okay, let's get those clothes dry, I'll fix you up with some shoes, clothes, we'll figure out what to do," he said, and backed out of the room. Jesus fucking Christ, was he supposed to put them out on the street now?

When the clothes were dry, Adam lent Amber a pair of Kira's athletic shoes and a jacket. Outside the wind gusted through the oaks, cold for the Bay Area, dark for daylight. At Target, Joey wearing his pajama pants and Polly's Mime Troupe t-shirt (it fell below his knees), Polly's old snow jacket. Adam browsed the electronics department while Amber shopped in the women's section, Joey in the top of the cart. Twenty minutes later he found her in front of the sock display, two black polyester thongs in the cart and a 2X pink tank top with Lusty Chick emblazoned in silver rhinestones. She held a pair of socks in her hand.

"Can I get these, too?"

"You're going to need more than that," he said, commandeering the cart, his body springing a big belly, white beard, red suit. He cruised the aisles tossing stuff in—two sweat suits for her, three t-shirts, two hoodies, a rain coat, socks, ho ho ho, a couple of bras...

"What size?"

"Hey! I'm not telling you my bra size!"

"Look, just get what you need, put it in the cart."

...four toddler pants, shirts, a tiny jean jacket, toddler shoes. In the pharmacy area, he stocked up on toothbrushes, toothpaste, deodorant, shampoo, conditioner, soap, Tampax, diapers, wipes. Amber trailed behind, came back with a small box of eye drops, an eyeliner, hair spray, and something that looked to Adam like a silver, skinny dildo.

"What's that?"

"Eye drops, for Joey. That okay? He really needs them for his eyes."

"No, that's fine. This."

She looked at him like he was insane. "A curling iron. For my bangs. It's on sale, $7.99. I got my mom's hair; desert hair.

Eyeliner's a dollar. You said get what you need."

"I did." Good thing she didn't "need" a computer. A chain saw.

He headed for the cashier, stopping halfway. "Need anything else?"

She looked into the full cart, stared at the scuffed white floor.

"Amber. Look, I'm buying. But now or never, so if you need it, speak it."

She shook her head. Then, "Can I get that Raiders shirt for Johnny? To take back to him?"

"Sure."

"Some gum, too?"

That was pretty much max on the credit card.

Back at home, Amber stuck the bags in the guest room, then sat on the couch and turned on the TV to the Home Shopping Network. She was so passive, it freaked him out—as if she'd teleported in, and that was it, she was there, ensconced in their house and never going to leave again. The couch already had an Amber-butt-sized dent in it, the carpet by the left side of her feet looked battened down—crop circles—by Joey's constant rolling there. He was obviously retarded. Developmentally disabled, Adam corrected himself.

He should drive them to the bus station. But he couldn't face her.

By late afternoon, he was back down in his basement studio googling "autism," "eyes don't shut," "no eyelids," "eye birth defects retardation," "congenital eye problems." Was it something genetic? If, and if, it could be his fault. If she was his daughter. He learned about potential causes for the eye deformation and developmental disability: telecanthus; Goldenhar's Syndrome; fetal alcohol syndrome (more likely to cause wide-set eyes and poorly developed optic nerves). Paralysis of the eyelids was sometimes caused by Graves Disease. Microphthalmia, to be born without eyelids, could be genetic or caused by x-ray, anoxia, pesticide exposure to the fetus in utero: benomyl, glyphosate, mercury, dioxins, methyl bromide, PCBs. As if knowing the reason why it had happened could help. As if he could help, unless he claimed them, doomed puppies at the pound.

The shiny metal heating ducts were warm and flexible. He reached high to hold one, warm his hands. Then back at the computer, he wiped the Google box and opened the tequila bottle. Typed: "Celebrity tits, free porn."

CHAPTER 3

"Like my scar?" Brady asked Polly during math. Under their long work table in the basement classroom, Brady pulled up the sleeve of his gray hoodie to show her a healing, raised red gash on his forearm, almost two inches long, running parallel to his wrist bone.

"How'd that happen?" Polly whispered. Mr. Anthony was looking their way.

"Scarification." He raised his chin, casually fixing his eyes on the board. "Do you like body mod?"

"I like tattoos."

"I do, too."

"You did that yourself?"

"Yeah. That's the point. You cut it and then you rub toothpaste in so it will scar up." He pulled his sleeve down, pulled his notebook toward him, and started copying problems from the board. Polly sat still. She'd never admit it to her best friend Nell, but she had a crush on Brady. He'd started the year preppy but was slowly turning more old school punk, spiking his hair and dying the front of it green, wearing stud bracelets. His dad worked at the East Bay Vivarium, so Brady knew a lot about snakes; he'd duct taped the front of his Converse hi tops. His iPod playlist was all The Clash and X and Siouxsie and the Banshees, stuff her dad liked. He was her math partner, and he was pretty good even though he was so throwback—they worked well together.

"It's called scarification?" she whispered when Mr. Anthony's back was turned.

He nodded. "A lot of girls think it's repulsive."

"I think it's cool."

"Why d'ya think I showed you."

Polly's face grew hot, and she ignored Brady for the rest of the day.

Scarification was even better than tattoos. Tattoos were for everybody, and even Amber had taken the one she wanted—she'd still get one, at least one, but she knew she had to wait. And by the time she was eighteen, tramp stamps would probably not even be cool anymore.

But scarification, that was fascinating. The body grew back. You cut yourself, your body grew more body. You could use it to carve your emotions in your skin, your barrier against the world. To express who you were now, so you would never forget, even when you were old. You could do it yourself—it didn't require parental permission, so you didn't have to wait until you were eighteen.

✍ KIRA

A long day at work. Once a year in February, The Center distributed arts funds campus-wide. She only had jurisdiction over a two hundred grand budget in small grants, but there were the orientation meetings to run, the Board to get together—a busy time of year. Two more weeks of this and things would loosen until April and visiting artist season. At least she had yoga to look forward to.

Wednesdays, Sarah stayed late and Kira snuck out a little early. As if she wasn't way over her 37.5 hours a week as it was. Wednesday, Polly's afternoon to carpool home with Amanda. She was old enough now to play latchkey kid if Adam was still involved getting Amber and Joey on the bus.

A small pang that she and Polly hadn't said goodbye to Amber and Joey. She pictured a black-belching bus crossing the snowy Sierra and the bleak Nevada desert, Joey staring endlessly out the window at endless gray… but should she have woken them this morning? And by the time she got home, they'd be gone. Back to normal. A small pang of relief.

Lunch at her desk, thinking about dinner. It was Adam's night to rustle it up. Usually he made something with organic vegetables from The Box—in January, summer's tomatoes and basil were long gone and they were deep into months of kale and garlic, lettuce, winter squash.

She called home before she left work, then his cell. Nobody answered either place. "Do you need me to swing over to Farmer Joe's?" she left on his cell phone; he never answered the damn thing. They ate out too often, despite Polly's pleas for more "at-home" dinners; they ate out because they were tired, because they could, because they lived in the Bay Area, with the best restaurants in the world except for maybe Paris or New York. Adam didn't call her at work, so Kira drove to the Y for Ravi's Intermediate class.

They were definitely too car dependent, she thought as she drove the four blocks from campus to the Y: Highways 580, and 13, and 80; MacArthur Boulevard, Broadway, Martin Luther King Jr. Way, a whole family continually fighting road rage. At least Adam drove a Prius—less environmental guilt. A "Pious," Polly called it. All the driving. To Polly's school in Berkeley, Kira's office at Cal, to Adam's freelance shoots, to their regular restaurants. El Huarache and El Centenario on International Avenue. Cheap Japanese food at Mikado on Grand, Kira's favorite. Vegan macrobiotic cooked by Tibetans at Manzanita Restaurant, though not when Polly could help it. Until the first Mad Cow scare they'd patronized East Oakland pho houses for rich, deep beef noodle soup. Soul food at Wilma's Catfish Kitchen on San Pablo, discovered the afternoon Polly and Adam met Wilma waiting next to them at the Touchless Carwash when they were washing Kira's Saab because some freak wrote "I wish my girlfriend was this dirty" with his finger on the back window. Doña Tomas; the best yuppie Mexican in town. Cactus, the cheapest yuppie Mexican in town. Pasta Pomodoro. The much-mocked, much-loved Café Gratitude in Berkeley, where the vegetables and nut dishes were raw and alive, and the dish names were affirmations: "I Am Welcoming," "I Am Evolved," "I Am Eternally Blessed."

Driving to eat locally grown food. Wasting resources, even in the Prius, but how else were they supposed to get around? The East Bay wasn't really set up for public transport.

Kira arrived at the Y ten minutes early, snapped off NPR, walked three flights down the pee-smelling garage stairway; she primped in the bathroom. Tired eyes from staring at the computer screen all day. Her hair looked terrible, curls flat in the back. A feeble attempt to fluff it... forget it. She entered the dimly lit Mind-Body center still five minutes early. Ravi reviewed his notes full lotus on his mat, back to the mirrors. Behind him, a small alter with a Tibetan singing bowl, a statue of Ganesh, and a single perfect pomegranate. The feel of small fruited seeds in her mouth.

Four long-haired women stretched and meditated on their mats. Two lay inverted in *salamba sarvangasana*, loose yoga pants gathering around their hips, exposing well-shaped, long, tan legs and pretty feet with toe rings. Ravi's girls. They always laid their mats near the front and circled him after class with requests for more corrections. "Pathetic," they'd whisper if they saw her checking herself in the mirror.

She went hunting for blocks and straps, then sat in lotus on her mat, trying to center herself. The room was filling up. Not just Ravi's girls, but men and women of all shapes—it was a popular class, maybe because Ravi was not the average Bay Area yoga teacher in his early thirties, the kind she and Adam made fun of for being too woo-woo Northern California hipster. Those woo-woo boys, the Burning Man boys: ponytails and generous sideburns, high clear foreheads, gentle tenor voices, steeped-tea brown eyes, surfer-boy legs sticking out of soy-based cargo shorts, Sanskrit and tribal black tattoos around wrists and biceps, loose walks, fake Eastern names changed from Brent or Brian. Several of those boys taught at the Y, matched sets with the Gitas and Shavitras and Lakshmis—blonde, taut women who, in the eighties, would have had names ending in "i," like "Debbi," and who would have taught jazz aerobics instead of yoga.

They laughed at those woo-woo new age people, she and Adam. Though how much participating could you do without becoming one of them?

Ravi was probably not born with that name, Ravi, though who knew, Kira thought, he was young enough to have hippie parents, maybe he was legitimately Ravi. Instead of Jesse or Jeremiah or Jason or Justin or Joshua like all the other men his age.

It had taken her months of attending class to notice not what he was *not* but what he *was*. Medium, not yoga-lanky. Solid thighs too big for his chest. That somebody that bulky was so flexible, so graceful, was a revelation, like watching an elephant dance without the comic value. After practicing with him for several months, she'd noticed his hands, large, block fingers. Never a fidget, every movement deliberate. Now she looked for them. *Sutra* hands.

Ravi was a good teacher, accurate and kind. He'd studied with a guru three years in the heat of Goa, eating rice and dahl and yogurt and dousing his intestinal parasites with vast quantities of lemon pickle. It had worked, he'd told the class, he'd come back clean. Forty pounds thinner, but parasite-free. Arriving to class early twice, she'd seen Ravi seated on his mat reading books by Maxine Hong Kingston and T.S. Eliot where she'd expect Thich Nhat Hahn or Krishnamurti. He'd mentioned once in a class, when the anatomical terms had flown thick and heavy and another student mentioned that he should be a doctor, that he'd dropped out of med school to follow a spiritual path, which meant he was brilliant and capable and evolved, able to see through the bullshit of the society at a young age.

Adam had barely gotten through Chico State.

Without looking at Ravi, Kira moved her mat further back in the room closer to the windows, tried to breathe, aware, even when her back was to him, of every time he looked up from his notes. Leave now, she thought. Go home. But it was just a little crush. She wasn't used to crushes, what was okay and what wasn't, so focused on Adam all these years.

"Okay, let's begin," Ravi said. He read from a small book: "Abiding in this ephemeral world, like a lotus in muddy water, the mind is pure and goes beyond. Thus we bow to Buddha." He bowed his head then raised it and surveyed the class. "Like this cross-disciplinary altar, the teachings from all the traditions are merely a brief reflective glance in a mirror. From these glances we can, maybe, get a glimmer of absolute truth. So, as we deepen our practice today, take a moment to find a comfortable seated position. Pull the flesh from your sit bones and send your energy down into the earth, rooting yourself. Align your spine and send the energy upward through the crown of your head chakra. If you choose to dedicate this practice to a person, a principle, a moment of trouble in the world, you can do that now. We'll begin by joining our voices together in three Oms."

Three times during the ninety minute session Ravi adjusted her, her body sinking against his hands. He moved from student to student, whispering to one, silently correcting another's position, paying as much attention to the hopelessly inflexible old men in the back as the show-off "Ravi's girls" in the front. He took his students seriously; even in this group drop-in class, available to any bozo with a Y card, he treated them like they were all committed yogis and yoginis.

"Kira," he called across the room when they were in warrior one, *virabhadrasana*, "Don't break at the wrist." But even before he got the words out, she felt her body make the adjustment he wanted. Just her name in his deep voice enough to remind her. And finally, near the end of class, as she lay in child's pose, *balasana*, he lay over her, pressed completely against her back so she could feel his breath radiating down through her. She lay covered, aware of every inch of his body. His heartbeat. Heat soared through her body. What was wrong with her? A crush. Just a crush.

She'd never thought she'd be attracted to a younger man. Or an older one. She and Adam, five months apart (she in August and he, the next year, in January) had always seemed the perfect age difference. The same age, but she with the edge of a school year on him. When they'd met at Tam High, she'd been a senior, he'd been a junior. That's how she felt about Adam—always—he was her junior, but just a little. She could boss him around—just a little. But they had the same cultural references. The same taste in music, clothes. The same TV shows growing up. The same community. With an older guy she'd be getting into that superior "I-was-a-hippie-and-you-were-too-young" attitude. Too much Rolling Stones. And younger men… she'd never looked at younger men. Too fresh. Too young. Their youth reflecting on her, making her too old.

Not that she'd considered either, younger or older. She and Adam completely bonded since they'd gotten together years after high school. Perfect for each other, in bed and out, fitting each other. Finishing each other's sentences like an old married couple after they'd been together only a week, and now she'd been monogamous for so long, it was habit. Only vague attractions, minor fantasies.

Near the end of class, Ravi encouraged the more advanced poses. Wheel. A back bend pose that always scared Kira, the feeling of maybe falling on her head. "Move into it slowly," he said. "*Urdhva Dhanurasana*. Feel your body one half of the complete wheel, the other half below you, circling through the earth." She felt her torso reach skywards, her arms strong, the cycle. Her head back, eyes open, noticing again the pomegranate on the altar, her favorite fruit. Had he known? He couldn't have known. Heart open to the sky, broken open.

In grade school in San Francisco, Kira had pomegranates in her lunch all Fall. She knew what six seeds felt like in her mouth; the cool, geometrical shapes, smooth surfaces, pointed tips where they grew attached to the thick bitter rind like baby teeth reversed—red on white instead of white on red. Six seeds, strong enough to swish and move through her mouth unscathed. Playing Persephone, holding the forbidden fruits in her mouth like a squirrel, testing gently with her teeth. Then biting down. Crunch. Sweet flavor, and her fate was sealed.

She held the wheel pose strongly a long time. Then his hands under her back. "Okay, slowly down now, don't collapse it. Beautiful." Then he moved to the front of the room again, dimmed the lights, and set up for *savasana*, corpse pose, the final relaxation. She tried to clear her mind, let her body totally relax. But her heart raced.

She took a long time rolling up her mat after *savasana*, waiting until everybody was gone. "Thanks," she said, turning back at the last moment, close to the door. "Great class."

"Yes," Ravi said. "There was amazing energy going on in class today."

Amazing energy. Adam would have snorted. But she was so tired of Adam's bitterness and irony, as if the cool that he'd generated for so many years had seeped into his bones and turned him brittle. Yes, he was funny. But so often, the humor ironic and mean. Ravi—okay, he was a little humor-impaired—but that was endearing. Like he could take the world seriously. And if you took the world seriously, then you could do something about it. She looked at her bare left foot. She needed a pedicure; a few chips of polish from last summer still lingered in the cracks of her big toenail.

"Hey, I've been meaning to tell you," Ravi said. "If you're free, I'm teaching at Studio Raza on Mondays during lunch. If you're free. Come on by. I'd be honored to work with you. It's a smaller space. More intimate. We can really focus in on your body." Her body. The heat of the blood flushing through her again. She felt her hips shift, her nipples press against her sports bra.

"We also work on some other practices, discuss other spiritual teachings as a small group. Do some reading."

Something she ached for. He knew things she wanted to know.

"Or I teach yoga privately, too. We could do a lot—you're carrying a lot of tension in your shoulders and hips. We could focus there."

"How tempting. Maybe I'll try to make it. Mondays are hard." *Tension in my hips.* She was already trying to envision her calendar, meetings moved earlier, lunch dates shifted. Her left hand throbbed, her wedding ring a barrier, as if she wore her heart on her left finger and it was banded, the platinum sank lightly into the flesh; the flesh welled up around it. She lost her nerve. "Well, thanks for class. I've had a hard couple of days; it was just what I needed today."

"I can see that, Kira. You're carrying a lot of sadness."

Am I sad?

"Well, namaste," he said, a twist in his imperfect upper lip that threw her over the edge again.

"Namaste."

He turned away, and she carried her mat and her shoes to the dressing room, kicking herself and thrilled. And then self-critical. Pathetic, she thought, driving home in her middle-class Saab. Look at me. He probably drove a biodiesel retro-fitted Mercedes, too cool for school. Ten years too young for her. Dancing at Burning Man, bending his pretty yogini girls into advanced poses and screwing them while chanting in Sanskrit.

No. He was different than that.

Three breaths to focus as she pulled into the driveway. This was bad for her. For her family. Like Persephone with her six pomegranate seeds, holding the little morsels of death in her cheek, testing them. She tried for more breath, filling her abdomen, diaphragm, and chest, releasing from the top down: chest, diaphragm, abdomen. She wondered if she'd dare fit in one more yoga class a week with Ravi—a public class, not a private one. I'm trying to deepen my yoga practice, she practiced saying to Adam. My spiritual practice. Would he laugh?

But as she opened the door to the house, the sky behind her roses and oranges and purples of late sunset, she realized they were still there; Amber and Joey, the diapers and the cigarettes and the blaring TV.

ひ ADAM

They discovered that night that Amber didn't ever eat salad.

"I don't like green food."

"Not even artichokes?" Polly asked. "With mayo and butter?"

"Never had that."

"That's my favorite. How about…" Polly's face worked hard, trying to think of green food that wasn't a vegetable. "…what's a good green food that Amber would like?" she asked Kira.

"Pesto? Olives? Lime jello?" Kira asked.

Amber laughed. "Nah. I don't like green food."

"Does Joey?" Polly asked.

"He likes carrots and peas."

Amber didn't eat almost anything at dinner, green or not. She drank a lot of Diet Pepsi.

"Um," she said to Kira, "can I get more Pepsi?"

In the kitchen after dinner: "She'll get hungry probably tomorrow," Adam said.

"So, how long is she staying?" Kira cornered him at the dishwasher, Polly had cleared the table and left for her room ("Homework!"); Amber was changing Joey's diaper in the living room.

"You're the one who insisted she stay."

"I said one night, Adam. You were going to take them to the bus today."

"I know. I'm sorry."

"Did you talk to her?"

"Not yet. I will. She's still limping on that ankle."

"Don't make me the bitch. You're making me the bitch, here. And my name is not 'Um.' She better start calling me by my name, tell her, you tell her that. Or she's out on her ass."

"Nice, Kira. Maybe she thinks your name is 'Om.' Om Mani

Padme Om. Let's give her a few days to get her shit together. Speaking of, I have to go take a dump." He left the room, aware of Kira fuming behind him.

❧ POLLY

Polly stood in the doorway of the living room; Amber sat on the couch watching TV and Joey whirled around and around, blocks in his hands. Amber didn't notice her. Or pretended she wasn't there. It's my house, Polly thought. I can stand here. Somebody yapped on about healing your inner child, and Joey spun and pawed his eyes.

Amber grabbed him, leaned him back on her wide lap. She uncapped a bottle of Visine and squirted it in his eyes, her hands harsh and tender, like Mishka used to play-growl and shake her stuffed Sheepie, then push it into Polly's hands to hold while she gently bit through the fur looking for fleas.

"Why do you do that?" Polly asked.

Amber turned. "Because his eyes can't blink. They get dried out, then they could get infected. He got microphthalmia. "

"When did he get it?"

"He was born that way."

"Do they hurt him?"

"Sometimes."

"Poor little kid."

"Yeah. But he's gonna have some operations later on, little buckaroo."

Joey lay relaxed, and Amber stroked his forehead, pushing his hair back, her hands shaking, her shoulders guarding her neck on each side. Polly wondered what happened when Joey slept, pictured the eyes staring straight ahead. Or maybe his eyeballs rolled back so that all you could see was the white.

Scarification had more of an aesthetic value than just cutting, Polly found out from the bodymod websites she found that night, self-banished to her bedroom to avoid the whole family thing—a couple of how-to sites with demo pictures of the results. Some of them were really scary. But some really amazing.

It was cool enough to have a simple scar like Brady's, but even cooler to have something more aesthetic. Polly planned a star on the flesh just above the short-shorts line on her right upper thigh. A five pointed star. When she got up the nerve. She drew it in ballpoint pen on her leg. You are cool, she thought about Brady, lying in bed before she went to sleep.

When it washed off in the shower, she drew it again and again with her finger, practicing the path so she'd know where to go, even if it hurt a lot.

❧ ADAM

Adam didn't say anything to Amber about leaving, and she didn't say anything to him. Instead of dealing with it, Adam started writing a blues tune, picking the chords gently until it sounded right. *"I sail the river called Denial, and it's not in Africa."* Fuck it, it would all sort itself out. No work gig until Monday, no place to have to be. For the rest of the week, Amber watched TV and sat, or talked on the phone and sat. God, the phone bill. He offered outings: tourist trips to San Francisco, to Telegraph Avenue. He offered trips to the grocery store. He went out for a run over to Piedmont Avenue and the cemetery and offered to take her, or Joey.

"If you move your body, you'll feel better. We can get hot chocolate at Gaylord's on the way back."

"Nah, I'm not the exercising type."

"What are your plans?"

"Waiting for Steve. He's gonna call."

When he got back from his run, they hadn't moved.

Steve, Joey's dad and Amber's kind-of-boyfriend, maybe partner-in-crime—he was on his way to Santa Barbara, she said. So maybe they would go there. She could get a job there; she was sick of being unemployed, though these days nobody could get work with just a GED. Or maybe it was Salt Lake. Or they'd go to Tucson, Amber said, where her Great Uncle Donny lived. "Sucks to be me," she said, two kids by two dads and a felony record. She was clean and sober, she swore to God; this week was unusual. Right, he thought. Just that Sandi—"Mom"—had been such an asshole, she said, and Steve was totally taking Mom's side and, 'cause she had to stay awake so nobody would steal Joey or nothin', giving her some toot. So here she was, she told Adam, outta work and shit outta luck. "Tada." Her intonation rarely left its dull note, only to yell at Joey when he yelled. How could he kick her out? Kira just said, "It's your business, it's your problem, you deal with it."

Joey wouldn't play with any of Polly's old toys except the blocks; he held a blue cylinder in each hand and drummed on the floor. He liked to look at books: *Baby Animals of the Forest*, the Richard Scarry books.

Adam sat in the torture chair. They watched Judge Judy. His big screen TV, bought for the movies he watched late at night, had rarely played anything but PBS and DVDs until now; it felt polluted. Joey gummed a cylinder block. All at once, when Judge Judy was barking at a plaintiff who looked too much like Amber, Adam couldn't stand how depressing it all was.

It wasn't her fault she'd grown up in a shadow world where casinos abutted desert malls and flatlands, where kicks and boredom combined into bouts of methamphetamine poisoning. It was usually easier for him to ignore the outside world of rotted teeth and facial sores and planetary dismay. He lived near the wooded hills of the best region in the West. He drank nice wine and ate well when he wasn't fucking his life up in a dark basement room. His daughter went to a private school—not a fancy one, but progressive—and all his friends voted like he did. He'd always thought of himself as an easy-going guy, a fun dad to Polly.

"Amber, I have to get work done," he announced at the doorway Friday afternoon. "Just knock on my basement door if you two need me." He descended again to the pit. A pity party in the basement, followed by breath mints and dinner.

That evening, he hung out. Polly and Kira tightened their faces, so similar when angry, and pulled him taut between them all: Amber and Joey stayed in the living room; for a while he read *Baby Animals of the Forest* to Joey, who watched the pages but never looked at him. Damn, Amber sucked up room, all the air in the house. The streetlamp flickered through the front window of the bungalow adding light, subtracting light.

He hung out with Polly in her room for a few moments, sitting on her bed, not commenting on the mess, and watching her paste together a collage of tattoo images. And late at night, when he came into bed, Kira finally hung him out to dry.

"What are you doing to Polly, allowing Amber and Joey to stay?" She sat in bed, and he saw her tension—two deep lines furrowed between her waxed eyebrows. "I'm going to ask you again," she said. "One more time, Adam. Do me the favor of answering me. Honestly. How long is she going to stay?" she asked.

"I don't know."

She stared at him.

"Well, you better figure it out. We have guests on Sunday. Did you forget about our dinner party? And I need you to get a DNA test. Because this is ridiculous. If she's not yours, it's a total free ride. And that's just her ripping us off."

He was going to say again that it wouldn't matter if there was a DNA test, that love and claiming wasn't a matter of DNA, did she really believe that? But her light clicked off, she flipped her back to him, and in her sudden turn, she took all the covers.

CHAPTER 4

⤳ KIRA

For days now the house had smelled of Amber's smoke—it clung to Amber's clothes and followed her into the house from the porch—and Joey's dirty diapers. His unclosing eyes leaked white goop.

Kira tried to be a compassionate stepmom. Step-grandmother. She took Joey by the hand, planning to lead him to the bathroom and gently rinse his face with warm water, but the moment she touched him he grew rigid. Was he autistic, retarded, abused, fetal alcohol syndrome? Was she supposed to take over and take him to the doctor? Her friend Clare had told her about the wonders of Omegas for autistic kids, not that her son Micah was in trouble, but Clare's nephew—and they'd had great results treating it with alternative methods. Flaxseed. Floor time, whatever that was. Confrontational interventions—"Look at me! You *look* at me!"—but Kira couldn't imagine talking to Joey that way. Not her place. They had flaxseed though, so she stood in the dining room with the small bottle in her hand. "Amber, I have some flaxseed oil in capsules. I think they might be helpful for Joey. I'll put them right on the door of the fridge. Maybe, you might want to open some in his juice."

"Okay," Amber said, perpetually parked on the couch. Her fat ass parked, Kira thought, her meanness providing a wall for her anxiety to lean against and rest.

"He's gonna talk the day he has something to say," Amber said. But Kira hadn't heard anything other than mouse sounds and his howl every time Amber left his sight. As if her small bottle of flaxseed oil would transform him, the situation, because what would happen when they moved down the road? She'd bet $100 that Amber wouldn't take the flaxseed oil along.

Amber all day on the phone with the TV on, staring at her dinner with dismay. "I never tried this before," barely talking to anybody except Adam, hitting her kid, upsetting Polly... "It's not good for Polly, and I have to protect my child," she wanted to say. She breathed. She thought about Ravi, a small group of students meditating together, learning to go deeper. Somewhere else to go instead of here. Something to wipe away her intruded-on house and life, the tiptoeing around the kitchen to avoid the big lump in the living room with perfect curled half-moon bangs, the staring child, Adam who never even answered his phone.

Adam seemed a million miles away, fuzzy, his face forbidding her to approach. So far from that first year when all they'd wanted was to stay in bed and talk and make love. (Last night a silent détente and the familiarity of his leg over hers, her foot tucked neatly into the arch of his foot.)

Saturday, Kira lured Amber out of the house with a trip to Costco. She dreaded Costco, but they had one roll of toilet paper left, and Adam had gone the last two times.

"That's cool, I'll go along for the ride," Amber said. "Joey don't like it, though."

"Adam can take care of him."

Amber pushed up from the couch.

"Give you a chance to be with Joey," Kira said to Adam in the hallway. "Give me a chance to check her out."

"Your funeral," Adam said.

"Adam, don't be a jerk. This is your problem, and I'm trying."

On their way to the Saab, Kira folded a ten dollar bill tightly, the way her great aunt Selma always had when giving her Mad Money. What was Mad to buy at Costco, she didn't know, but it seemed the right thing to do. She pressed the thick rectangle into Amber's surprisingly silky hand. Amber pulled her hand away fast, looked at the bill, and stuck it into her pocket. She didn't look at Kira, she stared straight ahead and presented Kira with her profile. From the side, Amber's nose did look a bit like Adam's, lightly hooked at the end, bumpy in the middle.

Kira waited for her "Thanks," which didn't come. Then wondered why she needed a thank you so badly, the interplay between giver and givee so complicated, so exhausting.

"Seatbelt, please," Kira said. "Otherwise it beeps."

On Amber's feet, Kira's cross-trainers size 8, $96 last year at Copeland's, the ones Kira had bought to use on the machines in the women's gym at the Y and worn exactly twice. Their treads had never touched soil nor sidewalk until Adam had passed them over to Amber. Kira was fine with that. She hadn't needed them. Amber did. It should be that simple, she thought. She backed out of the driveway, turned the car towards 580. Toilet paper, paper towels, two six-packs of Italian pasta in various shapes, Cascade for the dishwasher, sponges, one large jar of artichoke hearts, balsamic vinegar, some wines; her list, composed by Adam, not much compared to the huge flats of junk food most people piled on their carts. Amber was quiet; this was, Kira thought, the first time they'd been completely alone together, no kids, no Adam.

"Um, before I got there, I didn't think your house would be like that, no offense," Amber said.

Kira moved to the right lane in the MacArthur Maze, first making eye contact with the man in the black SUV who let her slide in, then twiddling her hand in the rearview mirror to thank him.

"I used to think about it all the time when I was little, like I was famous or whatever, and it was like this big house, like this big beautiful house, and I was this princess coming home."

Kira stared straight ahead. Made the curve and merged onto 80.

"So I'd knock. And I'd wait awhile, all beautiful with great highlights in my hair, and I'm all calm, then Dad answers. And I say, 'I'm Amber.' And he gets this wrinkled thing near his eyes, like doctors on General Hospital when they smile. He's this stud. 'Welcome home.' And then we hug." Amber's voice softens. "That was it. All the time I thought about that. I was always coming home to Dad. But your house, no offense or nothing, it's not that great."

Kira's stomach turned, she clenched her jaw. She wanted to yell, "Don't call him Dad!" All they had done for her—clothes, shoes, place to sleep, money for the lawyer. Food. Money for food. Mad Money. Traffic was clearer on the left so she pulled into the fast lane, Amber crowding her with her smell, her need. If it had been Lindsey, Clare, a friend, she could have listened. Nodded. Felt compassion. Amber had never asked anything about her, called her Um and Lady.

It's my house, she thought, my house is nice, don't mess with my house! Built with second growth redwood from the hills, it would stand forever, barring devastating earthquake, fire, direct nuclear hit. A dining room attached to the living room. Three bedrooms, plus Adam's illegally renovated basement office/studio space. They'd owned it almost a decade now, and all the stretching and skimping and begging from relatives to make the 15K down payment now seemed a joke, the market had gone so high; even leveled off they'd done all right. Okay, so it wasn't in a great neighborhood—near the Oakland Rose Garden (good) but too close to

Highway 580 (bad)—and it was Oakland, which automatically kept property values down. But they had a long double overgrown lot with room for a real garden—not just the vegetable patch she did every summer, the narcissus and daffodils she'd planted along the side—if they ever hacked out the weeds and poison oak. It was a house with charm, if not class. They liked old. The house had good bones. Some of the details people spent a fortune for at Ohmega Salvage: rose brass doorknobs and original pulley windows.

My house. My Adam. My life. No lotus flower dharma compassion in her, her yoga out the window. My shoes, too. You're literally walking in my shoes, she thought. She'd liked those shoes—sliding the charge card across the counter at Copeland's, she'd surged with hope, imagining her body tightening back to firmness, her abs and thighs powerful. Graceful at something, for once. If she stayed with yoga long enough… she imagined herself taut in the body, loose and soft in the soul.

"Sounds like you were a very imaginative child," she said to Amber, allowing a single drop of compassion, but when you were thirsty even a drop of water felt good in the mouth. Kira opened the window to get air—her eyes stung from the wind and the grit from the center divider kicked up by the trucking traffic ahead of her, behind her, on the right side.

The Central Avenue exit blissfully close; she hated Costco, the overt materialism, the sadness of the people who could afford so little buying so many tubs of mayo, boxes of sugar cereal, frozen chicken wings laden with hormones. As they pulled into the parking lot, Amber seemed thrilled, though, a dog smelling the air as they neared the beach.

They got out of the car. Amber said, "Can I get a frank? They come with a soda for $1.63."

"If you want," Kira said, feeling her own primness.

"Can I get two?"

Kira, speechless, opened her wallet and handed Amber another five dollar bill. Food wasn't what Mad Money was for.

Back home, they carried in the trunkload of supplies: frozen taquitos and ice milk. Chicken drummettes. Frozen pizza. Diet sodas. Their refrigerator had shifted time zones to the Midwest, Kira thought. The food was hideous. But now Amber and Joey would have something in the house to eat.

Amber and Joey did eat dinner that night. Because Amber cooked. Kraft macaroni and cheese, from Costco, fluorescent. Joey sat on two phone books on a chair at the table, picked up each pasta tube carefully between thumb and forefinger, placed it in his mouth, chewed, picked up another. His right thumb and index finger turned gooey orange to the first knuckle but the rest of him stayed clean. Polly ate the mac and cheese, too; Adam and Kira moved it around on their plates and rolled their eyes at each other.

That night, Amber talked and talked with Adam while Kira was in the bedroom breathing, and Polly sat there and pretended to read, and Joey said nothing, just a slight mewing.

"Do you think they'll shit orange?" Adam asked Kira in bed later.

"Adam, that's something I just don't want to picture. Do you mind?" But he'd made her laugh despite herself.

At 11:30, they turned off their lights. "I'm hungry," he whispered after a few minutes. "You hungry?"

"Starved," she sighed, suddenly tired of being furious at him. "Okay, I'll go. I hate to eat so late." She went to the kitchen, brought back dry roasted almonds, sun-dried apricots, and a bar of dark chocolate which they ate on top of the sheets, a quiet picnic in the dark.

"Oh God, this is so good," he said, his mouth filled with apricot and almond.

"Shh. Whisper. It's incredible. Try a bit of all three at once."

"Want to taste something else delicious?" He pulled off his sleep shirt in a mock strip tease.

"Adam!" But she carefully moved the bags of nuts and fruit and the empty chocolate wrapper onto her bedside table, folded the bedspread back again and climbed in. "I can't believe we were eating in bed."

"I love our bed," he said. "Nice bed."

The room was quiet, a shaft of street light on the dark wood floor sliced into strips by the Venetian blinds. The occasional car passed, and the dim but constant roar of the freeway.

Adam moved his leg against her. She wanted to slide against him. Her body needed smoothing, a cat with raised fur. But their bed stood against the wall shared with the guest room where Amber and Joey slept. Adam tugged gently at her silk-screened Buddha-imprinted pajama top, singing low in blues form: *"Gimme some nookie, baby. Love me all night long. Oh yeah, gimme some noo-uh-uh-uh-kie…"*

She laughed. "Adam. Shut up. We have to be quiet." But she felt a throb of arousal.

"I promise." Sliding his fingers up her shirt to her nipple, a gentle pinch. "No screaming. No pounding the headboard." He reached over, gently bit her neck. His warm breath smelled of chocolate and almonds.

"Adam, promise! I won't do it unless it's slow. Really slow. I don't want her to hear. I can't relax."

"Then you get on top. I'll just lie here. You do all the work, you do whatever you want to do to me." He leaned back, a pleased king, already erect. "I've got something for you, babe. Come 'n get it while it's hot."

She laughed, pulled off her pajama pants and straddled him, noting again the weight gain on his belly. Kissing him quickly, not too deep. His hand was already between them, probing her, working her open. She pulled his hand away and slid him in her. She closed her eyes, wanting water, to flow with him, shift from one *asana* to another, a pleasure palace, kama sutra style. Maybe if they redid their bedroom. Candles and Indian prints, chiffon, scented oils, the slow flow. But Adam was clumsy and fast underneath her, thrusting roughly, grunting despite his promise. Grabbing her ass too hard. His face tight and lost. She put her hand on his mouth, stopped moving.

"Slow. Breathe with me," she whispered. "Try this, just match your breathing to mine. Look in my eyes."

"You're the one with your eyes shut, Kira. Just relax."

"I'm too tense, this isn't working for me." She moved off him in a clump.

"Let me just make you come. You're really tense."

"I'll do it. Just hold me."

She lay on her back in his arms and rubbed her clitoris in circles, closing her eyes to picture Ravi stroking his hard penis over her naked torso bent back in *ustrasana*. Ravi, Ravi, Ravi. And with a shudder, she came hard.

"Yes. Now who's making noise?" He straddled her. She was soft and relaxed now, her hips sliding free, one leg wrapping around him *reclining vrksasana,* inner eye again firmly on the lump in Ravi's yoga pants.

Adam thrust down into her faster, hips pumping thrust, thrust, thrust, the headboard banged, banged, and he came with a small whoop, "Oh *yeah*!" and as he did, she came again too, see-ing Ravi's small smile, *"Namaste,"* biting her bottom lip against sound.

She snuggled against him, half of a whole, the silence friendly. A car passed on the street, making patterns of light on the walls. She was beginning to drift when he said, out of nowhere, "I just don't know if she's up for taking care of that boy. She's an adult but she seems so young sometimes, and he's got problems, it's not just the eye thing."

"I know," she said. In the dark it was easier to talk about it without fury. "I just don't know what we should do."

He stroked her curls. "Well, we're not doing anything about it tonight, pretty lady. Don't harsh the afterglow." He reached down to hold her hand.

◇ POLLY

The new relatives stayed. Sunday morning, they were out of milk and Joey had eaten all the cereal and it was too much for Polly to take. From her room, she listened for Amber and Joey sounds. Nothing. He creeped her out, the boy whose eyes wouldn't shut, like one of those gods she'd read about, all seeing, all knowing, with the unclosing eyes. Yet nothing about wormy little Joey sug-gested anything remotely holy. Snotty nose and crusty eyes; small, too, like a snake's—almond shaped and vivid blue, out of focus.

In Polly's Blood Drawer, the middle drawer in her oak bureau, under the socks, next to the tampons (as yet unused except in prac-tice) and near her cotton balls and single-edge razor blade, Polly kept a collection of postcards from Peter the Great's Kunstkammer, a strange museum in Russia. She'd found them in a used bookstore on Telegraph Avenue. "The Cabinet of Curiosities" the envelope said. Inside, eleven postcards of deformed babies and fetuses in jars, steeped three hundred years in black pepper-infused alcohol, dissolving slightly around the edges like softened soap. Twins conjoined at the forehead, at the chest, on their butts. In fifth grade science they'd softened hard boiled eggs in vinegar and pushed them through the narrow necks of bottles. The babies reminded her of those eggs: the color of piano keys and sickness. Skin loose and wrinkled, the wax in a partially melted lava lamp. Poor babies. Had their mothers loved them?

She slid the pictures in the envelope, put them in her Blood Drawer under the socks, and went back to the living room. Amber sat on the couch filing her pretty nails, Joey next to her. Polly came closer, reached over the couch back, and lifted one of Joey's baby hands. She stood there holding it, trying not to look at his face.

"Can I take him outside?"

"Go ahead."

"Come on." They walked through the kitchen, her dad at the table doing bills. "Daddy, me and Joey are going outside."

"Thank you for doing this, Apollonia."

Polly led Joey through the weedy lot. The air was crisp and cold.

"Come on Joey, this is sour grass. You can eat it, but not too much or you'll get sick." Joey chewed a piece of sour grass and seemed to like it. "Don't go over here, this is poison oak even though it doesn't have any leaves on it right now. Because it's winter. But we can collect old acorns, okay? They come from oak trees, which Oakland is named for." Polly wasn't sure if Joey understood her, there was something really wrong with him, though it wasn't as obvious as the jar babies in her Blood Drawer. But he liked the rain-blackened acorns with their little hats. They lined up a row of acorns on the deck.

Joey didn't look too bad once you got to know him, just his

goopy eyes. After a while he whined and pawed at them, and that hurt her eyes, too, so Polly took him back inside for his drops.

Amber reminded Polly of a big pinky, the baby mice Brady's dad fed the snakes at the East Bay Vivarium. As Amber worked on Joey's eyes, Polly said, "So what job are you going to look for when you get wherever you're going?"

"Some shitty place with a paper hat. I just need to find a place to keep Joey while I'm working."

"Can he go to preschool?"

Amber shook her head. "And my mom's got my Johnny already, she's his legal guardian. My friend Kelli, she's over near DC, she's waiting for an opening where she works, they've got these cashiers where you don't have to be on your feet all day, and she says her babysitter could take Joey. I wouldn't mind going out there. They've got a beauty shop in her town called Doug's Hair'em. Hair'em like a harem, that's like a brothel, only *hair*, like on your head. And then there's Dot's Hair You Are. Like 'here you are,' only *hair* you are. Really cute."

She set Joey on his feet, and he crawled up on the couch next to Polly.

"That's funny," Polly said.

"My last job," Amber said, "in a Marie Callender's, you ever eat at one of those? I gained twelve pounds just from the pie—at the end of the shift they had to give them to the employees or throw them out. These old people used to come down from the assisted living facility. It was so funny. You sit them down and bring them a pitcher of tap water and these old people, they sit there and say, 'Now isn't this water delicious!' 'Oh yes,'—this little old lady with a hat on says—'this restaurant always has the *best* water.' It's so funny, we'd all be just cracking up in the back. 'Oh yes, this restaurant always has the *best* water.' I didn't like the cooks there, though. They had attitude. Except this one guy, Marcus, he was hella hot. He quit, though."

"How old was Joey when you went to jail?" Polly asked.

"Prison. My mom pretty much always took care of this baby buckaroo. That's why I won't let him out of my sight now. He won't let me out of his sight either. That's why he was born that way. 'Uh uh, I'm not letting my mama out of my sight any more, ma'am.' I'm always in his sight. 'Cause of his eyes."

It took Polly a moment to get it and laugh.

"Can his eyes be fixed, ever?"

"Oh yeah. They've got these implants, like fake eyelids, but they want to wait until he's older so he doesn't reject them."

"Does it cost a lot?"

"Yeah. But the government pays the settlement. These kids, they're a separate breed of kid, I saw this article. And they're too hyper because they need all that energy for the next stage of evolution. They're going to lead the world out of the technology age into the age of the spirit, and they're going to be the leaders."

"Um hmm," Polly said, trying not to smirk. Amber was so ignorant.

"Do you smoke?" Amber asked her.

"No!"

"Good. My mom caught Johnny with a pack of Newports, he's only seven, bet he got him off Mel."

"Who's Mel?"

"Mom's boyfriend Melvin."

"Was he smoking them?"

"I don't know. She kicked Mel's ass good, though. He won't do that again."

"Did your tattoo hurt?"

"Yeah. Probably not too bad once you had a baby. Got this

big one when I was seventeen when we all went over to Boise to see Pantera. Joey hurt more than the tattoo, and Johnny hurt less than the tattoo. With Johnny, I had the epidural. Joey was sunny side up, his face was up when it was supposed to be down, so then they had to C-section him on emergency; that scar hurt like hell."

"How long are you going to stay here?"

"Maybe a long time, maybe a short time. I'm in the Lord's hands, just letting whatever needs to happen, happen."

Polly felt queasy. "In the Lord's hands." Like Amber had something wrong or different about her brain, that she believed in God without irony. She'd never known a religious person before, one who admitted to it. Sounded like the right wingers on talk radio. But maybe it was just an expression from where Amber was from, just an idiom.

ꙮ ADAM

Adam looked up from paying bills—robbing Peter to pay Paul—at the kitchen table to watch Polly and Joey collecting acorns, Kira Saluting the Sun on the deck. Writing checks pissed him off but the anger had no energy to it. Despite two cups of coffee, he couldn't bear the idea of getting out of his sweats and into his biking clothes today. And yoga wasn't his thing. He had little patience for Kira's recent foray into Namastes and Om-ing, though he supported the organic food and slow food movements more than Kira. "Yeah, it's a good stretch," he said about yoga. But Kira's woo-woo spirituality—even if she refused to admit it was that—bugged the shit out of him. She'd gotten so damned apolitical, too. Inner work indeed; she didn't seem any happier or clearer than before. She'd studied massage, Feng Shui, Reiki, Alexander Technique, meditation, always so fucking busy trying to get serene.

When Polly was younger and Kira was trying to do everything and had no time, her mocking cry was, "Serenitize Your Multi-Tasking." Now it was a bumper sticker on her car. Her damn car. Sixty-three grand in cash, the money from her dad's estate, and that was almost the end of their savings.

They shared money, but he balanced their checkbook. Stan did the business end for their production company. Adam just showed up for the shoots, operated the camera, pulled cable... basics, but he was still considered re-entry. Not much call for a failed geek/ex-musician who'd spent more years as a stay-at-home dad than was good for the resume. They were getting fewer industrials, they had a few debts going on—but Adam had cashed out okay when he left Zetrum with a load of dot com stock options pre-bomb, and he still got royalties from First Man's old recordings. Still big in the Czech Republic, woo hoo.

What with Kira's three quarter-time job, they were going to be okay. She hadn't noticed the bounced checks, the diminished savings account, the maxed charge card; he'd take care of it before she noticed. Had to cut down. He was doing too much bullshit—buying too much music, working too rarely, smoking too much, splurging on expensive food. Three times in the last month he'd taken himself to Oliveto for lunch, dropping fifty bucks on himself each time. He'd earned it. But it wasn't smart when money was getting tight. And he was gaining weight, too, his pants tight. He had to cut back on everything. A couple of times he'd bought Percodan from David, who had a prescription for his neck—"old people drugs," he called them. Taking away the aches and pains.

At forty-six, he was the old dude playing rhythm guitar in a band with three "flats"—the young guys with six-pack bellies and no bloat—though no gigs for a few months now, they hadn't even jammed since last summer—but it would pick up. He clicked off the radio whenever he heard Green Day. They'd been friends in the Gilman Street days before they sold out. First Man was always a better band.

Who was he fooling. It had all gone to shit. He had not finished being young, and now it was over. He was tired. Fuck it. Bills and jobs and being old. Fuck it all.

Kira stood on her head, her heels pressed against the sliding glass door. Unless she had eyes in her ass, she couldn't see him. Quickly, Adam swept up the unpaid bills and the checkbook and dumped them all in the kitchen garbage. Fuck it. Then, just to make his point, he dumped the used Peet's coffee grounds from the French plunge pot on top of them.

And when David called to say he was on his way over to get Adam for their Sunday bike ride, Adam cancelled, "David, man, we've got houseguests, Alcatraz and Coit Tower and all that... let this one go, okay?"—and went back to the basement. He opened his bottom desk drawer where he kept his stash in a Japanese cherrywood box. His talisman: the evils of the world in measurable portions, little bits of death in a controllable container. Two Percodans. Then back upstairs to fold laundry.

☙ KIRA

"I sail the river called Denial, and it ain't in Africa..."

"Daddy, want to play a game?"

Kira was still in her yoga pants. The three of them folded laundry on the living room floor; Amber smoked on the front porch; Joey napped in the guest bedroom.

"Like?" Adam said.

"Backgammon?"

"Let's do something we can all do. *I sail the river called Denial*," he sang. "Somebody give me the next line."

"Africa… hard to rhyme," Kira said. "You *are* in denial. This isn't working for me."

"Amber and Joey, too?" Polly asked.

"Ideally."

"They don't play games, Daddy."

"What's your song," Kira said. "The AA Recovery Blues?"

"More like, The New Age Woo-Woo Blues. *Oh my MasterCard is maxed out, and my 401K is gone…*"

Polly folded a shirt, looked at the crumple she'd made, made a face, and refolded it.

"That's the Yuppie Blues," Kira said. "More like this, *"My heart chakra's out of alignment, got a splinter in my Third Eye."* Snapping her fingers hipster style.

"Oh yeah…!" he joined in, *"My baby's heart chakra's out of alignment, woo! She put a splinter in my Third Eye."*

"Well, I'll do my kapalabhati pranayama… not sure that scans…"

"…and then I think I'm gonna die," Polly sang. "Hey, Mommy, can you pass me my underpants and my gym pants?"

"Oh, that's so funny," Kira said. "Let's finish it."

"I sail the river called Denial, and my yoga mat is tore. I sail the river called Denial, meditation is a bore. Okay, that sucks," he said.

"Just forget the river called Denial, it's not working."

"If we're not going to play a game, can Nell come over today?"

"I don't see why not. Sure! The more the merrier. Fill the house. I'm evolved. See how evolved I am?"

Adam ignored her. "I don't see why not, Pol. Does she want to come for dinner? Invite Lindsey too."

"I don't even know if she's available, Daddy. It's kind of late notice."

The dinner party! "Oh no!" Kira said loudly.

"What happened?" Adam said. "Don't wake up Joey!"

"Damn it, Adam! We have people over tonight! The dinner! You were going to cook! They're all coming! I reminded you!"

"Oh, fuck. Fuck!" He stared at her, then glanced around at the piles of clean clothes, still unfolded.

"Oh my God, you guys, how could you forget?" Polly looked panicked. "What are we going to do?"

"We have to cancel," Kira said. There was no way. The house was a mess. Amber and Joey. She hadn't even told Lindsey or Clare about them… "We're such idiots. I even confirmed with Clare last Monday. Hey. You didn't remember either," she said to Adam.

"But they're leaving for Colombia, Clare and Janelle and Micah. Don't know why they're taking that baby to a war zone. We can't reschedule. It's okay. Micah can play with Joey," Adam said.

"What…?" Kira said. "You want to actually have a party tonight? In four hours? The house is a mess. House guests for almost a week and nobody but me lifting a finger."

"They don't care. None of those people care. I'll make a quick risotto and salad, it'll still be fun."

"Fun? Are you out of your mind?"

"But can Nell come over now, early?" Polly asked.

"Fine, whatever," Adam said. Polly dumped the folded clothes off her lap and went to the kitchen to call Nell. "Jesus. She could have taken these with her and put them in her dresser."

"Adam, she's thirteen and a slob just like us, give her a break. I can't believe this. What about Stan?"

"What do you mean?"

"About Amber and Joey. Did you tell him they were here? Does he still talk to Sandi?"

"Eh. Fuck. I don't know, I didn't tell him they were down here.

And the others, we'll just play it cool like she's always been a part of the family. Who's going to ask?"

"Hello. Clare will. Lindsey will, too. What are my friends going to say that I've never told them you have another kid? *Might* have another kid? That's like a major withhold. From my friends. And telling Clare, she scares the shit out of me."

He nodded, a fake look of resignation on his face. *"No more river of Denial. Guess I've got to claim my shit…"*

She took a deep breath. "Claim your shit. Fine way to talk about a human being. Adam, I've about had it."

"You're right. I'm an asshole. Look, take next weekend. Go to Harbin, chill out by yourself at the hot springs. You deserve a break."

He was right, she did. "I can take off Friday, if I stay late on Wednesday or Thursday. I guess. But that's not fair to you."

"It's fair, Kira. Make the fucking reservation."

"I'm going to make a reservation. I am."

"Go for it. No really, you deserve it. *No more river of Denial. Now I wanna suck your tit…*"

"Adam! Are you stoned?" Noticing the vague eyes.

"No one can hear me."

She took a breath in, tried to breathe out her exasperation. "You better get your act in gear, if we're having…" she counted in her head, "eleven at dinner. I'm going to put these folded clothes away now. Bring the rest back to the basement, we'll just have to do them later. You do them. And you figure out how to explain Amber. She's not my problem. It's been five days, Adam. Five days."

"Not that you're counting."

CHAPTER 5

❧ ADAM

They all were coming. Lindsey, Kira's best friend since the Berkeley dorms, with Nell, Lindsey's daughter and Polly's best friend. Clare and Janelle and their little Micah, their favorite Berkeley "political" family—Clare had hosted a book group that Kira and Lindsey went to for a few years until it faded away. Stan: Adam's business partner, ex-roommate, and the drummer in First Man. They'd known each other forever. Then there were the three of them, plus Amber and Joey, which made eleven people, if you counted the two little ones Joey and Micah. He counted on his fingers again. Did they even have enough chairs? They'd eat buffet style.

To make risotto for eleven, he needed supplies. The house was depleted, so that meant Berkeley Bowl, which had more varieties of wild mushrooms than anywhere except maybe Market Hall and at half the price. Adam talked Amber into coming with him to the store. It might have been a good idea on any day except a weekend, when the parking lot was a twenty minute wait. When they finally found a spot up on Ward Street, Amber announced that she was going to sit in the car, her strained ankle still hurt too much to walk the two blocks.

"Okay, Joey boy, come to the store with me?" Adam asked.

"You want him, you got him." She took out her cigarettes.

"Could you please do that outside? I don't like smoke in my car. Actually, I don't like smoking. At all."

She opened the car door with a huff, climbed outside, shook her pack of Winstons. Adam fumbled with Joey's booster seat buckle. Joey stared sideways and clutched his blue cylinder blocks, one in each hand. "You can take your blocks, buddy. Let's go the store. Come to the store with Adam."

Joey looked directly at him, his thin blue eyes rimmed with red. "Ma."

"Hey, Amber, he said 'Ma.' Does he usually say that?"

Amber shrugged.

"Good boy, Joey." He was just a little kid. Adam picked Joey out of the car and slung him on his left hip. "Okay, let's go get some food, buddy. We'll be back soon, sure you don't want to come? Need anything?" She shook her head, blowing smoke.

Berkeley Bowl's aisles were so crowded Adam couldn't put Joey down, and Joey refused to ride in the cart, doing his straight-legged moaning thing.

"Come on, Joey, we're in a big hurry," Adam said, then decided not to fight it. He carried Joey with one arm, pushed the cart with the other, negotiating through the crowds. No Vialone Nano rice, he'd have to stop at A.G. Ferrari. Pissed Adam off; all this way for mushrooms and an onion, and now guests would arrive in three hours. Hope Kira's not too pissed.

He bought three baskets of raspberries for dessert, and got a good bottle of white wine, paying with American Express. In line, Joey kicked and moaned in his arms, flailing at his eyes.

"Just a little longer. Look, Joey. See the little doggy outside?" Joey didn't look. Several women gave Adam sympathetic glances. When Polly was a baby he'd suddenly become sexier, more in demand. Nothing hotter than a man with a baby. It took another twenty minutes to get through the Express line, Joey grabbing at the nutritional and yoga magazines.

"That your son or your grandson?" The checker, a big blond dreadlocked dude, asked.

Adam pretended not to hear.

"Maybe you should get him a tissue or something, his eyes are goopy, man."

"Thanks, man. He's got a condition. You want to just ring up my purchases? Okay?"

It had started raining while they shopped, and Amber sat slumped in the car. Adam wanted to yell at her, "Get a better attitude!" but refrained, silently buckling Joey in his seat. "He needs his drops."

"I didn't bring them. I didn't know we was going to be gone all day, Dad."

Dad. The word jarred. It was hardly all day. "Okay, I'll drop you two back before I get the rice, okay? And Amber, um…"

"What."

"Forget it." Dad was just a word. A sound. Did it mean more than Joey's "Ma?" He should do the damned genetic testing. Get it over with, he thought.

"Whatever," she said.

Dropping them back home ate up another half hour, Adam seething and swearing quietly at the idiot drivers, and then he had to go back to Piedmont Avenue and negotiate parking with all the rich Piedmont biddies in their old Benzes. He splurged on a bottle of extra virgin cold press olive oil; Kira couldn't taste the difference between cold and regular, she said, especially when it was cooked, but he could. Vialone Nano had gone up to twelve dollars a pound. "Shitload of money for rice," he said to the cashier. "Rice should cost nothing, fifty cents."

"But this is the good stuff," the young guy said.

"Put it on the card." Adam dashed across the street to Piedmont

Grocery for three more bottles of wine. They could drink while they waited to eat.

By the time Adam got back to the Moss Street house it was almost 6:00, guests arriving at 6:30, and the buzz of the Percodan had long worn off. He popped another—just one more—and began cooking. He assembled the ingredients, brushed the mushrooms, and began to trim them. Kira prepped the salad, silent and clearly pissed off. Polly and Nell wandered in, holding their newly-green fingernails away from their bodies like their hands didn't belong to them.

"Amber helped us do our nails. Like them? Can we have a snack?" Nell asked, draping her gawky frame halfway over the counter.

"Not now, unless you get it yourself. We're cooking," Kira said, shaking romaine lettuce over the sink.

"But our nails aren't dry."

"Then wait."

"Amber's on the porch eating chips and Slim Jims and smoking," Polly said.

"Polly, it's her body," Adam said. "We're not in charge of her body. But I'm in charge of your body until you're grown, and I don't want you having snacks now, before dinner. Especially shit like Slim Jims. Now please, girls, get out of the cooking zone before I lose it, we have guests coming in a few minutes. And can you and Nell clear off the table for food and set up chairs in the living room?"

Kira said, "No, we can all fit around the table. Can you put the leaf in, Polly? Do you and Nell know where it is? Hallway closet, behind the ironing board."

Polly looked at the piles of shitake, portobello, and black

trumpet mushrooms. "Are we going to waste the stuff from The Box again?"

"I don't see *you* cooking it," Adam said.

"Daddy, I don't cook the dinners around here. You do."

"Yeah well, then don't criticize. Actually, we're using parsley and lettuce from The Box. So there. Now scat."

"We'll be back," Polly said.

"And hungry for parmesan cheese," Nell said.

Adam put the frozen stock on to melt in one pot, extra hot water on in another, and began chopping two white onions. It felt good. It was stupid how rarely they hung out with friends, they should do it more often. In the old days, people's houses were open, people dropped in. Not so much growing up in the hills of Mill Valley because the houses were all so isolated from each other, and his mother was an anti-social type anyway, after the divorce—but other people. That's what other people did. And when they were in their twenties, big funky houses with lots of roommates.

The thing about risotto: it was a lot of assembly but very easy to cook, almost impossible to fuck up. He sliced the mushrooms with his sharpest paring knife, feeling like a surgeon, working to get the slices the same width. It didn't matter at all—some could be thick and some paper thin, but it was a game he liked to play with himself. Then he chopped the parsley, grated the cheese. He peeled and chopped three cloves of garlic.

Or maybe it was a myth, neighbors borrowing cups of sugar. People certainly didn't drop in on neighbors here: "Hey, do you have an extra egg?" Between last year's public street tree campaign and the recent push for a Neighborhood Watch association, he and Kira knew most of their neighbors, but in nine years none of them had ever come in the door. He couldn't imagine borrowing cake ingredients—maybe that was one of those fifties housewives things.

He poured olive oil in his biggest Le Creuset so it just covered the bottom and turned the flame on to medium. He added the onions, mushrooms, salt, pepper, garlic, and shook and stirred it until it reduced and the mushrooms gave off a dark water.

Stan arrived first, an anomaly for him. Adam heard the doorbell, Polly's yell, "I'll get it!" just before he added the Vialone Nano; one handful of risotto rice per person and one for the pot. He wasn't sure if the kids would eat, except Polly of course, ah what the hell, ten handfuls, make the whole bag, cooked it high for a couple of minutes stirring until the rice sounded crackly, then ladled enough broth to cover it (a big sizzle of steam), turned it down, and started the big stir.

Stan's voice. Then, a few minutes later, the doorbell, and Lindsey's. Halfway through the stirring process, the doorbell rang again, Clare and Janelle. Two-year-old Micah was crabby, so Kira got him a cup of apple juice and disappeared again to make the guests welcome.

"Can we get just a little snack?" Polly and Nell came in.

"You can clear the table."

"Mommy's doing that."

"Where'd she put all that stuff that was on it?" The bills, electronics, cords, objects to fix, objects to replace. Where was Amber? Out on the porch smoking, of course. Cold out there. She never seemed to mind. He heard Clare's loud laughter and Janelle's low voice. Polly shrugged.

"Can I stir the risotto?" Nell asked. "Will I like it?"

"It's just easier if I do it right now. Some other time, okay? I'll teach you how to make it. Where's your mom, Nell?"

"In the living room with Stan the Man."

"Ask her if she wants wine with dinner." He tasted the risotto. Done. He added a glob of butter and the parmesan cheese.

"Why'd you put the cheese in?" Kira back again. "You should put it on the side. Not everybody eats cheese."

"Everybody here does."

"How do you know? Clare might not."

"Clare goes to Colombia and eats monkey brains."

"Not. She's a vegetarian—she studies herbs and natural pharmaceuticals in the mountains of Colombia, and she might even be a vegan, I don't know."

"Kira, chill. I'm cooking, I'm the chef, you're the eaters."

"I'm the chef, too. I'm making the salad."

"Chill! I've had it with you!"

"Well, it's mutual." She left. A few minutes later she came back in looking for silverware and carrying a six-pack of Anchor Steam. "Stan brought beer. Do you want to serve it?"

"No, we're drinking wine."

"Stan brought beer," she said.

"It's like a host gift, we don't have to serve it. I don't want him getting loaded and being an asshole. Take this glass of cabernet out to Lindsey. Did she get some? Did you? Will you please chill out? Have a glass, you need it. Do you think we should offer Amber any? Oh, this is going to be so good," he said, tasting the risotto again. He poked his head out of the kitchen, "Did everybody meet everybody? Clare, Janelle, Lindsey, and Amber, you all know Stan. Stan, it's Amber, you know—*Amber*, Sandi's daughter. Joey's her little guy on the floor. Where's Micah? The girls? Food in one minute flat. Who wants wine?" Nobody responded, busy talking.

"We already did the introductions while you were cooking, Adam," Kira said. "Let's sit down, everybody!" She called down the hallway, "Girls and Micah, come eat!"

"Hey Amber baby, so how's your mama?" Adam heard Stan

say as he pulled back into the kitchen. "Come sit next to me."

Adam brought the risotto pot in, placed it near the salad on the table. "Pass your plates, everybody. Clare, more wine? We're all squishing in at the table? Okay. We can get cozy." But they were all deep in conversation already.

"It's really bad there now," Clare said. She had that do-gooder Brit look, Adam thought. Weathered blonde white lady with long, upper class limbs and snarled buck teeth. How did Janelle kiss that?

"From all the cocaine trade, right?" sexy Lindsey put her napkin on her lap, her boobs hanging out as usual. "Thanks Adam, this looks beautiful."

"Help yourself to salad." He served risotto to Polly and Nell, newly arrived from Polly's room, and handed the ladle to Janelle.

"I'll take a beer, there, when you get a chance, buddy," Stan said.

"Sorry, man, I'll get it in a minute. Amber, did you get enough? I think you might like it if you give it a chance."

Amber put a squirming Joey on the floor.

"More complicated, yeah, they've got the coca leaves, but they've also got these big oil and water reserves, so that's the biggest thing now," Janelle said. "Colombia's interesting because the indigenous people actually have great land rights, but it's only so long as they stay on their land. So that's the big move now, to get them off. It's terrible. There's a lot of spraying, just killing everything. This is great. Adam, man of many talents."

Man of many talents, right, Adam thought. Fucking pompous Janelle, tall and lean with a jawline, ex-venture capitalist, retired, cashed out at forty-one to be a do-gooder, rubbing in Adam's failures. He raised his wine glass to Janelle, toasted her ironically. You're a rich butch bitch! But your wife still has ugly teeth.

"The coca plants?" Kira asked.

"Pass the cheese, please," Nell said.

Lindsey said, "Leave some for everybody, Nelly."

"And corn, food crops, you name it," Janelle said.

Amber carefully separated her risotto into two piles, rice and mushrooms, and picked at the rice. From the side, she looked a bit like Sandi, Adam thought. A sweet tenderness around the cheeks; he had a strange urge to gently run his index finger over that pink vulnerability. She was still so young.

"Amber, can I serve you some salad?" Clare asked.

"Oh!" she looked up from her plate. "No, I'm good."

"It's really good," Lindsey said. "Everything. Thanks, you guys. Here's to the chef!"

"Everybody get enough?" Adam asked. "There's salad, too. Amber? Does Joey want some milk?"

"Why?" Polly asked. "Why do they spray the cocoa plants?"

"Coca. Cocaine. To get them off the land," Kira told her quietly. "So they have to flee. Polly, I need you to eat some salad."

"What about the guerillas?" Adam asked.

Janelle said, "They're a problem, they used to be a real liberation movement but they got cut off at the neck a few years ago, now they're just thugs. Kidnappers. When we were in Bogota last April…"

"I'll just stick with the wine," Stan said, "since the beer isn't happening."

Clare was breastfeeding two-year-old Micah. Micah's hand pulled gently, consistently, at Clare's earlobe. "The government, by that I mean the Colombian government but supplied by the US industrial military complex, is aerial spraying Glyphosate. That's the active ingredient in Roundup, but, like, four times as strong."

"I thought Roundup was banned," Lindsey said.

"In this country, maybe," Kira said.

"It's not banned. I've got Roundup in the shed," Stan said. Stan sat between Amber and Lindsey. He'd slathered his bread thickly with butter, now used his spoon to make a risotto sandwich. Lindsey watched him with a look of mild bemusement.

"Carbohydrate sandwich, mmm mmm. Just like Mama used to make back in the old country." He winked at Lindsey.

"Don't believe a word of his bullshit," Adam said. "Old country, my ass." Stan reached for the bottle and refilled Lindsey's glass and she mouthed a "thank you."

Damn, that woman is sexy, Adam thought. A little round, but that could be fun. Adam took another helping of risotto. It was pretty perfect.

✍ KIRA

Joey sat on Kira's lap. It felt good to hold a toddler again, his warmth melting against her. She'd filled celery sticks with peanut butter for him, and cut them into inch-long pieces; now he carefully licked the peanut butter out of each smooth section. Kira kept her plate to the side so she could reach it, and turned the risotto over with her fork. It was good tasting, but her appetite was gone. When Lindsey arrived, she'd been greeted first by Amber on the porch. Kira had opened the door. "Amber, this is Lindsey, she's Nell's mother. You met Nell earlier." Nell was already inside playing with Polly. "This is Amber and Joey."

"Hi! Nice to meet you!" Lindsey had said.

"Hey."

"Come in." They'd stepped into the foyer. "I hope you don't mind," Kira had said quietly as she hugged Lindsey in the foyer. "Stan's already here. And," her hands filled with Lindsey's winter coat, she'd stuck her chin abruptly in Adam's—in the kitchen's—general direction, "she's his *maybe* daughter from the old wild days."

"No way," Lindsey had said. "Wow. Never knew he had it in him."

"Yep. They're staying with us."

"What? Why?"

Kira shrugged. "We'll talk. It's complicated." She hadn't managed to corner Clare yet and explain. But Clare was savvy. She probably already knew; she could be so judgmental.

Kira maneuvered another forkful over Joey's slightly cradle-capped head. They were still talking about pesticides, the conversation flying over Amber's bent head, Clare and Lindsey watching her, both too smart for their own good. Ooh, she was going to get it later: from Clare, measured questioning about the family dynamic, from Lindsey, compassion and then, in a month or two, a confession that her feelings were hurt that Kira, in decades of friendship, had never confided in her about this. *I haven't told her about Ravi, either*, she thought. Kira reached across Joey for her wine, then glanced at Adam, who was swigging back his glass. Damn him, he was getting drunk, which meant somebody else needed to stay in control. As usual. She set her glass back down, well out of Joey's reach. The conversation rolled on.

"Glyphosate is actually a pretty safe pesticide," Clare said, "but not when it's four times as strong as the recommended dosage and they're doing aerial spraying."

"We eat mostly organic these days," Polly announced.

"We're members of a CSA; we get The Box every week. Some of this meal came from it, not all," Adam said. So self-satisfied.

"Monsanto recommends spraying from ten feet high but it's too dangerous to go in there because of the guerillas," Clare said. She'd barely touched her risotto. Micah sat up and flopped again against his mother's other breast, "Udder side, Mama."

"Does he say 'udders' for your breasts?" Adam asked.

"'Udder' is 'other,' but that's pretty cute, Adam," Janelle said.

"All about the boobs as always," Stan said.

"I used to get a CSA box too," Lindsey said. "But I'd never use all those vegetables, not with just me and Nell, and we had to go pick it up."

"So they go up, each plane, flanked by two US-supplied helicopters. And this is happening," Clare said, "because of the guerillas, from the air, not from ten feet. The Glyphosate's polluting the Punto Mayo river now, tributary to the Amazon. People and livestock dying, driven off the land. And the big oil companies, Occidental, BP, moving in for the oil reserves. Children are being born with just terrible birth defects."

Kira had stopped eating completely. Amber stared at her plate. Lindsey made eye contact with Kira, gestured with her chin at Amber, raised an eyebrow. "So Amber, what field are you involved in?" Amber looked up, quickly shook her head, then leaned away from Lindsey, to where Clare was still holding forth. Lindsey went on. "Where did you go to school?"

"She got her GED a long time ago," Polly said. "She didn't go to college. She was a teenage dropout mother."

"Eighteen! I was legal when I had Johnny," Amber said. "Gave him to my mom, though."

"Genocide. Ecocide. Suicide. All the 'cides. Colombia's really a crucible," Clare said. "We've lost a lot of indigenous pharmaceuticals, extinct."

Amber said to Clare, "That's sick. They're going to dump more rocket fuel and make another Superfund site and then the government has to give out even more money."

"They're talking about in Columbia," Polly said. "It's a country in Central America."

"Colombia. In South America," Adam corrected.

"Do you have any plain rice? I like this? But it's too rich for me," Nell said.

The politics went on and on until Kira couldn't listen any more. "La la la la la," she wanted to say loudly, her hands over her ears. She fixed her inner gaze on her breathing. Clare always made her feel so inadequate. She wasn't brave enough to face the details of destruction head on, like Clare did. If she knew what waste-lands faced her daughter in thirty years, she would curl up and die. Better to know but not know, focus on the deep solace of the redwoods in Joaquin Miller park, the promise of revealed myster-ies in Ravi's corrective touch. Dinner was almost over. Adam get-ting drunk didn't help. He always got so stressed around Janelle, poor guy. Pissing contests. The tension all through her body. If she could just release, relax, let it go.

Adam poured himself another glass of wine. Kira wanted to smack it out of his hand. "What kind of birth defects do these kids have? Like thalidomide poisoning?" he asked.

"I didn't see it first hand," Clare said. "But my friend Teresa did. She said she saw babies born with no skin."

"Ew!" Nell said. She turned pale. "But they can't live."

"No, of course not," Janelle said.

"Did you know your skin is your biggest organ?" said Polly.

"Not mine," Stan said. Nobody laughed.

A blast of rain spattered the windows of the dining room.

"You're making me sick," Amber said to everybody, "talking what you don't know shit about. Going to fix some other coun-try's problems when we have it right here in America. Me and Steve was living near Henderson when I got pregnant with Joey, all this perchlorate in the water and we didn't even know it. And we got mercury in Elko all over from the mines. And you all talk,

talk, talk. We might be a bunch of buckaroos where I live, but at least we're real. Thanks for dinner, Dad. Gonna go have a smoke." She got up and hobbled toward the front porch, exaggerating her limp. Clare shot a questioning look to Kira, who kept her face neutral. What had just happened?

"Well, still waters run deep, or something like that," Lindsey said. "She's got it going on."

"It's been a struggle," Adam said to Janelle.

"What's a buckaroo?" Nell asked.

"Like a cowboy, I think," Kira said. "I think their hats are different. Buckaroo, from the word vacaro, like vaca, cows. She comes from buckaroo country in Nevada."

Nell looked bored.

Stan got up and followed Amber, "Hey, baby girl, can I bum one?" Joey wriggled off Kira's lap and crawled after them. Lindsey smirked at Kira.

"Does he walk?" Clare asked.

Kira nodded. "Sometimes."

"Can we be excused, too?" Polly asked Kira.

"Please bring your dishes to the sink, Poodle," Adam said.

Polly glared at him and stomped off to her room.

"Polly!" Kira called after her, but sat still. Breathe. Let it go. Release.

"Nell, did you have enough to eat?" Lindsey asked.

"I don't get it," Nell said to Kira. "Is that your daughter?"

Adam said, "Oh no, she's the daughter of an old, um… of mine. Well, we're really not sure."

Lindsey put down her fork, stared at Kira. "What? In the hallway you said she was Stan's. Didn't you? Which surprised me because I thought he never got laid—shit. Sorry, Nell."

"No! I never said…" Kira said.

Lindsey glared at Kira. "When I came in. 'From the old, wild days,' you said."

"Maybe she is," Adam said. "Could possibly be. And believe me, Stan got laid. Right, Kira?"

Kira glared at him.

"Stan lived with Sandi for a few months. Or stayed there, or something," she explained to the table.

"Who's Sandi?" Nell asked.

"Amber's mom."

"But he's not her…?"

"They say no."

"Can I be excused, Mom?" Nell asked.

Kira turned directly to Clare, started talking rapidly. "I don't know how you do it, all this direct action. It's too much for me. I mean, we give money to MoveOn, NARAL, Doctors Without Borders—I'm happy to donate to any organization you think is great, you know, but I don't want to know the details. I'll give money," Kira said even faster. "But I can't have all this pain in my life all the time. It's happening, I hate it, I'll vote to change it. But maybe I can enjoy the moments before it all hits here."

They'd barely dented the risotto, and only Adam was still eating. Stan came back through the dining room into the kitchen, came out with two beers, and headed back towards the porch. "Beer and cigarette party on the porch, anybody wants?" Nobody moved.

"We can't all be activists," Clare said.

"Of course we should be," Adam said. "Kira and I are just selfish shits. More wine? I don't know about you guys, but I'm having another glass."

"No, thanks," Janelle said. "Okay, just a little."

"Adam likes to link his issues with mine," Kira said. "Problem with being married. We, we, we."

"This bottle's toasted," Adam said. "Okay, Janelle, come help me choose our next beverage. I've got a nice Elyse Zin I've been saving, pretty big for a Zin, or if you're ready we can switch to Porto." He pushed back from the table and went into the kitchen, Janelle following, leaving Kira, Clare with a sleeping Micah in her arms, Lindsey. The table was a mess. Lindsey started reaching for dishes and silverware.

"Wait," Kira said. "Let me just sit a moment. I'm so tired."

"I'm not surprised," Lindsey said, lowering her voice to a harsh whisper. "Look what you guys are doing for Amber and her little boy."

"Um, not really," Kira said. Damn Lindsey for bringing it back to Amber. "Mi casa es su casa or whatever. I just have to learn to be more serene about it. I'm not that evolved yet."

"Sounds like there's some doubt about paternity. Did you get a paternity test?" Clare asked.

"We don't believe DNA tests make a difference. Adam just has to decide what his relationship will be with her, with them," Kira said.

Clare said, "No. No. With the little one's problems, you need to know if it's genetic—for appropriate intervention, and for Polly, when she has kids."

"Amber said it's environmental pesticides causing his eyes, or could be mercury. There's a lot of mercury coming out of those gold mines where she's from in Nevada," Kira said, still surprised that Amber had spoken up. Is she playing us? she wondered.

"I heard that. More going on in that head than it looks like, right? And I believe it, considering the state of the water table out there in that desert," Clare said. "Last year at Burning Man we found out a lot about the mercury emissions from the mines."

"Jesus. I hate to desert you, but I'll be back, okay?" Kira pushed up to go to the bathroom. Excuse me, everybody." Breathe. Just a moment of space. Ravi's voice in her ear: "Take some time for you."

On her way to the bathroom, she put her ear to the door of Polly's room.

"My mom's hot for Stan, I think," she heard Nell say.

"Ew!" Polly's voice answered, "And what if they start going out? That's weird."

Nell said, "You can tell if people are having sex if they're tired all the time. Sex makes you tired. That's why they call it 'going to bed with somebody.' You want to play a game or something?"

"Remember when we used to play Candyland? Do you want to?"

Kira moved quickly away from the door and into the bathroom. She checked the door lock, then lay on the bathmat on her back for a quick *savasana*, total relaxation. Ravi's face, his smile. She could have invited him to the dinner. His pool-blue quiet pace would quiet things down. She'd stand over the sink, and he'd stand behind her, press against her, bend her. He'd lean down to bite her neck, leaving a blue bruise. She'd wear scarves, and in front of Lindsey, she'd let the scarf fall down a little, and then she'd be able to tell her about it over tea, share this thrill.

Savasana wasn't working, her body tense. Ravi, she thought. She pulled her pants down to her ankles, and lying back on the bathmat, quickly masturbated *Ravi Ravi ravish me* aware of the sounds of the party, muffled voices and glasses. Touching herself felt incredible. She came almost immediately in a quick release. Standing up so fast she was dizzy, she flushed the toilet to cover for herself, washed her hands, thought: what's come over me? On a whim, she grabbed Adam's toothbrush from the holder, blue and worn, grabbed Amber's toothbrush from the top of the sink, pink and toothpaste splotched, and stuck them in her back pocket, arranging the back of her sweater over them. Then she opened the bathroom door and almost ran into Lindsey, who was waiting outside.

"Okay, K, spill. What's the deal with Stan tonight?" Lindsey said. "He doesn't look so great. And he's been hitting on me all night, really weird, first time like that ever in like two decades, and now he's out there drinking beer with Amber. And what's the deal with Amber and her boy? I'm totally confused. You misled me, and I know that I acted like an ass about it, but you're holding out on me."

"I knew you'd think that, Linds. Oh shit. I'm so sorry." Aware of the stolen toothbrushes in her back pocket.

"Are you okay? You look really flushed."

"No. Yes. It's the wine." And the orgasm. "Okay. Look, she might be Adam's kid but we don't know. It's always been a maybe thing. Stan used to be involved with her mom when she was a baby, so it's complicated. Then they just showed up like five days ago. It's been a really shitty week. And I've been wanting to tell you about this other thing, it's just a crush but it's floored me, I don't know. I think I might be in love." Orgasms on the floor of the bathroom during a dinner party? "No. No. Not love. But I'm really messed up." Sliding easily into the old whispered confessional quality of the friendship, forged during crisis nights at Stern Hall, both of them peer counselors.

Lindsey grabbed her by the shoulders. "What? No. You and Adam might be going through a hard time is all. You love each other."

"This has nothing to do with Adam, I don't think."

"Right."

"Really! But this is more of a spiritual thing anyway."

Lindsey looked fierce, her green eyes squinted. "No. You are not going down that road. Okay. You need a hug. Look. Now's not the time, but we have to talk."

"Yes, look, okay, it's just a crush. I'm just feeling loving. Towards everybody. It's the yoga mind." What an idiot she was for bringing it up with Lindsey.

"Uh huh. That's bullshit. We'll talk." Lindsey turned and walked back towards the kitchen.

ꙮ ADAM

An hour later they were all gone. The kitchen was a disaster.

"See you later, Daddy," Adam overheard Amber saying to Stan as Stan left, and what the fuck was that about?

Kira heard it too. "What was that about? The 'Daddy' and the 'Baby' stuff?" She cornered him in the kitchen, piles of dishes on every surface, Amber putting Joey to bed, Polly back in her room.

He leaned against the sink, fed up with being blamed for everything. "I don't know, Kira. Maybe it's like an Elko thing, like elders are 'Dad' and 'Mom,' kind of like how in the African-American community everybody is your cousin."

"Bullshit."

"Or like a hep cat thing, 'Daddy-O.' Or because he lived with Sandi when Amber was a baby for like two minutes. I don't know, Kira, what the fuck was that about? How should I know? You want to ask her? Because I've had it for tonight."

"I'm too tired to fight, Adam." She looked sad, he thought. Stressed. "Maybe you need to find out whether she's really yours. For appropriate intervention. For Polly, if she has kids."

"And if she's technically from my spunk? Does that make her mine? I didn't raise her. I didn't have anything to do with the way she turned out. I don't like how she turned out. Look, she's an adult, I have no responsibility either way. Hey, it went okay, didn't it? The dinner? Did they like the risotto?" He reached for her. A brief hug.

"I changed your toothbrush," she said. "That old one was disgusting."

◊ POLLY

Polly waited until it was finally quiet in the house. It was just so lonely in their house now with all the people who didn't love each other. She didn't want to open her Blood Drawer. But she needed to look at her stuff. Because what if somebody had found it; her mom or dad putting clothing away, or maybe Amber sneaking around and going through her stuff. Do it, she thought, the words "do it" dark and secret, like the small half moons on her leg where she made designs with her fingernails in History, like touching her vagina until it ached but the sneeze she'd read about never happening, leaving her sweaty and sad. "Do it." The pin prick on the tip of her index finger, that beautiful bead of red blood and the taste in her mouth filling and satisfying that urge, that urge to "do it," to slice a line, watch it fill from end to end. To build up the strength, to "do it."

She held her breath. The razor blade and cotton balls were still there, inside the green socks, and near them the postcards in their envelope, "Cabinet of Curiosities." She slid her hand inside the envelope, plucked out a couple, any of them would do. Slid them into her copy of *Animal Farm*.

CHAPTER 6

KIRA

Kira woke up Monday morning a bear, though she held it together until a few moments before she and Polly needed to leave. Polly needed a check for yet another field trip, and Kira couldn't find the checkbook.

"You had it last," Adam said.

"I did? I don't remember. Maybe Amber took it."

"Fuck you!" He stormed off to his studio, slamming the basement door behind him. Kira winced.

"Uh uh. Don't you ever let a man talk to you like that," Amber said to Polly as she ambled out of the guest bedroom. Kira pretended not to hear. Had Amber heard her accusation? Too much this morning.

"What's his problem?" Polly asked.

"Me," Kira said, knowing it was a bad day, she was liable to flip off drivers after she cut them off, sideswipe a car, be late picking up Polly, accidentally erase her hard drive at work, snarl at a beggar, forward a nasty note about one of the professors she worked with directly to that very same professor. If she went shopping, she would wander, heart pounding, for an hour through the consignment shop, buy stuff she hated, and eat dessert, hating her thighs, rebelling against taking care of herself and being good. She longed to go to Ravi's lunchtime class at Studio Raza. No. She'd need a two-hour lunch, and the way things were going with prep for the faculty proposal workshop, there was no way. She'd go to his

Y class after work, her usual. Safer idea anyway. Because she was fantasizing about somebody not her husband, crazy on the floor of the bathroom. Stealing toothbrushes. Losing the checkbook. She'd been wrong to accuse Amber. Where had she put it? Losing control. "You're going to be five minutes late, Polly!" she shouted as she went into the bathroom, scene of her crimes.

When she got out of the bathroom, Polly, cowed, had everything together including her shoes on. Rare. Amber sat on the couch. Joey knelt near the front door with his hands on the floor in front of him, an Egyptian guardian cat.

And all the way to Pioneer, Kira hated Adam, hated how he grumbled about other drivers on the road when he drove. The Ravi spark was gone today. Who was she fooling; the flop of her belly, the cottage cheese of her thighs a natural chastity belt. She felt useless, shrink-wrapped in the same polycarbons that were destroying the planet. The world was dying and in her inaction she was a collaborator. She was spent. Nothing left. Which was precisely when you should go to yoga class, she knew. Ravi or no Ravi, it was the practice. But she was going for Ravi. And hating herself for knowing that, too.

Alone in her office, she tucked two Ziploc baggies containing the pilfered toothbrushes, Adam's and Amber's, into a manila envelope. A quick check of the Internet for DNA tests. Two hundred fifty bucks for "curiosity testing," much more for court approved tests. A filled-out form, a wad of cash from the file folder in her petty-cash-for-emergencies drawer, leaving it almost empty. Licked, sealed, stamped, addressed, and into the pile of outgoing mail.

Ravi's face lit up when Kira walked into the Mind-Body Center that afternoon after work. She nodded casually at him, feeling not casual at all, and went to the back of the studio. She placed her mat down to unroll it. She inhaled, couldn't fill her lungs. Her body flushed. Guilt, sexual charge, she stood, mat half-unrolled, her towel around her neck, barefoot, but she felt slammed to the ground, no wind left. She finished unrolling her mat and sat down to center herself.

It was a strange class. Ravi used her as the model for three poses, his hands moving and supporting her body, though she was nowhere near as strong or flexible as a lot of his "girls." What did they do in the noon class? The inner sanctum. It was maddening, all of it; she rolled up her mat instantly after *savasana* and put on her shoes in the corner. Because it was impossible. She had to give it up, this craziness; the garden going to weeds, work barely holding its own, the bullshit with Amber and Joey. She wasn't twelve, dying for love. She had love: Adam. Polly.

Kira walked towards the exit, past him. "Hey," she said.

"Hey," Ravi said, moving too close to her. "I'm going to get a cup of tea or something. Want one?"

She paused for only an instant. "Okay! I'd love a cup of tea." Her words despite her intentions. Follow it through, get rid of it, she told herself.

She walked casually next to him, around the corner and down Shattuck, past the bums and the BART station, as if he just happened to be headed the same way.

"Amado! Buenos tardes!" he stopped briefly in front of an old Latino man holding out a battered Starbucks cup, patted him on the shoulder, "Que pasa hoy? Bien suerte hoy, mi amigo." Kira dug for a buck, but only found a five in her jacket pocket, so she handed him that. They turned left on Addison Street to the Capoiera Café, where students jenga'd on the sprung floor, accompanied by a man with a berimbau.

"Chai latte, soy milk," she ordered at the counter, aware of him standing behind her a little too close for strangers.

"Separate or together?" the young woman looked at them.

"Separate," Ravi said from behind her. She didn't turn around. "I'll have a single espresso with a zest, if you have it," he said.

"A zest?"

"You know. The lemon zest."

"A twist," Kira said.

"Sorry," the young woman said. "We don't have that."

"Not a problem," he said. They stood awkwardly. She tried to make her thoughts opaque, a milky blue. Calm, calm, breathe.

"Coffee's my weakness," he said. "I have a tendency towards Kapha; in the Ayurvedic tradition that's the heavy, slow energy. I can use the speeding up."

That, maybe, was the stillness in him she was so drawn to. So different from Adam's—and her own—wiry energy. "I can use the slowing down. That's why I like yoga," she said. "I would have thought you were against caffeine."

"Because I teach yoga." He moved next to her. Magnets clicking into place. They watched the barista foaming Kira's soy milk. "Yoga, yes, it's a practice and a lifestyle, but it's something you can incorporate into your whole life. You don't need to be a monk to do this practice. Which is why we have a lot of wealthy, aspiring types in this work, involved in the world and in yoga. Like you."

"I'm not wealthy!" she protested. Is that how he saw her, rich middle-aged woman dabbling? "But busy, yes, making a living in the Bay Area, raising a family—it's hard work. And I take the traditionally masculine element in my relationship—my husband works part-time and does a lot of the house-holding." She felt her voice stress "husband."

"Ah. That's it. I can see the tension of that in how you walk."

"You notice me walk?"

"I notice." His eyes behind his thick glasses stared intensely at her. "I love to watch you walk. It's not just sexy—I mean it's so incredibly... " He stopped. Started again. "I don't mean to make you uncomfortable. Are you uncomfortable? But there's a tension between strong and vulnerable in that walk. Does your husband tell you how beautiful you are?"

The hiss of the foam. "Well... after so many years."

"He should. If I was married to you I'd tell you every day."

Wow. She grabbed the counter for stability.

They sat in the raised café area to watch the capoeira dancers.

"You're married," he said. "What's that like?"

He was a truth serum, eyes focused on her; he asked questions and she answered: "It's been a long marriage. How can I describe all these years? We love each other. It's work. We don't always see eye to eye. He's... well, he's a skeptic, early punk. A really good musician. I think it's hard for him to be in his forties and still in his twenties in his aspirations."

"Aging must be hard. Though I'm looking forward to that time in life, a slowing, less intensity."

She riled. *We're not exactly aging.* "How old are you, can I ask?"

"Thirty-four. But I've come to a spiritual path at a much younger age than most people. I began training as a Zen monk in my early twenties. So I might seem older to you."

"You're a good teacher. I've never been one of those people who looked for a teacher. But you're really good."

"When the student is ready, the teacher will come."

She looked at the table, wondering what to say. His big hands held his coffee cup. The left one trembled. "Are you still practicing Zen?" she asked.

He took a sip and put the cup back on the table, hands below the table on his thighs. "Oh, that was such an asinine thing to say, 'When the student is ready, the teacher will come.'" His cheeks were red. "I'm sorry. You shake me up, Kira. You're so…" he shook his head.

"No, it's okay."

He took off his glasses and put them on the table. "So, Zen. Not now. The austere nature of that path is really not my own, though the teachings are intensely valuable. Or maybe I'm still not done with ego-clinging. But I've learned I'm much more of a sensualist on this planet. We're given a body, this life's body—look…," he patted his belly, his thighs, "…it's big, it needs sensuality. I believe we choose a path to enlightenment that suits our individual temperaments, and our bodies. Food is more than medicine for me, for instance. Sex. I appreciate the human need for passion as well as serenity. Perhaps why I'm so drawn to you, your energy. Very Vata."

"What's Vata?"

"Among other things, very passionate. But I don't want to make you uncomfortable, talking like this."

Under the table, their knees touched accidentally. Kira left hers there. Ravi didn't move his, either.

"I feel like I'm in junior high school again," she said.

He smiled, looking at her. Kira couldn't look at his eyes. His knee was hot against hers, she slid her leg open—just an inch, so his knee was now slightly between her legs. She wanted him to plunge his knee deeper against her thigh. She felt her lips loosen.

"Can I say something about this energy?" he said. His head leaned closer in. "I'm feeling something strong, and I don't think it's just from me. But if it is, just let me know I'm a jerk and I won't say anything about it again."

She closed her eyes, and nodded. After a moment, she opened

her eyes. He was staring at her unblinking: big, brown. "I know you're married."

"I just thought I'd like to get to know you," she managed. "Make a friend."

"Yes. That's what we need to do." He gulped. "Kira, I think about you. I come to class and look for you. I wait for you to make a mistake so I can come adjust you."

"Me, too." This couldn't be happening. A sense of falling, impending doom, destruction, death... the bliss of a new drug. Bottle it, the world would go insane. I Am Insane, a new meal at Café Gratitude.

"You stand out of alignment so I'll adjust you?"

"No. I'm just bad at yoga."

"You're beautiful at it. Can I touch you?"

"Just a hug," she said, pulling away from the emotion. The birimbau plucked out the beat of the class; students in the center of the circle spun and kicked. "I'm not sure what I want to do with this." She gestured to her heart. "And with this," folding both hands over her crotch. "Just a hug, between friends, we can hug."

"Well then, stand up," he said, smiling. He was single, nothing to hide. She stood and they moved to the side of the table and embraced. The capoeiristas jenga'd. He was taller than Adam. Bigger. Her mouth came to his throat, and she moved to kiss it, just his throat. A friend could kiss a friend like that. But her mouth slipped open on his neck and she tasted him, denser than Adam. A slight bitterness that sang in her mouth. Her knees went soft and she clung on to him, dizzy. "My wees are neek," she murmured in his ear, and laughed.

He didn't hear it, or get it. "My wees are neek," she said again. "You mix up my words."

"Beautiful Kira," he said.

"I can't make love with you," she said, into his neck.

"I know. It's okay. Just let this be what it is."

"I should go." She gathered her mat and her bag, trying for dignity.

Driving home in traffic trying to meditate—failing. Walking seemingly calm into the Moss Street house, smiling lips only, "Hello, everybody! Sorry I'm late! Traffic. Should we order pizza? Who's for pesto and who's for pepperoni?"

"Forks down, spoons up, Kira," Adam said, as he unloaded the dishwasher.

"Sorry I broke the rules, Adam," she said, his name a jagged bottle cap in her mouth. "Guess I'm just a rebel."

His face, red with the injustice of being accused a tyrant, "It's not a rule, it's a... it's common sense. It's how you get dishes clean. It's what works." He held up a spoon with a hard thin coat of egg yolk.

"I guess I'm just *bad*," she said, her face hard. Hating him.

"Bad mood, anyway. I am not your enemy. Not yet, anyway."

"Leave it alone, Adam." She would kill him if he said anything about PMS. But he left it alone.

She found the checkbook. That evening, Adam and the rest of them watching a video in the living room, she tore the house apart. She searched the junk drawers, the piles of paper on the sideboard. She dug through the kitchen garbage to see if she'd accidentally thrown it out. She found it near the bottom, deep under risotto leavings, slimed with coffee grounds but still legible. Relief. And guilt. She must have been so distracted to toss it out like that. If she could just clear her head of Ravi.

She wiped off the plastic cover and slid it back in the kitchen drawer where Adam kept the bills.

ᘒ ADAM

"If you're going to stay here, we need to broaden your horizons," Adam told Amber. "I'll take you out to lunch." Over lunch he could ask her again about her plans.

"The amount of money you all spend in restaurants."

"Actually, we've been eating at home a lot," he said. "For us. And I really don't want to cook or think about lunch for us three. Let's go get dim sum." He was sick of the food pickiness. She looked puzzled. "Chinese food." He hoped she wouldn't blow it and make a ching chong comment or stretch her eyes.

"I like chow mein. Johnny likes Chef Chang's best. It's all good with me except I don't eat that beetle juice."

Adam didn't know what she was talking about but didn't want to go there. He was deeply in the mood for char siu bao, siu mai, har gao. Just basics. Nothing there to freak them out.

They were seated immediately at Peony, good thing, as Joey was keening and Amber fretting. He wanted her to be impressed by the high "quotient" of Chinese people at the restaurant, but she didn't seem to notice.

Chinese food in Nevada was not the same as Chinese in Oakland Chinatown, he'd forgotten. The first several carts were challenging. He turned down the chicken feet, jook, and turnip cake. Amber looked distressed. He ordered noodles for her, a bowl of white rice for Joey. Tried not to feel humiliated as he asked for two forks, one for her and one for Joey. Amber poked at the dim sum, a disgusted look on her face.

"It's just rice, pork, and shrimp. Seventy-five ways of preparing rice, pork, and shrimp," he finally said.

"How do you stay so skinny with all that food you eat?"

"Good genes, I guess. But I'm getting fatter." He patted his belly. "Trying to make peace with that. That's what happens when you stop obsessively exercising." How long since he'd actually hopped on the bike?

She slammed her fork down. "I'm done."

"Really? You don't want to try anything else?"

"Forget it. I get it, *Dad.* Keep your good skinny genes, and your gobbledygook food. I'll meet you in the car. You got the keys?"

"Amber, I don't even know what to say to you, with that racist filth coming out of your mouth."

"Keys?" She glared at him, hand outstretched. "I know where I'm not wanted. Still denying your blood." She looked disgusted.

"What did I do? What did I say?" But he handed her the keys, and watched as she picked up Joey, still clutching a pork bun. As she walked away, Adam noticed Joey's butt was covered with rice, and he remembered how Polly had done that, too, until she was ten or so, way past when she should have. Somehow she'd get up from a meal at an Asian restaurant and the back of her pants would be covered with sticky white grains of rice. Forget it, he thought. I tried to be nice. It took a while to get the bill, and when he got down to the car in the parking structure they were both strapped in, Amber listening to the radio, which she snapped off as he opened the door.

❧ POLLY

During English when they were doing silent reading of *Animal Farm*, Polly showed one of her postcards to Brady: a plump infant's leg severed mid-calf, the top tied with a lace cuff and the toenails painted black, floating in clear liquid in a narrow jar. On the back of the card, it said: "Dutch anatomist Fredrik Ruysch. To make the babies look tasteful and natural he adorned them with beads, flowers and lace."

"You're sick," Brady said, but his face was both freaked and admiring, and he wouldn't give it back, "I'll give it back later. I will. I'm not stealing it, I just need it for a moment."

"That one, or this one?" She offered the other card: a wide shallow jar of fluid. In it, the lower half of a baby's head, cut off just above the eyebrows and ears (brain exposed) and just below the jaw, the eyes shut as if sleeping, the cheeks and lips pink and natural, a puff of lace at the throat.

"Oh, dude! Both!"

"Brady, you have to give them back."

"I will."

He shared the cards around at recess. Craig turned pale and backed away, but what did you expect, he refused to participate in the dissections in Science and got a note excusing him from discussions of the human reproductive system. Nell shrugged loyally. "I've seen worse. Besides, what do you expect from a Goth? Polly's a Goth."

"I'm not a Goth, I'm Emo."

Sally from eighth grade insisted they were fake. Amanda said she was going to puke. Mr. Frank confiscated them, and gave Polly study hall. And he wouldn't give them back.

"Sorry," Brady smirked.

She hated him.

⋄ KIRA

Tuesday morning, Kira called in sick and crawled back in bed beside Adam. "I just need some time alone. You take Polly to school, please," she said. "I really just want a morning alone in bed."

"What about Amber?"

"You said they never get up before ten. I just really need a mental health day. A mental health hour. I need to not drive to Berkeley." Her voice steady and low.

"But I'm meeting Stan in downtown Oakland, and you're getting time alone at Harbin soon." Then seeing her face so stressed, "No prob. I'll take Polly and go from there."

"Thank you."

She put a pillow over her head.

Some sick day, Kira thought as the phone rang at 8:15, right after Polly and Adam left. She'd tried to motivate herself to the office, but it was too much. The scene with Ravi. Amber and Joey—the stress with Adam. Just one day in bed, she'd thought. A mental health day.

"Is Amber there?"

"Amber," Kira knocked lightly on the door.

"What."

"Phone call."

"Tell them to call me back."

"It's Steve calling from Salt Lake City."

"Okay."

Kira opened the door. Amber sat up on the futon, one side of her hair matted and snarled. Joey was still asleep on the floor in a puddle of blankets making little sleep whistles, his small hands curled into delicate shells. Kira handed the cordless phone to Amber and closed the door behind her. When she got off the phone, Amber announced she was going to Utah. Right now.

"Do you got any old suitcases we could put our clothes in? Can you get us to the Greyhound, or do we got to walk again?"

Kira felt disoriented, the floor soft below her. What she'd wanted, a surge of a *woo hoo!* But it was followed by a lurch of guilt: I should have been nicer. "You're sure? Oh. No, no, I'll take you. Do you want to check the schedule first?"

"Nah. Steve told me there's one at like 1:00 or 1:30. But I gotta be there early."

"Okay, then. Let me just check and see what I've got that you can pack in." She called Adam's cell, he didn't answer. All on her, as usual. She dug through the back of the hall closet, found an old carry-on bag with a loose wheel. Then felt guilty about the loose wheel.

Getting into the Saab, Amber lit a cigarette. "Amber, you know this is a no-smoking car." Kira worked to keep her voice neutral.

Amber opened the window two inches and stuck her hand, with the cigarette, outside. At the same time she exhaled a cloud of smoke.

"No, really. This is a non-smoking car, please put that out."

"I only just lit it."

Kira said nothing. After a moment, Amber dropped the cigarette. It landed on the concrete driveway. Kira turned off the engine, unclicked her seatbelt, opened the car door, got out, and went around to the passenger side. She stepped on the cigarette to put it out, then picked up the flattened butt with the tips of her index finger and thumb and carried it over to the garbage can. She got back in the car, closed the door, refastened her seatbelt, and restarted the car, saying nothing. They'd be gone in an hour. Amber stared straight ahead. Joey hummed in Polly's old booster seat.

On the way, Kira stopped for a container of chicken chow mein on Broadway so they'd have lunch on the bus—she'd slip Amber a few twenties at the last minute but didn't want to give her too much cash for fear that she'd get off the bus, turn right around, and arrive back in Oakland. The whole way, she fretted about how much was enough, how much was too much. We gave them clothing and food, I'm buying their tickets, she decided. Only a little cash.

A direct line to Salt Lake City; straight up to Sacramento, across Nevada, seven hundred thirty-two miles. Leave at 1:30 p.m., get in at 6:05 the next morning. Fifteen hours, thirty-five minutes. One hundred three dollars and thirty-five cents for both of them. But the clerk handed Kira's gold MasterCard back to her. "Denied. You got another one?"

There was no way it could be denied for a hundred bucks. The computers must be down. She didn't want to hassle it, the thought of piling Amber and Joey back in the car, driving them back home… She handed the clerk her American Express and held her breath until it went through.

The high-roofed bus station had not improved since the last time Kira was here: fuzzy P.A. announcements, the stench of urine and homelessness, big people squeezed into too-small orange molded plastic chairs. Trash cans overflowed with Burger King and Wendy's wrappers. Amber waited next to her, Adam's old carry-on flat on the floor with Joey sitting on it.

The printer finally spit out two cardboard bus tickets. Kira held them, walked over to where they waited. When their bus was called, "Salt Lake City, lane 3B. This is a boarding announcement for Salt Lake, lane 3B, departure in eight minutes," she walked with them to the bus. Amber held Joey's hand. Joey dragged behind, one cylinder block clutched his right hand, wearing his new jeans jacket. Amber didn't seem likely to say anything—she'd been silent since they picked up the chicken chow mein—so Kira said, "Well, bye, Joey. Nice meeting you." She bent to kiss him on his head and give him a squeeze. "Um, Amber, nice seeing you. Have a safe trip."

"Okay," Amber said. "Tell Polly 'bye.'"

Kira watched carefully to make sure they climbed into the bus. Then they were gone. She exhaled.

She drove from the bus station directly to Redwood Park. The fog was in, the bay trees and redwoods dripped condensation so dense it felt like rain. It wasn't the same, hiking without Mishka. They'd caught the rapist who, for a year or so, prowled these trails—a gym teacher at a nearby school. But this was still Oakland—it was wise to have a dog with you. Kira stepped carefully over the occasional banana slug. They were endangered now.

It took a long time to lift herself out of herself and into the woods. On Big Trees trail, she reached the Walking Stick Graveyard—a wide grove with piles of fallen five-foot-long branches. The redwood grove soaring high above her. Sky.

They were gone. The bus was east of Sacramento now. She had her life back, she could go home and open the windows. She stopped to savor it, but the wash of relief she'd expected didn't come, and she moved through the rest of the day feeling low-level anxiety and dread. Amber might come back, Amber might not come back. She felt a pang of pity and guilt over Joey, so small in his jacket. Now they really existed, even though she didn't want them to, and they could never not-exist again. The family was altered.

And all that was riled up between them all—her and Adam and Polly—things not so easy to air out as the smells of stale smoke and diapers.

CHAPTER 7

❧ ADAM

Adam and Stan spent the day working with fourth graders, filming them doing raku pottery, sand paintings, and then building a labyrinth out of paper mache "stones" made of balloons they'd spent weeks covering with fast food wrappers. The kids all marched through it, very solemn. It would be great footage for the MOCHA arts center promotional DVD. He'd brought Polly down to MOCHA a couple of times when she was little—just a great little organization. So good to get back to work.

"Talked to Sandi last night, she called," Stan mentioned as they reloaded the company van early evening. "She dumped that asshole Tommy, doing much better. Got a job as a nurse's aide."

"Yeah, I heard about that."

"How's the little visit?"

Adam shrugged. "Kira's barely talking to me, Polly, I don't know. But Amber's little boy, Joey, you know, he's got pretty serious problems, and I don't think she's up for handling it. So they're staying with us for a while, I guess."

"What's his thing?"

"Joey? The eye thing, but Kira thinks he's autistic, too. Amber's kind of in denial or just doesn't know. *I sail the river of Denial...* anyway, what can you do."

"What can you do. Wanna go to Barney's, get a burger?"

"Probably got to get home, make dinner for the troops. I'll rain check you." They slid the van door closed, climbed into the front.

Stan put it in gear. "Traffic's going to suck on 580."

"Yeah. Hey, Stan."

"Hey, bud."

"Ever think Amber might be your kid, not mine?"

Stan laughed. "Nah. No way, absolutely no deal. She's always calling me Dad, though, 'cause me and Sandi were together for a while. I say, 'Hey Amber baby, you make that million, set me up in the life of luxury, my own jet, then I'll be your old man. Until then, I'm Uncle Stan the Man.'"

"Do you ever give them money?"

Stan shook his head. "Hell, no. Like I got any."

"You don't feel guilty?"

"Not going to do any good. All I can do is listen to their problems."

"Hey, they're your responsibility, too."

"What? Why? What'd I do?"

"Because you might be her father just as much as me; you fucked Sandi that weekend."

"I'm not."

"You're so sure."

"Adam. Never got a lady pregnant, and when Lucy and I were trying, the docs said I don't have any swimmers," Stan said.

Adam grimaced: stuck my foot in it, big mouthed Me. "Man, I'm sorry." Jesus. Embarrassment, but something else, too: what he'd long suspected about Kira's first pregnancy couldn't be.

"No worries," Stan said. "News to you, not news to me. Makes it easier anyway, fewer contraptions to negotiate during the hot times. Hey, could have been Jumbo too, he was with her that weekend. Man, she was hot, Sandi. Not so much later on, but remember?"

Adam shrugged. A tight tee shirt, pink nipples on tiny

breasts… Dropped the subject. Traffic was still bad even so late. Stan turned on KFOG and they played air guitar, stop and go, until Stan dropped him off at the house—which was empty, no note, no Kira, Polly, Amber, Joey. Eventually he remembered to check his cell phone for messages. They were gone? Utah? He had a drink to celebrate or mourn, he wasn't sure which; a shot of tequila. And fifteen minutes later, Kira and Polly were home from dinner with no "to go" for him, so he pulled leftovers from the fridge.

❧ POLLY

Polly waited at Pioneer after music practice that afternoon. It was already dark, mid-January afternoon dark, and her mom was late, only swerving to the pick-up curb after everybody else was gone. Polly dashed through the drizzle, slammed her backpack into the back, and climbed into the front seat. "I'm cold. Why were you late? Why don't you have the heat on?"

"Hello to you, too," her mom turned on the engine and blasted the heat. "How was your day?"

"Good."

"Anything special?"

"No. Emily and Etani are going out. He asked her at lunch to be his girlfriend."

"What do you mean, going out?"

"I don't know. Going out. Seventh-grade-going-out, not eighth-grade-going-out." She shrugged.

"So does that mean they kiss? More than kiss?"

"Kiss. Sometimes, I guess. Why do you care?"

Her mom said, "Honey? Amber and Joey took off today. They said to say 'bye' to you."

"What? Where did they go?"

"I'm not really sure; somewhere in Utah. Maybe Provo? She said she had a job possibility. Joey's daddy's there waiting for her."

They were at a red light. Trapped! Polly scrabbled at the car door then stopped: what am I going to do, run out of the car? "That fucking sucks. Nobody tells me anything." They hadn't told her Amber was coming, they'd barely told her she was gone. In this family where they were supposed to listen to each other, and be equals, and respect each other.

"Polly."

"Why can't I swear, when you guys do all the time?"

"Daddy swears, I don't swear."

"And nobody does tell me anything. Like when Mishka died and I was at camp and you didn't even tell me."

"I know, Polly." The light turned green. "I'm sorry. I wasn't trying to keep this from you. It just happened." She flipped open her phone. "I'm going to try your dad again."

"Well, our house is way too small for everybody anyway." Polly turned her head to look out the window. The car's headlights left reflective flares on the damp streets.

They ate at Mikado. Her dad was still at a shoot. It was nice with just the two of them, Polly thought, sitting on the same side of the table as her mom so they could cuddle. The people at Mikado always brought her mom hot water without being asked. The miso soup was clear until you stirred it cloudy, with tiny treasure cubes of tofu and sharp tastes of scallion. The sushi was nothing special, but they liked it because she could order anything she wanted; nigiri sushi was only one dollar each.

"Do you think Joey would like Green Dragon rolls?" she asked. He liked rice, and small food you could hold in your hand and eat.

"Not sure, honey." Her mom looked distracted, worry lines

between her blue eyes, her frizzy hair uneven. Polly wanted to go home; she still had math homework to do and it was so late. That was the problem with staying after school for the music program. But it took a long time to get the bill, and then it was a hassle.

"Do you have another card instead?" the waitress asked, handing back her mom's MasterCard, and then, "I'm sorry, missus, we don't take American Express."

"Oh, that's right, I'm sorry," her mom said. "Can I write you a check?"

"We don't take checks. But for you, this time only."

"Thank you so much, thank you. I really appreciate it."

"Mommy, why don't you just pay cash so we can get out of here?"

"I'm low. I gave some money to Amber before she got on the bus."

"Good. Because I don't think she had any. Daddy kept giving her money for cigarettes and junk food." Her mom made a face. In some ways, it was a good thing they were gone, Polly thought, putting her jacket on.

❧ ADAM

The evening house was huge without Amber's stolid presence, the danger of turning a corner and seeing Joey's blank face. Like a visitation, rather than a visit, Amber and Joey had left a hole. The sag in the couch. The places where they weren't.

"Come have a snuggle, Polly," Adam said. "Watch Flight of the Conchords with me."

Polly looked dubious but sat down, a bit obediently. Great, he thought. Were they in for that, already? Teenage indulgence of dear old Dad? He put his arm around her stiff shoulders.

"So now I'm supposed to just forget I have a sister? And Joey?

And another nephew somewhere?"

Ouch. Adam didn't say anything. He stroked her head. She needed to wash her hair, it was lank and tangled. Her skinny arm, the flesh like crème brulee, baby skin. He nibbled, expanded his universe. How had he gotten so lucky? "It happened before you were born," he wanted to say. "It has nothing to do with my love for you. *You* are my daughter. It doesn't matter if she's biologically my daughter or not, I didn't raise her; she's not my daughter. Not the way *you* are."

He'd never say it that way. That wasn't how they talked to each other.

"Cut it out, that tickles!"

"Polly, it's fine. They're back to their lives, we're back to ours, and they may visit again, but it's really not our responsibility."

"Great. And what if she has nowhere to go, Dad?"

He sighed.

"Dad, how come you won't even answer simple questions?"

"These aren't simple questions. But Amber is a grown woman in her twenties, she has a mom, a boyfriend, and her own life."

"But what am I supposed to do?" she pulled out of his grasp.

"I guess just do what feels right, not just good, but correct."

"I don't know what you're talking about, Dad."

"I don't either." He'd lost the thread of the conversation, head fuzzy. "Now, time for bed. Get your ass in gear."

"So my MasterCard hasn't been going through," Kira told him as she turned off the bedside light.

"Okay, I'll check into it," Adam said.

✣ KIRA

Amber and Joey were gone, which meant life was back to normal.

Thursday evening, they all ate at Café Gratitude even though the scene was, even for their family, a lot too much Berkeley to take. The wait staff wore ripped and safety-pinned black T-shirts with "What are you grateful for?" printed on the back. They all had tattoos, one of them high on her shaved forehead; two had blonde dreadlocks. On birthdays, they all leapt about and sang—Polly loved it, Kira liked the food, Adam tolerated it.

"You are enlightened," the waitress placed a smoothie in front of Polly. "You are elated": Adam's raw "enchilada" of sprouted sunflower seeds and tomato. For Kira, green salad, raw nachos, almond hummus, "You are fulfilled. Enjoy!" the waitress bowed and backed away into the busy café.

"I don't feel elated yet," Adam said.

"Eat it first," Kira said.

"I'm getting the 'I Am Borderline Psychotic' next time." Adam poured Polly filtered water from the clear pitcher engraved, "Calm."

"That's not on the menu, Daddy."

"How about the "I Am Pathetic?" Kira said. The room was filled with yoga types. Ravi might be here, she thought. She glanced around, pretending to look at the graphics on the walls, huge posters with inspirational images and slogans: *"Can you surrender to how beautiful you are?"*

"I Am Neurotic," Adam said.

"You are neurotic," Kira crooned like the waitress. "Do I sound like her?"

"Daddy. I've got one. Next week, I'm getting the 'I Am Bulimic,'" Polly said. "It's a large plate of food, and it comes with a stick."

Kira and Adam laughed. "You Are Funny," Adam said.

She really was funny, Kira thought. That she could find the

absurd in situations, not just the ironic.

"…or the 'I Am Obese.' Same thing, no stick."

"I Am Amber. Same thing," Adam said.

"Adam!"

"Oh my God, Daddy. That's so mean. She can't help it. You have some kind of a fat phobia."

"Probably. That was mean. I'm sorry."

"I'm a teenage girl in this society, and you're going to give me an eating disorder, Daddy. Next time, I'm ordering the 'I Am Anorexic.'"

"What's that, Poodle?" Kira said.

"Half a glass of water."

Adam laughed, pointed his finger at Kira and shook it. "What a daughter. We made a good one."

Kira said, "Good one. Eat, Polly, stop talking. I'll have the 'I Am Full,' next time."

"I'm never full here," Adam said. "They don't give you any food."

"It's living food, it sustains you even if you don't feel stuffed."

From the juice bar, the evening manager called, "Arielle! You are calm and effervescent! Monique! You are *still* understanding! Please pick up your understanding!"

"Could you guys start calling me Apollonia?" Polly said. "You said you would. But you never do." Her chin quivered, a thirteen-year-old's quick shift into distress.

"I'm sorry, I do try to remember," Adam said. "Just that you're so *Polly* to me. You are Polly." Strands of shredded carrot clung to his lips.

Kira winced, handed him a napkin, "Chin."

"Then why did you name me Apollonia?"

"So we could call you Polly."

"Adam, don't be a jerk. It's so when you were a teenager and dramatic, you could change your name to Apollonia and walk around..."

"...with a rose clutched between my teeth. Mommy, you always say that."

"Polly, I'll try to remember," Kira said. "Apollonia. Are your friends calling you Apollonia?" Asking carefully. Don't scare the small wild animal.

"Some of them. Amanda. Nell isn't, she says I'm overly dramatic about it. Amber said she would, but then she left."

"You can call yourself whatever you want, Apollonia," Adam said. "That's your right. Legally, you can call yourself whatever you want as long as it's not for fraudulent purposes."

"I'm changing my name to Kiraswami Shakti," Kira said.

"Not surprised," Adam said. His voice had an edge. Did he know about Ravi? If she could only talk to Adam about it in a way that made sense, wouldn't threaten.

"Shut up." She fired a look toward Polly, then chewed one of her live falafels and stuck out her tongue, coated with off-white goo.

"Mommy, can I get an 'I Am Incredible?'"

"What's that?" Adam asked.

"Live pecan pie."

"No," Kira said. "You can be incredible without dessert."

The waitress placed the bill on the table: "Tell me one thing you are grateful for today." They all stared at her; Polly looked at her dad for escape. "It's our Question of the Day," the waitress said.

"I'm grateful for the opportunity to eat such good food," Kira said.

Adam said, "I'm grateful for not being asked personal questions or having my daughter put on the spot."

"Oh, it's not required!" The waitress left.

"I Am Broke," Adam said, paying the bill.

"That was mean," Kira said. "God, you're in a mood."

Adam shrugged, squeezed Polly's hand. "I Am Broke and I Am Morally Bankrupt," he said.

On their way to the car, they passed a man sitting in a doorway, selling copies of *Street Spirit*. Kira paused. "I've only got a twenty."

Adam dug out a dollar bill.

"Bless you," the man said, handing Kira the paper.

Polly said, "Don't bless us, curse the system."

❧ ADAM

On the answering machine when they got home: a message from Sandi: "Amber? Baby, will you please call me? Adam, I know you don't want me calling you, but I want to know where Amber's at, so if you know, give me a courtesy call."

Adam looked at Kira, who stared at him with an unreadable look on her face.

"She leave a number where she was going?"

Kira shook her head.

Polly glared at both of them, stomped down the hall and slammed the door to her room. "What?" he asked. "I don't have Sandi's number. I don't even know her last name anymore."

"You could call Stan," she said.

"Yeah. I'll do that."

When they were out of the house it was easier to forget that Amber and Joey even existed. But at home, because they'd been there for days and days, Amber and Joey had left heat trails. Stuff moved, touched, marked by their touch.

"You know, you could thank me," Kira said that night in bed. "You've never thanked me, and you've never apologized."

"For?" For the money, for the maxed out MasterCard, $800 in website fees for erotica… he forced his mind away from it.

"For? For putting up with Amber and Joey all those days. I didn't bargain for that."

"Jesus, Kira. Do you think I did?" But it was a momentary reprieve, he felt the tension drain from his neck.

"It wasn't them, it was the not knowing if they were staying, what the relationship was. Not being able to plan anything. You just left me hanging and hanging."

"Kira, I'm sorry. Let's not fight."

"No. I'm sorry. I'm a total bitch," she said.

"No, baby. You're not. Or, but if you are, you're *my* bitch." She smiled. He moved his hand across the mattress to touch her breast. "Do you want…"

"Oh, no. I'm sorry. I do want to want to, but I'm so keyed up. I'm such a bitch, I just have to get over myself. Can you just hold me?"

"Yes." He slid over, wrapped himself around her, a penguin father covering his baby with feathers. "How's this?" He held her until she fell asleep, wrapped by him, safe and hot. How did he get so lucky? Home, home, home.

Then he gently detached himself and went down to his workshop where he kept his stash.

❧ KIRA

Polly was spending Saturday night at Nell's house. Kira walked Polly up the long, narrow stairs to Lindsey's small wooden house, on a hillside near Highland Hospital. Polly and Nell ran off like little girls, the dogs chasing them out to the back yard. Lindsey and Kira stood in the dark wood foyer. Here, years of secrets told during drop-offs and pick-ups.

Lindsey hugged her goodbye. "Have fun, Miss Woo-Woo!"

"Lindsey, cut it out," she flared. Everybody made fun of New Age woo-woo types, but at least they were trying to go deeper, make sense of it all, she told Lindsey. She made fun of the woo-woos too, but meditation, yoga felt good. It lightened her body and mind, and...

Lindsey stopped her rant. "Shut up, you goose. I've been a Buddhist for seven years. Two months retreat at Green Gulch in 2007, remember? I went to Burning Man at the salt flats. I'm just keeping you real. You're so cute, getting the true believer glow."

Kira felt foolish. Going off like that. She looked at Lindsey, speechless, wanting to talk about Ravi. "I'm going up to Harbin next weekend alone to sort it all out."

"What about that guy?"

"Just a little crush, Lindsey." She never should have mentioned Ravi. He knows things, she thought of saying. Things I need to know.

"Well, doesn't matter where you get your appetite, so long as you eat dinner at home, my aunt used to say," Lindsey said, and hugged her. "Just... be careful, Kira, lots of psychos out there. A lot of sincere people with really good intentions, but a lot of... You're smart. Relax. I love you. I won't let the girls stay up too late."

"Thank you. She's been a bit moody lately."

"Nell, too. Hormones."

Kira turned to go.

Nell and Polly pounded back. "Can we get a snack?"

"Later," Lindsey said. "Why don't you show Polly our new

fish. Polly, you're going to love him. He's got the weirdest face."

❧ POLLY

"Thank you for saving me from the stagnant pit they call my house," Polly said, as they looked at Al Gore, the new fish. "I can't stand it. My dad's an old punk rocker and my mom's a woo-woo wannabe. I don't even want to talk about Amber. Or Joey. His eyes fuckin' creeped me out. I'm glad he's gone."

"You're just going from one pit to another."

"That's a matter of perspective. I like your house."

"Yeah, if you like small, cramped, and smelly," Nell said.

"It smells good."

Nell shrugged. Polly and Nell sat at the big table in Nell's dining room, beading. Their parents had gotten really irritating, Polly and Nell both agreed. Always in your face with their own issues. Then they talked about Amanda and Etani and Brady. They planned next summer, many months away—both together one week at each person's house until they got sick of each other. And maybe they should agitate for horseback riding lessons, if they weren't already too old to start.

They both were good with their hands. At seven and eight, they'd made costumes for their stuffed animals, Nell sewing with a darning needle, Polly a whiz with tiny gold safety pins. Fashion shows with draped scarves, hot glue guns and sequins; they'd made books—written, illustrated, and pasted together with cardboard covers from old shoeboxes. They'd made cloth hangings from iron-on shapes scissored from bright fabric scraps, trailing threads. They'd carved pumpkins, though last year was the first year they'd been allowed to actually wield the knives after drawing eyes, noses, ears, and broad scary mouths with marking pens.

They saved their allowance (five dollars a week) for bead binges, and today they made dangling earrings from beads and wires and fittings, twisting wires and swearing profusely when things didn't go well. Polly threaded three straight pins beneath the first layer of skin on the heel of her palm—"It doesn't hurt!"—enjoying Nell's reaction "Ew, Polly, you're so Emo!" and the way the skin looked translucent above the silver of the pins.

They had their colors, they had their styles: Polly fixated on black and silver. Nell loved red. No pink, for either of them, pink an anathema.

Tomorrow they would dye Polly's hair black.

Polly loved Nell's house because it was always the same: Nell and Lindsey, the crafts, the big dogs, the food: baked potatoes with all the fixings and salad with arugula from the wheelbarrow garden in the garden; fresh pasta (they hung the long strands on broomsticks parked between two chairs); pizza with dough Lindsey made from scratch. Lots of parmesan cheese. And they never, ever had to go out to dinner. Polly slept in a nest of sleeping bags and blankets on the floor of Nell's room, a dog snuggled on either side of her—and when the dogs spread out in the night, as dogs did, she always ended up squeezed out of her sleeping bag, toothpaste out of a tube. Waxing nostalgic with Nell as they ate pancakes in the morning, the sun streaming warm onto the dark wood of the dining table: "Nell, remember when we used to…?" "Hey, Polly, remember that time?"

Because they had already been friends forever through tantrums and summer camps and teachers; because they were both only children (until Amber…) they would be friends forever, Polly knew, sisters really.

"Even though I have a sister now, you're more my sister than she is," she told Nell. The same high school. The same college just like their moms, three cats and three dogs in their little house.

After breakfast, Lindsey set Polly up in the bathtub for the hair dying session. Nell knew her way around a bottle of hair dye, the towhead of her childhood long gone (first black, then blue, now mahogany). Polly sat in the bathtub, changing.

Before her parents came to pick her up, she glanced at her reflection in the high old mirror on the dining room sideboard, her face pale in contrast to her blue black hair. She stared at herself in the bathroom mirror when she went to pee. "This is what I look like now," she whispered to her reflection, stunned to see herself still a child. "Hello, me."

CHAPTER 8

✿ KIRA

In the grocery store. On campus. Every time she turned around, she expected to see Ravi. Hope and fear settled in her stomach, a roiling sun. He'd love this, she thought in the kitchen, admiring the orange of a freshly cut cantaloupe. She wasn't eating—she looked great. I'm on the Ravi diet, she wanted to say.

At the YMCA. Nobody in the small jacuzzi near the showers. She slid into the hot water. Her head towards the door so she could see if anybody was coming, she contorted her crotch against the jet stream, shameless and elated, and orgasmed immediately, a rush of release. It wasn't enough. Climbing out of the tub, she chose one of the few showers with a curtain, leaned against the white tiled wall with the water on full blast, using her right hand to rub herself and her left hand to pinch a nipple, running his words through her head: "I think about you. I come to class and look for you. I'd be honored to work with you." Now he held her on the floor, poised above her ready to enter her. His stare: "It's an honor to break my heart on you." She came again, then, knees weak, slid to the floor of the shower. And then did it again. She never fantasized about fucking him, always him poised over her, ready to enter. It didn't help.

It was ridiculous, this obsession. She had to say goodbye. Part of her knew she was cutting herself off at the knees by not going with it, saying no; he had so much to teach her. Yoga, that kind of loose bliss in her body, a kind of freedom, a path to deeper consciousness, an initiation into higher consciousness. No. Perhaps if she'd started younger, had fewer responsibilities.

Let me just go there once, she thought. Just in my mind, not in my body. Maybe I can get over him then. Alone in bed, she closed her eyes and, not moving, slowly made love to him, feeling every move between them; his hands would be here, her mouth would be there, his taste, his fullness, his words, her words, their orgasms. A full sense memory of a memory that hadn't happened, and would never, ever, ever happen.

"Goodbye," she told him in her mind.

Like that would work.

ADAM

Without Amber and Joey, the house was silent on weekdays. Be proactive, man, he told himself. Get your fat ass in gear. Adam made himself another pot of Peet's, wearing sweats because they didn't bind his belly. He'd write a "What's Next" list. He grabbed the message pad next to the phone, the house too quiet without the ticking of Mishka's toenails. Next door, Tansy barked. She and Mishka had played under the fence, growling and ridging at each other. We should get another dog, he thought. Every morning a bright and shiny day for dogs. Like an afternoon TV special where the dog died, things went south, then on Christmas morning there was a new puppy under the tree, or a stray rescued from a culvert, and everybody was happy all over again.

He looked at the blank memo pad, listened to the silence in the house. Just him and the coffee and the mist, and there was still a sense of possibility.

Maybe he should become a professional dog walker, get a van, pile the pooches in the back, and head for the hills. They always looked so happy, the dogs, and the dog walker too, loose and casual, draped with leashes. Kind of a dead-end job, but they looked like they didn't care, hanging out every day with the sweetness and danger of strange dogs who offered the possibility of instant love, but with teeth. Each dog with its personality in its eyes. A job for a twenty-eight year old.

"I'm on vacation for a bit," he told himself. "I'm hanging with the family, building relationships." But it didn't work, he was still a failure. His belly strained against the elastic waistband. He'd slacked on his supplements, wasn't exercising. Not being a success felt like an elephant was sitting on his chest.

He began to write DOG WALKING COMPANY on the pad of paper, but the pen died after DOG. Leaning back in the oak chair, he opened the kitchen bill drawer to get another pen. And there sat the checkbook he'd thrown out and dowsed in coffee grounds, back in the drawer, a silent reproach. Kira. She did know about the money situation. She hadn't said anything. Fuck.

In the basement, a couple of shots of tequila, fast and shuddery, the end of the bottle. A few tokes on a joint to cover up the smell of the booze. A mint to cover the smell of the joint. Even if Kira noticed, she'd never say anything.

From above, the phone rang. He got up the stairs just as the machine got it: "It's Sandi. Is Amber there? Tell her to call. I just don't appreciate the dump and run. Amber? You there? Listen, baby doll, Johnny and Joey need their mama."

Adam played it again. The dump and run? He hesitated over the Save and Erase buttons, then pushed Save. The machine rewound with a hum and the fast green blinking light became slow. His stomach growled. Hungry. Damned if he was going to call that bitch Sandi. How had Joey gotten back to Sandi's house? That was probably the best place for him anyway.

Time for lunch. He wanted a juicy burger from Barney's; the

steak cut fries served so hot they sizzled on your tongue, the out-side crisp, the inside white and mealy. A thick chocolate shake, extra chocolate.

✎ POLLY

It was winter between the rains. Foggy mornings, the afternoons clear and fresh, slanting light through January clouds. Polly felt glum too often—school was at the boring part of the year—the weather still bad and summer more than half way away. The next chocolate holiday to look forward to was Valentine's Day. With Amber and Joey gone, things felt normal, but not quite. She had changed, but nobody had noticed. Her dad had said, "Nice hair, babe," when they'd picked her up from Nell's, but her mom had just stared into space, and hadn't said a word about it, not yet, and the longer she didn't say anything the more Polly knew she hated it.

Finally she mentioned it after school when they were at Whole Paycheck picking up dinner: "Mommy, am I pretty?"

"What? Polly, yes, you happen to be very pretty. And smart and kind and insightful. What's up, honey?" She took a number for the fish counter. "Do you want salmon or trout?"

"Can we have trout? Do you like my hair?"

"Hair? Polly, you know I love your hair." Then she peered closer. "It looks great, Pol."

"But you never said anything about it."

Her mom looked confused.

"You didn't notice." Then, at her mother's look, "Mommy! You didn't even notice that I dyed it. Me and Nell! You didn't even notice."

Her mom looked pale. "Oh Polly, of course I noticed. I've been thinking how sophisticated you look. But when I first saw it, we were all talking and I didn't want to interrupt what we were saying, and we just never got back to it."

"Right." She could tell her mother felt guilty for lying because they went to Fenton's for ice cream before heading home, and that night, her mom insisted on sitting with her the whole time she did homework, even though math usually made her snippy.

✎ KIRA

Kira hadn't noticed Polly's dyed hair; though she'd covered it up pretty well, she thought, sitting at classic white marble tables over Fudgeannas and Black and Tans at Fenton's Creamery, their favorite dairy splurge. Yet as she'd spooned sweet caramel and chocolate and whipped cream into her mouth, Polly whispering, "Everybody in here is happy, did you see that, Mommy?" she was inwardly horrified at herself. How had she not noticed Polly's hair going from brown to black? Too focused on Ravi. So far from the days when she'd celebrated every almost-smile from infant Polly, every poop and pee; when she and Adam had gone out to dinner leaving baby Polly with Lindsey yet spent their date holding hands over the food, happily talking about Polly. Joined at the hip, the perfect couple, the perfect parents. They'd been on auto-glide as parents for a couple of years now. They'd had it easy with Polly—the rare school crisis or social dilemma—but now she was a teenager, and the hard years would begin. And the first symptoms had happened—dying her hair without asking—and she, unbelievably, hadn't even noticed. Guilt socked her. Had Lindsey noticed? It had happened in her bathroom. Had Polly lied and said she had permission? Had *she* given permission to Polly and not noticed, so distracted?

It was her feelings for Ravi, she knew. He was an addiction, she was strung out, and now it was even impeding her relationship with Polly. Not okay. I'm not okay, and it's not okay, she thought.

Cold turkey hadn't worked. Saying goodbye in her mind hadn't worked. She had to get over it before it destroyed her family. And maybe the only way out of the maze was through it. If she got to know him she'd demystify him. If she just touched him once, she'd get that he was flesh and blood. It was strong medicine, an inoculation: an overdose to frighten her system back to reality. Electroshock. Chemo. Radiation. She was desperate enough to try. She had to tell Adam. She pushed the ice cream away.

"Do you think anybody can ever finish one of these?" she asked Polly.

Polly stared at her half-eaten Fudgeanna, poked at the banana. "I'm grossed out. Do you think Daddy will be mad we ate these before dinner?"

"I'll get one to go for him. He likes the Saddleback Brownie, extra cherry."

"What about the trout?"

"Wow. I guess we can cook it and make it into cold fish sandwiches for tomorrow. Okay?"

Polly looked at her dubiously. "Oh-kay, Mommy."

"Don't worry, it will be fine!"

"I don't know," she said to Adam. "What do you think these days about polyamory?" They were lying in bed, still sugared out. He'd given a laugh like a friendly sneeze when she'd handed him his ice cream, then settled down happily at the kitchen table.

"What? Polyamory, Love of Polly?" he gently massaged her right shoulder. She snuggled against him, tucked the covers around them.

"Lindsey told me Janelle and Clare have an open relationship now, and Clare was the first to take a new lover. They made a formal agreement, and anybody they sleep with has to sign something, too."

He slid his hand down her torso, swept it under her pajama top and up to her breast, held a nipple between his fingers. "Oh, that's absurd. Sign something. That's what you want? And how about this?" A small pinch.

She pulled away from him slightly. "Gentle! No, the signing thing's absurd. But I'm thinking that it's probably not such a bad thing, for mature couples, just as a principle, if nothing else. We're old enough now, we should be secure enough to be able to have adventures without each other, and sometimes those adventures might be sexual. If the couple is mature enough, if they're committed, if everybody is up front about it and it's done with love and respect, then it seems like a more mature thing to do." She wondered if she sounded as rational as she was trying to be.

Adam looked distracted. The corner of her mind noticed the faint musk of pot on his breath. Stoned again.

"You're the one who didn't want an open relationship," he said. His other hand fiddled under her pajama pant waistband, moved slowly on her thigh.

"You mean before Polly was born? Well, yeah, you had about a gazillion groupies hanging all over you, and we had that scene with Sheila and Stan, and we weren't mature enough to be able to deal with the jealousy when it came up. I'd like to think we're a lot more evolved now."

"Mm. I'm always up for a random fuck with a hot blonde." Buried his nose in her hair.

"Are you really? Have you been?"

He pulled away abruptly and sat up in bed. "Kira. Are you into this at all?"

"Yes! I'm just asking!"

"Okay, is this some convoluted way of asking me if I've been fucking around on you? Are we back to Sheila?"

"No," Kira sighed. "I hadn't even been thinking about Sheila. Look, I didn't raise this to fight. Just that it seems like it's working for Clare and Janelle."

"You wanna sleep with them?"

"Clare, sure, Janelle, no chance. She barely talks. No. But somebody at yoga…" she flapped her eyebrows to lighten the news. If he freaked out, she could make it into a joke. But he didn't seem to react. "See, this could be a whole new development in our relationship. Bring a little heat home, or whatever."

"I knew your dykiness would come out sooner or later." He slid back down in the bed, his hands on her body, pulling her against him.

"I'm not a dyke. I'm…"

"Ah, you're a dyke who likes dick. I know. Want some dick, dyke?" He put her hand on his erection.

"Oh yeah, baby, baby, right here, right now, on the floor, at the door…" A twinge for letting him misunderstand her.

"Look, babe, I've always been into freedom, you know that. We're 'evolved' as much as Janelle and Clare, we don't need no stinkin' permission slips." He pulled her pajama bottoms down. "Do your thing. Just be honest with me? Now, let me turn you on."

A wash of relief came over her body. Maybe she could work though the Ravi thing now, get it over with, move on with her life. She felt a wave of desire for Adam. "Let me first," she said. She worked her way down below the covers, kissing his round belly, her tongue following the ladder of black hair down from his belly button, sucking his penis, enjoying the taste of him. *Him.*

"No, sweetie. My breasts are really sensitive," she said, when he pulled her toward him.

"Let me do you softly," his mouth moving down her torso

now. "Pretend I'm your yoga friend. Sorry I don't have breasts. Is she big or small? Probably small breasted. Am I too hairy?"

"Shh. Stop talking. Come inside me." And why would it matter if it was a man or a woman? she thought.

He mounted her, pinning her arms spread eagle to the bed.

Lying together afterward, his leg over her thighs. She felt good, bathed in warm milk. She'd broached the subject; he hadn't objected. She could learn the lessons Ravi offered, Adam didn't seem averse. She'd just tell him about it afterwards; they'd work it out.

Or, even, maybe she didn't have to tell him about it. If Ravi could teach her about transformation through sexual energy, well then, she could bring that home, and Adam would be none the wiser, and they would all benefit.

This was why she'd picked Adam, she thought, flaws and complications and all—like finding the perfect artichoke, knowing that the frost-tipped leaves might look damaged but signaled tenderness. They had an understanding now. She loved him and she'd be careful. She couldn't hurt that heart in the center of his prickly leaves.

CHAPTER 9

In the night, Kira woke to roaring. A storm. It took her a few moments to realize Adam wasn't there. She peeked through the blind: just wind.

The exercise, the careful eating, the meditation, the spiritual books, the asanas, all just the boxing coaches in the corner between rounds, stitching her wounds, icing her bruises, pouring cold water on her head and pushing her out for the next round. She'd thought she was progressing... then Amber had burst in, Cupid fired his bow from the stands, and she was down for the count. TKO. She scrawled on the pad next to the bed:

> You think it's the wild rain, the ground getting nourished, but it's only the disappointment of the wind. Pumpkin spiders spin last webs, give up, clutch their egg sacs, and die.

But she stopped there. Once, she'd written poetry, before she figured out she had no talents, nothing artistic to say: no music, no art, no words. She lay listening to the wind; Ravi's voice murmured endearments. She was a Café Gratitude dish: I Am Obsessed.

She moved her hands up her torso to where her breast melted against her side. That seam would only deepen, her breasts soften to nothing. So little time left to be desired. If it was dark, if it was candlelit, he would be kind. She felt the pomegranate seeds in her mouth, the tense smooth skins, the sharp point, redder than her mouth. Persephone had a choice. Kira moved them into place, and bit down. The poison spurted sharp and sweet and spread backward over her palate, spreading its magic—a little bit of death.

ADAM

Adam was taking out the garbage when the phone rang at eleven that night; he got back in the house in time to hear the machine get it. "It's Sandi. Just calling for Amber again. Amber, just come get your goddamn kids."

KIRA

Kira held her breath as she punched numbers on the kitchen phone, Adam taking a morning shower, Polly gathering her backpack. Barely getting the words out: "Can I schedule a private session with you?"

"I'd be honored," Ravi said. He could come over at ten on Friday, he said. "I'd love to practice with you, and play. Where do you live?"

The word "play" entered her ear and left, leaving itself lodged there. She couldn't hear it. She couldn't hear anything but it. She thought at it sideways. *Play.* Well, yoga was playful. Friday at ten. She was supposed to leave for Harbin that morning, but, then, Adam had a shoot and wouldn't be around—she could be ready, be all packed up, have her session with Ravi and leave after. She was allowed to have a private yoga session. It was her money, she'd earned it, she was the breadwinner, and work was particularly stressful right now. It would be good to relax before the drive up to Middletown. But she wasn't clear if Ravi would charge her, and how much he'd charge her. Play. What did he mean? Yoga was playful. That was all. She gave him the address.

She got through Thursday by focusing hard at work, clearing her desk to take Friday off. There was a lot to deal with: visa issues for a visiting Russian composer; an insurance issue for the student art gallery. Neither problem hard, and both a welcome hassle. *Play.*

On Friday, Adam was up at six, the alarm clock pounded off; he and Stan had an early call in Hayward which meant, for him, driving rush hour traffic down 880, the road from hell. For her, it meant driving Polly to school even though it meant driving to Berkeley, back to Oakland for her session with Ravi, and then all the way up to Middletown. Staggering in her robe, she murmured consoling words, slipped Adam a chocolate bar when she kissed him.

"Hey!" Polly said, sitting at the table eating muesli. "How come he gets that?"

"Because he's my husband and lover," she said, guilt roiling through her intestines.

"Trying to make me fat?" he said, slipping the bar to Polly.

Fine, she thought. I tried.

She got back from taking Polly to school at 8:45 a.m. The ride to school had been tense, the carpools leaving early for a field trip to San Jose—they'd be gone all day.

"Why don't you ever drive on field trips anymore, Mommy?"

"Polly." She snapped on the radio.

But Polly wanted to talk about possible high schools, and wouldn't get off it, even though they had another year to go before worrying about it. Stutter-starting through rush hour traffic on 580, it occurred to her that she might be committing adultery. But no, they had an agreement. She was free. Free to explore. He has so much to teach me, she thought. And I can bring that knowledge home.

"How come like every stop sign in Berkeley has something under it? On the sign?" Polly chattered. "Like 'Stop War.' And 'Stop Shopping.' What else? Mommy?"

She tried to focus on Polly. It wasn't fair to her that she was this distracted. "'Stop Driving'?"

"And, 'Stop Racism.' Oh yeah, there's this one near school, 'Stop Eating Animals.' Hah! But then in Oakland, none of the stop signs say anything. Did you notice?"

"No, I haven't noticed."

"How come, like, every one in Berkeley does, and none of them in Oakland?"

"I'm not so sure that's true."

"Well, I've never seen one in Oakland."

"We'll have to look. Have a good day at school and a great weekend, Apollonia. I love you. I'll see you Sunday night."

The morning light was dull with rain; through the bathroom window, the endless February sky of no color. This is what it would look like to be blind. Before stepping in the shower she felt her legs—stubble. She was between waxings. Dao would kill her at her next appointment, but she'd do the unthinkable. Just in case. Not that it would happen. From under the sink, she dug up one of Polly's leg razors behind their shampoos, conditioners, deep hair treatments, bath oils, mineral salts, packages of tampons and sanitary pads... Razor in hand, she stood up too fast. Lightheaded. She began to shake, a sudden acrid taste of stomach acid, afraid she would barf.

I can't do this. She was afraid to look in the mirror, afraid of seeing Old. What was she thinking, he was coming to do a service, a private class. She was a mother, a married mother. Adam's wife. Like Adam cared. Like he'd thought about her all those days with Amber here, imposing his crap on her life. "Breathe," she told herself.

She shut her eyes, waited for the nausea to pass, holding onto the sink. Opened her eyes, the eyes in the mirror shining: two thoughts pounded: I Am Beautiful. And I Am Doomed.

Naked in the kitchen, clutching her still dry towel, she called Lindsey, unclear of what she would say if she answered: "He's coming over. I think something might happen. I want it to, but if anything happens to me, it's my yoga teacher, his name is Ravi, he works at the Y." No. That was crazy. And telling Lindsey would only complicate things. The answering machine picked up. "Hey Linds," she said. "It's Kira. Just checking in. Give a call when you can, okay?" She hung up the phone, her eyes still doing something wonky. Back to the bathroom. She showered and shaved her legs, concentrating on her yoga breathing. The nausea was almost gone.

"Your *qi* is strong here."

He stood on the front porch. She could feel him pressed against her body, taste him. He looked like hell—crappy jeans and ugly jacket; he looked amazing. His legs looked a little stumpy. She hadn't noticed this before. She felt the physical force of him, wool cap, black hair in a ponytail, yoga mat carrier slung over his shoulder, and the windows of the houses on the block, accusing. The neighborhood dogs would smell it, smell her. They would howl.

"Come in!" She didn't know what to do, where to go. As if they'd never talked in the café. "Tea?" almost stumbling over her backpack for Harbin; a quick tea, yoga session, and she'd be in the car driving up north of Calistoga…

"I'm not thirsty," he said.

"Come in, this is the kitchen." Duh.

"You have a nice place," Ravi said. "It really feels like you."

What do I feel like? she wanted to ask. Who am I to you? When you look at me, who do you see?

He looked nervous. Out of his element, standing with his yoga mat strapped to his back with his legs spread.

"I haven't been sleeping so good," he said.

Sleeping so *well*, she thought.

He looked drained and nervous. "I'm sorry."

"Sorry for what?"

"You have very strong *qi*."

She heard Adam's hoot in her mind—"Qi! Is that a pot of Lipton's with three tea bags?"—stifled an urge to giggle.

"Give me a hug, please," she said. He clutched her hard, she could feel him trying to slow his breathing. "I have a proposition for you," she said, her voice coming from somewhere other than her head.

"What do you propose?" He released her, his hands holding her upper arms.

"Well, I guess a proposition. I'm propositioning you."

"That's what I thought you were going to say." His jacket still on.

Hanging.

"I don't want to do the wrong thing. What about…"

"My marriage? Open." On the refrigerator, the picture of Adam skiing, his broad smile, zinc oxide nose. Damn him.

"It's okay?"

"Yes," she said.

But he was frozen, staring at the floor. So it was up to her. She leaned in the two feet between them and kissed him. "You're so beautiful," she said.

He dropped the yoga mat and shrugged off his jacket onto a chair. They kissed. It was like falling into a soft place. New kisses—

good ones, soft, tasty, large. That's what didn't happen anymore in married sex—kissing. The smell of somebody new, the feel of somebody new's hands on your back, wanting those hands lower, around to the front, and not knowing how to ask.

The phone rang four rings. "Ignore it," she said.

"I want to lie down with you. Is there somewhere for us to lie down together?" he said, twisting her hair with both hands, turning her head from one side to another, gently stretching her neck. Had anything ever felt so good? Her breasts felt almost perky again, her nipples erasers, the tips on fire. Would he ever touch them?

But where? On the floor of the living room, bent over the kitchen table? (Lindsey's affair a couple of years ago with that famous defense attorney, two years of flirtation and when he came over he grabbed her, dragged down her jeans and fucked her abruptly from behind over the dining room table, saying, "I've been dying to do this since I first saw your ass." And then never called her. Didn't answer her calls. Haunting her from the newspaper headlines when he defended murderers.) No, not the kitchen. The futon in the guest room now piled with clean, unsorted laundry. The couch? Polly's room? No. Just, no.

The bedroom was the only place. She led him there. They kissed again; his mouth soft, a whole world. "I brought a condom," Ravi said.

"I have an IUD."

"Good, I'm glad. I'm glad you're taking care of yourself. I think we should use both. No diseases. No babies."

"No, absolutely not. No babies," she said.

"Though sometimes I think about it; I've pictured…" his hands shook.

"No." A wave of dread. What was she to him? "Yes," she

relented, "it would be a beautiful baby. But no. None of us needs that. No more babies for me." The phone rang again. Probably Lindsey calling her back.

"Let me, um…" She pulled away, disengaged his hand that clutched her arm, left him standing next to Adam's side of the bed and ran to the kitchen, caught it on the third ring. "Hello?"

"Hi, it's Sandi, I'm Amber's mom…"

"Yes, Sandi. It's Kira." Ravi in the bedroom, if he came out, said something… "Look, please stop calling here," her voice low but urgent, one eye on the hallway. "Amber's not here. We haven't heard from her. And Adam doesn't live here anymore."

The words came from her mouth unexpected and hung, betraying, in the dim kitchen air. Outside, the rain had finally begun. She heard the ticking of water through the drainpipe. Stood in Adam's kitchen too, looking at the door to his basement room, thinking: He's going to die, I've just committed him to die.

"Well okay, missy. I get the message, but she's my only daughter, and you don't need to be such a bitch." Sandi hung up.

In the bedroom, Ravi stood next to her bed, naked, his face frightened, then relieved, to see her. He was beautiful. His penis stood slightly sideways, the top split like a heart. She felt a rush—not power, power was cold, this was fire—that she could still dissolve a young man to erectness. She made a noise and dipped to kiss down his belly. His penis was heavy in her hand, the black pubic hair fine like baby hair, his body almost hairless. She sucked him into her mouth, bitter and dark as she remembered from that split-second her mouth had slipped open on his neck.

He pulled her up to a full stand and kissed her again, fumbled at her clothing. "I need to see you," he said.

She pulled, shed, tossed, stepped. "Well, here I am." Her

breasts burned, her nipples tender; they waited for him to touch them, but he didn't.

"So beautiful." He put his hand on the back of her head and pressed down. "That felt great. Do that again." She stretched her mouth over him again. He pulled her up again and they backed onto the bed. "Nice bed," he said. He moved on top of her, exploring her belly, tasting her vulva, her legs, her feet.

"He's kissing my feet," she said, like a sports announcer. She meant to be funny but he didn't laugh. The bedroom walls they'd painted, "Peaches 'n' Cream"—Adam on the ladder in the corner... .

"Are you ready?" he asked. Couldn't he tell? Wet from the moment they'd kissed. He sat up and reached to Adam's bedside table for the condom he'd placed there, then rolled it on, turned back to her, and pushed in, and began his rhythm.

He doesn't know how to let go and fuck, fully fuck, she thought. She missed Adam; so wrong to have this stranger in her bed, but her body was responding to the stimulation and without expecting it, she came, an arcing shock.

"Did you come already?"

"Yes, don't worry, I'll come again."

"You will?" As if that was strange. He thrust into her, his face high and distant; the seething zap they had in yoga class wasn't there now, when he'd lain on her back in child's pose, *balasana*, when they'd hugged at Café Capoiera and her mouth slipped open on his neck... but she could teach him, it could be a project... She was in her head again, damn it. But then he looked down at her, and the expectation in his eyes socked against her, a wave of tsunami that would pull her out to sea.

No. He needed something from her. Trouble. She closed her eyes and focused on the sensations. So long since she'd had sex with anybody but Adam. And it was still sex, the rawness, the in and out, the slide of bodies.

Except he'd stopped. He'd lost his erection. "I can't shut off my monkey mind. I don't know why, I never have any trouble staying hard."

"It's okay," she said.

"I really wanted to come in you."

He lay on top of her, heavy, molasses, drowning her in her own bed, Adam's bed.

"We'll try again later," she said.

"I want to make love with you forever," he said. Heavy and thick on top of her. Too heavy, far too thick.

"Please get off me," she said, lightly, afraid he'd kill her with his need. Walked to the bathroom. She looked at her reflection in the mirror. Ugh. Well, that was something less than great.

CHAPTER 10

༄ KIRA

Kira kissed Ravi and practically pushed him out of the house, paranoid that some neighbor had seen him arrive, would time his departure. "I'll see you in class, okay? I'll call you. I'm really sorry to cut this time short but I have to get going, thank you, thank you," another kiss.

He looked bewildered, a child's face on a man's body, how had she not noticed that?

"I'm honored," he said, leaning in for another slow one, which she cut off with a peck. Honored, my ass, she thought. Just another man, no answers. And how stupid to have him come over, what had she been thinking? All the neighbors who could be watching the house, wondering who had gone in, and when would he come out? An hour-long yoga session. That could stretch to an hour and a half, safely. On the right, Katinka, the hippie painter, always home. On their left, Tripp and Debbie, probably at work. Across the street, the Kim family, the elderly mother who sat in a window seat, three small Chihuahuas on and off her lap yapping in the window whenever somebody came too close. On the corner, Miss Loraine, the African-American woman in her early eighties who trimmed the hedges in front of her Tudor house by herself, thin bones balancing on a ladder; around the corner, the Laotian family who kept chickens and roosters and posted courtesy notices on local telephone poles to let people know they planned a ritual—Please don't worry: we will have gongs and firecrackers and incense. The houses with eyes.

Gone, the door closed behind him, her shoulders released. What had she been thinking? The things that the adulterous do. Changing the sheets, throwing the dirties into the hamper, heart pounding. Checking the kitchen, the bathroom, the bedroom for evidence of him. She didn't shower, not willing to relinquish the smell of his body on hers, needing his smell to make it real; all these years with no sex with anybody but Adam. She had now. "I fucked him," she whispered. Shocking herself—pleasing herself. Great sex or not (not!), she'd had the guts to actually do it.

Because she'd packed to go to the hot springs already, it took only a few minutes to leave. She scrawled a reminder note—SEE YOU SUNDAY NIGHT!!!—for the kitchen table. Checking to make sure the porch light was on; Adam would be home after dark and Polly couldn't be counted on to remember to do it, plus who knew what time her class would be back from the field trip. Don't worry about Polly, she's Adam's responsibility, she told herself; it was her weekend away. A quick memory of Ravi's hands on her body, the thrill of a stranger's hands. "Mm," she said out loud, the sound echoing through the house before she pulled the door shut. "Mm."

She'd actually had sex with him, risked and followed through. The thought sent another thrill from her groin up to her stomach, where it turned to nausea. I had permission, we had an agreement, she reminded herself. I won't tell him. He'll never have to know.

But she felt sick. The disappointment of Ravi's neediness: not so enlightened. Just a man. Don't think. Breathe.

Into the car, backing out of the driveway. Completely blank through Oakland, Berkeley, Richmond, San Pablo... finally through the traffic on 80 and onto 29, the ugly stretches in front of Vallejo and American Canyon, the construction going through Napa. Within an hour and a half, the slow green curves of Silverado Trail Road towards Calistoga. And yet, the taste of him on her lips, the weight of his cock in her hand, her nipples still burning, the zap of guilt and sex.

Three days to get her head together without facing Adam or Polly, how lucky to have that release. It was over, she'd done it, now it was over, she could move on to making things better with Adam. Three days to get it together. Freedom. I actually fucked him, she thought.

But just before turning onto Tubbs Lane for the trip over the mountain, her stomach churned, guilt, resolution, disappointment imploded with throbs of pleasure, bleach and ammonia, a volcano of toxic froth. The nausea was so great she had to pull the Saab over. Getting out of the car, getting to the edge of the pull-out, she leaned over and vomited into a ditch.

❧ POLLY

From the time Mr. Frank called out the carpool lists, Polly was in a bad mood. An hour and a half to the Rosecrucian Museum in San Jose in the back of Amanda's mother's minivan with Amanda, Davis, Jordan, and Brady. Davis was stupid, and Jordan worshipped Rush Limbaugh. Amanda was fine, though they hadn't been hanging out as much. But she'd avoided Brady since he'd stolen the postcards, even though he kept pulling up his sleeve to taunt her with his body mod. He stuck out his foot as she climbed into the van, as if she'd be stupid enough to trip over it. When she began her own body mod, she'd never show it to him. It was none of his business, and just because they were into the same things didn't mean they needed to be friends, to hang out together.

Now he sat next to her in the back of the minivan, not looking at her, as if she wasn't there.

"Brady, move. Amanda's going to sit there."

"I was here first."

"So? I want to sit with Amanda."

"It's Amanda's car. She's sitting in front."

That was true, that was the rule. If your mom drove, you got shotgun. The alternative, then, was sitting next to Davis or Jordan, and they were best friends, and they were sitting together in the middle seat giving each other noogies.

"Okay, then." She'd lost. She turned her face to the window. She'd watch the scenery. Why did he want to sit next to her anyway?

That was the beginning—all day he was right behind her in line, sometimes pushing, and just two people away from her during the movie in the auditorium.

The movie was pretty lame, most of it they knew already; they'd studied the Egyptians in sixth grade. Polly had done her report on the symbol of the Sacred Eye:

The eye is how the body perceives light. It is the symbol
for spiritual ability. In Egyptian times, the right eye was
the symbol of the sun. They called it the Eye of Ra. The
left eye was the symbol of the moon. They called it the
Eye of Thoth. When they show both eyes together, they
were called the Two Eyes Of Horus The Elder.

It was cool, though, to see real Egyptian artifacts and be able to say, "That's the Eye of Ra. That's the Eye of Thoth," and know what it meant. Brady wasn't at the same table in the cafeteria at lunch—the girls sat together and picked at bad mac and cheese and jello. After lunch they were going to go into a tomb, transported from Egypt stone by stone, with a mummy in the middle, the actual one they'd x-rayed in the movie they'd just seen. It was a young girl, a royal girl about their age.

Polly wasn't sure if she'd seen anybody dead in person before, even a thousands-of-years-old mummy—she knew it was stupid to be nervous, but she was.

"It's good luck to make out in the mummy's tomb," Amanda said. "Last year, Zoe and Gabe got together there; Mr. Frank caught them and called their parents."

"Why is it good luck then?" Polly asked.

"No, like *real* good luck. Like, you'll live to a hundred good luck."

"Brady's going to try to kiss you in the mummy's tomb," Nell whispered as they lined up for the museum. "He told Etani, and Etani said go for it, that you were hot."

"Ew! No way!" she said, but she felt dizzy, she was hot! And when they got into line to go into the tomb, she maneuvered herself so that she was right in front of him, and she entered the tomb terrified and completely hopeful.

It was black in the passageway, a thick black, darker than it ever was at home even in the closet at night. She walked a long way, feeling her way with her feet, pressing her hand against the stone wall to guide herself. A boy ahead of her made scary "woooooh!" noises. Giggles, and "Shut *up*, Spencer!" she heard Nell yell from behind her. "Silence in the tomb," a grown-up's voice. Then just murmurs and shuffles.

As they turned another corner, she felt Brady press up behind her, push her gently against the wall, his front to her back. A thrill ran through her—he was warm against her. "Turn around," he whispered. She turned, rubbing against him, her whole body feeling him against her. She felt like a cat, her whole body fur. Then she felt his lips, hot and dry, brush near her hair, slide over her nose, find her mouth. They were kissing. His mouth was soft and she felt his breath against her lips, he held her around her arms gently. She opened her mouth in case he wanted to French her, and she felt his lips open too, but then a kid bumped hard into them, "Come *on!*" and he let her go.

A few moments later they were all in the heart of the tomb, looking in dim light at the opened sarcophagus carved with the Eye of Thoth, symbol of the moon. And inside, the wrapped mummy, which just looked old and dirty and not like a dead person at all.

"Cool," Brady said. She couldn't look at him, she was too shy, but she still felt his mouth on hers.

The ride back to school was quiet, even through two hours of Friday afternoon traffic. She and Brady sat in the back seat again, and she pretended to look out the window and nobody talked much; Davis was carsick and had to sit in the front seat with the window open, holding a paper bag, Amanda fell asleep, Jordan looked at anime, and, down where nobody could see, Polly ran her fingers over and over and over the smooth ridge of Brady's scar.

↘ ADAM

Adam got home early but Kira had already left for Harbin, the note on the table reminding him. He settled with a beer in the torture chair, listening to the quiet in the house. With Kira gone for the weekend, Amber and Joey gone—(he should call Sandi back, figure out what was up)—he had Polly to entertain. Easy enough, a few DVDs and a bowl of popcorn with food yeast. He could have her invite Nell or Amanda—hell, Nell and Amanda—and not do much at all other than listen for screams of distress and shovel hourly snacks through Polly's bedroom door.

Then his old friend Desperado Dave called about Strum und

Drink's reunion gig at The Rickshaw Stop. Adam had jammed with them twice way back in the depths of when; they and First Man had shared the bill countless times. Back when he'd drink a fifth of whiskey before the show to loosen his throat, hips, inhibitions, throwing his all into it, *"pipe up, bong down..."* above the crowd, the beat beat beat, and he was the star, a cheering crowd screaming along with him, the set over, the applause, the throbbing crowd, his throbbing ears, and coming off the stage completely wet with sweat to smiles of oh so many beautiful women. Take your fucking pick. He did not want to think of the results: Perry in and out of rehab. Jumbo driving a moving van near Seattle, last he heard. Garcia with Hep C. He and Stan. Losers.

"I'll try to make it," Adam said. Damn. He could bring Polly along to the reunion, fit her out with ear plugs. Make her stand near the back away from the mosh pit—Jesus, did anybody still mosh anymore? He was that out of it—but the Rickshaw was a bar, so no Polly. He was too old to hang out like that anyway, fuck it, he would skip it; hadn't spent enough time just the two of them lately anyway, he and Polly. Kira at Harbin, no Amber and Joey to worry about, not even a dog to vomit in the car or find dog sitting for. A good time to be a better dad.

Polly got dropped off a little before six, and he opened the door for her, gently took her backpack from her and said, "Fuck it, Polly. Let's go to Disneyland."

"When? I just got home from San Jose, Daddy!"

"Tomorrow. Tonight!" He grinned at the surprise of it.

"Daddy, are you crazy? How are we going to get there?"

"Drive. You can sleep in the car and we'll catch a few more winks in a cheap motel. We'll hit the park tomorrow, play all day, drive back Sunday, get back before your mother gets home."

"But how are you going to tell Mommy? She's up at Harbin."

"She can't call anyway, her phone doesn't work up there, and I doubt she's checking email, so we'll be all, 'How was your weekend? Great! Ours was great too! We went to Disneyland.'"

Polly stared at him, then bounced with excitement. "Really? You're not kidding? Can we eat on the road?"

"Anderson Pea Soup? Sounds good to me."

"Okay! Okay! How long before we leave?"

"It's six o'clock now. Friday night... traffic should start getting better in, oh, an hour. Can you be ready?"

"Okay!" And she darted into her room to change and get her stuff together.

"Don't forget your homework!" he called after her. "You can do it on the road!" He moved quickly through the house, filled with more energy than he'd had in days, hell, since before Amber had shown up, checking on the porch light, checking the doors and windows, running the garbage disposal, taking out the garbage. He checked the phone machine but Sandi hadn't called again. Good thing—he'd deal with it Monday. Packing, he couldn't find his funky jeans; had he thrown them in the hamper?

Pulling through the clump of sheets and pillowcases in the pile of dirty laundry, something flew out and dropped on the floor near his right foot with a small plastic clicking noise.

A torn-open empty condom packet.

Which did not compute.

The drive was a blur, Polly babbling in the front seat in sweats that would double as PJs, a blanket wrapped around her, a pillow blocking his right side vision. She'd brought three stuffed animals, far too many clothes for the weekend ("It doesn't matter, we're driving, I don't have to pack light, Daddy"). Adam forced every ounce of his energy towards putting on a happy face for her.

Because it could have been anything—Amber's pockets are full, she drops the condom wrapper while digging for cigarettes, Kira finds it and tosses it accidentally into the hamper instead of the garbage can. Kira shows Polly a condom as a sex ed thing. Polly experiments with a condom as part of normal teenage curiosity. Or Kira fucking somebody. In their house, in their bed. Or, not! Could be anything!

Traffic was not good, getting out of town on a Friday night, thick traffic over 580 to the Altamont Pass, "Daddy, it's too dark to see the windmills," though once they got to Interstate 5, it loosened. Anderson Pea Soup was too far down, and, as he remembered now, way too expensive for green soup that usually came in a can. Hitting an In 'n' Out when Polly's whines got too bad ("Daddy, I've been driving all day to San Jose and back and now this, and I'm hungry"), ordering two double-double burgers no cheese with grilled onions and two fries and a chocolate milkshake extra chocolate to share, his own stomach too sour to eat at first, until the first bite, then, "Man, they do a good burger." Eating all his fries, half of Polly's.

"Do you want to sing a road blues song, Daddy?"

"In a bit."

"Daddy, do you want to play a car game?"

"In a *bit*, Pol."

"Hey, did you know about the symbolic eyes of Egypt?"

"What?"

"Forget it. You're not listening."

Polly climbing into the backseat, snuggling down. And then he was alone with his thoughts again. Could the condom be Amber's? Were the sheets from her futon? No, he'd washed those, hadn't he? Were they from their bed? How long since they'd changed their bed? He almost turned the car around, to check, had Kira changed the sheets? She never changed the sheets. He did the laundry. Who would she be fucking? Was she with him now?

The road spilled out straight and rolling, speed limit 75 but everybody drove 90. Headlights, dim shadows, not well lit but who needed it, Highway 5 a straight line artery through the core of California, down the valley, thick with agriculture and smog, pesticide-scorched land between the crop humps. The car needed gas. Maybe he'd just drive it into oblivion. But no. Polly. He couldn't ruin her life, too. It was only a fucking condom wrapper, no other signs of disaster, not the end of the world. Stopping at a gas station; Amex in, gas out, ready to go. Pedal to the metal, it should take six hours to LA—a cheap ass Indian motel and then another two or so—less if they were lucky—to the Happiest Place on Earth.

He had not taken along his cherrywood box.

✒ KIRA

A gray squirrel family chasing through the empty branches of wild fig trees. Fearless deer and their fawns. A living apple tree with no core. A flock of wild turkeys on the lawn. A quiet temple, free yoga classes, and the springs: warm, hot, and cold, fed directly from the deep earth water sources. Silence, meditation, wind chimes—they'd been to Harbin several times together, a clothing-optional retreat just beyond Calistoga. They'd come a few times, Kira and Adam, to hang out naked and not be parents, to make love quietly in the thin-walled 1920s-era lodging house. Harbin was the perfect place to come for contemplation, or to mark important changes. By the time Kira drove up the gravel driveway and through the Dragon Gate, she felt determined; three days to get herself together, to detoxify, and then she could face Adam.

They'd make it better, they'd work it out.

And half an hour later she walked regally nude down into the warm pool, felt the water hold and support her and wash Ravi away. She leaned with a sigh against the white pool walls. All would be well. Hours of soaking and meditating, each thought put into a soap bubble and sent floating away. Deal with it later. She slept well that night, *later, later,* quieted by the quiet, the rushing streams. Winter water.

❧ POLLY

Polly and her dad just cruising into the night, the comfort of snuggling up in the car (seatbelt still around her), the lights approaching and receding, like all that stuff with Amber and Joey had never happened, like it was just the two of them in a safe little spaceship, sailing out into a special world. She liked how she didn't have to always talk with her dad. Sometimes they could just sit in silence, comfortable with each other.

The motel: the feel of the car stopping and her dad's voice, softly, "Apollonia, wake up just a little, baby." Keeping one eye shut to hold in the sleep as she carried her blanket and pillow and stuffies, only a little self-conscious past the bored clerk, through the small dingy lobby with low pile stained green carpet, out the back door and along the cement strip to their room, two double beds, a coffee maker, a mirror, a couple of bedside tables, a desk.

"Climb right in and go back to sleep, sweetie. You can brush your teeth in the morning."

A strange bed. The cold harsh sheets woke her fully and she lay there thinking, her father across the room making sleep sounds. Snuggling her stuffies. She'd kissed a boy today. Brady. Was he her boyfriend now? Part of her didn't feel old enough to have a boyfriend. But she was. Old enough to dye her hair, make out in the mummy's tomb. She felt her dyed hair; it felt normal. In the dark it was the same color it had always been. Her brown had been ordinary, but it had been her hair. Even though it looked awesome now, jet black, she should have kept a small piece of it the color it was supposed to be, cut off, in an envelope with a label on it, "Polly's hair."

The room was cold and walls thin, a coughing man and a laughing woman. She should have done it, now it was gone forever, what she had looked like. She should have put it in her drawer with her milkweed pods her grandma had sent from back east, the white fluff softer and whiter than Mishka hair; her crystals—quartz, amethyst, crumble of serpentinite, clump of heavy hematite; dried baby starfish; the jar baby pictures; the fall maple leaves she'd pulled from old books, pressed between the leaves, leaves between the leaves... her razors, pins, needles...

She couldn't sleep. To hold something sharp in her hand, that sense of possibility. In her jacket pocket, her pushpin—she retrieved it from the chair across the room, her dad unmoving, held it loosely in her left hand, the point just pressing against her thumb pad. Warmer now, snuggled in, slipping back into dreams of long car rides, riding and riding, the sounds of passing trucks.

In the early morning, her dad a still lump in the other bed, she climbed out to go to the bathroom. Wondered how far they were, and how far they had to go.

❧ KIRA

Saturday morning—breakfast, then a long float in the warm pool, watching the interplay of all the naked bodies, everybody so flawed and so lovely. She sat on the shelf at the back end, neck deep in clear water, hearing the wind chime from over near the cold plunge, the murmurs of muted conversation.

She closed her eyes and let the emotions rise over her, a swirl of confusion and panic shame shame guilt thrill—Adam, the bond between them so stretched, too thin, silly putty trailing into nothingness. Ravi, her body aching to touch him again, to do it right, her brain shouting—no! that's insane! His neediness! And she could never go back to his class now, and what that meant, what she'd thrown away... What had she done? Weeks of craziness, her lust, the way she'd seduced Ravi, the way she'd denied Adam's existence to Sandi, the way she'd pushed Ravi out of the house, so paranoid. The way she'd vomited on the side of the road. She opened her eyes. A man leaning against the pool wall stared at her. I must drip with it, she thought. Infidelity, sex. No more, too complicated.

She moved away from him, half-swam across the long pool of warm water towards the steps to the hot water temple, dark and candlelit, and climbed down into the pool. The water so hot she felt a thin circle of fire around each leg as she descended. Slow dunk all the way under, the hot water burning her cheeks and scalp. Slow rise. She climbed out and walked up to the cold plunge pool shaded with fig and bay trees, icy water gushing directly from the mountain stream, a sign above saying simply, "Breathe." The icy plunge after the hot water hurt, then felt refreshing. She came up gasping. *I'm purifying.*

CHAPTER 11

≫ ADAM

Disneyland was expensive. A day pass $56 each not including California Adventure, then the food, more food, and souvenirs de rigueur. His Amex getting a workout this month—all those extras for Amber and Joey. No limit on American Express, which was good—last month paying it all from a cash advance on the MasterCard, maxing that out... At the ATM on Main Street he thought about pulling the last two hundred or so from the checking account so he wouldn't be so cash poor ($38 in his wallet) but didn't want to leave Kira without a buffer. In case she needed a massage or some other treatment shit up at the hot springs. Instead, he transferred another thousand dollars from savings into the checking account, leaving them with $1,800 total, give or take, and took a couple of hundred cash. Kira's next check would be coming in soon, his six-month royalty check in another few weeks, wasn't it? And Stan owed him a bunch, didn't he? Or maybe not.

"Can we get a hot chocolate?"

Three fifty for a hot chocolate. Don't think about money in the Happiest Place on Earth. And don't think about condoms, the conversation: "What do you think of polyamory?" She'd mentioned women, only women, hell, it had just been a sexy idea, hadn't it?... so what was with the condom?

"Whatever you want, Polly, within limits. We're on vacation. Junk food it up, girl. But you might want to wait until we get over to Frontierland, they've got beignets over there."

147

∾ POLLY

Disneyland was pretty much a blast. Because it was the off season, even Saturday wasn't too bad with the lines, and with the FastPass system they got to go to the front by reserving in advance. Last time she'd been to Disneyland she was seven and tiny, way too short to go on all the good wild rides. This time, they hit the Temple of Doom twice, the Matterhorn once, Splash Mountain four times, and Thunder Mountain, which wasn't so good. They skipped the lame Jamboree that she'd liked when she was little. They ran back and forth and her dad was so fun all day, from the Haunted Mansion, not scary! over to the Pirates yo ho, yo ho a pirate's life for me. Her dad kept saying "It's the happiest place on earth!" and she ignored his weirdness—he'd had a lot of coffee, stopping for more espresso every couple of hours.

But then over prime rib and a mint julep, Sprite for her, at the Blue Bayou for dinner, he said, "We're sitting on a shell, Pol. The 'happiest place on earth,' it's a damn hoax. They hose this place down every night, underpaid workers, all the trash swirling right down the drain. And beneath this it's all hollow. We're on like the second floor, and underneath us is the bank and the trash bins, and huge tunnels and offices and stairways and elevators and warehouses. That's where they keep the costumes and the green rooms. Cast members can't smoke up here, it's probably a cigarette haven down there, all yellow and smoky. Totally toxic, sealed tight. Snow White bitching to Mickey about the brats. All fun and glee up here, a happy show. But underneath." He took a final slurp of his drink.

"Daddy! This is fun, aren't you having fun?"

"This is fun," he squeaked, imitating her. "Not so fun for Mickey in the costume."

Polly felt sick. "Can you shut up? Can we just enjoy ourselves for once?"

"We're enjoying ourselves. But you can't think this is real. It's important to know about real life, how privileged you are. And don't forget it. And think about Amber, she never had this kind of opportunity to have this kind of weekend, it's just too expensive."

"I *know!* But now that we're here, can't we just enjoy ourselves?"

Her dad ruined everything. She'd planned to tell him about Brady. Her boyfriend. Now she never would. She fiddled in her pocket for her pushpin: If I push this button, it will all go away.

"Let's go. Let's get the check, if we can get their attention." Pushing aside his plate. "I think the fireworks are starting soon."

✸ KIRA

In the restaurant Saturday night, Kira saw the man from the pool again, ordering just ahead of her in line and getting the resident's discount. "I'm Martin," he said to her. "Saw you in the pool today. I'm offering free watsus tomorrow, and I wonder if you would like a session." His voice completely professional—in public—so obviously not a come on. "Do you know what a watsu is? It's water shiatsu."

"Yes, I've seen it done." Naked people with blissed out expressions swirling around the pool.

"Never had it? Like to try a brief session?"

"Okay," she said. Why the hell not, at this point.

"How about ten o'clock tomorrow, at the warm pool? Does that work for you?"

"I can do that," she said, not sure if she'd show up.

"I'll be working around the pool earlier, so please let me know then if you're not going to make it, so I don't wait around for you," Martin said.

"No, that's fine. I'll be there." He bowed a little and turned away. "Fuckin' new age hippie," she heard Adam's voice in her mind. Shut up, Adam, she thought. It's important to try things. Checkout was noon, she'd have plenty of time to relax with a free watsu in the morning, then hit the road home. Back to reality. A small wave of nausea.

That night, Kira went to the Unconditional Dance in the conference center. Kira loved the slow warm up. Trance music, she moved through Ashtanga sun salutations, rolling each shoulder, her head, her torso, her hips, rocking on her back in a gentle massage, feeling the flat smooth of the sprung floor supporting her. Then, as the music amped up, as the intensity got greater, the meditative dynamic shifted. The beat reached deep into Kira, pulling her pelvis into thrusts, her leg and arms doing a hot funky chicken. Moving around the room, feeling the grin on her face. Professional dancers parked themselves near the front mirrors watching themselves turn and pose, contact improvisers rolled around with each other, a tall thin man leapt up and down in the corner near the door, a pogoing pile driver. So good to release this energy, let it slide into the room, join the rest of released energy, ascend as steam.

Kira watched herself in the mirror. If Ravi saw her dancing like this, not the real Ravi, the Ravi she'd imagined—if Ravi saw her dancing like this, sinewy and sexy—better than yoga. They'd mirror each other, her on this side of the room, him on that, the flailing bodies in between not mattering, not seen. She danced the moves they'd do with each other, if Ravi –not the real Ravi—was there, smiled the smile she'd give him. Making love through space. Then he'd step behind her, press against her, his hands thick on her thighs, whisper in her ear.

She felt a man's hot breath in her ear. "You're on fire, and straight from Heaven."

Too abrupt.

She turned quickly—a white-bearded hippie dressed only in an orange Speedo. His sweaty belly slid lightly against her back. She continued swiveling her hips but pulled away from him slightly, smiled in his general direction, and pulled far away, dancing into the middle of the room. The music thumped. Now, a voluptuous dark-haired woman, wide smile and white teeth, moved up to her, shaking her breasts and waving her arms. Kira echoed the woman. I can, she thought. I can do this, be this open, this free. She glided away, back towards the mirrors, stepping around the group of three improvisers rolling over each other on the floor, sidestepping a man who made wild, large circles around the room, touching as many women as he could. DJ Dragonfly was upping the ante again; Kira thrust back into it. No thought, just body. No body, just dance.

Outside after the dance, the sky clear, the moon through the trees, small lights led across the wooden bridge, gravel pathway, stone stairway. Cool air on her sweaty body. Alone in bed, she suddenly missed Polly, felt the separation of miles, of deeds. A cringe for Adam, sleeping alone in their room, holding her pillow. So far from her. A restless sleep.

Kira moved towards Martin in the warm pool, the sky high overcast through the leafless fig trees. They stood neck deep in the water, face to face, both naked, very close to each other. "So you're working on a watsu certification?" Keeping her voice a whisper.

"I've still got a few classes to go. But I'm offering free watsu today as part of my spiritual growth path," he said.

"Sounds good." She tried not to feel self-conscious, everybody naked, bathers leaning against the pool walls, she in the center of the pool with him.

"Is there anything I should know about your body? Any

medical condition?" he asked.

She shook her head.

"We'll go about forty-five minutes. We start by breathing together, looking into each other's eyes. Then I'll have you lean back in my arms, and I'll support your head and shoulders against me, and your back from underneath. Just breathe with me. I won't let you fall. You'll know we're nearing the end when you feel me bring you to the wall. We finish with a small ritual."

She nodded.

"Don't be frightened," he said.

"I'm just nervous about getting water in my nose." A lie.

"I won't let that happen."

"Let's breathe," he said. She looked into his eyes, blue. She closed her eyes. He matched his breaths to hers, diaphragmatic yoga breaths. "Lean against me."

She leaned back into him, let her legs float up. He supported her head on his shoulder, one arm under her back. Cradled and rocked by him, his hands and arms holding her, supporting and massaging her as he moved her through water.

Sounds softened to the shushing of the water, the murmurs of people around her. Womblike. Not sexual, though their naked bodies touching, the occasional soft breath of his penis brushing her thigh as he switched her from side to side. He swished her and massaged her back with his free hand, deep pressure down her spine reaching in and freeing the tension, moved her, stretched her, swung her naked through the warm pool. The water buoyed and engulfed her, pale blue, like swimming in a warm sky. She was completely exposed in public, every inch of her available for inspection. Yet there she was, smiling, moaning, swished through the water. Letting it all go. Opening up to his breathing, the water sounds, lap, lap, lap. She knew he was working, earning hours, certification, but it wasn't work, it was flow. It was deeper than flow. It's a gift, he's giving me a gift, she thought. Drifting into almost-sleep.

At the end, he steered her to the side of the pool, stood her against the wall, his face inches from hers. When she opened her eyes, she stared into one big blue. It's all love, she thought. He placed their right hands on his forehead, then on her forehead, then on his lips, then on her lips, then on his heart, then on her heart. A ritual. I know you, I love you, she thought.

She kissed Martin on his forehead. "Thank you," she said. "That was…" What was it?

"I know," he said. "I just couldn't stand seeing you in the pool yesterday without a smile." Ah. More than just a ritual, more than just watsu hours for him.

He backed away a foot and she looked into the face of a stranger; she was wary again. "Not smiling all the time is not such a bad thing," she said.

"No, I know. We also have to honor the dark side."

"Yes."

"I'd love to work with you again, if you're going to be around," he said. His voice ragged at the edges, heavy like Ravi's.

"I'm leaving soon." Adam. Polly. Home. Work tomorrow. Looking at the clock on the fence—11:30. Checkout time in half an hour. He'd watsued her for ninety minutes? She felt disoriented.

"Next time you come up, anytime, just let me know, I'll try to put another smile on your face. I work on the pool cleaning crew, you can always find me here. Martin."

"Thank you." Near the steps to the hot pool, a young couple in love groped each other.

"Where do you live?"

"I'm in Oakland."

"Ah." He stared at her for a moment. "I come to Oakland sometimes."

What does he want from me? "Well, thank you," she said again.

"Oh." His face fell. "When you come up again. I'm happy to work with your body, release your pain. Put a smile on your face."

"Okay, thank you, Martin." No way to get past him without touching him again.

Finally: "Blessings." He bowed, backed away, kissing his fingers of both hands and then blowing them back to her, then climbed out of the pool and walked to the outdoor showers near the warm pool. She watched him soap up his hair, soap up his genitals and rinse. He wrapped a sheer sarong around his hips, tucked so high the tip of his penis swung beneath it, and sauntered down the path towards the swimming pool and La Sirena café.

I'm such an ass, she thought. The world was filled with Ravis, maybe with good intent, maybe just trying to get laid: Yoga Ravi. Watsu Ravi. What next, Tantra Ravi? She could do it, move from Ravi to Ravi, but how endless. The public pool's water felt dirty around her. Do people fuck in here? She wanted the anti-Ravi, the one she'd made a life with. Adam.

Time to check out, go home, and work it out with him.

Now, self-conscious in front of the other bathers still resting at the side, she got out of the warm pool. The clouds had thickened, a new storm front was coming in. In the co-ed dressing room, the white bearded 'you're on fire' man from the dance: "You sure looked like you were enjoying your watsu."

"It was nice." And it had been. Until the end.

"I'm sorry I keep looking at you," the bearded man said. "It's just that parts of you look like a friend of mine."

Old Hippie Ravi. Yuck. Time to go home.

With the rain, the winding road over Mount St. Helena and down into Calistoga became instantly slippery. Other times coming home from Harbin, she'd drive this road fast, but the rain beat hard against the windshield and she felt no urgency. Too much to face at home. She'd fucked up. Literally. At the summit of Highway 29 at Robert Louis Stevenson State Park, the rain briefly turned to sleet and she tightened her grip on the steering wheel and slowed further. Even going thirty, she came up to a Calistoga water truck heading from the spring down to the processing plant and had to slow to twenty.

She imagined coming in the door, Polly and Adam waiting. "I got a watsu," she said out loud, practicing telling Adam. But then she'd have to explain why she hadn't paid for it. And that wasn't the point anyway.

"Look, things haven't been so good between us. Yes, I need you to deal with the Amber stuff better. But I know I need to change, too. I've been distracted."

She tried again. "You know how we talked about polyamory? How we agreed it was okay? Well, I fucked my yoga teacher. I got obsessed. But the sex was bad and the guy's not what I wanted and I'm over it." Her voice in the car sounded harsh and stupid. Because then he'd ask, "Well, what did you want?" "I don't know."

I do know. To evolve, to grow up. Which you don't seem to want to do.

But that was blaming.

The rain was so heavy that she could barely see the green truck in front of her. Rain, rain, rain. If she slid off the road, careened over the cliff and landed in the trees, nobody would ever know she'd fucked her yoga teacher.

No. Maybe not tell him at all?—"How was your weekend, Kira?" "Fine, relaxing…"—but the one thing he'd asked for was honesty. And to hold a secret like this forever would drive the wedge between them deeper.

Figure it out, Kira. Figure it out. She'd be home in less than two hours.

She'd tell him. She had to. They'd always told each other everything, honesty the foundation of their marriage, of their family.

She tried again. "You know how we were talking about polyamory? Well, I had a brief affair. And it's over. And it didn't mean anything." But that was a lie, too. "A crush gone bad." Just a crush gone bad.

Breathe, she told herself. Let it come to you. Figure it out.

✎ ADAM

Polly on Splash Mountain laughing her head off, Polly wanting but not wanting but really wanting to go on the Tea Party ride even though (because?) it was for little kids. At night, the fireworks over Sleeping Beauty's castle, his heart lifting, soaring, exploding, watching Polly, head back grinning, still his same little Polly girl—how lucky he was, things with Kira would work out, money was intangible, just a concept, it came in, it went out, and they would be fine.

They slept that night in the Candy Cane Inn, $100 cash on the barrelhead. Breakfast at HoJos, bad coffee, hitting a Starbucks on the way out of town. God, he hated Starbucks. The drive home was harder, six hours in daylight, thick smog and dull groves of olive trees, the condom wrapper in his pocket, looming clouds of confrontation. Then again, maybe "don't ask, don't tell" was a better policy. At least she'd had safe sex.

Party time over. The dull hangover of real life. Somehow he had to get his own shit together.

They were home forty-seven minutes before Kira drove up, and then, once parked, she sat in the car a long time before coming in the house. He waited in the living room. Armed with presents for her, Adam would not mention the condom wrapper in his front pocket; water under the bridge.

He greeted her at the door with a big smooch, "How was Harbin, babydoll? Are ya rested, relaxed, and Harbinated?"

"Very nice," she smiled. Hugged him, grabbed Polly and back-walked her over to the couch (Polly giggling) where she tipped her over and sat on her. "Ah… what a comfortable seat!"

"Good yoga classes?"

"Oh! No I didn't take any…"

"Mommy! Wait! Aren't you going to ask about our weekend?"

"How was your weekend?" Wiggling around to get comfortable on top of Polly. They were almost the same height, Adam noticed. So lovely. His heart turned over. Would he lose her? All that he'd been risking.

"We went to Disneyland!" Polly, triumphant, from below her mother.

"What?"

"For real, babe. Spur of the moment R and R." Sheepishly presenting the Minnie key chain, the Mickey hat (on the back sewn in cursive: Kira).

"Well, wow!" She shook her head a few times as if clearing it. "Did you… you didn't fly down, did you?"

"Road trip!" Polly said. "We stayed in *two* motels. Zip, zip."

Kira looked questioningly at Adam, who nodded. "Gotta be spontaneous."

"Well. Okay then. Advantage of no longer having a dog." She looked a little stunned, but not upset. "Tell me all." She slid off of Polly, sat next to her on the couch, mouse ears on.

"Babe, let's make dinner first, can we talk over dinner? We're starved. In 'n' Out both ways."

"Can we go to Ethiopian?" Polly said.

"Pol, we've been eating out all weekend, your mother's been eating out all weekend, and Ethiopian's expensive. I'll cook."

"Oh, honey, you drove all day. You really want to cook and clean? Let's have a nice relaxing dinner out. Ethiopian is fine with me," Kira said. "Did you know that teff is alkalizing?"

"Whosis is whatsing?" Adam asked.

"Teff, that's what they make the Ethiopian bread, injera, from. Alkalizing food is better for you than acidic food, and the only alkalizing grains are the little round ones: millet, quinoa, teff, what's that other old one…"

"Boring, Mommy."

"Polly, don't talk to me like that. Amaranth. That's it."

"Babe, it's kind of expensive. I can cook."

"Adam, don't be silly. Polly, your choice. Do you want to go to Asmara or Addis, or that other place on Telegraph Avenue."

"They're *all* on Telegraph, Mommy. All six of them."

Fine. One more meal wouldn't make or break them. "Kira, you're driving. You drove two hours, I drove six, I'm driven out. And I'm low on cash, so you're paying."

"That's fine."

Dinner a success—Kira's "parts of you look like a friend of mine" line howled at; "I wanted to take her picture with Winnie the Pooh but she's too old for that," "Daddy!"; both Adam and Kira relieved to be in public, normal, a family; dipping injera-clad fingers into the large family platter of goro wat, drinking honey wine, Polly smiling from one to the other.

Kira seemed chipper, that was the word, more present, more

active, more... she's trying too hard, he realized. He touched the outside of his front pocket to feel the crunch of the condom wrapper, weirdly comforting, gulped his tej and poured another glass of the sweet, medicinal wine.

"I'm sure you're very tired, Poodle," Kira said as they got out of the car. "And we're all tired, so, Polly, I think it's a good idea if you went to bed early, okay? You've got school, and you had a big weekend."

"I'm not really that tired, though."

"Polly, listen to your mother," he said. Shit. It's about to hit the fan.

"Well, *fine*. I'll just go to bed *now*, then."

"Goodnight, sweetie," he said. "We had fun."

"Have a good sleep, sweetie," Kira said at the same time. They were barely in the house.

CHAPTER 12

❦ ADAM

Now they were alone, the mood less celebratory.

"There are things I need to tell you," Kira said. She stood, her back to him, facing the sliding glass doors in the kitchen, her reflection a black outline.

From his seat at the kitchen table: "Yes, I bet there are." So dizzy from fatigue, the honey wine. When he shut his eyes, the endless drive of Highway 5, the motion of the car still reverberating.

"And there are things we need to talk about."

"Yes, indeedy."

"Adam, this is serious."

To haul the condom wrapper out of his pocket and simply hand it to her would kick start the conversation. Then what? He could picture her going to the kitchen drawer and wordlessly handing him the checkbook, and then they'd be even, wouldn't they?

"I have something to tell you," she said as though cold reading a script. "I had a brief affair. I had sex with somebody. Last Friday." She turned to face him.

"Yeah, babe," his face unable to move, only his mouth opening and closing. "I know." He reached in his front pocket, then opened his hand. The condom wrapper crinkled and expanded on his open palm, a chick fresh from the egg.

Her body sagged. "Oh, Adam. Oh, no. I'm so sorry."

"In my bed."

She didn't say anything.

"You're an asshole, Kira. You talked about wanting women." His voice was quiet, the long numbing drives, the weight of the weekend of not knowing pressing on him.

She looked at him. "We made an agreement," she said. "I feel bad. It was something I needed to do. But it's over, really. I want to work this out. I'm really sorry. It's not anything, just a crush gone bad."

"I don't remember agreeing to your fucking some guy. Who was it?"

"Remember? We talked about it. About polyamory. You were not averse. We talked about how we could both be more open, bring back new experiences…"

"Theoretically. During sex; it was sexual. But you didn't ask me, 'Look, I'm thinking about sleeping with somebody, and I want to do it in our marital bed. Is that okay?' because there's no way in hell I'd go, 'Oh fine, whatever.'"

"I didn't ask for Amber and Joey to appear out of nowhere and then be here for a week in my marital house."

"Jesus, Kira. Don't gunnysack me."

"Okay, that was out of line. I'm sorry. I am. I can see how that would be a terrible shock," she pointed to the condom wrapper now sitting on the kitchen table between them. She shuddered.

He took a breath, tried for rationality. "Look, conceptually, I'm not morally against polyamory. But you lied. And you did it in my house. My bed! So who was it?"

"My yoga teacher. Ravi." As she said his name, the left side of her mouth turned up in an uncontrollable smile. His stomach flipped. Jesus. Her face looked like that when she came. She covered her mouth with her hand.

"*What?* You told me somebody at your yoga class. A woman."

"No, not explicitly! And please be quiet. Polly." She turned away.

"*Fuck* Polly."

"Adam." She came closer to the table and lowered her voice. "And why does it matter if it's a woman or a man?" she asked, her mouth seeming in control again.

"There's a huge difference, if you can't see... Your goddamn yoga teacher? That's fucked! That's unethical." He stood up from the table, scraping the chair—he'd like to scrape it through the floor, rip the linoleum—began to pace in front of the stove. "Look, you're a victim here, he's your teacher, we should report him, that's completely unethical, I'll report him. I'll sue his fucking ass. Fucking over my wife."

"No! I did this. This is my responsibility. I propositioned him. Don't treat me like I'm some victim, some little woman who doesn't know what she was doing. You agreed, we talked about it."

"We talked. And you lied."

"Haven't you ever lied to me? It's what humans do."

"Yes, goddamn it!" Now he was raising his voice. "I've lied by omission, I've fucked up. Yes, we're in deep shit financially and it's all my fault. Is that what you want me to say? It's all true. You don't need to keep letting me know you know all about it by your hinting, and putting the checkbook back in the drawer, and leaving hints, like condom wrappers, that you're onto my issues and you're sick of them. So fucking passive aggressive. Why don't you just ask me about it?"

She looked puzzled, "Wait, you just said we're in deep shit financially? Polly mentioned you gave Amber money. You told me when you sent her that five grand for lawyer's fees, you're like, 'This is the only time I'm sending money, I'll tell her to stop calling me Dad.' Now what? You're supporting her? Are you claiming her? Am I a stepmother? A grandmother?"

"What, Amber? No! What are you talking about? I gave her like twenty bucks. I thought you were talking about the money. Our money."

"What money?"

"The money, the shit I've been doing. You know about this. You put the checkbook back in the drawer. Why do you need to drag me through the mud?"

"Stop. I'm confused. What are you talking about? I thought we were talking about Ravi." Again her mouth did that reflexive smile thing, her mouth so pleased with itself.

"Ravi, the asshole who's destroying my marriage?"

"He's not... I'm not... Oh, Adam." She sagged, the opposite of the faux-chipper she'd been in the restaurant. Jesus, he thought. She's playing me.

"Does he have a big dick?"

"Big dick? Why are you so foul? Why can't we have a normal conversation like normal people?"

"Mommy?" Polly's voice from down the hall.

"See?" Kira said.

They stood silent, faced off. The purr of the traffic on 580, a distant siren, the refrigerator's hum, the sky outside not quite dark, it was never quite dark in Oakland, the high overcast sky reflecting the urban lights. Kira said, "I'm going outside until you can talk to me normally."

∾ KIRA

It took most of the night, both of them dizzy from fatigue. Storming out to breathe three times (her). Pounding the wall (him). The porn, the money, the drugs.

"I told you, a little. At Café Gratitude I told you I was broke.

'I Am Broke,' I said. That was me telling you."

"How bad is it, Adam? How much do we owe?"

He stared at the table, then looked up at her, defiant. "Only around twelve. Thousand. On the card. Like a couple of grand left in the savings. Okay, the savings are toast. Don't look at me like that. I blew it. I just blew it. But it was all there for you to see, if you'd been paying any attention and not fucking *your goddamn yoga teacher*!" His voice broke out.

She held out her hand. "Shh."

He took a moment. "Your check's coming Friday, we're okay for now, I'll make it up. It might take some time, but I'll make it up. Stan owes us money. You know I can ask my mom for a loan, she's always offering."

"You'd ask your mom."

"If necessary, yes!"

"The savings are toast. My dad's money. The Zetrum money. The cushion. Polly's college fund. Wait. We had like 18K in that savings account!"

"Jesus, Kira. Not for a while."

"The money from my dad?"

"You spent all that on your car, Kira. And why haven't you been looking at our money? It's your money, too, you're earning a lot of it."

"Most of it."

"Hey, that was my money from Zetrum when I cashed out. It's our money. It was my money, too. I blew it, but you weren't paying attention."

"You blew it on porn? Drugs? What drugs?"

"Just stupid stuff. I'm just chipping."

"Oh my God, you're not okay."

He shook his head. "No. I'm not."

"Do you need help? Do you need therapy? What are we going to do now?"

"We've been in the hole before. You're still earning money. I'll talk to Stan about more gigs. I just need to pull myself together."

What now. She tried to breathe in the same room as him, the same air. The air pressed in on her. The kitchen needed the floors washed, nobody had cleaned the bathroom since who knew when. Now she couldn't call a cleaning service and ask for a "deep clean." Her face needed a deep clean, pores blocked. A waxing—her eyebrows all stray. Three days since she'd slept with Ravi (an unbidden zap down to her crotch) and her legs already spiky. Back to cheap razors and Polly in public school, the house on the market? Back to peanut butter for dinner, the dull ache of money stress always there. How long before they lost the house, the three of them pushing shopping carts on the streets of West Oakland? Like Amber: no shoes, no money, desperate. He would do that to the family? To Polly? Goddammit.

She tried to modulate her voice, head pounding, "You lied to me about the MasterCard. You're like, 'I'll look into it.' Why didn't you tell me it was maxed? Am I so awful that you can't even share something that concerns both our lives with me?"

"Because I was embarrassed. Because you're not available— emotionally—to me. I didn't trust you, and I guess I had good reason not to. Why did you go fuck somebody else?"

"Maybe because you're not available emotionally to me." And then she remembered the mail order DNA test somewhere off in Ohio. She hadn't told him about that; another breach in the honesty. And it finally occurred to her, a big duh, that their marriage was in trouble. Real trouble. "Adam, I'm too tired. I can't do this anymore." Three a.m.

"Go to bed. Just go to bed."

Their bed a release, a relief not picturing Ravi there. But Adam didn't come in, so she tossed and turned, went back and forth to the bathroom. At five thirty she found him on the love seat. "Come to bed."

"Sleeping," he muttered. "Took a couple of extra Percodan. Wake me up to take Polly to school."

❧ POLLY

Polly felt their voices before she heard them, seeping toxic gas through the walls, sliding around her, filling the room, hissing snakes. So eager to get rid of her so they could fight. Well, she wasn't tired. She organized her backpack for school, set up her new Mickey stuffie on the stuffie shelf. Changed into her PJs. She was scared to go get a glass of water, but she was thirsty from the yebig tibs at Ethiopia House and she had to pee, so she slid out the door and down the hallway.

Coming back from the bathroom, from her parents' bedroom, her dad's voice, "Does he have a big dick?" and her mom said something she couldn't hear. Then silence. She got to the door of her room. Before she closed the door, "Mommy?" she called. They just kept talking to each other.

She closed the door and sat on the edge of her bed, first shoving the books, old homework, and dirty clothes onto the floor. Tomorrow she'd see Brady again. Her heart pounded. Too young to have a boyfriend. But the feeling of Brady's hands, soft and rough, in the mummy's tomb. The smooth ridge of his scar.

She stayed in her room. The fighting went on and on. Through the walls, their voices: "...your goddamn yoga teacher!"

Blood of my blood, she thought. If I just give a blood sacrifice it will stop.

Now she held the single-edged razor blade she'd pilfered from her dad's basement. She looked at the arch of her foot, creamy white.

One tiny nick. Just one. She held her breath until she had courage, then quickly jabbed in a corner of the razor blade. A small jolt of pain. A single bead of perfect ruby blood welled up. She waited until it was about to lose its teardrop shape and then gently touched it with her index finger. It ran—relieved, and she released her breath with a whoosh. Her shoulders relaxed and slid down her back. She felt a dull stinging and an ache. Pressed the cotton ball against it, hard, until the bleeding stopped.

Now she could sleep.

Monday morning her mom woke her late, Daddy sleeping on the couch. "We had a late night."

"I heard you fighting."

"Did you sleep okay, babe?"

She shook her head. "Can I have coffee to wake up?"

"What? No way. Caffeine jacks you up and then drops you down. Has your dad been feeding you coffee? You can rest in the car. I toasted you a bagel to eat on the way."

Disneyland already seemed a long time ago. Her mom took her to school even though it was her dad's morning on the calendar. Another Alaskan storm was coming in, big wet cold drops. Stop and start traffic.

"Can we listen to the radio? Daddy lets me listen to the radio."

Her mom ignored her. "Polly, people who live together sometimes fight."

The rain made harsh silver blasts against the window. "I forgot my umbrella."

"Well, I'll pick you up right after school."

"You're not going to yoga?"

"Not today."

"Right." She snapped on the radio, and her mom didn't do anything.

"Went to Disneyland," she said casually, when Nell asked what she'd been up to.

"Lucky! You *always* get to do the fun stuff," Nell said, and changed the subject.

All day, Polly avoided Brady, wondering what would happen if they were alone. He didn't look at her. Fifth period they were going to watch scenes from Zefferelli's Romeo and Juliet in English because they were reading the Shakespeare play, but Miss Ann had forgotten to bring down the video machine.

"Brady and Polly, can you please go up to the third floor and get the VCR cart, it's in Mr. Sebastian's room. Here's the elevator key, it's just up and down, no playing. And you'll return it immediately."

Polly's face turned red; she stood up to leave the room, dreading. And hoping. "Ooooh," a low murmur from Nell and some of the boys. Emily's face tightened and Polly looked away. Davis whispered something to Brady.

"Davis, do you need something?" Miss Ann asked.

"I'm cool."

Brady walked out of the English room without looking at her. Polly followed. They didn't take the elevator—they were quiet walking up the stairs, Brady taking them two at a time, Polly hurrying behind. Every step a small pinch on her instep where she'd cut herself. I'm like him, she thought. Nobody was in Mr. Sebastian's room. The cart was in the corner, near the big world wall map. Polly went directly over to the cart, started to push from behind.

"Come here," Brady said. He grabbed her around the waist, and then they were kissing behind the cart, a real kiss, tongues too, he tasted like gum; a moment later their front teeth clunked together hard and he pulled away. "Sorry."

Polly felt flushed, her hair in her eyes. "It's okay." Her left front tooth ached. "Can I touch your scar?" she whispered. Brady pulled back his sleeve. The scar was a thick pink line. She touched it—he was warm. She wrapped her fingers around his forearm and held it.

Brady looked down at his shoes. "We better get back."

"Yeah." She let his arm go.

They pushed the cart out the door, awkward, not saying anything, and waited next to the elevator, listening in silence to its approaching slow hum.

"Da *da* de *dump*, Da *da* de *dump*!" Davis sang the wedding march loudly as they wheeled the cart in.

"Shut up, asshole," Brady hissed.

"Brady!" Miss Ann said, turning toward him.

Polly looked at nobody, afraid her lips were starting to smile. Then out of her peripheral vision, she saw Amanda and Nell grinning at her. She gave them a shy thumbs up.

"Yeah, *woooo*!" Amanda yelled.

"Go Polly, Go Polly, Go Polly!" Nell chanted, most of the other kids chiming in, until Miss Ann raised her voice—"Now settle down!"—and Polly sat back down in her seat, staring at her notebook, pleased and embarrassed. Miss Ann cued up the movie. The rest of the period, Polly felt the echo of Brady's scar on her palm. Its twin, the small ache on the arch of her foot. Nell elbowed her twice but Polly didn't look at her. So embarrassing to be watching Romeo and Juliet, today of all days.

That night they had take out from Silver Dragon, and

everybody was quiet at the table. Polly ate her won ton soup. I have a boyfriend, she thought. He's really my boyfriend. And wondered what would happen next.

❧ KIRA

Lindsey would call her stupid, Adam would hit the roof, but Kira went back to Ravi's class. As she parked in the Y lot, she listed her reasons to herself: One: before she'd found Ravi as a teacher, she'd tried everybody else at the Y. And he was by far the best practitioner, that's why his classes were always so packed. And with the money issue, she couldn't afford another class somewhere else on top of the Y membership. Two: okay, she admitted it, it had been about Ravi, yes, him, and what he offered her in terms of emotional recognizance, spiritual growth. The sex factor too. But she was over it, that hadn't worked, she was over it. More than that, Three (or was she still on Two?): it was about the yoga. The yoga was important to care for her body, her sense of well-being. And now that she and Adam were fighting, she had even extra stress. She'd given the fantasy of Ravi up, and good riddance! But did she have to give yoga up, too? Yes, she could study with somebody else... but then she was back to reason number One.

She slammed the trunk lid and walked with her yoga mat down the garage stairs.

So she had reasons. She wasn't being stupid, she was adult enough to handle a few uncomfortable moments, and he was doubtless used to this, all those little yoginis in the front row. And they would go back to normal, him as yoga teacher, her as student. She'd stay in the back of the room. No more cafés or meeting privately.

She waited until class was starting, standing at the water fountain outside the Mind-Body Center until she heard through the door his words, "Okay, let's begin. Take a moment to find a comfortable seated position." Then she quickly walked past him to the back of the room, slipped off her shoes and unrolled her mat. The floor paved with mats; the most popular class at the Berkeley Y. She was almost anonymous.

The familiar words. "Pull the flesh from your sit bones and send your energy down into the earth, rooting yourself," he said. "Align your spine and send the energy upward through the crown of your head chakra. We'll begin by joining our voices together in three Oms."

"Om," she chanted. She was here because it was a good class, a public class, and because she had a right to be here, and she liked it.

Her heart thumped hard but she focused on her breathing and didn't look at his face. He didn't come to the back of the room, focusing on his fan club near the front. He was just a man, she thought, look at him lusting over those young girls, so typical, and she would get over him. Stretch and hold, another downward dog, *adho mukha svanasana*.

He didn't come to the back of the room, and she made it through.

When class was over, she quickly put on her shoes, rolled her mat, passed in a crowd towards the door. Ravi lay on the floor demonstrating hip lifts. But as she walked past him, he reached out and grabbed her ankle, his grip sending shivers up her legs and deep into her womb.

"Stop," he said, looking from flat on the floor up into her eyes. "Hang on, okay? I want to talk to you."

His eyes were so beautiful. She nodded down at him; impossible to say no.

"Chelsea, text me if you have questions, I have to talk to Kira," he said, dismissing the lean girl he'd been working with.

Ravi kept a hold of Kira's ankle, thumb and fingers pressing and massaging. People flowed around them and disappeared, and her body pulsed with his touch. Then it was just the two of them in the large silent studio, Kira standing, still holding her roll of mat, facing the exit, Ravi on his back on the floor, one hand outstretched holding her ankle. The sounds of the Allston Street traffic came through the windows and across the room.

"Gotcha," Ravi said. He let go of her ankle, sat up, and then stood up, looking at her face. "How ya been?"

"Hey," she said. Looking away, unable to look at him; she'd fall in and never climb out. Reasons One, Two, Three went poof. She'd needed to see him. Their connection was real. They'd both been too nervous—the first time people had sex it usually wasn't perfect, not like in the movies. If we learn each other's bodies, she thought. Learn what works for us. She pictured them in a field, in the sun, out in nature…

She pulled herself from the fantasy.

"I can't do this," she said quickly. "I just can't. I'll come to class sometimes, maybe, but it's too complicated for me. Nothing more. I'm sorry." She looked to see his reaction.

"Okay, then." His mouth twisted—disappointment. Pain. "I see. Okay. I get it."

"Namaste," she said, waiting for his response.

He turned away from her and walked to the equipment cabinet, so she left, Persephone climbing back to the light. Outside their house when she got home, fighting blue jays, clear sky, rain-drenched trees, rivulets in the garden mud.

Now that she and Adam were stalemated, they acted ordinary—ordinary on ice. The morning rush, the evening dinner dance, done in formal speak, broken by glares, then a return to formality. No more laughter. At night the fights, quiet, trying to keep it from Polly. Standoff across the Formica kitchen table. She took over the checkbook. At work, she plowed through piles of paper. She and Adam teetered on a cliff but there was still the driving to do, up and down the highways and the streets; and the traffic—thick and thicker. Back and forth, and to and fro. School and work and gas stations and grocery stores and to the Food Mill for supplements and bulk organic, and never shopping big at the supermarkets because that wasn't the kind of family they were; they ate European-style, buying fresh food and bread every day. Occasional runs to Costco, and they were almost out of parmesan and wine and paper towels and toilet paper again, all the big bulk items. All the cooking because now they had no money to buffer it all, they had to budget and fret, a deep ditch to climb out of. And laundry. Endless piles of dirty, and (worse) clean, because then they had to fold. Dishes rinsed and then put in the dishwasher and then put away. Once a month the heating ducts should be vacuumed but that was ridiculous, maybe once a year if they were lucky. Holes in the wall from pictures hung and rehung. Cracks in the walls from earthquakes. Dust under the bed. The house trim needed paint. The trees pruned. The deck resurfaced. Where would that money come from? Mucking out Polly's stable-room. Flaxseed oil for Joey, still in the refrigerator, she'd won that bet with herself (you're a winner! You're a no-brainer). Sweeping and dusting—what's that? When was she supposed to exercise? Because she was getting fat, her stomach tight against her pants—and someday, osteoporosis and heart disease and diabetes and Alzheimer's, and would she ever have time to hang out and go to a movie? (Too expensive now.) Learn to do something creative? Checking the mail every day for the DNA test results, not that it mattered. And answering email. Email, email, email. Don't even think of calling on the phone—though she always answered on the second ring. At work she'd fallen asleep on her desk twice today. The garden, waist high in weeds. Oxalis. Poison oak. Food for Polly's lunches? When was she supposed to help Polly with her homework; when was she supposed to have her life? The weeds kept growing and there was no way out of it now, no fantasy of Ravi, no quiet blue island of calm.

Her belly felt bloated, she rubbed it under her desk at work, a thick feeling in her abdomen. She'd been eating too much dairy, her energy stagnating from no yoga. Work a blur, hours of email and the usual plethora of phone calls.

Sneaking in calls to Lindsey to let her know what was going on. Sarah was in the office next to hers, and unless Kira closed the door—standing up and crossing the room—Sarah would hear it all.

"Hang on, Linds."

Sarah was typing, iPod earbuds on. Kira closed the heavy office door.

"It's not like we had a bad sex life. It's good sex. It's just always so comfortable. I mean not now, right now it's all a mess, we're so messed up with the money."

"Spice is nice."

"And I know I don't want Ravi, I'm not nostalgic for Ravi, I'm nostalgic for how he made me feel. I wanted something he promised. Like, I thought he could teach me something. Like there were secrets and he had the keys to doors, and I didn't even know there were secrets. And I didn't know there were doors. And I didn't know there were keys. And now I don't know if there are any of those things."

"Are you talking about spirituality?"

"I guess so."

"What does having sex with Ravi have to do with that?"

"I don't know. He's just this guy, and the sex was terrible but then when I think, fine, I'm over him, and what an idiot I was, I hear something that sounds like his voice. I thought I saw him at Star Market yesterday, and it wasn't him. Or I think about a yoga asana. And I get zapped with it."

"You're a midlife mess."

"Is that what this is? Midlife crisis? I hate you. It's like the energy between us got plugged up inside me. I'm constipated, and I think some of it is psychological."

"Get a colonic irrigation."

"I've just got to move this energy."

"That's what I'm saying, colon hydrotherapy. They flush out the colon, drain all the toxins you're carrying. Your colon carries like twenty pounds of sludge encrusted in it, like baked-on lasagna. Elvis had sixty pounds of impacted shit in him when he died."

"That's impossible."

"The hydrotherapy flushes it all out. So you feel all clean. Purified."

"Did you ever try one?

"Hell no. But you try it, and let me know how it goes."

She looked it up, but colon hydrotherapy was seventy dollars and that was a lot of money now. So none of that. No more massage, watsu, Harbin. She could use that $250 she'd sent off for the genetic testing, probably a hoax since she hadn't heard back.

She called the Y and cancelled their family membership. She was the only one who used it, so it had turned into $150 a month for three yoga classes a week—stupid extravagance—and she certainly wasn't going anywhere near the Mind-Body Center now.

And then Ravi called her at work, had she even given him that number? "Haven't seen you at yoga, is everything all right?" His deep voice cracked on the word "yoga." Deep breath.

"A lot's been going on," she said. She sat still, listened to his breath. Outside her window the sky was pale blue. Cold. Her feet pressed against the electric space heater under her desk.

"I miss seeing you. I wonder if I offended you, or hurt you. That's not my intention, Kira."

"Well then, what is? Your intention?" A flood of moisture down her body, and her pulse raced.

He didn't say anything. She clutched the phone, imagining his eyes as they'd looked down on her, his weight on her body. Missing that weight.

"Look," she said. "I've got a lot going on. It's not a good idea." Her heart was huge, filling her chest; she felt it tear. How could you actually feel your heart? she wondered.

"I've got to go," she said, "Don't call me again." And hung up the phone.

That evening, as she sat in bed, Adam stood in the doorway. "I think we should just get a little space from each other," he said. "I'm sleeping downstairs."

"Oh, honey." A big swell of sadness. The beginning of the end? He stood waiting for more reaction. For her to beg him to stay? She set her mouth. "Probably a good idea," she said, and opened her book. As soon as he left, she closed it. I deserve this, she thought. Sick of it all, she got out of bed, poured herself a water glass full of vodka and ice, and drank until she dozed off.

ꙩ ADAM

He'd tried. For days, they'd shared the same bed but not the same space. If they touched in the night they both pulled away, preferring the cold corners. His body felt brittle; if he moved too fast he'd snap. Adam took his pillows and a nightlight and dragged the tri-fold futon down the narrow basement stairs. The foam was getting a workout, its edges soft, a sag in the middle from where Amber, elephant girl, had compressed it. He hated lying where she'd slept, the strange forced intimacy of sharing the same spot, even weeks apart. Like a bedspread in a motel room, sleeping with the skin flecks of strangers. Where was she? Why hadn't Sandi called again? But until this blew over, he needed to be out of Kira's sight, her pretty face twisting at the sight of him. He needed to not see her as she slept, deep creases between her eyes.

Legs tucked in his sleeping bag on the futon, drinking tequila, eating pretzels and Cheetos, and listening to old Delta blues recordings.

CHAPTER 13

❧ POLLY

Having a boyfriend at Pioneer in seventh grade meant that you sat together at lunch, that you Facebooked each other at night, that sometimes you texted, and that sometimes you kissed in the hallway when no teachers were around.

At least that's what you were supposed to do. Tuesday, Brady sat next to her at lunch out in the yard, so close they were almost touching. The storm was over and birds swooped down near them. The sky was blue with a few clouds, and they sat in a shaft of sun. She wondered if this was what love felt like.

But after a few minutes he jumped up and spent the rest of the time doing Reverse Sumo, shouting "Hai *yah!*" and backing into Jordan with his backpack and vice versa. So maybe they weren't going out, she fretted, but then he brought over two anime to look at, and brushed against her "accidentally" and kissed her cheek as they were lining up to go in from lunch, even though Ms. Paula was there. She decided he was just shy. On their way home from school, Lindsey driving, she had Nell write their initials with a sharpie on her arm where she couldn't reach well, encircled by a heart, but, too embarrassed to let him see it, wore long sleeves the next day.

But then Wednesday he ignored her completely. At lunch he sat next to Emily. "They're going out now," Nell said, and Polly hated the glee in her voice. Polly pretended not to hear.

"Emily and Brady are going out," Nell said again. "They got

together after school yesterday. He sure gets around: baby boy slut."

"Whatever," Polly said. "He's gross, he likes to cut himself, you know."

Nell looked alarmed, and Polly felt like she was going to vomit.

A flock of crows had set up camp on the light post across the street. They cawed loudly when Polly and her mom drove up. A bad omen for a bad day. Polly was first up the stairs to the house, her mom moving slowly. Taped to the door, a folded in half piece of paper torn from a yellow legal pad, and on it in block letters, KEERAH.

"Mommy, is this for you?"

"What?"

Polly opened the paper and read it:

Open wide your heart, Lover, as you would open the
window to the shining day. In the courtyard below, the
peacock's blue tail spreads wide. The peahen saunters
brown. Fling yourself through the window, Beloved.
I will catch you. I would join with you as flame joins
flame, in a single surge of light, of heat. Heart to heart,
and all around the world fades away. Open the love
window.—Arshya

> My heart,
> Ravi

"Mommy? Is this for you?"

"I don't think so," her mom took the paper quickly from her hand.

"The love window?"

"Polly, that note did not have your name on it."

"Did it have yours?" Polly looked quickly at her, but her mother looked normal, like nothing was wrong. But Polly had heard the name Ravi, hissed and shouted, deep at night. He was the yoga teacher; that's why her mom had stopped going to class. ("…your goddamn yoga teacher!") Her stomach dropped; she felt sick. That's why they'd been fighting, over Ravi. Her mom had a boyfriend. ("Does he have a big dick?")

Daddy was working late, her mom said. Polly stood in the kitchen while her mom cooked, waiting for her mom to turn, cry, make an announcement that she was leaving, going to an ashram in India. But her mother prepared dinner like normal, stir-frying tofu and vegetables and setting plates for both of them though she didn't eat, didn't laugh, only stared at the stove, moved the food around on her plate and sipped ginger tea.

Polly ate, though her stomach hurt and she hated Emily, the way she could just love Etani and then just love Brady. Love window. Just yesterday Brady had loved her. She lined each tofu square up around the edge of the plate and put a piece of vegetable in between each one, a stir-fry star: tofu, broccoli, tofu, carrot, tofu, red pepper, tofu, asparagus. But her mom didn't notice. When she did her scarification—Brady didn't have the monopoly on it. Not a star. Everybody had a star. She wasn't going to be a star, stars were too distant, and, like unicorns and rainbows, something for little girls; too common.

She needed something else. Something to slice herself into her skin so she could keep herself forever.

✎ KIRA

Adam arrived home as they were washing dishes. Outside the window was dark from the winter and the overcast sky.

"Not tonight," he said when she asked, dutifully, if he wanted to talk again. He spent a few minutes with Polly in her room, then took his burrito down to the basement, a definitive thump to his footsteps. Her belly in a knot, she welcomed the time alone. She'd torn the note into small pieces in the bathroom, flushed twice, now fretted about the old plumbing barfing up the evidence.

So tired. Polly doing homework. She should help her. But just to lie down for a few minutes first. She tossed. Their bed so lonely with her alone. Adam loved this bed. And below her, in the basement, was he drinking? Smoking pot? Jacking off? Gambling online?

She slept: A man rubbing her back, trying to get the tension out of her shoulder, she sat backwards on a chair wearing only her black cotton panties. A man like the bearded guy at Harbin. Something wrong with her shoulder and he was going to massage it out. He had a new technique; "I can get the problem out," he said. His feet were long and bare with thick yellow calluses. He touched her butt, mumbled, "I really shouldn't go there."

She elbowed him. "No, don't."

"I'm sorry, I'm sorry, it's just so hard to resist." He massaged her right shoulder in large round swipes, working deep: "I can get this." Now he rubbed in a numbing agent, getting more and more into it, a trance, a sexual fervor, getting it out, big circles, working out her pain. "I'm going to get it, I'm going to get it." She couldn't feel the skin on her shoulder and arm. He pulled her arm back, "I'm ready to get it. Are you ready?" She felt a hard pressure, a long line of pressure. "The-e-e-re," he moaned. He'd released it—released himself? She turned her head to look; he'd sliced her skin from her wrist to her shoulder, a thin line of red just to the quick, the flesh separating.

She woke shaking. She'd been so vulnerable. She'd let Ravi get off on her need for a teacher. Yes, she was to blame; but yes, he was to blame, too. Adam was right: he was the teacher, in a power position. She was the sucker. Goddamn it. What a cliché she'd become. And what did Polly think? "The love window." She was afraid to go to the window, afraid he'd be standing there under the streetlamp, solid and waiting, hunched in a blue jean jacket. And if Adam saw, if Polly saw… How would she ever mend it with Adam, what would Polly think, how dare he? She felt a rage rise in her along with the fear. Her fault, his fault, whatever. Her family was bleeding. He wasn't taking no for an answer; well, she'd make him, cut *him*.

In the dark, reaching for her cell phone, the number she'd memorized without realizing.

"Hello?" Ravi's voice thick with sleep.

Her words propelled by the pounding, the image of the dream, low so nobody would hear, forced. "It's Kira."

"Kira." He sounded happy.

She took a breath. "No. Stop. I'm not happy you left that note. You can't. Look, it's obvious it won't work out, and you've been inappropriate in a gazillion ways, including sleeping with me. That's breaking the teacher-student trust. Yes, I know I wanted it, and I'm sorry for encouraging this but it was your responsibility to say 'no.' I opened myself up to you, and you hurt me. Okay, I'm a grown woman. I can handle that. But when you leave a note on my door like a, I don't know, a high school kid, messing with my family? That won't wash. How dare you? You stay the hell away from my house, from my family, from my life. Stay *out* of my family."

Now his voice was leery, alert. "Whoa. Slow down. I'm sorry you misunderstood. I just sent you a sweet note; there was no hostility and I'm sorry I misjudged our connection. There was nothing in that note that said anything about anything, and you have an open marriage, you're jerking *me* around... you, you invited me in." The hurt in his voice.

She ignored it. "I'm inviting you out. Do you want me to report you? To the... YMCA, and the yoga board of certifiers, whatever that is..."

"I thought there was something real between us."

"You stay the hell away from me," she hissed. "You get anywhere near Moss Street again and I'll get a restraining order on your ass!"

"Okay, calm down. You're clearly unstable. Look, I'm sorry. Maybe it's me, my egoic connection is too strong. I don't know what I did, but I'm *sorry!*" but it was shouted, and he didn't sound sorry, or calm, and his anger and dismay deeply satisfied.

Good. She'd broken through that fake serenity. Welcome back to the real world, Ravi, she thought. She snapped her cell phone shut, and the snap felt so comforting she opened the phone and did it again. *Snap.* Not evolved at all. But he'd gotten the message just the same.

ꙮ POLLY

Polly thought about Brady. After Nell had told her about him and Emily, she'd ignored him the rest of the day, and Brady had ignored her. I shut my eyes to you, she thought. She loved that idiom. But what if you couldn't ever, ever close your eyes? Polly lay on the floor of her room in underpants and her bathrobe, keeping her eyes open as long as she could without blinking. Joey was such a little boy, not even potty trained, but she knew why he moaned—sometimes there was too much to look at. Sometimes it hurt him because he couldn't stop looking, not even when he slept.

Joey and Amber had left only a couple of weeks ago, but it

was like they'd never existed: we've shut our eyes to you. Nobody talked about them anymore. Nobody talked—her parents were still in a terrible fight. Just quiet intense voices from the kitchen, small shouts from the bedroom at night. A chill, evil and awful. Her dad didn't know about the love window note. She didn't know if she should tell him.

She traced the Eye of Thoth with her finger in the air. What to do about Brady? If she told her mom she'd had a boyfriend, that he'd dumped her, her mom might say, "You had a boyfriend? Well, I have one, too!" and that would be unbearable. Or she wouldn't say anything about it, and that would be unbearable, too.

"Polly, are you still awake?" Her mom's voice, whispering through the door.

"Come in!" She tucked her feet under her so her mom wouldn't see the nicks in the arches.

Her mother in pajamas, pleading. "Polly, Apollonia, do you want to sleep in the big bed with me tonight? Daddy's having a private time in the basement again, and we could have a sleepover."

Polly looked at her, her mom jumpy all the time, the fights—could she really think she didn't know what was going on? The idea of her mom, warm and suffocating and too soft, snuggling next to her in bed. Something gross about that. She used to want that, she used to climb between her parents, warm and smelly, and snuggle down, head in her dad's armpit, a big jumble of bodies and snores.

"You can stay up as late as you want reading. I'll just doze off next to you."

"No thanks, Mommy." She'd rather die, snuggling against that wall of need.

"Okay," Kira said, "Goodnight again, Poodle."

But a few minutes later, her mother's sad look too sad, Polly put on socks, collected her stuffies and other stuff, and climbed in next to her in the big bedroom. "Don't bug me though, Mommy. I want to read."

"Hey, sweetie." Kira sounded relieved. "I'll read, too."

Polly tucked a wall of pillows between them and opened her book. If she'd been in her room she could play her music as she went to sleep. Or write in her journal.

But her mom wanted to talk. "Remember we used to do this when Daddy went on a trip? And then I'd make you scrambled eggs and children's coffee in the morning."

Polly barely remembered, then a flash of yellow eggs on a metal plate with ducks, a grown-up cup half filled, sunshine in the pale blue kitchen. "So that's why I like coffee so much."

"It was only a tablespoon of coffee in a half a cup of warm milk. But it made you feel so big. That was nice. Tell me about school."

"What's to tell?"

"Tell me what's happening with Emily and Etani."

"Oh, they broke up. He decided she wasn't hot enough."

"Jesus. Hot? She's twelve."

"That's okay, she's going out with Brady now."

"Don't you have a crush on Brady?"

"No. I hate him." She kept her voice casual.

"What happened?"

"Nothing happened, Mommy, *nothing*. I'm just moving on, okay?"

"Okay. But I'm sorry." Her mom looked like she was about to cry about it.

"Sorry that I don't like a dickhead anymore? It's okay, Mommy. Let's just go to sleep." She leaned over her mom and turned off her bedside light.

"Thanks, Pol. I love you."

Her mom fell asleep almost at once, and she snored. So Polly packed up in the dark (stuffies, quilt, books), and went back to her own room. It was easier to sleep there.

CHAPTER 14

◌ KIRA

"7:15! Polly, get up! Get *up*!" Adam yelled in the door of Polly's trashed room. Slamming the door.

"Hey! Adam, don't talk to her that way." They bumped into each other at the dishwasher, in front of the refrigerator. She stumbled over his foot reaching for a roll of plastic wrap.

"Ow," he said.

"Well, excuse me."

"Jesus, Kira, don't use that tone of voice with me."

"Do you need to start this early in the morning?"

"Who started it?"

"All I said was 'excuse me.'"

"It's the tone of voice."

"You're projecting."

"Mommy! Daddy? Could you guys please cut it out?"

"Glad to see you've decided to join us, princess."

"Look, now you've made her cry, Adam."

"Fuck it all. You do breakfast." The slam of the basement door, he thumped down the stairs.

In the silence of the morning kitchen, Kira tightlipped at the stove, frying tofu with food yeast and tamari. This was what she'd decided to keep?

Polly assembling her English essay into its folder to turn in. Polly quietly at her shoulder. "I'm going to need a lunch."

"Do it yourself. You're old enough. There's probably some

187

almond butter. Enjoy it while you can; you'll be back to cheap Skippy for the next jar."

"*Fine*, Mommy. You don't need to be such a bitch to me and Dad."

Kira turned to face her. "Watch your mouth. And if you're not in the car by 7:50, it's leaving without you. I'm not telling you again."

Polly's face red with indignation. "You're a *bitch!*"

Adam stood in the basement doorway again, holding a plastic laundry basket of dirty clothes in his hands. "You will not speak to your mother that way."

"Adam, leave her alone."

"Well, if *you* ever lifted a finger around here, washed a god-damn dish, when's the last time you did laundry, Kira? I'm sick of this. You could clean your own shit once in a while!" Hands gripped tight on the basket, he flung the clothes at Kira. And missed.

The clothes landed on Polly.

Polly cringed, small and thirteen, under the shower of dirty underpants, socks, jeans, shirts.

They all stood there. Then Polly ran to her room, a long wail down the hall, and slammed the door behind her.

Kira and Adam stood in the same positions, floor littered with dirty laundry. Kira didn't raise her voice. Just: "Enough. I will not stand for violence. Get out."

"You're one to talk."

"Don't change the subject. I don't care what I did—that was in our agreement."

"Under duress! That was not a theoretical agreement; you were on your way, and you just wanted permission. Which I was such a dick to give."

"I don't ever need your permission, Adam. I'm not that kind of wife. And it's over. Completely over. But beyond that. Polly didn't do anything. You will not be violent with her. Ever."

"I didn't touch her, I lost my temper. At *you*."

"Tough. You're out of here. Leave."

"You leave. It's my house, too."

"Do you want me to call the cops?"

"Are you fucking serious?"

"I am."

"Fuck you. Fuck you." Crying. His face red, eyes streaming.

Her face fisted and brittle, eyes slits. "I'm going to work. We'll talk later."

ADAM

Adam called and cancelled The Box, permanently. "No, no, no. We love you, really support what you're doing. We're just in the kind of family upheaval which means we're not cooking right now, and I hate to see those beautiful vegetables going to waste. Yes, we will. We will. Great. Okay, we'll give you a call real soon. Okay, and thank you."

He hung up the phone. Silence in the house, a winter wind through thin sunlight outside. The dirty clothes still lay scattered around the doorway to the basement stairs. He piled them in his arms and walked back down the stairs. At least he could do the laundry. Tripping as he entered the basement room. Socks and underpants peeled off and fell to the grungy floor: concrete, dust, flecks of food, ancient crumbs. He dumped the clothes in the washer, measured the detergent. His job. He was the one who kept the household running, not Kira.

His eyes snapshotted around the room. Lava lamp. Amp. Grateful Dead poster, corners gnawed by years of thumbtacks.

His toolbox. Inside it, his old rig. In the corner, the clutter of poisons: the can of Ortho killer Diazinon from last year's explosion of houseflies, their soft black bodies dead on every windowsill. The rat poison pellets. Borax, Lysol so old the can rusted at the seams. Upstairs, too, throughout the house, so many poisons. Ammonia, bleach, matches, disinfectants, pine oil, drain cleaner, oven cleaner. Fabric softener and detergent, spot remover, indelible markers, super glue and epoxy, printer toner. Some of the houseplants. Charcoal lighter, kerosene, paint, paint remover, paint thinner, snail bait, antifreeze, herbicides, insecticides, turpentine, suntan lotion, shaving lotion, rubbing alcohol, boric acid eye wash, deodorant, wart remover, hair dye, iodine, nail polish, nail polish remover, Nair, perfume, prescription and non-prescription drugs.

But they chose to live like this, surrounded by toxins in the dark places under the water source. They stepped carefully.

"Danger and delight grow on one stalk," the old English proverb his grandfather used to say. Danger and Delight.

The Japanese ate fugu as a delicacy—blowfish sashimi, the most tender and delicious treat the spoiled and overwrought palate could imagine; savory, tingly, yes, mood altering, with only one drawback—or was it? The flesh of the blowfish, incorrectly prepared, was deadly. The poison paralyzed and caused almost instant fatality. Amanita mushroom, "death caps," destroyed the liver, caused convulsions, foaming at the mouth, terror, agony, death, yet their cousins, the sweetest mushrooms on earth, were furtively hunted by the same people who sought fugu, or who skydived, or searched for crack on late night Oakland streets. Choose your fruit: was it pleasure or poison? Russian roulette. He imagined a fruit tree: "Florida Citrus Party," a Frankenstein-mix of grafted lemons and limes and oranges, some delightful, some deadly. Take your chances. Would you delight or die?

The furnace hummed as he sat down at the desk and opened his cherrywood box, looked at the Percodan. Two left. Poison. He took them.

There. That was over.

And now? Leave? She wanted him to. Go where? He booted the computer on the old desk and looked up the weather in Elko on Accuweather.com: 21F°, RealFeel® 19F° and snowing. He pictured Amber with no shoes, standing in the doorway of a smoky casino.

Or he could stay, honor the commitment. Until death do us part. They'd danced naked with the fire dancers on Maui after their wedding, Stan and Lindsey, too, Kira pregnant with Polly, Lindsey pregnant with Nell. Already together off and on five years then, though they'd known each other forever. ("You're going to do this?" he'd asked. "Have it?" "People have babies, I guess we can," she'd answered. "I'm having it, and it's up to you if you want to stay. But I'm not ever having another abortion.") The hard curve of her belly and his hand on it feeling the thump. The arcs of yellow fire against the sky, reggae and surf. Some people just had weddings, DJs in hotel lobbies; they'd gotten married. Leave? No. My house, my daughter, my wife.

He stood up. He'd get more work, earn more money. One yoga fuck didn't wipe out years of lovemaking. She'd get over it. He'd get over it. It would all be fine (the Percs already fuzzing the edges).

"It's my house, too," he said when she got home from work.

"Fine." She barely looked at him. "But I can't deal with you. Sleep in the basement."

He nodded. He'd be the troll under her bridge, the monster in her dungeon. Down there again.

Later that evening, though, the silence. A troll alone, what the fuck was he supposed to do down there? Poisons to play with, invite in. Depression. Never going all the way. Never taking control of anything, no responsibility—life happening *to* him, never any goddamn choice.

He scrambled in his toolbox for his old rig. What could he shoot—wanting out of it, oblivion. Grabbed the bottle of Ortho insecticide off the shelf, opened it, smelled the sweet soapy scent. He put his lips over the mouth of the bottle, ready to raise it, ready to begin. Go all the way, take it to the end. No more flirting. He'd raise the bottle of Ortho and swig, and swallow, sweet and soapy, more and more until he started to feel sick and spacy, ringing in his ears, a bad high, a bad, bad high. Then he'd put it down. Pick up the rig. He'd stick the needle deep in the bottle and pull the plunger back, and tie off and find a vein and plunge it, the poison hot and burning, and he'd stick the needle deep in the bottle again and pull the plunger back, and too dizzy, to sick to find a vein again slam the poison down into his thigh, a definitive slam, the final blow. And sirens, sirens and then he'd be in the ICU sweating and dying, and…

Adam put the bottle of Ortho down, paced the basement, eyes shut.

He'd be in the ICU, but he wouldn't be dying, just stupid, sick as a fucking dog, and finally they'd call Kira and as she paced and paced and moaned and waited for them to call her back, the phone would ring, and it would be him, and he'd say, "You see what it's like? Ha ha ha you bitch…" No, no, that wouldn't work because he'd be in the ICU on the bed with a respirator, and then in the TCU dozing in and out, and it wouldn't be until four days later, after pneumonia developed and he'd been moved back from the TCU to the ICU that he'd blurt out to the nurses that he hadn't just shot it up, he'd swallowed almost a half gallon of it, too, and there'd be brain damage, affecting the synapses controlling his involuntary reflexes so he'd tic and drool. He'd drool, and Polly would visit...

And Polly.

Fuck.

Polly stopped the fantasy cold.

Goddamn it. Goddamn it to hell. Polly. Son of a motherfucking bitch, Polly. He slammed his head hard against the wall, sat down hard on the futon. Polly.

Fifteen minutes later, he called Stan. "Spur of the moment thought. Friday night: we're too young to be old, let's hit a bar. Meet you at King's Lucky Lounge in twenty minutes."

"Hey, I'm watching my show."

"Tivo it. This is important."

"Ah, fuck you. Give me thirty minutes."

He checked his wallet; twenty-seven bucks in small bills. The days of "emergency hundreds" crisp in his desk drawer gone. Twenty-seven would buy a few. Stan owed him a bundle.

Adam walked out of the house, not saying a word to anybody, the house silent and blaming, Kira and Polly in their bedrooms probably asleep. I can leave. I'm only the troll in the basement. A twelve minute walk down the hill.

❧ POLLY

Her parents were in their separate places again, Daddy in the basement, her mom in her bedroom probably doing yoga. *Yoga.* It made a sour taste in her mouth; stale spit. The love note from Ravi had immediately disappeared, and was nowhere easily findable. Going through her mom's stuff was about the only thing that made Kira freak out totally, so Polly had learned how to be discreet. In her recent forays through her drawers, though, nothing good had turned up. She wanted to see that letter again; it shocked her all the way to her feet, but made her feel sickly excited, too.

The clock ticked loudly. Eight thirty on Friday night. She wasn't tired. And she wasn't going to call Nell—Nell, so happy that Polly didn't have a boyfriend now. Just jealous, but still. Your friend was supposed to be your friend. She could ask her dad to take her to Video Room but she didn't want to knock on the basement door. Her mom? Breathing, probably, thinking about that guy. Her boyfriend. Her mom thought she was so blind.

She opened her Blood Drawer to look at her things. Her Kunstkammer pictures, the ones that were left after Mr. Frank had confiscated the good ones. Her Mishka hair. She closed the drawer and went to the bathroom. Silence in the house, dark like the mummy's tomb. But not peaceful dark, the dark of fighting and hissing and things falling apart. There was nothing she could do about it but she had to do something.

On her way back down the hall she got it. Her scarification. Not a star, but an eye, the Eye of Thoth, an open eye on her body. In honor of Joey's eyes. To make Brady see her. To make her mother see what she was doing to the family. It was the perfect symbol. The only one that made sense. Without the Eye, she could see what was happening with her parents, and the fighting and the silence that went on and on, but with the Eye—and the blood sacrifice of cutting it—she would have the power to fix it.

Nayanonmila. They had studied this, too, in Social Studies when they'd studied Hinduism. Hindu sculptors always carved the eyes on a sculpture last. It was a special ceremony, called Nayanonmila, the "eye-unclosing." Because the eye was the last organ to become active; in the womb, the fetus used all its organs except its eyes. Unclosing the eye meant enlightenment. She would unclose the Eye.

The Eye of Thoth was complicated. She took off her jeans and put on her bathrobe so she wouldn't be cold. She sat on the floor. On her right thigh, down near her knee, she drew the Eye of Thoth with her thin Sharpie. Horus used the Eye of Thoth to revive his sleeping father Osiris so that he could rule the underworld, she remembered from her 6th grade Egyptian report. Her dad was in the underworld too, under the house.

She could use the Eye, too, to bring her dad up, make him realize he missed them.

Six strokes of the pen. The top lid, the bottom lid, a half circle—arc down—denoting the eye. The eyebrow, a short line from the outside of the eye. A long curved line from the inside of the eye. Then she stood up and looked at herself in the full-length mirror on her closet door, trying to imagine it in raised red flesh, in scar tissue.

It was upside down when she was standing up.

She thought for a long time. Which way was right? If she wanted it looking back at her when she sat down and looked at her thigh, she should keep it this way. But it looked stupid when she was standing up. If she wanted it looking out at the world, it should be the other way, the bottom of the eye facing her knee.

She started again on the left leg, drawing it upside down, tracing lightly in pen, six strokes. She stood up again. Perfect.

Surprised—she'd never gotten the star that perfect.

Another sign.

No time to think it through. Magic happened when the omens were right. The crows on the lamppost. And Thoth was the bird-headed god, the god of magic and the moon.

She moved into action: Her Exacto blade from the Blood

Drawer. It should be sterilized. Cotton balls. In the bathroom, she found a plastic bottle of hydrogen peroxide from when she'd had her ears pierced; an empty cottage cheese container in the kitchen. Back in the bathroom, she poured a puddle of hydrogen peroxide into the bottom of the container and dropped the blade in, not knowing how long it would take to kill the germs. It fizzed a little, the blade magnified against the white plastic bottom, she counted a minute: 58, 59, 60, then carefully poured the hydrogen peroxide down the sink and maneuvered up the blade, careful not to touch the edge.

She sat on her desk chair and propped her left leg on the desk. She had to move fast, six strokes just tracing the pen. She'd start with the eyelid: top line, bottom line, quick curve of the eye itself.

The Eye of Thoth.

At first it didn't hurt at all, just an electric shock-like feeling, a terrible buzz. By the third stroke, Polly was terrified to stop, terrified to go on. She bit her lip and moaned. It didn't hurt that much but it would hurt, it was going to hurt bad any second, and the blood, dark red and insistent, ran down onto the chair, running and running, she should have sat on a towel, but it was too late, she had to keep going or she never would. "Oh no, oh no," she gasped, "oh no," but her hand kept moving and carving the lines, the straight line of the eyebrow, the short deep line, the long curved line stretching from the inside of the eye, and she finished the final line and grabbed the clump of cotton balls, "Oh no, oh no, oh no." Her throat choked, tears streaming down, sobbing, her leg on fire, and her heart broken, her heart ruined, her skin ruined, her life ruined, and she missed them. Missed her mom, her dad, Brady, Nell, Amber, Joey, missed Mishka, her soft white fur, and how they used to lie in the corner and she'd whisper her secrets; missed herself.

The clump of cotton was soaked through, bright red. More. It wouldn't stop. "Daddy! Mommy!" she moaned. But nobody came. She grabbed her shirt and wrapped it around her leg, held her leg, running to the bathroom. Sat in the tub. Oh no. Oh no. There was nobody to come for her. She had the shivers now, patches of black, and she had to work, work, work to keep her eyes open.

ADAM

By the time Stan got to Lucky's, Adam was two tequilas into it, standing at the end of the bar watching the pretty girls and their playa men.

The bartender came by again when he saw Stan perched on the stool next to Adam. "Name your poison."

"More tequila," Adam said. "Hey Stan, ever tried this Añejo? Awesome aged tequila, goes down smooth. And I should know."

"Give it a shot."

"Dos more of those, Señor." Welcoming the bit of slur in his speech, the tongue relaxing with the booze. "Stan the Man's in the house. He's buying, 'cause I'm broke."

"Look at you go, big boy," Stan said. "Long time since we hit a bar together. What's up with the familia?" He lay a twenty on the bar.

"Oh, fuck 'em for a moment. Just drink." Later, staring at the fingernails on his right hand still kept long for the guitar. How long since he'd played? "I'm having a problem."

Stan was quiet. Adam felt horns grow on his scalp, springing through the flesh and hairs; fool. Cuckold. Idiot. Who cares. "Hey, man, you listening?"

"Got your back, bro," Stan said.

"Just to say that... Oh, man. Kira's got a thing going on with her fucking yoga teacher. First she asks me for an open relation-

ship, next thing—next time I even talk to her—he's boning her."
Tossing the rest of shot back—he hated tequila next morning
but it was oh so sweet at night. The words "in our bed" wouldn't
come. Didn't matter, Stan not his fucking confessor.

Stan shook his head. "Sorry, guy. That's fucked up. I heard this
comedian once, funny guy. He's like, 'If a woman tells you she
wants an open relationship, that is not rhetorical. That cowgirl's
already got another horse cut off from the herd, saddled up, and
ready to ride.'"

"I'm not finding that funny."

"That's because it's true, man."

Adam drank the dregs of his drink again. "Let's get totally
fucked up. I am so fucking sorry for myself right now. Conversation
over. Tell me about something I don't give a shit about." Music on
the jukebox, a great collection of blues. He didn't do this often
enough, trapped in that house with so much female energy. This
was what he needed, more time with friends; so long since he'd
hung with Desperado Dave, and with Stan. Usually it was just
at work. Stan was taking it easy, but Adam had another shot of
tequila. Añejo. The word so sweet in his mouth. A party of five
young people came in, clustered near the bar. Too loud.

"Let's go sit," Adam said. Definitely feeling it now, that head-
over-no-feet feeling, looking through an aquarium, but the feet
were still moving so hey, he couldn't be that fucked up yet. He
wanted to taxi it home, roll out, lose it in the gutter. That kind of
blow out. They moved to a small table in the back. Still, a relief to
have Stan know, even if they never mentioned it again. A reason to
lose it, deep end dive it down. Music in the background, Muddy
Waters. Not a bad soundtrack to his life.

Stan said, "Kira and you will work it out. She's worth it, she's
the real thing."

"Why's she pushing me?"

"Sometimes you just have to go to the bottom and eat worms."

"What the fuck's that mean?"

"My Mormon aunt used to say that. But I'm not sure if it's a Mormon thing."

"I like it. I'm eating worms. Oh yeah, I'm eating worms."

"Have another drink," Stan said.

"Get me a beer?"

In a while, Stan was back with a couple of drafts, the foam so soft he could curl up and sleep in it. "Hey," Stan said. "I think I saw them at Café Capoiera together like a few weeks ago, a month ago. Some guy with a ponytail. That him?"

Adam shrugged, "How the fuck should I know?"

"They had yoga mats rolled up like little burritos, that must be him. I didn't want to say anything to you. But they looked like they were into each other. Way into."

"Fuck you!" It exploded out of him. Knocking over the beer onto the table—it felt good. Raising his fist up in Stan's face. "*Fuck* you! Why didn't you tell me then? Why are you telling me now? What the fuck good is it going to do now? Do you know how fucking humiliating this is? Can you even imagine? No. I bet you *fucking* can't, because you're a *fucking* dick. I should've cut off your fucking dick and shoved it down your throat years ago, asshole."

"Whoa, calm down!"

Nobody close to them noticed, except the bartender across the lounge who fixed him with an evil eye. "No. I'm not calming down. And that, by the way, is an absurd way to get somebody to calm down, to tell them to. You ever think of that?" But he was calm. Exhausted. He lay his head down in the beer, and first it was cold, then warm. "She didn't want another dog. That's when you know it's over, man. When she can't even commit to another fucking dog."

"Okay, let's go, bro. I'm driving, but you cannot puke in my van, get it?" Stan was putting money on the table, pulling him.

"I can walk, man."

"Let's go." A blur of traffic lights and queasiness. He wanted to sleep, like he'd slept in the back of the old woody station wagon growing up, his mom carrying him into the house long after he was too old for it. "Get out of the van. You're home, dude."

The house was quiet. The streetlamp outside Kira and Adam's bedroom flickered—they always forgot to call about it during the day when PG&E was open and, like the proverbial man with the leaky roof, they only remembered at night. I'll call tomorrow, he told himself. Fumbled the key into the lock.

It was his house, his bedroom, his wife. The bedroom door was open. Kira lay there alone, not sleeping, even drunk he could tell from her position—side-lying but not relaxed. He took off his clothes, leaving them collapsed in small unoccupied piles, slid in behind her, put his arms around her. This he couldn't lose. His bedroom. His Kira. "Open your eyes, baby."

She moved her body back into him, "...bad dream... birds with beady eyes and you weren't there and I missed you...," and then he was rolling her over on her back, kissing her deeply, and pushing into her, "I'll fuck him out of you," so hot, so sad, both of them clutching, moaning, "I'm sorry, I'm so sorry," the room spinning and spinning *añejo, añejo,* and they fit together so well, so hot. Like they were supposed to.

When he struggled from sleep, out of the empty master bed and into the empty kitchen, it was midmorning Saturday, another storm front on its way this afternoon. A note on the table: Kira

and Polly had already left for the Grand Lake Farmer's Market.
They were out of coffee, so he put on shoes and a raincoat and
took a walk down to Peet's.

CHAPTER 15

 ADAM

When Adam got home, head still two sizes too large despite the caffeine, they were sitting on the front porch damp from the rain: Amber and Joey and Johnny, two old Samsonite suitcases neatly near the door, two black umbrellas open to dry. Amber looked exhausted but her hair was clean, a maroon sweat suit, Joey clean too, chewing on his cylinder block and sitting next to a little boy, Johnny—it must be Johnny—a normal looking seven-year-old with a Game Boy, blond and freckled, with a small scar near the side of his eye. Adam felt a rush of relief. They were okay. Not that he'd helped them or anything. Then a sinking feeling—oh, the complexity. And could the timing be any fucking worse.

But: "Hello!"—his body running up the steps, he felt his mouth stretch wide in a grin.

He reached to give her a hug, then stopped himself. Amber said, "Hey, Dad. We didn't have nowhere to go." Same flat voice.

Goddamn, couldn't she be there without him being "Dad"?

Adam scooped up Joey, "Hey, buddy!" Gave him a kiss on the top of his head and, still holding him, bent to kneel in front of Johnny.

"Hey. Are you Johnny?"

"Hi, Grandpa," Johnny said, dutifully.

It jarred, but not as bad as Amber's "Dad." Hers seemed pointed, even malicious; it wanted something from him. His was just a little kid, doing what he was told. "Wanna see my Bionicle?

He's a Kirop. And I have a Solek, too."

"Well, that's cute," Adam said, looking at a fierce plastic monster thing. "Call me Adam, okay? And my wife is Kira. And our daughter is Polly. Okay? Adam, Kira, and Polly."

"I have to go potty, Adam," Johnny said.

"Well, come on in, then. We have a toilet with your name on it, we call it The John." Over his head completely, over all their heads. "Amber, we're going to have to talk about this. Not sure exactly what we can do about it."

With him, the troll, on the futon in the basement, where the hell would the troll's other family sleep?

⌁ KIRA

Kira arrived home with Polly twenty minutes later. They were all in the kitchen; Kira heard Amber's voice from the front doorway, froze. "Our company is back," she said to Polly.

"Oh no." Polly, sullen and draggy all morning at the farmer's market, sagged in dismay but Kira could see a little smile on her face, the first one all day—how could she actually be happy about it? "Guess this place is like the Hotel California, Mommy—'The roaches check in but they don't check out.'"

"That's the Roach Motel commercial."

"What*ever*." And dashed ahead.

"Polly! Take off your rainboots!"

When she walked into the kitchen, there they all were: Amber with her Diet Pepsi, Johnny slurping a bowl of cereal with milk, Adam drinking coffee from a large paper Peet's cup, Joey sitting on Adam's lap, sucking his thumb. Joey's eyes looked crusty. I can't do this again, Kira thought. This is not my life.

"Well, hello," she said, from the doorway, trying for normal. "Hi Joey! Hi Johnny, nice to meet you!"

Thunk. Neither child said anything. Her gesture lay on the ground, a bird flown into a plate glass window.

Polly gave Amber a shy wave and a smile.

"Go on, say hi to your grandma," Amber said to Johnny.

"Hi," Johnny said, and waved with one hand the way Polly had. He was cute. The grandma thing though, she thought, it was absurd. And remembered, again, the DNA test. What a waste. Like ripping up money. A pang of guilt.

"Hey," Amber said to Polly, "Like your hair, looks good black. I was telling Dad about this job I almost had at the casino in Battle Mountain where Steve's cooking, but then Steve and me had a fight and he sent me back to my mom's, and my mom sent me here with the kids. She says she can't raise Johnny no more. I'm so tired of sitting on a bus."

Kira didn't understand. How could she just go, be sent, move from place to place by default? "So you just came back here because she told you to?" Wondered: did Sandi say I told her Adam doesn't live here? She dismissed the thought. Don't borrow trouble.

"Where else am I supposed to go? Steve's an asshole, my mom don't want the kids no more, and I don't want Social Services to get them. You try walking a mile in my shoes, lady."

"My shoes." Amber was, still, wearing her shoes. Impossible to shape her face into false happiness. "Look, let's get you all settled for the night but then we need to talk about it. All of us. We can't have you live with us right now."

"Dad already told me." As if it didn't matter, none of it mattered, move her here, move her there, as long as somebody was paying attention long enough to move her.

Polly swung her head back and forth between them all: Kira, Adam, Amber, Joey, Johnny, back to Kira, like she was trying to figure it all out. Kira looked at Adam—shoulders stooped, hair shaggy, unshaven; the small boy on his lap. Clean up your act! she wanted to scream. Stop sulking! But the way he'd touched her last night, hands sliding over her perfectly. He was looking at her, too, eyes soft. He bit the left side of his lower lip at her, a small flirt for her eyes only. The sulk and hangover only a coat he wore, beneath it something determined.

She set the vegetables down. She'd meant to make a winter stew, beans and greens. Cheap food to last the week; she'd started packing lunches for work. Now what would she feed them all? Money felt tight and hot and hard; the kitchen, too small anyway, felt tight and hot and hard. Her mouth tasted metallic. All morning she'd walked carefully through the produce stands, shopping for the cheaper foods, balancing organic and not organic. Supplies rather than surprises. Less wastage than The Box. She craved cool water, a bowl of it, maybe the big blue ceramic bowl they used for company pasta. Clear water with ice; sliding her hands in, her hands splashing it up to her face. Refreshing. Cleansing.

Adam said, "I told her she might have to stay in a motel, that we had to talk, me and you." He only looked at Kira. "*Voulez vous couchez avec moi, c'est soir,*" he sang.

"We will see, mon amour," she said. "That might need to happen. Logistically." Because who would pay for the motel?

Amber stared at her hands, waiting. Johnny fiddled with his Bionicles. What must it feel like to know you're not wanted where you've always lived? Kira wondered. But meanwhile, the rest of life never stopped. Belly sore. Where was the time? What a mess I am, she thought. Real issues, real problems, but here they were, the storm about to hit, in the kitchen of their mortgaged house, with Amber and her kids who had no place to go and no resources and—for the moment—until it all crashed around her—she was still so privileged.

I need to do the right thing, the honorable thing, Kira told herself. She took a breath to fight her nausea. "For a couple of days only," she said. "Only. Adam will bring up the futon for you."

Amber's shoulders lowered an inch.

◐ POLLY

"Adam, can we watch the Superbowl at your guys' house?" Johnny asked.

"I don't see why not," her dad said. "When is it?"

Johnny and Amber looked at her dad like he was crazy. "Tomorrow," Amber said.

"*I* knew that," Polly said. Her parents were so out of it. She still felt dizzy from what had happened last night.

She'd sat there a long time, in the bathtub, until her head was clear again. She'd slowly taken off the t-shirt she'd wrapped around her leg. The bleeding had mostly stopped. She'd slathered the area with toothpaste so it would scar up, then wrapped her leg with gauze and strapped it with tape. She'd tied her bathrobe tighter around her. Then she'd turned on the shower and rinsed the blood down the drain, and still nobody had come. So she'd put the bloody t-shirt in the kitchen garbage buried under lots of stuff, taken two Tylenol, and gone to bed, snuggled up with her stuffies.

"Alors, we're not really a *sportif* family," her dad said. "But why the hell not. We'll do beer from the can and chips Amurican-style. Do you think it will be on a regular channel? We don't have cable."

"Man-oh, man-oh, man," Johnny said, and shook his head. "My grandma told me you was California weirdos."

Her dad laughed.

"Hey, Grandma Kira," Johnny said, pushing back from the table and coming up to where she still stood next to Polly in the doorway. "Want to play with my Bionicles? This one is Solek, and this one is Kirop."

Polly watched as her mother knelt down so she was eye-level with Johnny. "Hello, Solek. Hello, Kirop," she said. "Oh, hello, Johnny! Let me know when you're ready for a hello hug, okay?"

He leaned for a moment against her leg, then pulled away from her. She smiled at Polly. "Cute!" she mouthed.

"Those are cool," Polly said to Johnny, not smiling back at her mom. She hated boy's toys.

Johnny said, "You can play with them sometime if you want, Polly. I'll let you."

She saw Amber nod approvingly at Johnny, shove him gently between the shoulder blades. "Go on and play with Polly."

Polly didn't want to deal with the Eye. She left the bandage on and didn't peek. It was kinda cool to see Joey again, though Polly couldn't tell if he remembered her. Johnny was into video games and liked some sports but not "boring ones like baseball." His Game Boy was loaded. He was at that age where boys didn't talk to girls too much, especially girls who were older. He was almost as bad as Joey—he wouldn't look at her, mostly he wanted to play his Game Boy, vroom vroom his Bionicles, and get stuff to eat.

Slim Jims. Slurpees. After they got settled in, Amber and Johnny and Joey walked to the 7-11 for more junk and she went along, holding Joey's hand. When they were all hanging out on the porch, Polly's ears aching from the cold air, Amber said, "Johnny. Give me my smokes," and he took a cigarette out of the package and walked it over to her, balancing it vertically on his finger on the way. "Just give me my smoke. Don't be cute."

Johnny turned to her. "I got a zoomer rifle at my house."

"What's that?"

"Duh." But he wouldn't explain.

That afternoon she sat with Amber in the living room.

"What's it like to go to jail?" she asked Amber.

"Prison. Sucks."

"Do you mind if I ask you a personal question?"

"Yes, I do."

"But is it a personal question to ask how you got caught?"

Amber stared at her. "Being stupid."

"But is it a personal question to ask how you were being stupid?"

"Okay, here's the truth. Guys do stupid things, and they want you to do them with them, or come along, like I was coming along on the way to SLC when Steven knew this Moron—that's a Mormon—who wanted some drugs and didn't know how to hook it up. Steve's got this friend out in a ranch near Jiggs who cooked meth, so Steve said we'd drive for a fee. And then we did it again, a few more times, just driving the truck. Hanging out. I drive, then Steve drives, and we listen to tunes. That's all we do anyway— drive—just about everything's two hundred miles away. Making deliveries like the milk man, only it's the meth man. Bad shit, don't try it. In prison, they show you pictures of this meth lady, she starts out like normal, pretty, and then nine years later she's like Michael Jackson but not from plastic surgery. And I didn't like it, because when you go to Utah and Idaho you're crossing state lines. But Steve is just stupid, and I guess I'm stupid too, and five years later, wah lah."

Polly didn't understand everything she said, but most of it. "You and Steve are still together?"

"Kinda. When he's not a flaming asshole. Don't got a lot of choices, and rivers run deep, you know. And he's Joey's daddy. Johnny, doesn't matter he lives here or there, he's fine. Anyway, he's my mom's now, though she don't want him no more. But Joey, who's gonna love him unless his mommy and daddy do? Steve's part Indian. My mom says I am, too, Shoshone on my dad's side. That's why I'm so big; they're big fat people. Fry bread and shit."

"Uh uh. No. Dad's Jewish. My mom's English and Greek, that's why my name is Apollonia. We might have some Gypsy. But not Indian."

"Nah, I'm talking about my other dad, Jumbo. Want me to French braid your hair? Go get a brush, and if you got any hair ties."

"But you can only have one dad of your blood," Polly said when she came back with her brush and ponytail clips. ("Is your homework all done? her mother asked. "Almost. Or I can finish tomorrow. But she's going to do my hair up, it only takes a minute I think.") "You can be adopted, but there's only one father of your blood, and one mother of your blood."

Amber patted the loveseat next to her then held out her hand for the brush. "You know how dogs can have different dads for the same litter? I'm not saying I'm a dog, and I'm not saying I'm a litter. But my mama had herself a wild weekend and there was three she's telling me about, and maybe they're all a bit of a part of me. For real, I don't know who the real dog was, but it's okay. Gives me options."

"But don't you need to know? Or want to?"

"Not really. You want two braids or one down the middle?"

"Um, two braids." She leaned her head in, and Amber began brushing.

"So, Stan's been most my daddy because he stayed with my mom awhile and changed my diapers; anyways took my dirty diapers in the trash can out to the curb. But she dumped him and he moved back to California. He don't help with money, but he might help with his van. You ever get into trouble, you call Stan the Man with the Van. My mom says you have to know which dad is which.

"And," she said, brushing firmly, "then Jumbo, but I ain't no Indian dog. Those Indian ladies are scary, and they like their beer. Jumbo's somewhere North, but he's maybe where I get my Sight. This psychic in Winnamucca told me this one time that I had the Sight, that I just needed to develop it. Then I had Joey, and he's a retard from the chemicals but he's got the Sight, you can tell by his eyes." She began the right braid, pulling Polly's hair tight across her scalp.

"Then there's your daddy. I think he's my real father, and my mom always told me he is too. Even though I don't look like him and I don't look like you. I didn't weigh what you weigh since I was Johnny's age. My mom told me that Adam was my ace, and you don't go showing your ace around all the time. That he was kinda a wimp, not a real man, but rich and pretty good looking and he would take care of me when I really needed it—but to be careful not to push too hard. He's the only one who done shit for me—he sent me five thousand dollars when I got arrested. Only a real father would do that. But maybe that's because he's Jewish, so he's rich."

"We're not rich! And we're not really that Jewish, my mom's not, and they're always worried about going out to dinner, and how much everything costs nowadays." And my dad's not a wimp! she thought. And wondered if she should tell her parents about all this. But how would she explain?

Amber shook her head. "Little rich girl. You don't even know what not having money is. Tip your head." The braiding was really going fast now, pull, pull, pull, *yank*, as she worked her way around her right ear and down. "Your hair's a little hard cause it's Jewish nappy and you got so much of it. But I do it all, even the nigger hair on my friend Tricia."

Polly jerked up. "You can't say the n-word, that's racist!"

"She's my friend, she don't care. Tilt again."

"I bet she does care."

"Well, she is a nigger. If an Indian's a dog I call them a dog. If you got nappy hair, I call it nappy. Just like I'm a fat ugly trailer trash bastard, and Joey's a retard, and you're a rich Jewish princess. Are you gonna tilt?"

It was all wrong, and it made her feel weird and terrible. But she didn't know how to explain it right.

"You do got it tough, though," Amber said. "Better you than me, living here, all the time careful about how you talk, what you say."

"But I thought you wanted to live here."

"Nah. Might be okay for Johnny though."

Tug, tug, tug, *yank,* tug. "You got those bands? Okay, now switch sides with me." Polly stood, Amber moved over, and Polly sat down again on the other side of her.

"I still think it's weird having three dads."

"None of them is really my dad, though. You're lucky. Your dad might not lift a finger to help me no more, but you get to be his little girl forever. Don't be a spoiled brat, now."

"I'm not a spoiled brat." But Nell had called her that, too, because she got stuff she wanted. So maybe she was spoiled. Maybe not compared to Nell who just *wanted* everything, but compared to Amber and Joey. Compared to Johnny who came from Elko where people were racist and poor, and she didn't even know if he liked it there.

❧ ADAM

In the early evening, Adam folded the tri-fold futon, dragged it back up the narrow stairs, and leaned it against the hallway wall. Kira in the bedroom. Amber's voice from the living room sounding so much like Sandi's, the dryer in the basement rotating towels ka*chunk* ka*chunk,* Polly and Johnny and Joey quiet. Having them back again—Joey and Johnny on the futon in the guest room, Amber on the couch—put him and Kira back into bed together. Fine, he thought. Circumstance was forcing the issue, fate putting him back where he belonged. Le Troll was out from under le bridge again.

"What exactly did you tell her?" Kira asked.

"That it wasn't a good time, that I'm taking her back to her mom's house. That we'd talk—you and I—about if we could help them out a little but that we had our hands full here. Can you move your arm a little? Thanks."

"Adam, how are we going to help them out when we're totally screwed financially right now?"

"How many times do I need to apologize?"

"I'm not picking another fight. But you need to call Sandi and find out what's really going on, not just drive five hundred miles and dump Amber and the kids in the middle of Eastern Nevada. 'Cause she'll come back. Okay? Plus, she's not a child, she's in her mid-twenties, she's done hard time, and we keep treating her like she's a helpless teenager or something. I feel so bad for that little boy Johnny. He seems sweet."

"Stop. I'll call Sandi." He put his arm over her. For a moment her body stayed rigid, then she backed up a few inches so they were touching.

"They sure are getting cozy, Amber and Polly," Kira said. "Wonder what Polly's making of it."

"Polly's smart, she's got good values. She can handle whatever hick bullshit comes out of that mouth."

"Adam, she's not very well educated but she's not stupid."

"No, believe me, I don't think she's stupid. She's got street smarts. Desert smarts. But Polly's got smarts, too."

Kira was soft and sleepy against him. "Night, sweetie," she murmured.

"Night, mon amour."

☙ POLLY

"Look, I'm not about to watch football," her mom told her dad after brunch. "You all go ahead. I'm not sure what's wrong with me. Maybe just the weekend. I'm just so tired. I'm going to lie down, okay?"

It was an "Amurican" party, her dad said, and he went to the store and got Ruffles and Cheez-its and a six-pack of Coors and some watery fake guacamole and spray cheese and RITZ crackers. "I don't think our guests get the irony of this," he said to her as he set up the food in the kitchen. "But middle-American cuisine has its own aesthetic, and I'm sorry, if I'm going to watch football, I gotta do it with a can of beer in my hand. Voila! I got you and the boys ze orange Fanta."

Her leg still throbbed, her special secret. It wasn't too bad if she put most of her weight on her right leg. She wondered what it looked like now under the gauze, if it would infect, and if it would scar. But her dad was out of the underworld.

They all sat on the floor in the living room and snacked. "There's ants in the bathroom," Amber announced after the first quarter.

"Just wipe them up with Simple Green under the sink," Polly said. "That's what we do."

"I can't deal with bugs," Amber said. "You can't just wipe them, you gotta spray them."

"Yes, we have ant poison," her dad said. "We'd prefer not to use it. Just wipe them up. They're just looking for high ground, a way to get out of the storm."

Polly went in to pee. The chrome around the side of the shower was black and moving. "*Daddy!* There's so many! A whole thick trail!"

He went to get the ant poison from the basement, and Johnny followed him downstairs. "Okay everybody, stay out of the bathroom for a few minutes until this dissipates. I've got the window open and the door closed."

"Hey Joey, want some ooey gluey cheesy Cheez Whiz?" she sat down next to him and offered him a RITZ. "Do you want me to do his eye drops, Amber?"

"Nah, he's okay. Make friends with Johnny, okay? Johnny needs somebody to play with."

"Okay. Sigh. Hey, Johnny, can I look at your Kirop?"

On the TV where the Superbowl was, it was not raining. Outside the big storm had come in. "Le Yin, Le Yang. We'll make something organic for dinner," her dad said.

"Is the ant poison gone enough? Can I pee?"

"Go ahead, Pol."

She flushed and the toilet overflowed. "*Daddy!*"

Her mom woke up from her nap and came in. "Hey, *Adam!* Bring those funky towels, would you?"

Polly heard her mom plunging over the roar of the game, but in a while she came out, a grossed out look on her face, her hands away from her body, and said, "I think I just made it worse. Call the plumber!" Her mom went into the kitchen to wash her hands.

Polly wasn't that interested in the game, so she stayed with her dad in the dining room while he went through the Yellow Pages—first they had to find it in the pile of stuff on the table. Then he called at least three places before one answered. From the living room, Johnny's and Amber's voices, "TOUCHDOWN!"

"*What!* Two hundred and thirty-six dollars? Are you out of your skull? Uh huh, uh huh. Okay, we'll call you back." He hung up. "Superbowl Sunday. Double-time. Jesus. Ants. Plumbing. Not to mention…," he flicked his chin towards the living room then stood up sighing and went in there. Polly followed. "Bathroom's off-limits for a while again. Maybe it'll settle down. I'll throw some Liquid Plumber down there."

"Don't do that, call Stan," Amber said.

"Nah."

He went back into the kitchen. Polly followed again. She didn't want to be with the relatives.

"Good idea," said her mom. "Stan's got everything. Maybe he has a snake."

Stan had a snake; "But he's watching the game and he's not leaving." Her dad came back into the kitchen. He grabbed a double handful of Ruffles from the open bag. "I'll be back with Le Snake. Le Snake for la toilette."

"Okay, that's enough! What's up with the fake French these days?" her mom asked, smiling a little. "Adam, you're dropping crumbles."

Her dad gave a fake French shrug, hands out, elbows close to his sides. And her mom snorted and turned away. But she seemed to be in a better mood than she had been since the fighting had started. Even with the ants and the relatives and the plumbing. Which didn't make sense. Unless the magic of the Eye was starting to work, a slow bloom.

Now Polly watched the game again. Which she didn't really

understand the rules of. Her leg throbbed and burned and she wanted to check it but she was afraid it would start bleeding if she unpeeled the gauze, and then she'd be gone a long time and people might come find her.

"Come help me get this thing out of the car?" her dad said, coming back into the house. "It's really heavy." Commercials were on, so they all went outside. "You're all getting wet, you don't all need to help," he said. The rooter was in a little cart in the back seat of the Prius sitting on spread-out newspapers. "Let's get this on the porch. Can you help, Polly? I'll look online how to use it."

"Nah, don't bring that in the house," Amber said. "I can do it. Where's your cleanout?"

"I have no idea," her mom shrugged. "We just usually call the plumber. Polly, go back in the house, you're getting wet."

"I don't care," Polly said.

"I want to see, too," Johnny said.

First Amber got some tools from the basement with her dad, then they all walked around the house until they found the cleanout, and Amber unbolted the cap. Water gushed out. Then she switched on the machine and stuck the cable down. "It's just a soft blockage," she said after a few moments. "I got it."

"Thank you," her mom said. "I'm impressed." She looked relieved.

"Yes, thanks a lot," her dad said. "I can't believe they wanted two hundred thirty-six bucks for that. Sports-crazed Amuricans."

"They always charge more on weekends," her mom said. "And I guess because it's the Superbowl."

"Pretty stupid to spend more than two hundred bucks for only that," Amber said.

"Yeah," her mom said. She looked really happy. The magic of the Eye was definitely working now, and Polly loved her.

"Mommy, can I hug you?" Her mother opened her arms, and Polly gave her a huge hug, careful to keep her leg out of the way, and they stood hugging even though the rain was really starting to pour, and laughing at how long they were hugging outside in the rain, for a long time.

CHAPTER 16

Kira and Adam held each other. "What a day. Ants and toilets. Like the house is exploding under us," she said.

His hand moved to her breast, resting, palm against her nipple. "Just be here with me. Feel me."

She sighed. Habit, connection, emotion, history, fate, whatever. He fit so well against her. She thought of the Buddhist Sylvia Boorstein—'It's not what I wanted, but it's what I've got.' "Make love to me?" she wanted to hold this peace even if just for the moment.

"You betcha, baby."

But, "What do you have in there, teeth?" he asked—pulling out after several deep thrusts. She put her fingers inside herself to check her IUD string. She felt a plastic knob coming out of her cervix. "Oh no, my IUD must be coming out."

"What? How does it do that?"

"I don't know. It's not supposed to."

"Fuck," he flopped on his back. "Does it hurt you?"

She shook her head.

"Well, it hurt me." He made a face.

"Really?"

"Nah. Maybe a little. Just felt a little hard in a very tender spot. How about a gentle rub?"

"I think we can arrange that." He folded his arms behind his head as she reached for the lube. "But now I have to go the clinic.

218

This is crazy."

"Shh. Do your wifely duty." The words a caress.

"Oh shut up," she said. "Just 'cause we can't fuck right now doesn't mean it's not your turn next."

"You do your wifely duty, and then I'll do my husbandly duty." He flicked his tongue rapidly at her, smiled as her hand moved on his penis.

So good to be back on track with each other, even if just for a moment.

✣ POLLY

Her leg barely hurt at all, only when she accidentally bumped it getting in and out of the desks at school. At home, she made sure not to limp. Life was actually better now that the relatives were here again. Her parents couldn't fight as much, her mom was smiling, her dad wasn't hanging out in the basement. They'd had to eat dinner together Saturday and Sunday and now Monday, and they were eating real food again, not just quick pastas and take-out. Not counting the Amurican food fest.

Her parents were being so nice to the relatives, letting them eat junk in the house. Diet Pepsi in the refrigerator, though when she asked her mom if she could have one, she just said, "Polly." And that was that. "What would happen if we took them to Café Gratitude tonight?" she asked her dad, trying to make him laugh.

He did, a little short "Ha!" Her mom wouldn't have laughed— she would have just looked exasperated: "Polly. We can't afford to take all these people out to dinner anymore." Missing the point entirely.

They came from Elko, Nevada, and they were going back there. Her dad was driving them back. Five hundred miles exactly. She sat at the kitchen table and did her math homework with her mom. When she wasn't looking, Polly used her erasable pen to trace her own journeys on her arm. East to the Sierra for camping and back home, every summer. Down to Disneyland. Up to Seattle once. Down to Mexico. Back home. And over here, right on this freckle, Elko, where Amber lived. She loved the sound of the word "Elko," like elks and cowboys, horses and rodeos, dust and sagebrush and tumbleweed.

"Why can't I come to Elko?" Polly asked her dad before dinner.

"Numero one, school. Numero two, room in car."

"Does Johnny go to school at all?" she asked.

"I don't think he goes much."

She'd never been to Nevada. Except the places on her arm, they rarely went anywhere outside the Bay Area. Some years up to Tahoe or just Donner Summit for a snow trip. But mostly on the same line: up and down and a little to the side. Cutting a groove up and down and east, the repeated cut scarring. Was this on purpose? Her mom and dad talked about living in a bubble, and the scary world outside their safe environment, where people were religious fundamentalists and voted for religious fanatics and gave the country a bad name. But just east beyond the tunnel, just over there in Orinda, Pleasanton, Walnut Creek, it started. Amurica.

The kids at school—oh, Jordan's family was Republican, and that kid who loved guns so much who graduated a couple of years ago (*not* a friend of Polly's)—but everybody else joined in war protests and thrift-shopped for peace sign pendants from the '60s. They talked about diversity, but though Etani was black and Amanda's dad was Guatemalan and there were lots of Asian kids in her school, mostly adopted from China with white moms, they all seemed the same as the white kids, except those parents were not as interested in organics and yoga and stuff. But now, in her own family, Amber and Joey and Johnny, and they were not the same at all.

After everybody had gone to bed Monday, Polly started to worry. Her leg throbbed. She knew you had to clean wounds but it had been three days and she was afraid to look. If she opened the bandage alone and it was gangrenous, she might pass out. Brady would know. But that was not an option.

Her mom and dad silent in their bedroom, the boys in the guest room. Amber was sleeping on the couch. But when Polly peeked in the living room, Amber wasn't there.

On the porch, Amber stood smoking, blowing smoke out into the rain.

"Hey," Polly said. "Can I come out?"

"Your porch."

"Um, I want to show you something, okay?"

Amber looked at her.

"It's on my leg. It's a secret."

Amber stubbed out her cigarette on the railing and put the butt in her pocket. "You gonna show me?"

"Not *here*."

Amber had never been in her room. Joey or Johnny either. She had never invited them, and they had never asked. Amber wasn't that fat even though her dad always muttered about it, but she was bigger than her mom and dad and as she stood near the bed, near the bookshelves, near the bureau and the desk and the chair piled high with clothes, the small space in the middle of the room, the room seemed even smaller, and somehow dingy and dark, despite the overhead light.

"Shh," Polly said. "Don't look yet." She took off her slippers and then her pajama bottoms, tied her robe closer around her, and held up her left leg. The gauze had a blotch of dull red dried blood.

"You hurt yourself?"

"Look."

"Oh, girl," Amber said. "I'm gonna pass out. I can't look at blood."

"No, it's okay. It's old, it didn't just happen right this minute," Polly said. She rested her foot on her desk chair, touching her bandage then peeling off the tape slowly, wincing. She unwound the gauze. Unwrapping the mummy. Amber stood in the middle of the room, looking like she was holding her breath. It stuck a little at the end, but she closed her eyes: be brave be brave.

Then they were both looking at her wound in swollen red lines, the toothpaste pink from blood and crusted up, but the wound itself perfect, as if it had always been there and she'd only stripped away the covering; a wound so close to the surface, protected only by her skin. The Eye of Thoth.

"What's that goo? Pus?"

"No. Toothpaste."

Amber sat down on the bed with a thump. "No, girl. That's not okay. Don't you be a cutter. Cutters are rich girls who don't have enough normal to worry about."

Polly felt a wave of dismay. Again the *rich* accusation. This wasn't about that. She had honored Joey, and then they had shown up. She had needed her mom to realize what she was doing, and then they'd laughed so hard and her mom and dad were getting along again. It was magic, and it had worked.

"I'm not a cutter. This is scarification. It's like tattoos. Body art. It's esthetic. It has power. You have tattoos."

"Don't you shit me, Polly. It's cutting."

Suddenly she wanted to giggle. "So you're saying it's cutting no matter which way you slice it?"

Amber didn't laugh. "It's nothing to laugh at. You want pain?" She stood up in the middle of the room again and lifted her shirt. "See this? Emergency C-section for Joey. It's up and down instead of across because they had to do it so fast." She pulled down her shirt and pulled up her left sleeve. A huge thick white V near her shoulder, the skin around it puckered and sewn back mismatched. Polly's stomach lurched.

"Barbed wire tear. Running from assholes who set the dogs on us. Seen enough?"

Polly nodded. Amber pulled her sleeve down.

"I used to like tattoos and I got some but now I think it's stupid, letting somebody make you hurt like that. In prison, they got girls who will cut you. For real. Not like cop shows. Not like rich kids doing body mod. Johnny's got a scar from where somebody threw a rock at him for saying don't make fun of my brother. You get your scars for things that mean something."

The scars were terrible. Polly took her foot off the chair and put it on the floor. Her robe closed over her leg. "Be quiet, please, don't wake up my mom and dad, okay?"

Amber sat down again. She lowered her voice. "You only get a certain number of lives before you die, like a cat. You might of used up one of your lives. Only spoiled rich girls hurt themselves like that."

Polly started to cry. She melted down to the floor. "You're into tattoos. I thought you'd understand."

"Your folks don't know, do they."

She shook her head. Her parents would say "Oh no!" and "Poor Polly!" And blame themselves and take her to a therapist. Her dad would cry. Her mom would fret. And at night she'd hear them worry about how much money the therapist cost and whether they should put her on meds or weird supplements. She shook her head again. Amber shook her head. They both stood there shaking their heads.

"Are you going to tell?"

"I won't tell them if you promise me you won't do it again."

Hard to talk crying: "I actually don't like how it looks when people are all sliced and diced. I just wanted *one*. A little one."

"Promise."

"I did it, I got my one. That's all. I promise." She meant it. "I might still get a tattoo when I'm eighteen, though."

"You need help cleaning that up?"

Polly shook her head. She needed Kleenex.

"Keep it clean, put some ointment on it every day. Try and get it some air. It'll heal right up. Might scar some. But you want that, don't you." She shook her head again at Polly. "Stupid." She stood up again and opened the bedroom door. "Clean it up and go to bed. You got school, a good school. Don't mess it all up."

Polly took a few more sobs and then stopped crying. She looked at her face in the mirror in the bathroom for a long time, eyes swollen, nose red. She washed her face with water. Her eyes stung more than her leg, now just a low, dull throb. She blotted her wound with wet toilet paper to get off some of the blood and toothpaste. Then she squeezed more toothpaste on the area (it stung a bit), spread it gently, and re-bandaged it. She felt calm.

There were things so powerful you only did them once, and if you did them again, they were just things that you did. At restaurants they called it "first-time-itis." When the restaurant was a discovery and you couldn't believe how delicious everything was. Her dad patting his belly and saying over and over again in the car home, "Not one false note!" and her mom saying, "I could eat there every night for a month." And then they'd go back, and it was good, but it wasn't as good, and one of the appetizers wasn't gelled in the middle like it was supposed to, and there *was* a false note. And then on the way home they were disappointed. And then they'd go again, and they'd start knowing how to order, and then they were regulars, and it was just part of the cycle.

Scarification was like that, she thought. If she did it again, she'd just be a cutter. One of those sad emo girls from Piedmont who sat in waiting rooms at Kaiser huddled in their jackets even in summer. That's not what she was about. Amber was right. She was done. It was over.

◎ ADAM

He didn't call Sandi. He couldn't deal. What, ask Amber for her number and explain that he and her mom were deciding her fate? What, call Stan and explain why he needed the number? What, call Sandi and explain why he'd shined her on all those times she'd left worried messages about Amber? Technology had its uses, but there was nothing like face-to-face confrontation. He'd arrive, he'd get the lay of the land, he'd figure out what to do.

They left mid-morning Tuesday, Cheetos and Slim Jims and all, a scrambled morning of getting shit together after Kira and Polly headed off to Berkeley. Clear weather over the mountains, the weather report said. Good, he had no tire chains. He rummaged his cherrywood box for supplies and came up dry. How would he get through it, no Percs to pop? In Kira's bedside table, he found her bottle of codeine. If necessary. He foresaw headaches, slid the bottle into his pocket. Stan had nothing scheduled for them until Friday; he'd be back by then.

They were out of the house by 10:45, the Prius seeming stuffed with four people despite the small amount of luggage—Amber's two Samsonites and Adam's backpack; only 501 miles to Elko, a straight shot on 80 East. Hard to get lost.

The first half hour was quiet in the car, monkey brain in the head. Amber looked out the window, Adam negotiated the traffic on 580 and 80 through Berkeley, Pinole, Benicia, Vallejo. He was a father bird distracting danger away from his nest. He was dragging away these bad spirits; bad for the family, for him… though they didn't mean to be. All had been well until they arrived. All would be well once they were well gone. He was the huntsman, going to take Snow White into the forest to kill her—he wouldn't do that. But he would leave her deep in the forest, in the desert, in Elko, with Sandi.

"When we get to Lovelock, that's like tomorrow, the bus always stops there, they have more jerky than any other place. The kids like that, okay?" Amber said.

A rack of beef jerky. Whatever. Two days of this. Sleep in Reno? If it was as he remembered it, Reno casinos had cheap rooms, loss leaders, places for kids to play while their parents pursued desperation. Hope, hope, hope on the roulette table, yes or no, win or lose.

Peppermill. Harrah's. Circus Circus. Silver Legacy. Sands Regency. Atlantis. Boomtown. El Dorado, where First Man had gigged, where he'd knocked up—*maybe maybe baby* knocked up—Sandi. Did Amber know?

If he brought Amber back, if he talked to Sandi, maybe it would stick, they'd get it: Not from me, I'm tapped out. Relationships have to be a two-way street. He wondered what Sandi would look like now, more than twenty years later of hard life. Matronly, a nurse's aide in a cowboy town, big hair, make-up and fingernails? Still a freckled waif, wrinkling now in that tight scrawny way some women got? He wondered how different he looked; less hair, bigger belly. The lines around his eyes. They hadn't aged so well, Stan and he. All those years of decrepit living. Kira still looked so great because of her yoga, the best-feeling skin in the world… oh hell. Don't think about it.

Three separate times he'd slept with Sandi. That infamous party weekend, the band all teasing each other that now they had groupies—gropies, as Stan called them—they must be really on their way to the big time. A weekend at the El Dorado 1849 Saloon. How the hell had they pulled it off landing that gig? Not Nevada material, SF garage band-punk, pre-grunge. The cowboys hated them, not even enough to throw bottles at them, they sneered as they strode by, all boot, buckle, and hat. Crowds never materialized, but in the front of a lot of empty tables, a couple of girls who wanted to get to SF but stayed stuck in Nevada: Sandi and oh-hell-what-was-her-name? who didn't stick around after, though Sandi did. Danced wildly through both sets the first night, tiny tits in a tight tee-shirt and cute cowgirl jeans. So drunk, he fucked her in the gratis room on the floor between the double beds, and the next night she was with Jumbo, and maybe Stan, he wasn't sure—that whole weekend so fucked up on Jim Beam— no pot (paranoid of Nevada, another state). "I wanna have your baby," she'd said. So stupid. To whip it out anyway, fuck her any-way… and then again that morning of the last day, up against an alley wall, "I wanna have your baby," she'd said again. "What?" Sober enough to realize. "Aren't you on the pill?" "Oh yeah. I'm on the pill." What kind of pill was that, Sandi? A pre-natal vita-min? And then the third time, in San Francisco in the Stanyan Street apartment, baby in the corner in a nest of Indian fabric the week before Stan sublet to Dave and followed Sandi back for six months before she dumped his sorry ass… Three times. Because she was cute, because she was into him, because she made him feel like a rock star. How pathetic.

"Can we stop to get something to eat here?" Amber said as they passed through Davis.

"Ma, I have to go to the bathroom."

"Yeah, we'll do that, too," she said.

"Wait a bit," he said.

"But I've really got to go!"

"Okay, Johnny, but it's only been an hour. We can't stop every hour, we'll never get there." He drove through the Sacramento valley, foothills. He pulled off in Auburn. At Ikeda's, he bought them all hamburgers and onion rings.

Into the mountains, green trees turning to white, the sky colored like nothing, the highway clear but icy, dirty snow piled high on the sides. A terrible wreck just outside Truckee, a long hauler and a t-boned SUV curled like a comma or a question: what next when all is lost? And a man with hair circling a bald spot, his face buried in his hands, sitting and rocking alone on the side of the road. Emergency vehicles already on scene. The kids watched quietly through the window, Amber put her face in her hands: "I can't look at blood." Just another few hours, then they'd be over and down into Reno—used to be cute in a dragged-out way, quaint despair, the underbelly so much more in evidence than Vegas— and then, tomorrow, the long straight flat of nothingness desert, bleak as future, cold and rain and snow flurries, driving a carload of people he'd rather not know existed.

Amber quiet in the front, eyes shut. He'd get them there, talk to Sandi, say goodbye, drive back and fix things with Kira. He'd forget about her yoga fuck. They'd solve the money problem, he'd get out from under the depression, he'd done it before. Alone, on the way back, he'd be able to numb out, surf the country music stations and not have to talk or respond to anybody.

Hours of napping, all three of them, Polly's old pink baby

blanket over Joey's head to shield his naked eyes from the light, and he tuned in radio station after station, Sacramento heavy metal lasting until way past the Tahoe turnoff (Highway to Hell!), barren snow-covered hillsides remnant of the huge wildfire last summer. Down through Toiyabe National Forest on the Eastern side of the Sierra, arriving in Reno just after sunset.

✎ KIRA

Tuesday morning, Kira called in to The Center to let Sarah know she'd be late. Again.

"Do you want me to start sending the packets out to the advisory board?" Sarah asked.

"Sure. That would be great." Her head so far from work that she frightened herself. If she couldn't pull it together, if she lost her job, they were sunk.

She dropped Polly at Lindsey's for a tag team carpool and drove to the downtown Oakland clinic, a dingy office in a dingy building on Pill Hill, where the young nurse told Kira her IUD was almost half out—natural expulsion sometimes happened—but that they'd have to remove it now. "How long have you had this IUD?" The woman snapped off her latex glove, tossed it in the garbage and washed her hands using the foot peddles on the sink.

Kira sat up, retrieved the blue plastic drape sliding towards the floor. So hard to be dignified half naked on a table with stirrups. "Not so long, like six months or so."

The woman stood next to her. She wore that compassionate "therapist face" that Kira hated.

"I thought the IUD was very effective—I got pregnant twice on the Pill. Second one's my daughter. This was supposed to last twelve years, my 'final solution.'" The woman didn't get the joke.

"It sometimes happens. We need to remove this because it's

about half way out. But if you were pregnant, you would probably lose the pregnancy or there's a big chance of the fetus suffering damage—birth defects."

"Go ahead and take it out."

The woman dispensed another pair of purple latex gloves, and snapped them into place on her hands.

"Lie back again."

It hurt like hell. Not worth it anymore, the agony getting it in, the weeks of cramping, now the discomfort getting it out. Back to the diaphragm, Kira decided. Not condoms. She'd never be able to broach condoms with Adam, not after the thing with Ravi. Tender bellied, she scheduled an appointment for a fitting.

Kira had to get back to work, despite womb ache. Feeling so bad, her period still not here, a few days, a week late? Eight days late? The days of digestive problems… nausea. Burping. Her sore breasts. Her hunger. Oh shit. Pregnant.

But no, she was forty-six, so not pregnant. Impossible. Menopause. But just in case, she stopped at Longs to get an EPT. She did the math in her head. Her period a week late, so conception about three weeks ago. So if she was pregnant, it couldn't be Ravi, they'd had sex only eleven days ago, with a condom, and he hadn't come. So Adam. But when? No. Menopause.

Feeling foolish as she undid the plastic wrapper in the bathroom at work, peeing on the stick and watching as, almost instantly, her future pulled into view. Two bright red lines.

Pregnant.

"The final egg."

She vomited in the sink.

Two lines on a stick. And an hour before she needed to pick up

Polly and the other girls. Kira drove to the Mountain View cemetery and parked high on the hill, near where the deer ran, where at dusk red foxes peered from drainage holes. High above the acres of stone monuments, crypts, tombstones, memorials. The day on the verge of rain.

She sat in the car, pulled the seat back. Queasy. She did the math in her head again. It must be Adam's. What would she tell him?

But if somehow it were Ravi's. If they had made a baby; a pretty baby, his dark hair, her blue eyes. Her light brown hair, his black eyes. Like Polly, only… no. The thought was terrible. One thing to cheat on Adam—she hadn't—another to cheat on Polly. Another child?

Another child was one thing—they could do that. But this would be a baby.

A baby. Little feet, the endless nursing that filled and subtracted. The impossible love of that eye lock, nipple deep in his mouth. Polly as a newborn, that heaviness on her chest, "Open your eyes, little baby."

How to have another baby, and how to not have another baby? Not ever? The weight of time pressed her back on the seat. If this was true, if she was pregnant, this was the last time in her life. How strange to be feeling so infertile, so old, even as she stared at the two lines on the stick in her lap. Could it be a false positive? But there were no false positives. You either had the pregnancy hormone or you didn't. She rechecked the packaging. Two lines = positive. Pregnant. How to tell Adam? And why now, this moment, the money the porn the drugs and Amber and Joey and Johnny…

The warm feel of Joey on her lap, of Johnny leaning against her for the moment, "Grandma Kira? Wanna play with my Bionicles?"

How did she feel? She tried to check in with herself, shutting her eyes to the scenery below her in the cemetery. Nothing, her heart as dead as the granite and marble monuments below her crumbling gently under weather and decades.

She'd continue the pregnancy, have a baby. How absurd. If nothing went wrong. But the IUD. And what if it came out wrong? The hot pool at Harbin, 116 degrees. The full glass of vodka—fetal alcohol syndrome. She could do a child. But a disabled child, a child like Joey… Nine months of hard pregnancy and then heartbreak. A special needs child. No.

"The baby shop is closed," she'd told Polly when she was seven, begging for a little sister. Her life. Their life together, her and Adam and Polly. This world and its troubles. An absurd thing to consider a baby at all—she'd lose it anyway now, her cervix already opened by the IUD removal, the little boy weight of Joey, his delicate hands, his damaged baby bird face. Another damaged child.

No, she could not have a baby.

Not a baby, and not this baby.

Kira looked over the monuments, snapped the radio on for the comfort of a live human voice. War talk. She snapped it off.

And yet not ever another D & C, a waiting room with impoverished sixteen year olds, nausea and Valium, Adam pacing in the waiting room. Not like that, the breeching and shock of it, professionally kind strangers, the wrench of sudden death. Not another abortion. Absolutely not. None of it.

No baby. No abortion. No pregnancy. Just. No.

CHAPTER 17

♭ KIRA

But things didn't stop just because you needed them to, and it was her turn to drive carpool. The pregnancy test stowed safely in her purse, Kira sat in the car outside the school until Polly came out, followed by Nell and Amanda, all three girls with multicolor pen all over their arms and hands—spider webs, fake tattoos. Backpacks and sweaters in the trunk, they climbed in. Tired kids, the traffic on Martin Luther King on the way to 580; traffic not stopped but stagnant, no flow, so she had to really focus. Polly in the front seat, Nell and Amanda in the back, long legs twisted.

"What's that on your arms, honey?"

"Body art," Polly said. "Amanda did me, and Nell did Amanda, and then she did herself. Like it?"

"I hope it's washable."

"It's Sharpie, it will wear off."

"Oh, great. Sharpie."

"Didn't you ever do anything like that when you were our age?"

"Oh, probably. I was the first girl at my high school to wear safety pins through my ears. But that was just like earrings, I just dulled the ends and stuck them through my earring holes."

"*You* were a punk?" Amanda asked.

"My dad was part of the San Francisco Underground," Polly said. "Did you ever hear of First Man? They're famous in Eastern Europe."

"That's so cool," Amanda said. "You guys were so cool when you were young."

Especially Adam, Kira thought. Grinning wide, pounding out the beat of music everywhere, the rhythm of the road when they drove in the old Lincoln, howling with the chorus of evening dogs out his and Stan's Shrader Street apartment window, his charisma on stage, Sheila behind him looking fierce, bass, bass, bass; Jumbo on sax, Stan wailing on the drums.

"And my mom was a groupie."

"You *were?*" Awe. Amanda leaned forward and stared at Kira.

"Not really, Amanda. There's a big difference between band girlfriend and groupie."

"There *is?*"

"Mommy, did you bring anything for us to eat?"

"We're going to go home and make dinner. Moussaka." As if she could eat now.

"But they didn't give us any kind of snack at Drama." Nell said.

"Don't they usually?" I'll call him tonight, she thought; tonight he's in Reno, tomorrow Elko, he'll drive home Thursday; drive fast without the kids, home Thursday night. They'd deal with this together, cry, hold each other. Big problems trumped smaller problems, and they'd set the money, Ravi, to the side, come back later, after the crisis.

"Yeah, but snack always sucks," Amanda said. "Like graham crackers like we're five. Today Ms. Felice let us run up to Starbucks before Drama."

"So you're all drinking coffee now?" She pictured them in a few years, draped over rattan chairs in Paris cafés sipping demi-tasses, looking carefully blasé but filled with adventure and hope. Save them from the pitfalls, she thought. Amber. Pregnant at 18, barely out of Elko and now sent back. She wanted to lean over the back seat and kiss each girl on the forehead, a blessing to keep them safe through the years of cheap beer and pushy boys and "cool." So much loveliness ahead of them, so many pitfalls.

Sucking in a deep breath, not thinking about the plastic strip, two pink lines.

"Well, *yeah*, I drink coffee," Polly said. "When you let me."

"I get herb tea," Amanda said. "Mint or chamomile."

"I get decaf," Nell said.

Not thinking about it. Not thinking about it.

"I get coffee," Polly said. "I drink it black."

"Polly, did I 'let' you?"

"You weren't there. I used my judgment. Dad lets me."

"Oh great," Kira said. But if she called Adam now and the test was wrong… No. She'd wait until she was sure. Were they in Reno yet? (His tender hands sliding down her body just last Saturday night, fitting so well… when *had* she conceived?)

"And then she got so caffeinated," Nell said.

"You should have seen her," Amanda said. "She sneezed in English and fell off her chair."

"Yeah! I'm like, 'I know, I know!' and I raise my hand and sneeze and went *down!*" Polly said.

Nell reenacted, "'I know! I know!' KABOOM! And it was so funny."

"Now *that* was embarrassing," Polly said.

"Great," Kira said again. Stopped at yet another stoplight (where is all this traffic coming from?), she made it to the corner and spontaneously turned left, breaking out of the traffic, galumphing the Saab over speed bumps just to fight the claustrophobia.

I'll call him once I'm sure. He's got too much on his plate.

"Mommy, this is the wrong way. Why are we going this way?"

"Just for a change."

ꙮ ADAM

They got to Reno just before he felt he'd lose it, shout, and weave the car on purpose just to break them out of their dullness. Amber wanted to go to Circus Circus—she'd leave the kids in the arcade watching the circus acts, hit the slots (with whose money, he wondered) but he was in a bad mood. "This is not a vacation."

"I didn't want to come here."

"I know, Amber. But unless you come up with another plan."

"This is *your* plan." And she slumped back in the seat.

Barren hills beneath the Sierra, green from the rains, patchy white from snow. A glop of metropolis on the edge of the endless desert, carved from the thick of cattle ranch. On the edge of town, he picked the diviest motel that didn't look rat and whore infested. "We're here, we're sleeping, we're leaving tomorrow early." Pulling into the lot.

"This hellhole? Cathouse putting on a good act," Amber said. "You wouldn't make Polly stay here."

So, deeper into town, down the strip. The lights! Brilliant against the overcast sky. Driving down the four-casino strip, a mini-Vegas, a surge of excitement, road trip! They were on an adventure. Reno so changed! Glitz! Glamour! He reached for his cell phone to call Polly, "Polly! I've got to bring you here!" But Johnny only stared out the window. He looked over at Amber, the lights no more affecting her than the mountains. Of course, this was home for them, Nevada. Casinos. He put down his phone. Did anything rouse this young woman from her stupor, a zombie through life? And that's why she couldn't be his daughter, no energy. "No, Sandi," he wanted to tell that young woman she'd been—what would she be like now?—"Baby Amber is *not* just like me." He'd see Sandi again tomorrow after the endless winter desert nightmare of it all.

He turned left and left and back through the arch, The Biggest Little City in the World. A quick nod to the Thunderbird Motel, "There okay?"

"You really want these kids sleeping there? Would you take Polly there?"

"Yes, I would, actually. But fine." Tomorrow would be the last day of her. He took another left and pulled into the Circus Circus turnaround. It was $85 with the AAA discount and before tax but what the hell. Give them a little fun. He forked over the American Express for the cheapest room with two queen-sized beds, high in the towers on the 21st floor, the smell of smoke and cleaning solvents permeating even the mirrored and red-flocked elevator. "Honest Injun!" a woman walking past the elevator exclaimed to her husband as the doors slid open, and Adam smiled: they weren't in the Bay Area anymore.

Amber squawked about sharing the room, sharing the bed with Joey. "Don't I even get my own room? You're sick, wanting to sleep with your daughter."

He snapped. "Amber, there's two big beds. We all have pajamas, it's like a camping trip. You'll share the bed with Joey or we can make him a nest on the floor. When you're paying, you can arrange the sleeping places, and we could have had three rooms for the same price at the Thunderbird." She shut up, turned away. Lit up a cigarette.

"This is a non-smoking room."

She didn't say anything, so he didn't either. He supposed he'd be in a bad mood too, dragged back home to where she'd run from twice.

They hit the Courtyard Buffet for dinner—a pale imitation of Las Vegas's excesses yet still the glutton's delight. He'd imagined tasteless and colorful industrial food in vast quantities and bloated people pushing to get to the front of the trough, all-you-can-eat, but it wasn't so bad: yes, the expected pink prime rib, breaded popcorn shrimp, MSG-laced pot stickers, wilted iceberg with ranch dressing, baked potato with all the trimmings (when's the last time he'd had bacon bits?), soft-serve ice cream with chocolate fudge; but on the side he found beautiful green-lipped mussels, crab legs, fresh shrimp, and a nice array of Mexican.

Johnny piled his plate high with boiled jumbo shrimp, ate deliberately, pulling off legs and heads until he had a pile of bodies then sliding each one into his mouth, his face concentrated and blissful. "Grandpa, can I get some more?"

Adam felt his swollen stomach rumbling and churning, a mess of calories and fat—"It's all you can eat. How much can you eat?"—the dimple in Johnny's cheek when he laughed.

Joey picked. Amber ate almost nothing, drank a large Diet Pepsi from a plastic glass.

He hadn't realized that the three big casinos were linked underground—you never had to go outside here. They walked for blocks and blocks, Joey on his shoulders, past faux Venetian fountains, cowboy bars… where was the 1849 Saloon? Now a brew pub… and everywhere the zing and clatter of slots.

"We playing?" Amber asked. In the arcade back at Circus Circus, Johnny won a stuffed Spongebob Squarepants throwing quarters in open milk bottles. Joey slumped on Adam's shoulders, overwhelmed by the noise. Amber won thirty-seven dollars and change at the penny slots in fifteen minutes. She cashed out, handed the bills to Adam, "Here. To help pay the room rate."

"No, no, you keep it. You won it. Thank you, that's so sweet," he said.

She held the bills out again.

"You're going to need it." And she nodded and folded the money into the front pocket of her sweats.

Back up in the tower room, Johnny slept next to him in the bed closest the window, a small, self-contained lump. That kid had been moved around too much. Amber a large silent shadow on the other bed, Joey invisible behind her. Adam barely slept, nodding in and out, evil dreams driven by the conglomeration of food in his intestines. It wasn't Kira he missed so much as Polly. And the damn dead dog.

◎ POLLY

"I just felt like comfort food tonight," her mother said as they sliced the eggplant and sautéed the ground lamb. Polly loved moussaka even though she was usually leery of eggplant. It was her grandma's old recipe, and her mom loved it more than almost anything.

It was different cooking with her mom than with her dad; her dad dramatic and swearing and stirring flamboyantly, her mom following recipes and working steadily and quietly. They both were great cooks, though.

The moussaka was outstanding. Things tasted best when you made them yourself, she'd noticed. But when they sat down to eat it, just the two of them in the kitchen, they'd made way too much for two people and that was sad. And even though Amber would never touch eggplant and lamb, Polly missed the idea of her shoving it around her plate, a sneer on her lips. Johnny might try it. She'd seen him sneak parmesan and feta cheese from the fridge. Joey, he'd just stare and stare. Because that's all he could do. Stare.

"Brady was my boyfriend for a while, kind of," Polly said to her mom.

"He was?"

"He kissed me. Twice. Once in the mummy tomb and once in the history room when they sent us to pick up the VCR for English, and it was empty. The history room."

"Did you like kissing him?"

"Mommy!"

"I hope you liked it, it should feel good to you. Only do it if it feels good to you."

"Our teeth clunked." She winced.

"Oh honey," her mom said. "It takes practice. You have time."

"I'm mad at you," she wanted to say: "I cut myself, I have a scar. And you never even noticed. And you never even care." But choked out instead, "Mommy... that note. On the door. The love window note to Keerah."

Her mom took a quick breath. "Oh no. Oh, Polly. I'm so sorry you had to see that. My yoga teacher—he didn't understand—he got confused."

"I *hate* yoga."

"Oh Polly, come here."

She got up and came around the table, sat on her mom's lap and put her arms around her neck. Her mom wrapped her arms around her and stroked her head. Her mom's eyes leaked tears. Some fell on Polly's arm.

"Do you want to watch Singing in the Rain?" her mom asked.

Polly nodded.

"Let's leave everything. We'll clean up later."

Later, they packaged the leftover moussaka, putting more than they'd eaten into the freezer in Ziploc bags.

ADAM

By the time they got done with bottomless acrid coffee and bacon and waffles, the maple-flavored syrup thick, it was almost nine thirty, not the crack of dawn he wanted. The Prius, as promised, made great mileage on the straightaway.

At Lovelock, they stopped at the in-station minimart. Corn dogs fifty-nine cents in the warmer. The biggest selection of beef jerky he'd ever seen. The floor of the car piled with junk food wrappers. In the middle of the desert the radio was all cowboy music and Jesus talk: KHWG, "…we don't forget where country came from, we'll keep you from thinkin' where it's gone." Deep in Amurica.

Pulling over for bathroom breaks at every rest stop to let the kids stretch and pee. In Cosgrove, "Excuse me, darlin'," a man said to Amber, holding the door as she left the outhouse. She nodded, serene, "How's it goin'?" A real cowboy, he thought, noting the jeans, hat, boots, big belly, blue button down shirt. In Oakland, she'd been freaked by the homeless people and huddled against him whenever a black man passed, clingy even on Grand Avenue.

"You want me to drive now?"

"You have your license?" Looking at her face for reaction.

"I used to have one but I lost it with my wallet. I'm legal, I just need to get it replaced."

Good. "I'll drive."

He wanted the control, anyway. Feared she'd drive like she lived, underwater slow motion.

Back in the car.

Seven hours, twenty-one minutes estimated drive time total over two days, not too bad. Five hundred and one miles, door to door. He worked on making it in only six hours, okay, six and a half. What the hell was he doing, driving with Amber across the desert, the two kids in back, Johnny beep boop beeping his Game Boy, Joey keening because he didn't like the booster seat. ("Tough shit, this car is not moving again until you get him in it.") Get them there, leave them there, go fast on the way back. Clean up his act. You had to bottom out before you could climb back up. In his pocket, the codeine he'd found in Kira's drawer. When Amber was sleeping, he fumbled quietly, came up with two and swallowed with his spit.

"If you hear the train I'm on, you will know that I am gone. You can hear the whistle blowin' five hundred miles."

Nobody joined in. Amber woke and stared out the window, probably jonesing for a smoke. The stink of Joey's diaper wafting from the back. Half a thousand miles in the car with them. Straight on 80 across Nevada. Keep the pedal to the metal, he could do it faster. No heat in February, even in the sun. The desert beautiful and desolate, stark snow dusting mountains, flat valleys, dry sage brush for hours, yet it kept changing—salt flats, rock formations, mist and sand flurries, and the sagey vegetation in colors of muted reds, greens, browns, yellows, the gray of the sky, the occasional fields of snow.

Winnamucca for lunch, Winner's Casino: pork chops, poached eggs, hash browns. "You doin' okay, honey?" their waitress, Vickie, asked as he slid out of the booth for the bathroom.

This was where they'd grown up, small town Nevada: Fallon, Winnamucca, Elko. First Sandi, then Amber, now these boys. Ranching families gone to the mines and to the wars. Sandi's rebellion to like punk instead of metal, loving that Seattle and SF street scene (too many needles) but back to the desert because… because of him? Or Jumbo, somebody else. So hard to rip yourself out by the roots, single woman with a baby. He was so fortunate to grow up in the Bay Area, everything easy, even the weather.

Driving, deep into the Zen of it, the whoosh of the trucks passing them making the car shake, the glare of the road when the sun broke, passing car after car, eyes ahead for highway patrol, nothing in sight. A federal penitentiary rose and slid behind them (road signs forbidding stops or hitchhiking), they shared the road with semis, flatbeds, SUVs, the rare sedan. Train track to the left of them, and they were faster than the trains. Limbo, limbo, limbo, the space between two things. Joey whimpered, Johnny's Game Boy beep boop beeped.

CHAPTER 18

🌢 KIRA

An unwanted pregnancy was a time limit. A bomb in her womb. All evening, she checked every few minutes for bleeding, sticking her finger inside herself and checking to see if she could feel the cervix loosening. Closed up tight. She had to start bleeding. So pregnant. You were or you weren't. Queasy and her breasts enormous, nipples on fire—how had she thought it was Ravi making them that way? Having to pee every five minutes (have I started bleeding yet?), exhausted. How ironic that she'd made the appointment for a new diaphragm fit.

In the morning, she called in sick, and Lindsey swung by to take Polly to school.

She gardened. The air was crisp but clear, shafts of sideways sun and good-smelling earth, birdsong. She battled oxalis: clover leafs and bright yellow flowers on sour stalks that choked the good plants. If she just kept eradicating, in a year the problem would be down to manageable size. But two hours and a bucket full of weeds and roots and bulbs, and half remained, and when it rained again, the same thousand square feet of yard would glow again in the un-chosen green of oxalis and wild onion. She worked with her back to a riparian slope tangled with blackberry, wild fennel, and poison oak in all its various forms—shrub, vine, tree.

On her palm, a half-dollar-sized red mark from turning over the earth, picking out the crisp roots and small brown-papered bulbs. Now she attacked a patch of wild onion, their oniony scent immediately releasing. Her stomach turned over like the trowel full of earth in front of her. She delivered a small pocket of sprouting onion eggs from the earth. She yanked at the tops of the plants, knowing that she would have to cut them back again and again until they weakened and died. She moved over to the flagstone path, almost obscured, grabbing handfuls of weeds, pulling with her thighs until the roots gave with soft ripping sounds and broke free, bringing a big clump of dirt with them. Careful not to stand up too fast or the nausea would catch her. The worms she gently moved to another patch of earth. When the area under each flagstone was clean, she shoved the earth smooth again, reset the stone, and refilled around it with sand. This year she would plant a real garden, sweet and savory. Golden thyme, rosemary, oregano, sage, rose geranium; plants that broke open wild aromas as she brushed through.

Kira stripped off her gardening gloves. She stretched, standing on the back porch overlooking the garden. The sun was thin but wonderful on her shoulders, birds chittered, a small ruby-throated hummer buzzed, hovered, dove, and soared straight up with a rapid set of cheeps.

Back to the bathroom. Her body had betrayed her, but also it hadn't. How wonderful that her body could still do this. Sometimes when she checked her underwear she hoped she wouldn't find blood. And then she didn't, and was crushed again.

In the afternoon, at the clinic, she fought to keep from crying. "How did this happen? I was using birth control."

She sat on the exam table, pants-less again, in the small white room rimmed with an appliqué of cheery baby bottles and smiling teddy bears. It was a different nurse, this one older, gray hair to her shoulders and turquoise earrings that clanked as she moved her head.

"Well, I don't see any sign of miscarriage. You might still pass it naturally, but since you're not bleeding and your cervix is tight, that might not happen. I think it's time to think through your alternatives. You could try to keep it, though there are risks. If so, we need to get you immediately on folic acid, and no alcohol or drugs, of course. If you choose to terminate, we can induce a chemical abortion, or you can wait a few weeks for a D & C."

"I can't have this baby." The words out loud surprised her with their solidity.

"I'm sorry this is happening to you. It's hard." The nurse put her hand on Kira's shoulder. "Why don't you schedule an appointment for next week, and see if you miscarry naturally before then. You still have a 30% or more chance of that."

Hard to process.

"What's a chemical abortion like?"

"It's essentially a miscarriage, done in the privacy of your own home, and we don't need to wait as long as for a D & C where you'd need to be, oh, about eight weeks. This way, the sooner the better. We use a combination of Mifepristone and Misoprostol. There's always some risk there, too, but it's small. I can give you some literature to read at home, and then you'd speak to a doctor." The woman gave Kira's shoulders a hug. "I'm so sorry."

"I feel like such a fool." A fool for feeling that stupid lust for Ravi. Had that made her body more receptive?

The woman shook her head. "It happens."

"How much does it cost? The chemicals?"

"Do you have insurance?"

"Yes." So fortunate to have that.

"It may cover it, it might not. If it doesn't, it's about $475. Is that a financial hardship?"

"No. Not really." In the big scheme of things. "But it should be free."

"Yes, I agree." The nurse looked at her, waiting.

"I have to tell my husband."

"Of course. This is a family decision." The nurse snapped off her gloves and left Kira to get dressed.

She picked up Polly at Clare's where she was babysitting for Micah until almost her bedtime. The evening was bitter cold again, moonlight slanting through breaks in the high clouds.

Her hands were cold and she fumbled with the keys. "Sorry, Poodle."

Polly danced on the porch to stay warm. "Micah's cute, Mommy."

"He is, isn't he. It's great that you're starting to babysit, Pol."

"I really started with Joey, didn't I?"

The key turned, the house was warm. They shed coats and shoes in the foyer.

"You can stay up a little later, finish your homework, but I'm not feeling well. Is it okay if I go to bed?" Kira asked.

"It's okay, Mommy." Polly gave her a hug. "Feel better soon. I won't stay up late."

So rare for Polly to relax into her like this anymore, her body fitting against her. She gave her a tight squeeze then moved her to arm's length to look in her serious face. "You're getting so grown up! I appreciate your sense of responsibility so much. Have a good night, Apollonia. I love you."

"I love you, too."

◊ ADAM

On the satellite map, Elko had been a gray-green patch along a strip of emerald river on the brown plain of the Great Basin. From the outskirts, Elko was any town: Office Max and gas stations. In a parking lot as they pulled into downtown off Mountain City Highway that stretched from Idaho into the Rubies, a taco truck, Las Brisas Tacos y Mariscos, next to a shiny black traveling tattoo trailer with orange lettering, "Experience the Pain!" on the side.

"Got my little tat here when he was through here couple of years ago," Amber said. "My rose."

"How are the tacos?"

She shrugged.

Elko proper was flat and gridded out. Willow, Walnut, Elm, Maple, Ash, Fir, Cedar, Oak, Juniper. Forests in the desert, worn clapboard houses on small lots. On Laurel near Third, they pulled in front of a small wooden house. Adam walked behind the kids, ahead of Amber who dragged up the walkway, resigned and miserable.

When Sandi answered the bell to his ring, pushing the screen door open but keeping the door ajar behind her, she looked wizened, an apple doll of herself. Her hair was thin and short. It was impossible that he'd once had sex with this old woman, that she was only a few years older than he was; he had the urge to run back to the car and recheck his own reflection in the mirror. But then as he looked at her, her face morphed and she was Sandi, and he felt a wave of fondness. Jesus, whether or not Amber really was his, their lives had been entwined now for a couple of decades.

"Well, hey, look what the cat drug back in."

"Hi, Sandi." He came forward to kiss her hello but at the last moment he stuck out his hand. They shook, and he backed away.

Joey sat down on the ground in the doorway, cooed at a rock. Johnny said, "Hi Gramma," and leaned his head against her side. Her arm went around him for a quick squeeze, then she gently pushed him away. "Johnny, you know you gotta stay with your mama now."

"Hey, Mom." Amber's voice sullen, a young teenager caught in the act of being bad.

Sandi ignored Adam, looked at Amber, her lips tightening. "Hon, okay, now what. You gonna go hire a babysitter and drive a truck out at the mine, now? They gonna be baby buckaroos?" Her voice rose to shrill. Johnny turned quickly away, disappeared around the side of the house. Adam wanted to follow.

"Told you," Amber said to Adam, lighting a cigarette.

"And now you got him to bring you all the way back. Well, he can bring you back the way he brung you." Sandi said.

"Fuck you, Mom."

Sandi's mouth opened and shut, and she sighed. "Now get off before I get Big Tom out here."

"Tom's back? Melvin's gone?" Amber said.

"Uh-uh. I'm not going to engage here. I love you, baby, but I can't do it. Nice to see you, Adam." Sandi stepped backwards inside and closed the door; Adam heard the sound of a bolt. He looked at Joey—how much did he register of this?

"Okay, everybody," he said, trying to keep his voice positive. "Let's go get something to eat and we'll figure out what's next."

"I'm not hungry," Amber said.

"Well, I am."

"I'm not coming back here."

"Amber, your mom is surprised and upset. She'll calm down."

Adam and Amber walked back to the car, Joey trailing. Where was Johnny? They got in and sat there, Joey climbing into his booster seat without complaining. The air was stale and smelly, but when Adam opened the window, an irritating cold wind blew dust in his eyes.

"Just a minute," Adam said. "I'm going to go back and talk to her."

He walked back to the door and knocked. "Sandi! It's Adam."

She unbolted the door and opened it again.

They looked at each other.

"I'm surprised she got you going with this goose chase," she said. "I would of thought she'd hit up Stan, not you."

"What do you mean?"

"She's in a needy stage of her life, or that's just how she turned out after her wild and woolly years, but I'm not going to accommodate any more. I can't do it. Got my own career now. I'm done raising kids. You've got one too now?"

"Polly."

Sandi nodded. "Nice name. She's a tough one, Amber. You be careful now. You're looking good, you know. Nice to see you again. Have fun with my grandbabies." She shut the door, leaving him standing there. He didn't know what to do. So he walked back to the car and got in. They sat without talking.

After a few more minutes, Johnny came around the side of the house and quietly got back in the car, closed the door, and reattached his seatbelt. He didn't say anything. Adam felt so bad for him, stray dog moved from pound to pound. "You okay back there, Johnny Rockboy?" In the rear view mirror he saw Johnny swallow and nod.

Food always helped. "Somewhere you like to eat around here?" Adam asked Amber.

"Stockmen's got a $9.95 steak dinner, unless you want Chinese, Chef Cheng's over on Idaho."

"Oh yummy," he said. But he saw she was crying, staring straight ahead, jaws tight against sound, tears flowing.

Adam pushed the button to turn on the Prius. "Okay, then.

Stockmen's it is. There's Kleenex in the glove compartment. Hey Johnny Rockboy, know why they call it the glove compartment?"

Silence from the back seat.

"That's where they used to keep their driving gloves. Back when they used gloves for driving."

"Grandpa, can I get my own steak?" Johnny asked.

"Go straight through at the light here, then make a right at Commercial's," Amber said, pointing. "They got the biggest polar bear ever killed in a case there."

☙ KIRA

Kira took the cordless phone into the bedroom and sat on the bed. The barriers between her and Adam so high, the spaces so vast; the Sierra and the desert between them. He should be in Elko now, or turned around to come home already? She was stunned when he answered.

"Hang on," he said through static. "Maybe reception's better down the hall." Then a moment later, "Fuck it's cold. I'm next to the ice machine. Can you hear me?"

"Pretty well."

"Sandi's not letting them stay, so we're at the Big West Motel. I sprung for two rooms, but they're cheap, just need a little privacy. Jesus, this is a fucking hellhole of a nothing town. Cute, but totally cowboy. We're waiting for her to come to her senses."

"Sandi?"

"She's had it. I can see why. What am I supposed to do now?"

"What about friends?"

"Amber's friends? Apparently she's burned through them."

"Yeah, I can see that happening."

"Jesus. I feel like I'm trapped in hell," he said.

"Adam." She took a breath. "Listen. I'm pregnant."

"What?"

"I'm pregnant."

She imagined his face crinkling and collapsing. "Fuck! What about your IUD?"

"I'm in the tiny percent that it happens to. But I still might miscarry naturally, they said. I'm not ready to have this."

"It's not mine," he said.

A cascade of ice from an ice machine five hundred miles away. Here, in their house, only the drone of the highway.

"What? Yes, actually, it is."

"*No*. You've never gotten pregnant with me unless you've wanted to."

That old discussion lumbering up from the dead—had she trapped him with Polly? "That's not true. And the abortion…"

"Don't even start," he said.

She couldn't sit still. She walked through the house into the kitchen, Polly quiet in her room. She refilled the water in the dish of the succulent cuttings on the window sill; they had sprouted roots and small branches. She had not even had hope or intent, she had just watered and ignored.

"Jesus, Kira! You have this baby, you're having it alone."

She spoke quietly so Polly wouldn't hear. "I didn't say I was having it. I called to tell you we can't have it. Because it would be damaged, and we don't want it, and I don't think *we* are in a place to even consider having it." She put the kettle on, waited for water to boil for ginger tea.

"Whatever! It's not mine, and I won't have you pawn off responsibility on me."

"It is! I did the math. I can't believe this."

"Fuck your math! Don't you think it's a strange coincidence? No pregnancy in thirteen—in fourteen—years, and all of a sudden you screw around with Mr. Yoga dude and boom. You know you're more likely to get pregnant with new sperm to you than old sperm?"

"What kind of bogus fact is that?"

"Heard it on NPR."

"Adam, damn it, listen! It's not possible. He wore a condom and he didn't come."

The silence stretched across the states. Silence. The house on Moss Street echoed with it.

His voice was small. "Oh Jesus, Kira, that was too much information." Then it broke, she could hear him crying. "Why did you rub it in like that? Do you have to be this cruel to me? What did I ever do to *you*?"

"I'm sorry." Watching the silver metal on the kettle fog up and then disperse. Silence. "I'm really sorry. But you pushed me."

Dead silence.

"Adam. Please talk to me. This is terrible—and even if you think it's not happening to you, it is, because it's happening to *me*. Can I get some support?"

Again a long pause. Turning off the kettle before it began its rumble. Sitting down at the kitchen table, the phone clutched tight against her ear. She imagined an empty hallway, him at the end of it. All those closed doors.

"Exactly what kind of support do you want, Kira?" he finally asked, voice choked and furious. "You want me to just lie back and take it up the ass from you? I'm delighted you're not having this baby—*his* baby—and fucking up our lives completely. But this is your fucking problem. Not mine. Not mine! So I'm going to drop Amber and the kids off as soon as Sandi gets it through her fucking head, and then I'm going to stay away a while. Clean your own mess."

"Listen. Adam, I understand that you think it *could* be his, but he and I had sex after I already had these pregnancy symptoms."

"Save it. I'm not doing this again! Did you even hear what I said about not coming back for awhile? Do you ever listen to me, or am I just shouting into some fucking void, here?"

"How long? Where are you going?" The kitchen, once empty with possibilities, now just empty.

"Do you hear me? I'm not going through another abortion with you."

"You're going to just stay out in the desert from spite? I can't do this alone."

"Well, you're going to have to, aren't you?" Spat through tightened jaw.

His voice so frozen angry, and there was no way to pull back on the bungie cords of energy that usually stretched between them; they seemed to have dissolved, or hung so slack she wasn't aware of the linkage, just the heaviness of holding her side of the line.

"Call me, okay? I can't believe this is happening," she said, hearing the pleading in her voice. Stranded, ditched, abandoned. She could barely keep her eyes open, the fatigue pressing her down.

"Kira." It sounded like he was trying. "I'll call you. At some point. But this is beyond what I can do right now."

"Yeah." It was beyond what she could do right now.

Silence.

"Good night," she said. She let him hang up first so she could sit, phone in hand, and pretend they were young lovers in a spat, he'd hung up in a snit… so much easier to take than this cold emptiness, the nausea. Moving to the bathroom, knees on the rug, she puked, hoping Polly, in her room down the hall, couldn't hear. A sour taste. She rinsed her mouth, her stomach tender. She turned the thermostat up to 72 degrees. She was so cold.

Huddled on the couch, a throw blanket over her, she called Lindsey. "I'm pregnant. And I can't do it, Lindsey. All those poisons. Scraping. I don't want it, but I can't do it. And Adam's being a dick about it. What am I going to do?"

"Oh, no! Oh, honey."

"Can you come over tomorrow after work? Bring Nell. We'll sit in the garden, sip beers."

"Beers?"

"I'm not keeping it. I can have a beer."

"Okay, I hear you," Lindsey said, her voice careful, "but don't jump to conclusions, promise me? I'll bring some really nice juice."

The house so big around her without Adam. She got off the couch and climbed into bed, too weary to fold her clothing, leaving pants and underpants sprawled open on the floor, falling deeply asleep.

℘ ADAM

He turned the cell phone off, sat down next to the ice machine, and rested his cheek against the rumble. Bounced up. Heart pounding, Jesus, how high was his blood pressure? Heart attack. Stroke. She'd be sorry. He'd thought he was over it, over her betrayals; they had moved through them, hadn't they? Their bed those last nights a boat of calm in a rough sea. Blindsided again. How could she do this to him? So unfair. No way it could be his. What made him such a target? A sign on his back: Trick Me!

Sandi: "Yeah. I'm on the pill."

Kira: They were twenty-four. They'd fought about it for weeks. In bed. At the Pork Store café over Sunday brunch. At Laundryland. Low voices and loud voices, a conversation in circles. "A baby's a baby, it doesn't matter whose genes it has. That's not how you make the decision if you want a child," she said. "The question is, do we want a child?"

"It matters to me if it's another guy's child. I've been screwed once already."

"You don't want a kid."

"Maybe I might. Don't I have any rights here?"

"I don't think I want it. Not now."

"Can you pick and choose, Kira?"

"Yes, I can. It's my right."

"What about *my* rights?"

"Do you even know what you want?"

Fought and fought.

"It's yours, it's not Stan's, but if I wanted the baby I wouldn't care."

"None of you do. You just make all the decisions and we men have to live with them."

"Don't lump me with Sandi."

And then him waiting in the clinic waiting room and waiting and waiting for hours and hours, each time the door swung open half-standing to greet her, and the young girls coming out and out and out…

He stood up, strode down the hallway. Damn card key. Sliding it in three times before the light turned green and he turned the handle and pushed. He grabbed his jacket from the bed, closed the door behind him and walked down the stairs, across the parking lot, across the quiet highway to the Red Lion Casino. Free drinks if you gambled. He'd gamble, then.

"Not this time, Kira. I'm not doing this again."

Clank, whir, ka*ching*. I'm not doing this again.

Waking in the night in the Big West Inn and reaching for

her in the empty bed. Then the smell of solvents and smoke and his own drunk gluey funk. Alone. And her alone in pain. And then the rage came back, a roar—fuck her. Fuck her fuck her fuckherfuckerfucker*fucker*!

He pounded the pillow into a better shape. Fuck her. She would have to do this one alone.

CHAPTER 19

They wore jeans and fleeces with hoods. Lindsey moved around the deck, dumping last week's rainwater off two of the moldy canvas camping chairs; all this chaos, though even before Amber arrived they hadn't prepped the deck for winter. Lindsey was walking her like a dog, caring for her like a wounded animal.

Okay, she was that.

In February dusk, they sat on the porch pretending it was summer, Polly and Nell doing homework deep in the silent house behind them. The breeze bit. Her nipples inflamed, her pants already tight, like the world's worst case of PMS. She'd vomited at work after lunch, telling Sarah she had the flu. The pile of proposals on her desk shaming her. Embarrassing, her age and knocked up. "I feel like hell, Linds."

Lindsey shut her eyes, slumped back in her chair. "Okay. Let me just say this. I can't believe you're not even thinking about having it. Are you sure? Especially doing it—the abortion—without him."

"But what if he doesn't come home?"

"He'll come home." Lindsey sat up and stared at Kira, who turned her face away, sharp smell of mildew from the chair. In the house, the girls thundered, galloping and giggles. Where had it started, this ball of mess, of snarled string, and weeds and more weeds? The more she pulled out of the ground, the more to pull.

"The garden looks better, doesn't it? I did some weeding."

258

"You guys could have this child. People who can have kids, who are good parents, who are smart and educated, should be the ones to have kids. Not like Amber, she just has kids randomly, and every crack whore down the block, and all those fundies…"

Kira sat bolt upright. "Wait. Lindsey, you can't choose for her, or for us."

"You're right." Her jaw trembled from tightness. "It just hurts me that you guys are so messed up. I danced at your wedding. You guys were so amazing. It was embarrassing because you'd be making out on the couch after, like, ten years together. You were so into each other, always using 'we' in every other sentence. Then this thing with Ravi. Now this. I don't get it."

"You never know the inside of a relationship unless you're in it."

"Yeah."

"But I need to be able to turn to you. You're my Burning Building friend."

"Look, I never wanted Nell to be an only child, and no man in my life. And you have two men, or had two. And kids in your life. Polly. Joey and what's the other one? Johnny?"

"But exactly. It's too much."

"I'm not in a position to argue with you. It's a bad topic with me, you know that. Okay. I can't be there. But talk to Clare about this."

"Why Clare?"

"She knows about herbs from her Herbal Women's Symposium thing. She can help. Maybe it will be more natural."

Oh Lindsey, she hated this but she was helping anyway. "You know I love you." She felt like a child, younger than Polly.

"You'll get through all this. We all will. We're going to go home now, Kira. Nell's got a bunch of stuff to do, and I have to do laundry. You'll be fine."

She didn't look as though she was storming off: casually standing up, bringing glasses to the kitchen sink, gathering Nell—"Nelly, *now*. We have groceries to buy and dogs to feed!" But Kira knew she was, and there Kira was, alone in the burning building, the air too cold in the deceptive sun.

✆ ADAM

His head hurt. Amber's snores echoed through the wall. The TV blared—they must sleep with it on, how could they sleep? The constant barrage of voices, clatter, soundtrack, laughter. The Big West Lodge smelled of coriander and cleaning fluids—it made the tip of Adam's nose itch. What a dive, even at $90 a night for the big room, $65 for his little one, even though the thin industrial carpet was fairly new and the brochure glossy:

> Big West Lodge Inn & Suites is conveniently situated in Elko, Nevada, in the center of northern Nevada's Great Basin. We welcome you year round! Come stay in 'The Best Town in America,' and enjoy Elko's annual powwows and festivals!

He'd been paying night by night—the card would go through for small amounts, he hoped, and it had, though he could tell that the Patel daughter, whichever one was on, doubted it would—and every morning they were entitled to "breakfast" at the tiny lobby buffet next to the front desk and a single small slot machine.

"Don't play motel slots, they're tight as your ass," Amber said. "Paki motel owners. You'll never win a dime."

"Amber!" Adam said. "Don't be racist."

"Call 'em like I see 'em," she said, and poured a pale glass of orange juice for Joey.

Adam closed his eyes and prayed for Tylenol.

"Ma. Ma. Ma." It was just babble, no words, Joey's tiny hands reaching for the glass.

Breakfast: a gummy Danish sealed in plastic, a mushy red apple, thin coffee with fake-o powdered milk substitute, watered-down frozen OJ.

Amber made the kids eat the Danish, "It's free."

"It's not free. It's included. I paid for it. And you don't need to eat it, Johnny. We're going out to breakfast—I want me more of that greasy cheesy grit shit at the casino. And real coffee."

"But I want it, Grandpa." Johnny licked at the Danish icing.

"Ma. Ma. Ma."

"Shut it, Joey," Amber said.

"Then eat it. I have no control over you. You need to learn to make your own decisions about what to put in your body. Don't listen to me, for God's sake, don't listen to your mother. I've never seen a parent force her kid to eat junk food before," Adam said, pointedly, to Amber. "And what are we doing today? I can't just sit here and wait for you to get it together."

"I know. I know. I know. I'm gonna make some phone calls."

"What about Johnny's school?"

"Don't know if I want him at that place, bad teacher and he missed so much already."

Adam shook his head. Opened his mouth and shut it.

"Don't look at me like that. He's my kid. Parents are supposed to decide about their kid's education, right?"

It felt like a dig, her unspoken sarcasm, "like you decided on mine." He thought of Polly, right now at school, twelve hundred a month for nurturing and the best science and English programs in Berkeley. "He should be in school, Amber. Unless you're going to homeschool him."

"Well, maybe I just might."

He sighed. That would be worse.

Josie Patel sat at the desk on a stool, the bulletin board next to her head advertising gold mining tours, cowboy ranches, local brothels, hiking trips up the canyons. "Will you be staying another night?"

"Yes," Amber said.

"No, I don't think so," Adam said. "We're moving to Stockmen's. It's only $35 a night per room."

Amber shook her head. "I'm not moving these kids to Stockmen's."

"I'm moving to Stockmen's," he said with false patience. His head throbbed. "And if you want me to put you up for another night—two max—you can move with me. Or you can go to your mom's. Or you can find a friend. Or you go to hell."

She sighed loudly.

He lost it. He was done with bullshit. "This is a boom town! You've got gold coming out of your asses here. You've got jobs at the mines, jobs at the casinos, jobs at the cathouses. You're in your twenties. You have two legs, two arms, two eyes, a mouth and a nose! Earn some money, save some money, move to Mexico where you can support your kids on ten dollars a day! Who are you? Stop feeling so fucking sorry for yourself! What makes you think I should support you?"

"You want me to work at a cathouse?"

He stopped his rant.

"I'm getting my stuff," she said, her eyes in a tight mean squint.

It took only thirty minutes to move.

Stockmen's Casino and Hotel, across a huge parking lot filled with pick-up trucks, Saturns, and old panel vans from Commercial's Casino, was an old-style building, three stories, the top two of them hotel rooms off a long dark corridor. Cash only. The $35 per room included tax. The sign on the desk had the date, Friday, Feb. 8, and then it clicked through his caffeine-starved brain, Oh hell, I've got a work gig. Now. Today!

"Two nights, max," he said. Johnny stared at him, puppy eyes. "I'll take us to lunch," he said to Johnny. Then turned and headed up the stairs with his bag to his room on the non-smoking floor. His room looked out across the parking lot to Commercial's—Liberal SLOTS!—"Bet that's the only thing liberal in this town," he muttered. A single queen-sized bed with a mud brown headboard and a red-orange geometrically-patterned spread. There was too much space in the room, nothing on the white walls, an uncomfortable-looking armchair in the same pattern as the bedspread, the dark maroon carpet as wide as the desert. He lay down fully clothed on the bed and closed his eyes. Kira. Damn you.

After a few moments he turned on his phone to call Stan. He only had one battery bar. Oh shit, didn't bring the charger. Message machine. "Hey, man, did not mean to blow you off today! I'm off with your old lady—ha ha—well, kinda. I'm in Elko, trying to negotiate a truce between Sandi and Amber. I'm sure you understand. Couldn't make it back. But if you want to reschedge for, like…" he counted in his head, Saturday, Sunday at the latest, the drive home… "…Monday or Tuesday, let's say Tuesday, I'm ready to rock and roll." He hung up. Muttered again: where can I get a phone charger in this town.

Lunch: "What's your pleasure," he asked, down in their room around one o'clock.

"You choose, I don't care." She changed Joey's diaper on the bed, "We got to get more wipes on the way back, Dad." Put drops in his eyes.

"I want KFC bowl." Johnny said. "Or Burger King."

"Whatever," Amber said.

Fast food. He gave in again. So many choices: Wendy's on East Idaho Street. Domino's, Pizza Hut, Burger King, Subway on Idaho Street. Arbys, KFC, Taco Bell out on Mountain City Highway. McDonald's on Idaho Street and Mountain City Highway. No Carl's Junior, No In 'n' Out Burger.

"Okay, let's go."

Quickly through the lobby into the parking lot. It was bitter cold. Johnny said, "'We start with a generous serving of our creamy mashed potatoes, layered with sweet corn and loaded with bite-sized pieces of crispy chicken. Then we drizzle it all with our signature home-style gravy and top it off with a shredded three-cheese blend. It's all your favorite flavors coming together.'"

"What's that, Johnny?" He picked up Joey and put him in the car seat. "There you go, buddy."

"He memorized that commercial," Amber said. Loading her suitcase beside Joey, slamming the door.

"We start. With a generous serving of creaaaamy mashed potatoes, layyerred with sweet corn. Loooooaded with chicken. Layyerred and loaded, layered and loaded, *lock and load!*"

"Johnny! Get your butt in the car."

"It's okay, Amber. He's just bored." He should be in school.

A quick drive up fast food row. KFC—Kira would be so disgusted with him. The thick fried smell made him queasy. He ordered a roasted chicken Caesar salad, feeling a bit self-righteous, and picked at it, nauseous by now, as Amber ate fried chicken parts, and Johnny gulped his layered and loaded KFC bowl, and Joey picked off the fried crust of his drumstick and ate it, leaving a stick of smooth gray meat on the chicken bone. The salad was bad—he'd expected no better. He reached across the plastic table, took a breast from the tub of chicken in front of Amber. The crunch of the fried topping, the hot spurt of oil and chicken grease, the chewy meat. Who was he fooling. It was delicious.

"How about I take Joey and Johnny Rockboy for a while this afternoon, to the park near Eightmile Creek or something, while you make your calls?"

Johnny looked hopeful.

"Nah, they don't like parks."

Johnny stood up on his chair, "Layered and loaded, *lock and load!*"

"Get your butt in that chair!"

"It's my catch phrase!"

"Johnny. Come here," he said. "Sit on my lap."

"I'm too old."

"No you are not. Polly sometimes sits on my lap still, and she's almost twice your age. I'll tell you two a story."

"Nah, boys don't sit on boys' laps," Johnny said.

"Johnny, for the last time before I start hittin' it, get your butt in that chair. Adam, stay the hell away from my kid."

"Whoa, Amber..."

"'Or you can go to hell...'" she parroted his words this morning.

"Amber. Okay. I'm sorry I said that. But I'm not okay with you hitting your kids."

Johnny sat down in his chair.

"He's down, so I'm not hitting him." Her voice flat.

They ate the rest of the meal in silence.

◊ KIRA

Clare met her for lunch at The Musical Offering, seven minutes from Kira's office, nine or ten from Clare's. Over salads, Clare's voice was almost a whisper; there might be staff, faculty, students they knew around. The Native Americans thought of it differently, she said. They took herbs to bring on their cycles. There wasn't the heavy concept of abortion. Just evening out what was uneven. "And of course, they had fewer accidental pregnancies because the men would go to the sweat lodge before they came in to the women, and killed so many of those little swimmers from the heat."

"I like that. Evening out what is uneven. There are still people who do this?"

"Of course. We still have the old knowledge, it's just underground."

"The old knowledge." Hocus pocus womyn's power, herbs by moonlight. Her old skeptic's voice. Shh, she told herself. Clare knows.

"A lot of women have success with vitamin C and herbs, rue, or cohosh. It's natural and you're not in the medical maw; a lot of women find it very desirable to take control of their own bodies in that way."

She knew the medical maw: She was twenty-four. The doctor came in. Kira slid down. "You'll feel something cold, and something pressing as we widen the opening," she said. "This is a shot to numb you. This will take about two minutes. It may seem longer." The round woman held her hand. "You squeeze as hard as you need to. You can't hurt me."

Now: "Yeah. I'd rather do it naturally if I can."

"I'm not talking about bicycle spokes and umbrella ribs, rat poison. You have to do it right. And you can't start later than the sixth week."

"That's this week, no, early next week. I conceived three weeks ago, no, like maybe three and a half weeks ago? So this is technically week five, almost six. So I would have to do this soon. Am I too late?"

"You'd need to start soon," Clare said. "And you need to be prepared to terminate another way if this doesn't work; it's only got a fifty percent chance of working, better if you have fewer doubts. The women who are sure have a better success rate."

"I'm sure. And I already have an appointment at the clinic for backup." The medical maw: "It's okay, baby. It's okay," the woman holding her hand. The machine throbbing, scraping, sucking stripes of pain, on and on, then, instruments withdrawn, the doctor disappearing, leaving the pain behind. "You're okay, baby. Now walk." "I can't." "You can."

"What about Adam?"

Kira didn't answer. Clare didn't know Adam was gone.

"And you need to say goodbye to the fetus."

"Bye-bye fetus!"

"No, seriously, Kira. You need to do a ritual around it."

"Will you help me?"

"This is for you and Adam to do together." Clare leaned across the table, grabbed both her forearms. "Be smart, Kira. Make sure you have somebody with you, like Adam or Lindsey, and if you start bleeding too heavily, be prepared to go in right away. Do it cleanly. Say goodbye to the fetus. Get medical backup. Make sure your bases are covered."

Feeling apologetic—she's the one who had instituted The Center's open door culture—she shut the heavy wood door so Sarah wouldn't hear. She called the clinic, spoke to an advice nurse. "I'd prefer to miscarry naturally. What do you know about herbal abortions?"

The woman was shocked. Kira could hear it in the measured

tone of her voice, as if she was afraid to move too fast for fear of spooking Kira into hanging up and killing herself in a dark alley with a coat hanger shoved up her cervix. "Chemical miscarriage is a safe procedure, done under our supervision but in the privacy of your home. We're very fortunate this is still a legal option for women. Don't mess around on your own."

"You're probably right. Thank you," Kira said, though she wasn't convinced.

"Ma'am, we don't recommend self-medication for something this serious. Just because something is an herb doesn't mean it's safe. You're basically inducing a miscarriage the same way the chemical miscarriage does. Why is it better if you get an unregulated, untested herb to do the same thing? Do you hear what I'm saying?"

"Yes, I do. You're right." But she had an image of herself riding on a horse alone into the desert, as if she had ever ridden a horse, oh, a pony or two…

Kira felt rebellion rise up in her. The memory: "Here's some ice cubes." A thick pad between her legs, blankets and ice cubes, elevated feet. Shock. Still sick, her body still thinking it was pregnant, dumb blind body. "Here's a bag if you need to vomit." Ginger ale and soda crackers. Even her pregnancy with Polly medically controlled. Adam gone, so angry; Ravi in the dream, "I'm ready to get it. Are you ready?" moaning, "The-e-e-re"… Who could she trust? Only herself.

Abortions on the verge of being illegal, and what would Polly and her friends do if they got pregnant and abortions were illegal? If they all knew the old wisdoms, how to take care of it safely. They would need to go underground, form underground railroads, retake control. These were things the ancient women knew how to do. Not always, and it was not always successful. But with a backup, there was no harm in trying and potentially a lot of good, not just for herself, but for Polly, for Polly's friends.

❧ POLLY

Her mom picked everybody up. The minute they dropped Nell off (Amanda dropped earlier), Polly asked, "Where's Daddy?"

"Still in Elko, I guess."

"You don't even know? Typical. You never notice *anything*. He said he was going to be home by today, he had a gig."

"Well, he's not."

"That's not right." And you don't even care, Polly thought. She focused on the side of the freeway. Why was there always so much garbage there? For weeks, she'd seen some poor kid's stuffie, a bear, lying on the side of the fast lane where it must have fallen out the window, or somebody had thrown it, and nobody found it, picked it up, and it just got more and more grimy as the pollution and dust turned it gray.

"How was school?" Her mother's voice an intrusion.

"Fine. Mom, I don't want to talk, just give me some space, okay?"

"Okay." Kira turned up the radio, an easy listening station. Sappy seventies music filled the car: *"There's seven ways you smooth me, move me, love me up and groove me, groove me…"*

"Mom, do you mind? I've got a headache."

"Oh, I'm sorry." The radio snapped off.

"So when *is* he getting home?"

"I'm not sure, honey. He's taking a couple of days in the desert, I guess."

"But I miss him, and he said he would be home tonight."

"I miss him, too," her mother's voice soothing, and something in it fake, like she was trying to calm down a little kid.

"I doubt it!" It exploded out of her, the first words clearing the way for the next words, until they spewed out of her. "Mom, you totally drove him away, you made him leave, you made *them* leave, and where are they going to go, huh? What are they going to do? Amber's going to get some shitty job wearing a paper hat, and Johnny thinks M.L.K. Way is Milky Way, not Martin Luther King Jr. Way, and he doesn't even know who that is, not that Amber's going to teach him because she calls people *the n-word* and *dogs* and *spoiled*, and Joey needs a real doctor who can fix his eyes and his brain and not somebody stupid at the free clinic in Elko. And you sent them back there. You. They're our family! For the first time in my whole life I wasn't an only child. And I miss them, Mom. I miss Daddy. I miss *everybody*."

Tears streamed down her face. She would jump out of the car, hit the ground running, run and run and find a soft green field to flop in. But they were on the freeway in the middle of the city and she couldn't do that. She imagined the sound her body would make, the thump, the next thump, as it was hit and tossed from car to car, the screeching tires, the smell of rubber. She lay back against the seat, eyes shut, trying to fade into the leather, thin herself down and just disappear.

❧ KIRA

Kira drove with her hands clutched tight on the wheel, keeping her eyes fixed firmly on the road. Polly's words ricocheted around the car, hit against her ears, sound bullets. Everything ached, and she was dizzy. It was hard to hang onto the wheel, but she had to, she had to get them home where it was safe, where she could hold Polly in her sadness and anger and just rock and rock, folding her girl's long arms and legs into her. Just rock and rock and rock. They could do it without Adam. They'd get through it together.

They'd have to.

She didn't say anything until they took the Harrison Street exit. Heading up the hill, she turned to Polly. "There's tissue in the glove compartment. Do you want to go right home or should we go to Piedmont to get steak? We could both use the iron."

Polly nodded, wiped out. "Steak."

"Hey Pol, when did you stop calling me Mommy?"

"I'm sorry. It just slipped out." Blowing her nose loudly, storm over. "I just think I should call you Mom now. I don't know why, I just do."

"It's fine, honey. Really. And steamed artichokes, okay? With butter and mayo?" Polly's favorite.

"Okay. Mom."

She turned left off Harrison down the hill towards Piedmont Market through beautiful old homes they'd never live in, deciduous trees stark in winter; her sadness, fatigue, heaviness, the watery haze of early pregnancy making it hard even to drive.

❧ POLLY

She missed her dad. It was cool, getting more responsibility because now it was just her and her mom. Made her more like Nell who did her own laundry and bought her own clothes already, probably because she didn't have a mom and a dad living in the same house. But she missed him. Even the other three, a little: Amber because she'd never had a sister before; Johnny with his Bionicles; Joey, the way they'd lined up the acorns for the squirrels to eat, and his little hat, and the way he saw everything.

She missed her dad so hard. She put her hand on her Eye and traced the numb ridges. "Daddy?" she whispered into the dark of her bedroom, the moon forcing stripes of light through the blinds. It was the full moon and she was trying wicca magic, trying to send her quiet voice out over the mountains to him, sending it on the force of her need and love. "Daddy, we need you to come home."

But it didn't sound convincing, because she knew she needed him to come home, but she still wasn't so sure about her mom. Without her dad here, Kira could just fade off, stop being a mom even.

On her way to sleep, Polly became Thoth, the ibis-headed god of the moon, of magic. He Who Balances. She soared still and fierce on the wind drafts. Her powerful shoulders thrust her wings. She sat up in bed to practice, her shoulder blades sinking down and back, sternum up and forward, her neck lengthening in the back so her chin tucked under, her beak curving moon-shaped, her eyes beady and watchful for any movement in the marshes below. A frog. A snake. A fish. She tucked her wings back and, head down, dropped, wind whistling through her feathers, stomach flipping in excitement and hunger. The wind cold through the feathers on her face, around her beak, eyes open as the water neared and neared and she plunged, gently snapping her beak around her prey.

And once she had eaten, she would soar to Nevada, water bird across the desert. She would drop a single feather and it would waft back and forth slowly down to her dad. He would know it was time to come home.

❧ KIRA

When Kira woke in the night, she stopped on the way back from the bathroom and quietly entered Polly's room. Polly had fallen asleep with her reading light on. Kira watched her sleep, the curve of her cheek still puffy from childhood. Her hands as big as Kira's now, the nails bitten short, the cuticles peeled and inflamed. Her sleep breaths. The adolescent shell melted into sleep; she would be pretty someday, not beautiful—Adam's nose, a little bulbous. Her own low hairline. But beautiful eyes, wide smile, the combination of wise-ass humor and enthusiasm—so winning. She would be sexy.

So many possibilities. And none for the little fleck inside her. She didn't touch Polly, just quietly clicked off the reading light and left the room.

Back in bed, she lay clutching herself. She'd heard that when the Dalai Lama killed a mosquito he said, "Better luck next time." She wasn't sure if she believed in reincarnation or not. Probably not. And a human fetus was not a mosquito. A damaged human fetus burrowing in an unwelcoming womb. A spark of life misplaced.

Time to say goodbye.

"Good bye, little one," she said out loud. She pictured a little boy, bright eyed and dark haired. "Go find another mommy and daddy. This is not the right place or time." She felt silly saying it out loud—but not as silly as she'd thought she'd feel. Because the little boy was listening to her, his face questioning.

"I really can't," she said to him. It was true. She felt tears spring hot in her eyes.

The little boy stared at her—he had Adam's jaw. She saw his face crumple in disappointment, a small wrinkle in his forehead like the one Polly got when she was troubled. His thin shoulders drooped, his head hung low. Then he raised his chest, looked at her, and nodded. Turned away. Something untangled in her.

She looked at the clock next to the bed, Adam's bed. 3:28 a.m. She wanted him home, his leg sliding over hers in the night, her foot resting on the arch of his foot. It was so wrong to have to do this all alone.

CHAPTER 20

꩜ KIRA

The old knowledge was on the Internet: once a woman was six weeks pregnant, natural abortifactants were not likely to work. After the eighth week, it was actively dangerous. She had a small window, and she was at the edge of that window. It might only take a bottle of vitamin C, no bioflavinoids. You might need to add Black Cohosh. Beware of Pennyroyal: the oil could kill you. The earlier you began, the better rate of success. It was a no-turning-back path. If you began the process, you had to continue to the end, until the pregnancy was gone, the miscarriage complete—whether that was natural, or chemical, or surgical. You could not change your mind. Once you had made the irrevocable choice, you had to be consistent. The vitamin C must be taken every hour in the correct dosage, every hour waking or sleeping. Even if your tongue blistered and bled—which it would. Until you sweated and cramped with gas. Until the herb tea doubled you over in the kitchen, the bathroom. Until you bled, passed clots, cramped, and cried.

It was not for the faint of heart.

She took Polly to Lindsey's to hang with Nell, then stopped at Longs for a bottle of vitamin C. Eight dollars. She began the C in the morning, popping it every hour. Her stomach got gassy, though that could have been the pregnancy. She set timers on the microwave, alarm clock, and phone. She gulped water. The massive doses went to her bowels, the water to her bladder. All that day and night, waking herself up to take more.

That first night alone in the bed, her mouth inflamed, feverish from no sleep, she dreamed: snake skins, insect carapaces, webs. She dreamed: the fabric of the furniture ripped and chewed looking, something had tunneled inside. Mouse droppings in the storage area, a musty metallic odor. What had gotten into their papers and books? You could not keep the vermin out in wet weather. The insects built spiral nests, segmenting their eggs. She opened a grapefruit; the same clusters of cells. "We are made of cells, too," she said in the dream, and could not eat it. Her legs grew lean, her thighs ropy. Terrorist cells. Cancer cells. The mutilated rotten mouse. Something rotten in the state of the Den. In the garden, snails and slugs. The old dream of the bottlebrush tree and trailing slugs sliding into her hair, caught in the curls. After the apocalypse, the smell of burning bone.

In the morning, she brushed her teeth and spat blood, her tongue blistering and bleeding. Her head pounded. Drinking a lot of water. Every hour, the vitamin C. The success stories were the ones who were relentless. Convinced completely. Committed. But she already felt less pregnant, the nausea receding and her breasts less swollen. Every day, round the clock. The hardest parts were the nights.

ADAM

Mornings at Stockmen's, the sky was misty with long pink streaks, the sounds of semi trucks. The sheets were so scratchy he got rug burns if he moved too fast. He shut his eyes: I won't do it. "Wake up," he told himself. Dozed again until after 8:00. Breakfast alone, biscuits and gravy with bacon. $2.29. Inedible. The coffee stale and thin. Then he'd meet with Amber and the kids, pay for their breakfast at McDonald's, drop them back at Stockmen's to make phone calls, and drive to the Red Lion and sit drinking real coffee inside a normal-looking Starbucks whose "fourth wall" was the casino floor. Joni Mitchell and the sounds of lattes being steamed mixing with the beeping of slot machines.

He did not ask Amber what she was doing those long days. Friday night, Saturday night. His two day max came and went. Lassitude, torpor, his limbs heavy, his head achy, the buzz of too many bad free cocktails at the slots, his (Kira's!) codeine gone now. He didn't turn the cell phone on. He didn't leave town. To get back in the car and drive 500 miles through desert, snow, and mountains. He was gambling lightly, a little blackjack, a little roulette, a lot of slots. And against all odds, he was winning. Up a few hundred—paying for the hotel rooms at least.

On Sunday mid-morning he dropped them all at Sandi's so they could go to church and drove himself up to Lemoille Canyon through thin snowflakes. Gray wide skies stretching to the Ruby Mountains, the glacial canyon winding up and up through stunning rock formations. He waited for the beauty—stark trees, icy streams, sharp-cut cliffs—to do their nature-number; give me a plan, make me feel again, he asked the cold air; but the beauty was icy as the road. Somewhere back in Oakland his life was on hold, his wife, child, job hung in a jar of formaldehyde, turning and staring at him. How are they managing? Who's doing the laundry? Is Polly upset? Is Kira in pain? And here he was, five hundred miles from home, listening for the lonesome train whistle.

"When you hear the train I'm on, you will know that I am gone…"
He hadn't planned to be this gone.

He woke early on Monday. The sunrise in Nevada looked different, more sun-like, the edges less fogged by the breath of millions of people. The animals that had encroached on their own homelands, now streets and houses and roads, retreated back to the desert. The desolate Ruby Mountains retreated in the distance, the Humboldt river flowed in its broad bed, opaque gray water among the sand and weedy bluffs. The sky lightened. Adam stepped out of the hotel onto the cement of the parking lot.

It actually wasn't so bad if you didn't have to live here, he thought. Elko still felt like a settlement town, cowboys and Indians and old whores named Cindi and Sue and Dee, legal cathouses (Mona's, Inez's Dancing and Diddling), buildings weathered by desert winds and sun and snow. Skins, too, dried and easily cracked, hair, so far from the ocean breeze, more brittle, dull—Sandi's hair. The harsher light of the eastern Mohave desert sun.

But he didn't have to live here. He wanted to go home.

Returning from Starbucks (already a regular: "Just a tall coffee no room fer cream, right, hon?"), he knocked on Amber's door. Through the walls, he heard only the static roar of the television, Johnny or Joey thumping around.

"Ma's in the shower." Johnny, the Game Boy loose in one hand.

"Where's Joey?"

"Watching cartoons."

But the TV so loud.

"You want to come out with me for lunch, just you, let your mom make phone calls? I want to hit that taco truck near the tattoo place, Las Brisas. Okay? A little carne asada with me?"

Johnny shrugged, then nodded.

"Good. And I need you to tell your mom something, Johnny. When she gets out of the shower. I'm leaving town tomorrow, okay? Tell her that. Tell her I'm taking you out to lunch later, and I'll talk to her then. Okay?"

"Okay." His little face was tight. This kid didn't believe adults, Adam realized. Of course not.

"You got that?"

Johnny nodded. Back to his room to call Kira.

❧ KIRA

Adam reached her at work in the middle of day three. "So we moved to Stockmen's a couple days ago—it's like living inside a really used ashtray. Goddamn, it's hard to find a quiet place to talk around here. The walls fucking vibrate. Damn TV has to be loud, not just loud, blaring. Nobody must have any eardrums in Nevada, man. It's totally Jerry Springer meets John Wayne around here."

"Hi Adam."

"That fucking Sandi! Living out here in this desert hellhole. And Amber's about as proactive as a slug. Like she's sitting waiting to die, and that can take a long time when you're twenty-five, and I don't know what to do, how to motivate her. I told her to call her friends, figure out where they can stay a while. I told her I'd help her out—give her a few hundred for an apartment, or help her write a resume, check into a women's shelter or something, but she has to take some initiative—she's just sitting on her ass. 'Thinking,' she says. Like the world's waiting for her to show up. Talk about being battered down, no ambition—not even any ambitions to save her kids, anything, not even sending Johnny to school, and he's a smart kid, Kira. He'll end up a redneck racist like the rest of them. They should give people licenses to reproduce, and she wouldn't get one. I'm ready to dump and run, I'm about stretched to the maximum here."

Kira counted to ten.

"Are you there?" Adam said.

"I'm here."

"What's the matter with you? Don't you have anything to say to me anymore? I would think you'd have sympathy for somebody here, even if it isn't me. Maybe an idea or two, because I'm out of them."

She was silent.

"Why aren't you talking to me? Did something happen? How's Polly—is she okay?"

"Polly's fine. Why don't you ask me how *I* am?"

A pause. "Sorry, Kira. How are you?"

"How do you think I am? I'm having a miscarriage."

"Oh good, you didn't need the abortion. Are you okay? Should you even be at work?"

Kira felt her anger melt into tears. "You are so clueless. Why didn't you even ask about me? Launching into your own rant. I'm sorry it's not going well for you."

"Fuck, Kira." He was quiet for a moment. She clutched the phone, trying to breathe. "You call the shots and I react. I'm afraid to even ask you what you're up to now."

"Adam," she said quietly into the phone so nobody in the office would hear. "Number one, this is an inappropriate place to call and rant at me. Number two, I'm fine, it's going fine, thank you for your concern, not even calling over the weekend."

"I miss you. My cell phone…" he began.

"Save it. Number three, if I make decisions, it's because you never do. And I'm going to hang up now."

She took another deep breath. The alarm on the computer went off, and she took another two vitamin C tablets.

ADAM

The tacos were decent. Not for Mexico, not for Oakland's

International Avenue, but they actually had decent tortillas and not-half-bad asada, and the carnitas melted in the mouth. Cut limes and pico de gallo. He loved to watch Johnny eat. If he was his biological grandson, he sure had gotten the food gene.

Eating was one thing (perched on stools on the side of the open truck, Mexican Cokes in front of each of them), talking another. What did you ask a kid like this? "How's school?" Right. He's in second grade but he doesn't go. Does he even know his teacher's name? "Who's your dad? It's Mike, right, not Steve?" (Fuck. Even better yet: "Who's your granddad.")

"What's your favorite kind of candy? I like Snickers, do you like Snickers?" he finally asked.

"Yeah. But I like Milky Way best."

Hey, the kid's got pretty good taste.

"Adam? My grandma says I can't live there now because of her work. I told my mom I want to live with you and Polly now and she said, 'We'll see.' That it's up to you."

Adam choked on a jalapeño, drank Coke.

"Oh, John. I'm not sure it's up to me."

"Okay. I also like Red Whips. And I think Polly does too, just to let you know if you ever wanted to buy her some candy that she likes when you get home and she's hungry and she wants some candy."

"Thanks, Johnny Rockboy." Poor brave puppy. He didn't give a shit if Johnny thought he was too old to sit on a lap. He picked him off his stool from behind and sat down again on his own stool with Johnny on top of him.

Now all Adam had to do was talk rationally to Amber, be nice, adult, and explain that he was done. That he'd tried. Then he could go home and deal with the fallout. Until then, he refused to think about that. One problem at a time.

"Did Johnny tell you? I'm leaving tomorrow?"

"Suit yourself."

"Okay, we'll go out to dinner tonight? A goodbye dinner?"

"Not the kids. Mom said she'd watch them tonight."

"You talked to her? She's okay watching them? That sounds… like maybe a breakthrough between you guys."

"Nah, it's only 'cause they're gonna go to Big Tommy's birthday party. But not me, and not you."

Better yet. To get one last chance to talk with her, find out her plans, help her form one.

"Did you talk to anybody else this morning, or just your mom?"

Amber's eyes lidded over, the invisible curtain of the reptile, protecting her gaze. "No."

"Did you call that women's shelter?"

"That's for tribal people. I'm not no Indian dog."

"Jesus, Amber, will you please cool it with the racial slurs. I don't need to listen to that shit."

She shrugged.

"What are you going to do? Where are you going to stay?"

She looked at him. He sighed. Lead a horse to water, dunk its damn head in the water, pry open its mouth, insert syringe full of water…

"Johnny, get your jacket on," she said into the room behind her. "Tie those shoes."

He gave up. "Okay, what time's that party? When do they need to get to your mom's house by?"

Amber shrugged. "Whatever time's fine after she gets back from work. They're just there, you know. They ain't never going nowhere, no place to go, unless Big Tom's driving. But it's his birthday. Aquarius."

"Where do you want to go to dinner?"

"I just ate some chips, I can't be thinking about dinner. But you want to go somewhere nice?"

"Somewhere nice."

"The Star's best."

"What's that like?"

She shrugged again. "Steaks as big as a toilet seat, lamb. I don't know. Basque, I guess. Family-style food. It's good."

"You follow three leads this afternoon, I'll take you out to the Star."

"Whatever."

"That attitude will get you far."

POLLY

The mail piled on the living room table. On her way into the house Monday afternoon, Polly reached in the mailbox for mail, maybe even a postcard from Elko. But only bills addressed to Daddy, and an intriguingly thick manila envelope for her mom.

"Ooh! Mom, can I open it?"

"No, Polly, you cannot. You don't open other people's mail."

Polly knew she was talking about the horrible love note on the door, and shut up, went to her room. She hated that man, the yoga teacher. The envelope was probably from him. She hated her mom.

Polly lay in her bed, tired of the silence, ready to jump up, turn on music loud, make a noise, anything to drown out this feeling of being useless, unable to bring her dad home. How long could you hold a secret before it exploded out of you like a mean thing you say in a fight? It was fine now, they all wore long pants or skirts and tights. But in the Spring, in shorts weather, her Eye of Thoth, healing now to a beautiful white keloid scar, would be out there for everybody to see. Plum sized. Not private. It was on her forever. And that was great—or it would be once the yelling and concern was over.

Telling things was better than having them found out. But how do you go up to your mom and say, "Mom, I'm not the innocent little girl you think I am anymore. Look what I did."

✍ KIRA

Kira put the thick manila envelope, return address The Ancestor Project, on the bottom of the pile of Adam's mail on the dining room table. The results from the DNA test were inside. She couldn't look at it. Couldn't open it. Because when it came right down to it, it wasn't her business. It was Adam's. If he ever came back, she'd tell him what she'd done.

CHAPTER 21

❧ ADAM

He hadn't brought anything nice to wear. An extra pair of jeans, a decent enough sweater, his ski jacket. They would have to do. After they dropped the kids off at Sandi's, Johnny leading Joey in while the Prius stood at the curb—Sandi yelling out the door, "Come back for them!" "No problem!" he yelled back—they parked in the Stockmen's lot and walked the two short blocks to Silver Street, wide enough for a herd of sheep, the rooftop sign a single red star on a barren scaffolding, like the stars he'd seen before the fall of the Iron Curtain in Prague. Inside, the restaurant bustled, no reservations taken.

"About forty-five minutes. You can wait in the bar, I'll find ya. What's your name?"

"Adam."

"Enjoy a couple punches; we'll get you a table in no time."

He steered Amber through the crowds, his arm looped through hers. Something was different, maybe because they were without the kids, Kira, Polly. Had they ever been alone together? Maybe because she'd made an effort to look good. She'd done up her hair, moussed it or something, it stood tall, and she'd put on a tight blouse that showed her ample cleavage. A skirt, no sweatpants. He tried not to look; she looked like a woman, he was out with a woman, not somebody who could maybe be his daughter.

He relaxed. What the hell. No reason he couldn't enjoy himself, last night in this hole of a town.

"Wanna get a drink?" she said.

"Sure. Whatever you want." Thinking tequila, and lots of it, that night at Lucky Lounge with Stan, Stan's ease with the situation: "She's always calling me Dad, but I'm Uncle Stan the Man," and the way he'd fallen in the gutter that night outside the house, that fuzz, the blue aquarium of too much tequila, and he needed that now.

"Picon Punch. That's the specialty."

"Two Picon Punch," he said to the bartender, a sixty-ish woman with a stiff hair and a squint.

"Two punch, for you and your lady."

"My daughter." He tried it out and the word flowed. Say something long enough and you got used to it. Maybe he could get used to it. But the bartender's back was already turned.

The Picon Punch tasted mild, though he thought—knew—it was deceptive. "What's in this?" he asked the bartender when they ordered a second round.

"Brandy, grenadine, Amer Picon, soda. Nice, huh?"

"Nice."

He'd meant to ask Amber about her phone calls this afternoon, grill her. Remind her he was leaving, she had to check out of Stockmen's take her kids somewhere else. Where? Where else? But the drink was strong. He was tired of cracking the whip. Amber leaned on the bar, her right breast spilling over a little, a pillow soft as the potato gnocchi at La Strada—what the hell was he thinking?

"Nice to get rid of those kids for a while." She rolled back a little, her breast off the bar and pointing right at him.

In the dark light of the bar, the bottles glowed, backlit, the candles flickered on the small bar tables. Noise of the loud speaker calling diners to dinner, "Mr. and Mrs. Adams, party of two!

Bidart family, party of six!" Saddles on the walls, rough beams, board walls, hardwood bar plain and straightforward. She fit here, Nevada girl. She was pretty here. Too fat, but nice skin, hard to believe with all the shit she ate. Wouldn't be able to get away with it for too many more years.

"It must be tiring to have both boys to take care of all the time," he said. "We were lucky, only had Polly, and two of us, Kira and me, to lighten the load. Two for one is hella easier than one for two." Polly two years old, curly hair and enormous eyes and round belly, balanced on his shoulders as they strolled through Rockridge, Kira next to him nervous that he'd drop her: "I can take her, Adam," "No, it's okay."

Amber looked away from him, tightened her mouth. Reached for her drink again, After a long moment he realized what he'd said, how she must take it. "Oh shit, Amber, just that it's a lot of work to have kids. Not that we were lucky to just have her."

"Mr. and Mrs. Adams, party of two," a voice at his elbow, the hostess. "Your table is ready."

"She's my daughter," he said to the hostess's back as she fed them through the crowds again, Adam holding Amber by the arm again, which felt so good, soft, warm, in this place of buckaroos and tighty whitey Mormons, and the brandy in the punch had really kicked in, halle-fuckin'-luja.

Dinner was forty bucks a person, six courses. They ate sitting next to each other on the same side of a long table covered with oilcloth, boarding house-style, an unlabeled bottle of red wine in front of them—"It's included," Amber said. "Drink up. Get your money's worth."

It was good. They sat with a bunch of families, loud and laughing, a woman who kept yelling, "Well, *Adon* thinks it's funny, *don't* you, Adon? *Don Don*?" Family-style for two people was soup with some sort of chorizo, a plate of innard-y appetizers: bacalao, tongue, squid, pig feet; tepid salad; Basque beans; two over-cooked vegetable side dishes, green beans and green peas (frozen, thawed, cooked, gray), a braised lamb dish with lots of garlic, and then, when he thought it was over, a wide white platter of well-aged chateaubriand.

"Too much!" he said, but he was happy, drunk on the thick red wine. Amber poured him another glass, her left breast brushing against his arm, her thigh next to his thigh, and damn it felt good. So damn long since he'd had physical affection; so nice they were getting along, getting closer. The steak succumbed easily to the fork, his teeth, juicy and aged.

"Save room for dessert, Daddy."

Something sickly sweet about her voice. Don't call me Daddy! he wanted to say. But Stan was okay with it, it was just a figure of speech. "What's dessert here?"

"Usually just ice cream, maybe flan." Rhyming with plan. "Coffee, tea. Haven't been here since prom."

"Booyah. Might as well dairy-load, because that's what's done here; when in Rome, baby. When in Rome. I'll take me some *flan*." Rhyming with swan. Prom? She'd dropped out. When had she gone to prom? Fuck it, he thought. Drank again. A strand of hair swung from her hairline and into her mouth, he reached up a tender hand to move it away. She had such a pretty smile when she relaxed like this.

He leaned in, their heads close together, time slowing, the loud crowd blurring into wine and Picon Punch soaked dizziness, her breath, the air so sweet with her…

Oh fuck, he'd almost kissed her. He pulled away.

She'd pulled away from him like he'd hit her. "You've got problems, dude," she said loudly, her face repulsed.

What the fuck was he thinking? Both hands over his mouth, in shock. "I'm sorry."

"Fuck you." She hadn't moved. Still staring at him like he'd crawled from a sewer. "Why can't you just be a normal dad? Why are you such a freak?"

The words burst out. "Because I'm not your dad! I don't give a shit if you take a DNA test, I don't give a shit. You're not mine. I don't claim you. I don't want you. I drove you here and I'm leaving and I'd be glad never to see your fat ass again. Fucking up my whole life."

Amber's eyes were blank.

The sounds of the restaurant filled in all the gaps, pressed in on his eye sockets.

He reached for the wine. There. I've said it, he thought. But his intestines lurched. Snake of shame.

"Suit yourself," she said, her eyes mean. "You're my asshole father, whatever you say. Hey, whatever, dude. I was going to ask a big favor, but I should have known you'd never lift your little finger for anybody but yourself."

"But that's not true!" he wanted to say. But was it? "I gotta take a piss," he said, pushing abruptly back from the table. He staggered to the bathroom, needing to piss, unable to piss. He stared into the mirror. Asshole.

He paid the bill in grim silence. They picked up the kids. He waited outside Sandi's house and, as the door closed behind Amber, he rested his foot on the gas pedal, practicing what it would feel like to press down, slide the car forward and drive forever, scrape her off of him, dogshit off a shoe. But his foot wouldn't move. A few minutes later Amber stomped toward the car, Joey on her hip, Johnny trailing behind.

Monday night at Stockmen's Casino in the room behind the craps tables, a band played, gold lamé curtains behind the raised stage, a huge room that seated two hundred at tables, and a dance floor. Amber and the kids wandered upstairs. Adam dragged his sorry ass and free casino beer in to listen. Total audience including him, five. These guys were pretty good, he thought. Lame jokes and self-promotion and cowboy hats, but they knew how to play. They'd had a national hit a few years ago that brought them to Nashville—"Unrepentant Redneck." Their act was tight, and even with five silent souls nursing beers scattered through the empty seats, they performed like they loved it, so he stuck around and bopped his head to the music:

> *Well, I run outta luck with my pick up truck*
> *Done dropped my load on the side of the road*
> *but my guns are racked and my lady's stacked*
> *and I hold her tight and I feel alright*
>
> *And I got my God and I got my guns*
> *and we got them liberals on the run…*

And he was nodding and tapping and laughing and laughing: I'm losing my shit! And it had its moments; a great back beat and trucks and guns and rednecks and beer and God and my lady and it's alright, picturing them all rockin' out, he and these guys on national tour, startin' here in Elko, Winnamucca, Lovelock, Fresno, every hick town, Stan sittin' in on drums, Sandi dancin' in the front, *not a "g" to be heard at the end of a word…* and his head down on the table. Son of a fuckin' bitch what am I doing—no, it's what am I *doin'* –

What am I doin'? What the hell had happened with Amber in that restaurant?

He stood up. "FUCK YOU FUCKING ASSHOLES!" he screamed at the top of his lungs. "I'M A BRIE-EATING JEW

FROM CALIFOR-NI-AYY! I LOVE BLACK PEOPLE AND INDIANS AND CHAR-DON-NAYYYY!" Nobody looked at him. "MALCOM X! GLORIA STEINEM! ALICE WALKER! TONI MORRISON! SI SE PUEDE! FREE HUEY NEWTON! FREE LOVE! AT-TIC-A! AT-TIC-A!" and the lead singer laughed happily, "Well, fuckyouverymuch, buddy, glad you're enjoyin' the show," and the other four men in the audience didn't turn a head.

So he wandered back through the casino, up the stairs: hadn't even noticed the carpets all hats and lassos, a fucking cowboy-themed carpet... and slid the card key. Red light. Slid the card key. Red light. Fuck. Slid the card key. Green light. Climbed into bed.

Woke in the night. Have I bottomed out yet? And the voice in his head, Kira's voice: "No. But you did just act like a total dick."

He tossed. He tossed. He tossed. Casino lights shone through the window. Fifty years of cigarette smoke seeped out of the walls. He was a black lung. He tried to get comfortable, still roaring with a sick lust—the feel of Amber's body against his, and hating her. Sick. Goddamn it. Still so drunk, a horny drunk Drunk, he pulled on his jeans, ski jacket, shoes, and crawled his sorry ass downstairs and into the lobby.

"Stockmen's: If you liked us before, you'll love us now!" the slogan over the empty front desk. The lobby bulletin board unwitnessing—Adam pulled a glossy card for Edie's House of Pleasure from the board—down on Third Street, just a few blocks away. Fulfill a fantasy, wallow in it—every guy's gotta try a prostitute sometime, and here, at the edge of the desert, why not go all the way down the road. A last hurrah, then home to deal with Kira.

Even in his fogged alcoholic haze, he noticed it all, imagined himself narrating to Stan: "It was a house, man, a real house of ill repute." A tiny square house on the corner of a big square block. He parked in front. A large sign out front painted on wood: "Edie's: Don't bother knockin', ring the bell, and CUM on in!"

He turned the door handle, pushed into a short hallway. It stank. It walloped him with the smell of smoke and disinfectant and mildew and what must be old sperm. On his left, a half-open door and inside, an Asian woman in a China doll wig and white lacy lingerie sprawled on a round bed, a crumbled blanket across part of her, limbs askew. When she saw him she sat up and posed.

Terrified, he walked past the door, and into a small living room. One end was a homemade bar, two other doors were curtained with old red velvet. The room was dark, the smell even more dank. A weathered-faced woman in her fifties stood behind the bar. "Howdy!" A big smile. Toothless. Toothless! "Come on in! We're open! You here for a party? You been here before?"

"First time."

"First time here, first time in a brothel, or first time?" she winked.

"First time in a brothel. I live in California." *(I'M A BRIE-EATING JEW FROM CALIFOR-NI-AYY!)*

"Okay! Well, glad you're here, we'll take good care of you. I'm Deb. The bartender. Have a seat. If you're looking for company, we got five girls here, but three is busy tonight, so you can meet Kelly and Kimi. You like red heads or exotic girls?

"Thought I heard the doorbell?"

"This is Kelly."

"Hi!" She was pretty. He couldn't look too closely.

"Do you want to meet Kimi?" The one sprawled on the round bed.

"No. Kelly's great."

Deb handed him a "menu" and he scanned it, chose the House

Special, $299 for "a little sucking, a lot of fucking." He forked over cash from the slots.

"Can we get two Sprites, Deb?" Kelly took his hand and led him behind the curtain, down the hall, past a dark kitchen to another bedroom. "Lie down, baby. No need to be nervous, we got as long as you want."

He didn't want long. He fucked her hard and fast on the lumpy bed, her body thin but slightly flaccid, her high screams of "pleasure" so rehearsed, embarrassing him. The act was fine, just sex, just wallowing. But her faking.

"Don't fake," he said. "Just don't fake it."

"Oh, baby, you're so good at this, I'm not faking it, you make me cum so good."

"Please," he said, "just don't pretend." His orgasm almost lost in the waves of drunkenness.

It was cold outside. Desert dry and frozen. At around four a.m., Adam wandered down to Buckaroo Bob's 24 hour coffee shop on Fourth Street and frittered away quarters in the electronic slot machine at his table where the juke box should be, drinking bad coffee to thaw, and savoring the full-out Amurican experience: orange naugahyde and soft rock on the system and red white and blue flags on everything, paper flag on the toothpick in his club sandwich. Thinking: God, I hate this country.

At nine, when the banks opened, he took an eight hundred dollar cash advance on the American Express, all they'd allow. He tucked six of the one hundred dollar bills in a deposit envelope and returned to Stockmen's. On the envelope he wrote: DON'T use this for bus tickets. Apartment deposit and food money only. Good Luck! Love, Adam.

After he'd written it, he hesitated over the "love," but scratching it out and putting "best wishes" or "XO" or nothing would show he'd crossed out the "love"—he couldn't be that cruel—and he didn't have a second envelope anyway. And he hadn't signed it "Dad." A thief, a coward, an asshole, he slid the envelope under the door, knocked on the door three times hard, and walked quickly back to the car, slammed the door, backed up and zoomed away. Too fast, as if they could pursue him on foot, zombies on speed.

A mile from Elko on 225—singing *"take it to the limit…"* fucking Eagles, arguably the best American band of all time. Arguably. He hated that word, *arguably,* and he hated the Eagles—he pulled randomly over to the side of the road and looked at the names of local ghost towns on the map: Arthur, Jiggs, Ruby City, Battle Creek, Bullion. Foundations and rubble. Land of gold and diamonds. And crystal, ice—meth labs in the desert.

Amber had told him how they'd driven out there, bought the drugs, then all-nightered it to Salt Lake City, where they tripled profits. "Morons," she'd said, shaking her head. "Fucking ass hypocrites." And the bust those years ago, just that side of the border, stopped for speeding, Steve's sooty green glass pipe and blackened foil sitting stupidly on the back seat of the Dodge. Blaming each other even as they sat, terrified and sullen, Amber pregnant and nauseous, for more than two hours in the back of the highway patrol car, waiting for all their info to be called in. No water, and she had to pee so bad. At the station, one phone call, not to a lawyer, but to Sandi. "You have to take Johnny again, Mom. I'm arrested."

It didn't matter where he headed. A random side of the road, a rest stop where he could sit out back. In the glove compartment, a tiny sealable plastic bag of glass-like shards, $100 of rock he'd scored from Kelly the hooker. An extra $38 for the new rig and spoon. "You know how to use this, baby?"

"Been a long time, but yeah."

"You need a lighter, baby? I got a nice souvenir one for five bucks."

He'd been totally ripped off, for all of it. But what the fuck. Go down flailing. Like he had a choice. And at least he and Kira were even now.

He'd go out to the desert. An old fashioned vision quest, find some ghost towns, Indians with peyote, an adventure, a horse into the sunset; find something. Find himself. Bottom out for once and for all. And anyway, what more could he have done?

❧ KIRA

On day four, Tuesday, she went back to the clinic. Her HGC numbers registered no pregnancy. Disbelief—had it been a mistake? She dug the pregnancy test out of the bottom of her bedside drawer, its two parallel lines still pink and bright. But she still had not begun bleeding. She had been pregnant. And the nausea, swollen breasts; all the symptoms. And now, apparently, she was not.

Now she just needed the bleeding to begin.

At the Food Mill, she bought Black Cohosh in gelatin capsules. Even the name sounded evil—Black Cohosh, the hiss of a devil. She was swallowing night. Within half an hour she felt a dull cramping. She took another capsule, and in another fifteen minutes she found bright red drops in her underpants.

Then a lurch, cramping so hard she lost her breath as if punched in the solar plexus. Then it truly began. She lay on the couch, wearing a pad, willing herself to check it every fifteen minutes. A hemorrhage would be a full pad more than once every hour. She was doing fine, on the verge of it, but still fine. It was just like a bad period. And breathing and meditating in between.

When Amanda's mom dropped Polly home after school, Polly found her curled in around herself and a hot water bottle on the couch, her eyes shut.

"Mommy?"

"Hey, sweetie. I'm not feeling so well. I'm having a really bad period, but it's okay."

Polly ran over to her, stood over her as if afraid to touch her. "Oh no!"

"It's okay. I'm fine." The contractions were hard now, taking her breath away. She felt another blurt of blood into the pad. "Can you heat up some water and refill this hot water bottle? Without burning yourself?" It was important to keep Polly from freaking out.

"Um, sure." Polly went to the kitchen. Kira heard the water run and the kettle clunk onto the stove, then Polly came back out. "Do you want some Tylenol or something?

"I'm fine. Do you have a lot of homework?"

"Fair amount."

"Then go to your room and get to it, Poodle." It was all she could do to keep from moaning out loud.

֍ ADAM

There was nothing in the desert in winter. The desert was deserted. He drove for miles, headed south on 225 towards Jiggs where, Amber had told him, there was an old saloon with a two-headed calf on the wall. Thirty miles on paved, icy road with nothing—snowy cattle range—on either side until he reached Jiggs. A few old battered buildings. A single gas pump outside the saloon. He parked the Prius and got out, fuck it was cold, and pushed, John-Wayne style, through the saloon doors. It was dim and cold and high-raftered. And empty. "Hello!" he called.

Adam walked around. There was a two-headed calf head mounted on the wall, looking dismayed. A stuffed jackalope, the seams showing; in a glass case, a few moth-eaten deer heads, a white porcupine, a coffee cup of eagle feathers; a pool table, old mining gear.

Finally a guy came out of the back. "Howdy. Help you?"

"Thanks, just passing through. But uh, any way I can get to any old ghost towns from here?"

"Right here, standing in one. This bar's historic. Jiggs is on the National Registry. No ghosts though, none that I've seen in forty-odd years. We got UFOs though, we're one of only thirty-five suspected UFO alien bases in the United States."

"Oh wow." He picked a postcard of a jackalope from the wire rack on the bar for Polly. "I'll get this." He put a dollar on the bar.

"You lookin' at ghost towns this time of year? Can't really do them dirt roads in winter 'less you got a 4-wheel drive."

"Guess not. Don't want to end up like that family in Oregon."

"Wise move. Need gas? Somethin' to drink?"

"Maybe a drink." Knee jerk. Man, he was tired of alcohol. He didn't even like it.

"What's yer pleasure, cowboy."

He was tempted to order a tall milk. Smartass. "Johnny Walker, up." It sounded like a man's drink.

He'd have his drink, he'd find a place to smoke his meth, he'd have a vision. He'd figure it out. He sat there.

Eleven-something a.m. on a Tuesday in February in a bar in an almost deserted town in the middle of a desert in winter. He was an Unidentified Flying Object.

Noon-something on a Tuesday in February. UFOs. Two-headed calves. What a baby. He pushed the shot glass away: I don't even like to drink. He took the meth and pipe out of his pocket and put it on the bar: like I'm really going to smoke it.

He took out his phone and turned it on. Like a fucking KFC bowl, every conversation with Kira layered and loaded. Pregnant. And now she wasn't. Who have we lost this time? But the cell phone had no battery. As if there would be a signal here anyway. He put the phone near the baggie of meth.

He took out his wallet. Useless credit cards. He stacked them on the bar next to the whiskey, the drugs, the phone. Which left him with $49. He put a twenty on the bar. He stuck the wallet back in his pocket, picked up the jackalope postcard, and walked out of the bar, the saloon doors swinging hard behind him. It wasn't like in the movies, though. He stopped just outside the door… it's cold! and one of the doors clunked him hard on the back of the head. Don't let the door hit ya on the way out.

He got in the car, reclined the seat, and fell asleep. Waking close to dusk, drove back to Elko. Fourteen miles before he got there, the Prius ran out of gas.

❧ POLLY

Her mom lay on the couch for hours. Cramps. Polly knew she could make dinner for herself, probably should, at least, put potatoes in the toaster oven to bake at 450 degrees. Instead, she ate a microwaved package of Trader Joe's lasagna, offered her mother tea ("No thanks, Polly, I'm good"), finally retreated to her room. The house so quiet.

Polly took a compass—point in Oakland, pencil in Elko, and proscribed an arc on her arm. Five hundred miles. When would Daddy be home. She closed her eyes.

"Polly!"

Her mother's summoning voice. "Polly, *now* please! Honey, I could really use more hot water. Fill it from the sink so it's not too hot."

"Not boiling?"

"Oh no! That would be too hot. You can make me herb tea now too, that would be nice. Chamomile!" she called into the kitchen.

But when Polly brought the tea, lovingly presented on a tray with a honey bear, spoon, and small dish to put the used tea bag on, her mom left it alone.

✒ KIRA

Kira didn't touch the tea; now she remembered that they used chamomile to treat severe menstrual cramps, and how would it combine with the cohosh? She needed to feel what she felt, bleed it all out of her. It was worse than it should be. She stood up too fast, and suddenly she stared at the ceiling, and Polly stood over her. "Mommy! Are you okay?"

"I'm okay," she said. "I think I just passed out a little." She crawled back on the couch, and Polly sat next to her, arms around her. "Help me to the bathroom, honey." She shut the door and lay on the cool tile floor.

When she was twenty-four: In an unmarked three-story office complex near Cow Hollow, Kira sat in a small room with three sixteen-year-old girls. They brought her ginger ale and soda crackers and the Valium. In the little waiting room so long before they called her, the TV blaring talk shows, the pregnant kids sullen and wrapped in blankets. After a while, the Valium took her out of time and into fuzziness…

"It's yours, it's not Stan's." That one night, drunk, giving in to Stan's pathetic drunken pawing—Adam gone home with Sheila the bass player. She and Stan had done it twice. Once at night, once again in the morning: his old Honda hatchback, darkness, not wanting to go home, mad at Adam for his lack of commitment, for being off with Sheila… maybe if she slept with Stan she could hurt Adam into wanting her…

"You'll feel something cold, and something pressing as we widen the opening."

…and Adam came home in the morning and saw her discarded maroon half-boots she'd left deliberately in the living room. He'd lined them neatly by the door to Stan's room…

Nothing resolved, except that Adam would pick her up, drive her home—she needed a ride. Who knew if they'd stay together.

The instrument cold in her: "Take a breath, now," the doctor said. A breath. Sharp! She cried into the pounding, her womb seized in a roll of pain; pierced, breeched. The world slid into gray and black spots.

"You're okay, baby. Now walk."

"I can't."

"You can." Somehow: the next room, a row of partially reclined beds, the other women so serene, so quiet. She hadn't known. To feel the cold moment of death… she moaned, gagged, a spectacle; broke a sweat, nauseous, dizzy. It wasn't the pain and it was the pain, the dull ache.

Was it then, or now?

"You're okay, baby. Um hum. A little shock." In the recovery room hours longer than all the others; they came, they went. Blood pressure checks. Cold compresses. Sips of water. Gentle hands. She slept. Hours later, they'd helped her out to Adam, still angry and helpless.

But he'd stayed. He'd been there. Not this time.

She missed him. Not the roiling, fuming, self-hating Adam he'd become; their laughter, his crude silliness. The rise and fall of the cramps. Her mind walked the old trails of him; they'd loved each other so much. She'd have to ground herself now, stay focused. Get a scholarship for Polly's school, do more parent hours. Up her hours at work? Maybe, if he didn't come back, rent out the basement to somebody for storage, or as an office…

Grief hit, volcanoed up to her head. Grief and cramping. Big drops. Gelatinous globs. Dark strings. Shocking blood blurting out from her, dark red, the color of life. Waves of red chunks. Her womb cramped and released, a clenched fist in her belly.

On the bathroom floor. The cold floor against her cheek so good, her eye focused just ahead of her an inch away, the small crack in the tile. It was over.

A surge ran through her, power. The old knowledge. She'd brought it back into her own hands. It's real, the old knowledge, she thought. Touching life and death like this was a solid touch of the universe itself; this was what she needed to teach Polly to revere. This depth.

The bleeding slowed.

Finally she rested, slept on the floor.

She was surprised at the sound of a man's voice and boots, Stan standing white over her. "Kira, you okay?" Polly behind, "Mommy, I sat outside the door for a long time but you didn't come out, so I went in, and you lied there for a really long time, and there was so much blood in the toilet so I called Daddy, I'm so sorry! Then I called Lindsey because Daddy didn't answer. He didn't call back. I'm sorry! I didn't know what else to do, but she didn't answer her cell *or* at home, so I called Stan. I was going to call 911 if he didn't answer, but he did."

Stan looking down at her, so concerned. When you were young you made friends casually, you messed up with them, slept with them drunk—Adam had never mentioned it, just sly digs about her liking the "big boys like Stan," and her making dirty cracks about Sheila, who had gone off and married somebody in Argentina and come back with some immune disorder... Had they ever talked about it, him and Stan? And what had she done to Stan? And all these years later here he was, "Do you want to go to Emergency? Are you okay?" You made those friends and you didn't realize that decades later they were still going to be the people in your life.

"I had a miscarriage. It's over. I was just sleeping."

Polly stood in the doorway behind Stan, her face twisted. Her brave girl.

"It's okay, honey. You did the right thing. Come here." But she didn't open her sticky hand, didn't want them to see. A dark clot; a tiny amniotic sac like a purple plum; a quarter-sized placenta with yellow branches.

CHAPTER 22

◊ KIRA

It was over. "It's okay, I'm okay," she said again, and sat slowly up. I'll be out in a minute."

"Are you sure?" Stan said, and she nodded, looked at Polly, pale and peering from behind Stan.

"Polly, I'm fine. I was just resting. I'll be out in a minute."

The bathroom door closed and she slowly stood, her hand still holding the large clot she'd expelled. Her heart. Impossible to flush it, to throw it away.

On the side of the towel cabinet they kept handkerchiefs and washcloths. She wrapped the clot in a lace handkerchief her grandmother had given her when she was a child. A shroud. And now what to do with it? Blood stained through the handkerchief, a dark menstrual blood, darker than rubies, almost black. She needed something to put the handkerchief in. A plastic bag seemed a travesty.

Bending at the knees so she wouldn't pass out, using her free hand, she opened the cabinet under the sink. She found a small six-sided jar that had once held bubble bath. She put the wrapped handkerchief inside, and put the lid back on. Then she washed her hands and face, checked her pad, and put the jar into the pocket of her robe. Sliding past the open doorway of the living room where Polly and Stan waited, she carried the jar to her room and placed it under her socks in the bureau. She'd wait for Adam and they'd bury it beneath the fig trees. In the garden, near where the poison oak encroached.

Polly had tucked her in, Stan standing awkward at the bed-room door, unwilling to come in. "I… I reached Lindsey. She's on her way over, hope that's okay."

"That's great. Stan, thank you. I'm really… thanks so much. For everything."

"Yeah that's okay, you know. Whenever. You're okay now, right?"

"Yes. Thank you. Really. It means a lot that you came."

"Polly's getting her stuff together for Lindsey's house. Do I need to lock the door on the way out?"

"It's fine, it clicks automatically. Thanks again."

Resting. She lay in bed—*my bed, Adam's bed,* a dull ache in her empty womb, its contents still trickling into the pad, Polly down the hall, disappeared into early teenagehood.

"I did it myself, the old way," she thought about telling Adam. "I really did it." Pride and sorrow. She missed him, the way they always looked at each other and laughed. She felt the ghost of him between her legs, his breathing with hers. Come back. So many years the two of them living enmeshed—like the pair of fig trees planted too close together in the backyard—entwined so tightly that she'd touch him and not know if she was touching his leg or her own for a moment. How much she'd damaged, how much she'd hurt, trying to be her own tree. Standing alone.

The pain filled and spilled over. Refilled. She'd birthed her heart and it was in a jar in her sock drawer: all the boys she'd ever loved; Adam when he slept, his face so vulnerable and sweet. Even little Joey, his damaged bird-face, even Johnny with his dimple, sweet boy. Little lost boy.

She felt nauseous. Not pregnancy—that was gone and there was relief in that—but remorse for it all.

Before this rift—Amber, Ravi, money—they would have

gone through the abortion together. He would have rubbed her back and they would have lain belly to belly when she could. She would have stroked the patch of wiry hair at the base of his back right above his butt, and complained about how wiry it was, and he would have joked about getting his body waxed—"Dip and rip, baby"—and they would think about the future and cry as their maybe-baby dripped from her. They would feel old and sad together.

She'd hurt him. So ashamed.

He had not been there for this. She had not been there for him, either, forcing him to face the Amber situation alone, and her grudging and resenting. How hard for him. It's not an epiphany, she thought. I never planned to leave him, I just never thought he'd leave. It's just missing.

She got up slowly to go to the bathroom, a little light-headed, wincing as her womb lurched. Back in the bedroom, she stood for a moment in *tadasana*, growing her roots down, letting her energy move up her spine. Then she moved into slight back bend, forward bend: *uttanasana*. No inverted poses, she told herself. Not while you're bleeding. Her hands barely reached her ankles. They used to land flat on the ground behind her heels, elbows slightly bent. Don't push, she thought. Let it flow. Right leg lunge, then moving into down dog, *adho mukha svanasana*. Starting from scratch.

❧ POLLY

Her mom was in bed resting. Stan was gone. A miscarriage. That meant she'd been having sex, and who knew if it was even with her dad. The thought zapped down her body, bad lightening. She paced. So scary, her mom on the floor so pale, the toilet filled with blood. *Blood.* She wanted to slice herself, to watch the beading and the running, but that was over. She placed her hand on her Eye and practiced again, saying, "Mommy, I cut myself." But it was so long ago already—tracing the raised red lines, fading to white. It was over, and she didn't need to worry them. By the time they saw it, it might even be gone.

She opened her Blood Drawer, took out the envelope of fetus postcards. The whole twin knelt in penance in her glass jar, supported her parasite beneath its legs and rear. Her eyes were shut as if weary. Her fine cloud of blond hair floated in the solution. Her perfect ears. A parasite twin like a supermarket chicken, no heart and only a knob for a head, emerged from her chest, hung like a baby in a front pack. Her perfect hands held the whole twin around the neck. A miscarriage.

She slid the postcard back in the envelope; she'd never look at it again. Any of them. Ever. She kissed the envelope goodbye, tenderness welling for the jar babies, three hundred years never born, three hundred years floating so lonely. Cold in the dark at night in the museum. Dead, their eyes never opened.

She carried the babies with her to the quiet kitchen and buried them deep in the side of the kitchen garbage, a sick feeling in her belly.

There was one more thing to do before she went to Nell's for the night. She tiptoed. Silence from her mom's room. She found The Ancestor Project manila envelope on the dining room table. While her mom was curled on her bed, she steamed the flap open with steam from the kettle. Her heart pounded—if anybody came in, she'd pretend she was making tea again. She quickly looked at the pages inside. Then she reglued the envelope closed, and— safe!—placed it back on the dining room table where it had been.

Sitting now on the floor of her room, she shoved pajamas and underwear into her backpack. Life was weird. Everything was the same, and everything was different, and now she knew the answer to the question of Amber. And she would never tell anybody that she knew.

✏ ADAM

Sandi answered the door on his fourth knock. "What. This better be a good one." Then seeing him, "Okay, get your sorry butt inside here. It's cold."

"Sandi. I'm so sorry, but can I make a phone call? I have to call my wife. Kira. She's sick, and I'm not there." His voice shook, he leaned against the door frame. "My phone battery died. I left my car… my credit cards, I can pay you for the call, I have some money left…" He fumbled for his wallet, his hands too frozen to get into his pockets.

The cold side of the road, with cars only every five minutes or so. An hour's worth had passed with a roar, the last driver the only one to look at him, hands up and shrugging. Finally just before winter-dark, a pick-up truck. "Outta gas?" "Outta gas," he'd said. "Hop in the back. Goin' to Elko." "Perfect. Thank you." The truck bed cold despite the plastic liner, the Prius disappearing in the distance. He'd walked the mile or so from Mountain City Highway.

Sandi sighed. "Okay, come in. Big Tommy's out on a haul for a couple days. Amber's already gone, said to say goodbye."

"What? Where'd she go?"

Sandi looked confused. "With Steve! To Boise! She didn't tell you?" and then at his face, "Guess she didn't tell you the plan. Steve's mom's taking on care of Joey, you know."

"No. I don't know."

"Told you not to get on that sleigh ride. My daughter's slick, pulled one over on me, too, left Johnny here. She was supposed to talk to you about him, guess she didn't. I got nothing good to say about that girl right now. I love that boy to death, but you know I have other things going on. It's not right I have to take him on again." She walked into the small house leaving the door open behind her.

He trailed her in. "Thank you. I need to call home, call my wife. I'll pay you back."

"Your wife told me you don't live there no more."

"What?"

"She said you don't live there."

"That's insane. I've got to get home, to my wife, to my little girl."

"Just how are you going to do that, no car?"

"It's just twenty miles or so down the road. I've got Triple A. Can I call them, too?"

"Suit yourself. Better pay me for the calls."

Sandi's house. A grimy brown wood veneer table, Fruit Loops cereal box, stacks of bills and cut out coupons, toy trucks, one of Joey's blue cylinder blocks (Polly's!), a single filthy boy's athletic sock, a giant entertainment system. On the way to the phone, Sandi's voice behind him: "Steve's mom's in Boise. She's an upright lady. Steve gives her all sorts of trouble but she's okay, she can take good care of that little one."

"What about Johnny's dad?"

"Mike's not been seen for five, six years. Never did claim him. Johnny's always been the problem, didn't you get that?"

No. He hadn't. He hadn't gotten anything. Fuckin' clueless. Taken for a ride.

No answer at home, his own voice on the phone machine. He called Lindsey. "Lindsey?"

"Hello, Adam." Lindsey's voice was tired, full of tired hate.

"She's fine. Polly's fine, everybody's fine, it's fine, it's fine, don't even bother with it."

"What happened?"

"You know what happened. She had the abortion. She did it herself."

"What? She said miscarriage."

"Induced miscarriage. She did it herself. She's fine."

Pressure on the chest, yawning in his stomach. If he crawled inside that yawn it would be red and raw. A gray wolf eating him from inside out. He'd left Kira alone with it. "Don't be an asshole to me, please, Lindsey. I didn't know. I'm in Nevada. Kira was telling me she was fine."

"Okay, suit yourself."

"Is she okay? Really? Please, don't cut me cold, here. Please. Tell me slowly."

"Adam. She's fine. Polly freaked a bit. Stan was there. It's fine. Really." Her voice softened. "Really. I wouldn't lie."

Stan? He clutched the phone; the other abortion, hours of watching women coming out and out and out and no Kira and no Kira…. The refrain in his brain: what an asshole I am. What a fucking asshole.

"Call tomorrow, Adam," Lindsey said.

"Why aren't they answering the phone?"

"I told her to turn it off. To rest."

"How's Polly? Is Polly okay?"

"She's here. She's fine, the girls are watching a comedy. Call tomorrow."

"I need to talk to Polly. Can I talk to Polly? Let me talk to Polly."

The screen door slammed, the door shut. Johnny came in, stood silently near the door. Adam gestured, come here, come here! and Johnny came over for a hug.

"I need to talk to my daughter."

"Adam. Calm down. Everybody is fine. Call tomorrow."

"Lindsey." He waited.

"Okay, hang on."

While he waited, he squeezed Johnny against his side, whispered, "You okay, Johnny Rockboy?"

Johnny nodded and stared at the floor.

"Daddy?" Polly's voice high and scared.

"Polly. Are you okay?"

"I'm good."

"Listen, Poodle. I'm coming home tomorrow, okay? It might take me a little while to get out of here, but I'm coming home, okay?"

"Yeah." Her voice so young. Six, four years old.

"Are you really okay? Are you okay there with Nell?"

"I'm fine, Daddy." This time her voice sixteen. Rallying.

"Everything's going to be okay. Okay?"

"I know. I know it is."

"Okay, love. Go back and watch your movie. I love you. I'll be home tomorrow night. At the latest, Thursday."

"Okay. Bye, Daddy. Have a good drive."

He hung up the phone. Johnny velcroed to his side. "You okay, Johnny Rockboy?"

"I forgot my Kirop in Steve's truck."

Poor puppy. "Come sit with me on the couch. We'll get you a new Kirop, kiddo," he told Johnny. Johnny stared at the floor.

"You staying for dinner? Sleeping here? You can get your car in the morning." Sandi was looking at him suspiciously.

"I think I'm going to have to. Thank you, Sandi. Really."

"Good thing I'm not on the schedule tonight."

Pacing in Sandi's back room, door closed, an old bedroom used for storage with a foldout couch, a funky lamp with a ripped shade. A wall of old paint and pesticides, a photo pan, photographic solution, pool chemicals, thinking: What? They don't have a pool here... boxes labeled "Sandi's stuff," "Amber's stuff," unlabeled boxes, an open tool box with a rusty box cutter on top, tired stuffed animals willy nilly, a tangle of old Barbies, a box labeled "X-Mas." Every house had its underside. He didn't know these people at all.

"Dinner time. We got Domino's. Come out and eat now." Sandi's head in the doorway. Over pizza, Johnny sitting between the two of them on a telephone book, "The daughter's a handful. Hope she gets it together soon, but it's hard, you know, based on where she's been, where she comes from."

"I fucked up."

"Yeah, you fucked up," Sandi said. "Recently. Before, you was a kid, that's all old water under a bridge. But recently, yeah. You fucked up. Should never of brought her back here."

He looked around the cluttered kitchen/dining room space. Sandi looked at him through narrow eyes.

"A lot of assholes in the same boat as you," she said. But her eyes were fond. She was so hardcore, Adam had always liked that about her, game for anything. One night she'd run naked into the ice cold San Francisco bay in the middle of the night, right down at Aquatic Park, making him follow quivering in his Fruit-of-the-Looms. He'd been such a fucking wimp. She'd tapped into his wild side, his rock star flail-on-the-stage-with-the-mike side. And a tiger in the sack. Yeah, she looked like an old lady now, but he could remember her knocking back a shot, "Another?"

"Okay, Johnny, go get your hands washed," she said. When he left the room: "Don't know what I'm gonna do about that kid. I don't want to call Social Services, put that boy in the system, but I swear, Adam, I'm tapped out."

"I'm taking him." The words surprised him.

Sandi looked at him dubiously. "You."

"Sandi, I'm taking him home with me. Give me permission. You've got legal custody, right?" The reality grew stronger the more he said.

Sandi leaned back and smiled. "Well, then. Thank you for stepping up." She pushed her plate away from her. "Didn't think you had it in you. 'Bout time you grew a pair." She stared straight into his eyes, a challenge, a look of respect. "Now don't go jerking that little boy around none, he's had enough of that. If you say you're gonna take him, you take him. I got legal custody. I'll give you permission. I'll take him summers, you don't want him, but he's gotta go to school, and he's gotta be in a happy home, and I'm off work tonight but that's rare. Thank you for this. You're his blood, too."

"I don't know that. I've never known that, Sandi."

"I do."

"I have to talk to Kira," he said, realizing what he'd done. Somehow it would be all right with her. He would make it right; he had to. This was the right thing to do.

"You do that."

"Tomorrow."

"You do that."

❧ POLLY

Polly snuggled in her nest of blankets and pillows on the floor of Nell's room and closed her eyes. If you stared at the inside of your eyelids, what did you see? She thought about Joey, out in the desert, wandering around. Joey with his open eyes, wandering, looking at things—the big horizon, the rabbits and the elk, seeing the cowboys, Indians, reservations, cattle and horses, sheep and cactus, mountains, rivers. He would see everything, because he had to. And when he was bigger and could talk, he would tell her what he'd seen.

She opened her eyes and stared around the comfortable dark of Nell's room. Then she shut them again, and began to drift. If you had eyelids, you were safe. You could keep the truth in.

❧ ADAM

In Sandi's spare bedroom, Adam sat on the foldout staring at the wall of junk, people's detritus: if she'd pressed him, if he'd buckled, he would have had a box up there with the other boxes, "Adam's Stuff." He would have moved here with the two of them, Sandi and Amber, raised Amber, managed a restaurant, played in a local band, helped organize the Elko Cowboy Poetry Festival every year. Instead, Kira and Polly. A rush of relief.

Three hours of fitful sleep, dozing in his clothes, not wanting to climb into the funky foldout couch smelling of mildew. Then, wakefulness, his body needing to move, to drive, to get to Kira, now, *now*. Six, the sound of an alarm clock beeping in another room. He must have dozed again.

The sound of the shower running down the hall, rustles in another room, finally the slam of the front door. Tiptoeing into the kitchen so as not to wake Johnny. Poor kid was going to have a long day. Time to get on the horn and start honking.

❧ KIRA

She'd never spent the night completely alone in the house before. She slept solidly until almost seven, woke rested, plugged the phone back in and gingerly went into the kitchen to make coffee.

She left the light off, the dawn lit the room enough, and under the kettle the flame was a beautiful blue. Another day of faux Spring, the sky streaked pink and birds twittering. The phone almost immediately rang: "Hey, babe."

"Hey," she said. So relieved to hear his voice.

"Before anything," he said. "I need to apologize. I wasn't there for you, I'm never there. I'm an asshole. I need to be a better husband to you."

"Adam, no don't…"

"Hey. Let me. I went a little crazy in the desert. Quiet crazy."

Maybe it was the dark kitchen, but she felt calm and expansive, the rest of her life stretching forever in front of her. "Adam, we have time for this."

"We do? You're not dumping me?"

She didn't answer. They had arrived at the edge of maybe.

If she let him go, they'd all survive. They'd grow distant. Polly would grow up, and time would pass. She'd measure time through the erosion of objects, the Saab getting scratched and dinged, blue jeans running through their life cycle from good jeans to casual jeans to funky jeans to gardening and painting jeans to rag bag.

Or. If she kept him, time would pass anyway. Ten years from now this would be "that time we almost broke up," a deep scrape scabbed over and healed from the outside in, the inside yellow and tender for a long time.

"Well, it wasn't your finest hour," she said.

"I'm so sorry. Listen, Kira," he said, his voice urgent. "I'm so sorry and there's so much I need to tell you. But mainly, I want to bring Johnny back with me."

"Here." She had no words. "To live?"

"To live. For at least until summer. Amber took Joey and moved to Boise. Johnny's odd man out."

"Wow. Adam. You're sure." She heard the conviction in his voice but wanted him to say it.

"Yes. I want to talk to you about it, but yes. And I'm not saying it would be forever."

"Oh, Adam, you know there's no such thing as forever. People promise 'til death do us part, and half of all marriages split up anyway." She paused. "Hey, where are you?"

"Sandi's house, Sandi's phone. She's at work. Johnny's in his room, packing."

"Packing? Wow, Adam. This is a lot."

"I know."

"Okay, then," she said.

"So can we make this work, Kira? Please say you aren't leaving me. I did stupid things. I'm so sorry."

Kira turned off the kettle just before it boiled. "I have something to tell you, too," she said. "And maybe you won't want me to stay." She took a breath. "I did a paternity test. On you and Amber. That's where your toothbrush went. So that might affect bringing Johnny home for you." The relief of saying it loosening a tension she didn't know she'd been carrying. She waited for him to jump on her, to accuse her.

"Wow. I thought you threw it out because it was so grody."

"Nope. Stole it. But it was grody." She laughed a little, testing the waters.

"You did a test? A paternity test? Wow."

She heard the purr of the 580 morning commute. "So," she said. "There's an envelope here with the results…" She walked into the dining room, fished it out from under the piles of mail.

"And?"

"I have it right here. I didn't open it. I don't know why. I sent for the test. But when it came, I figured that was for you to do.

If you want to."

A long silence. Then he said, "No, I don't think it affects anything. Either way."

"No?"

"Babe, I can see how you would do that, get the test, the way things were. Is it weird that I really don't want to know? Before, I was scared of finding out. Now, it just doesn't matter one way or the other. Think of it this way: if we'd adopted Amber from an orphanage, she'd be our kid. And then Johnny would be no question, right?"

"True."

"So I really don't want to know, especially since Amber doesn't want to know. It feels like it would intrude on her. That's her life, she should decide. I don't think it's avoidance or bullshit, not this time. And if we ever need to find out, we can."

"That actually makes sense, Adam." It did. From the stand of eucalyptus trees two blocks away, the yammer of crows cawing.

"I just want Johnny to be with us. With you and me and Polly. That's the weird part."

"It's not that weird," she said. She stood, holding the envelope in one hand, the cordless phone in the other.

"Hey, but Kira," Adam's voice got soft but pointed. "You need to come clean. Anything else you're holding out on me about? No more paternity tests or lovers or any other shit? No Jerry Springer? No Oprah?"

"No. Oh," she remembered, "I had a watsu for free at Harbin. But that's everything." And it was true. She felt clean.

"Okay. I believe you."

Though it was impossible, she could hear his shoulders lower. "Good. So what should I do with the test results?"

"I don't give a shit. But if you open it, don't let me know."

"No. I don't want to know if you don't know. I could put it in a drawer. But then we'd be tempted, next time we have a fight about it. Let's throw it away. Unopened."

"Burn it."

"What?"

"Put it in the fireplace and burn it. Don't forget to open the flue."

"Duh." She moved into the living room, removed the screen, opened the flue, and placed the envelope on the grate.

The envelope took a moment to light, and then a couple of minutes to burn, the glue sparking slightly, the envelope turning in on itself, black and red and manila yellow. The remaining black ash was flaky and complicated and beautiful. Gone, done, moving on. "I did it. It's gone."

"Good." His voice so soft, like they were lying together, his legs over her legs, his voice in her ear. "And? So. You and me?"

"Maybe," she said, hanging on to the if of it. Then she let it go. "You and me. And Polly and Johnny."

She heard the relief in his sigh. "Say it. We're not splitting up, are we."

"No. We're not splitting up."

"Oh good. Jesus, I'm hard right now. I really want to make love with you."

"Me, too." A shiver worked its way up her spine. "Adam? Sounds like a lot of logistics, but we'll work it out." A small bit of flame remained in the fireplace, turning the black flakes to white ash. She replaced the screen and walked back into the kitchen.

Adam's voice was energized now. "I know, we really have to talk. There are logistics, like whether Pioneer can take Johnny in the middle of the school year, tuition, if he can get a waiver or discount because Sandi has legal custody and she's still fairly low income, you know. But, Kira, we can do this. Remember how we pulled together to get the house? We'll do it again. And it's on me. I get that. I need to talk to Stan. Not for more work or money. I need to do something else with my life; he's my best friend but I can't work with him. I need to move on, like maybe open a doggie day care; it sounds stupid but dogs are huge right now, and people need places to keep them. And I'm sorry. I'm sorry I wasn't there."

She was quiet. "Adam. I'm sorry, too."

He paused.

"Adam. I'm really sorry. For everything."

"It's going to be okay, babe."

It was. They had things to work out, but it was. She wanted him. She wanted him with all his flaws, the tender heart of an artichoke. She imagined them broke, and him covered in dog hair and happy. And then, years from now, through with the hard times, comfortable. She wanted to grow old with him, to be buried next to him, to renew their vows, to hyphenate their names, to stand whole but leaning, to have each other's backs.

She clutched the phone, her mouth hurting from smiling so hard. "When did you know it was going to be okay with us?"

"I don't know. Just, this is our life, you know?"

She sighed. "We just missed each other too much."

"We did."

The kitchen was getting lighter. She turned the kettle back on.

"Do you think we need to ask Polly?" he asked. "About Johnny?"

"I don't think this is Polly's decision."

"Yeah. But I think she would actually like it."

"I think she actually will. Sweetie," she said. "If you ask me, I think you need to get off the phone and get you guys home."

"I know. I don't want to end this call, though. I love you."

"I love you, too. Now get."

She put down the phone and stood silently, the only sounds the hissing of the flame under the kettle, then its whistle. This is the quietest this house will ever be, she thought. She made her coffee and sat down with it at the table, enjoying the stillness, silently narrating their mornings to him all the way in Nevada: "We wake up and groan, and I get up, and you don't for a moment. I fill the kettle and measure three scoops of coffee beans into the grinder and grind. You wake up Polly on your way into the kitchen, and the kettle whistles. You turn it off and put the coffee grounds and water into the French press. I make my fruit shake, and you cook Polly's eggs and sit with her. I pour coffee and run back to our room to get dressed and get into the bathroom while you make her lunch. We'll have Johnny. More eggs. More driving. It will be double the trouble, Adam."

But she didn't care. She wasn't sure what she felt about Johnny, but her ambivalence wasn't Johnny's problem; love would come later. At first, caring and kindness would go a long way.

She imagined saying it to Adam: "It's what I want, Adam. The living together things."

You don't forget the other things, she thought. About Ravi and Sheila. About Amber: the family breached like her womb, and how not dealing with the undercurrents all those years had hemorrhaged into a big mess. You don't forget the betrayals of money and drugs. You don't forget—you're not able to forget, it's part of your life together. But you don't just toss the good stuff away, either.

Then she got ready to go pick up Polly and Nell. Her turn to drive carpool.

❧

ACKNOWLEDGMENTS

Much gratitude to the people and places whose lives and stories provided the nuts and fruit for this fiction blender smoothie. This includes the denizens of Oakland, Berkeley, Harbin Hot Springs, and Elko, Nevada.

Many thanks to Armand Inezian and the team at Last Light Studio as well as many others: Joel Friedlander, Elizabeth Bernstein, Erika Dreifus, Jane Roper, Masha Hamilton, Gayle Brandeis, Saill White, Susan Ito, Annie McManus, Seth Mendelowitz, Johanina Wikoff, Michael Alenyilov and the Freewriters, Luan Stauss, Rebekah Edwards, the SPW community, WOM-BA, Alison Luterman, Coke Nakamoto, Rebecca Chekouras, Mark Pritchard, Davina Kotulski, Michele Rabkin, Ami Zins, Tilly Roche, Sebastian Teunissen, Jessica Lutz, Clay Fried, Arthur Lutz, Karla Lutz, Robert Marshall, Sara Young, Jessica Barksdale Inclán, Gina Hyams, Rebecca Steinitz, Kristina Riggle, Caroline Grant, Maria DeScala, Literary Mama, Bill Sonnenschein, Anaya Sonnenschein, and the Casa Colonial in Oaxaca, Mexico and the Virginia Center for the Creative Arts (where the tracks for this book were laid).

Sometimes it's a long journey, navigating the sticky strands.

CPSIA information can be obtained at www.ICGtesting.com
Printed in the USA
LVOW I00356210112

264932LV00004B/2/P